Usha Ananda Krishna graduated from the School of Planning and Architecture, New Delhi, and worked as an architect in Bangalore and Kolkata. In 1980 she began writing advertising copy, interspersing the two careers for many years. Her first novel *A Turbulent Passage* was published in 1995, followed in 2009 by *Fallout*, a family drama written in the mordantly witty style that characterizes her work. Her interests are reading, architecture and contemporary art.

The Escapists *of* J. Mullick Road

Usha Ananda Krishna

SPEAKING
TIGER

SPEAKING TIGER PUBLISHING PVT. LTD
4381/4, Ansari Road, Daryaganj
New Delhi 110002

First published in paperback by Speaking Tiger 2018

ISBN: 978-93-88070-31-7
e-ISBN: 978-93-86702-04-3

10 9 8 7 6 5 4 3 2 1

The moral right of the author has been asserted.

Typeset in Garamond Premier Pro by SÜRYA, New Delhi
Printed at Sanat Printers, Kundli

The Escapists *of* J. Mullick Road

1

'Hey, you! Stop that!'

'Huh?'

'Get away—*now*!' Breathing hard, Biren dug his fingers into the thin shoulder. 'Out!'

'K...k...ke...' stammered the man he'd pounced on. 'Ki?' Fumbling at his crotch, 'What are you doing?' he cried. 'My pants are wet! I'm an old man, can't you see?'

He *was* a wizened specimen, Biren realized, feeling a bit ruthless. Under the shirt he still clutched, the bones felt like whittled sticks. The hair, what little there was to see, was white. And those pebbly, genderless spectacles, circa 1940, were only worn by the elderly—or the impoverished—in these parts. He released the ancient with a little push. 'You should know better then, grandpa. Next time spray your own doorpost. Not this column, for fucksake!'

His captive slunk away. Swearing under his breath, Biren drew out the bottle scrunched under his arm in a paper bag. It was an unnecessary ruse here, the paper bag, especially in the dark, and one that would fool no one anyway, but *some* niceties had to be observed, else you'd become what you fought against. He unscrewed the cap, tipped his head up—and stopped, transfixed.

He'd noticed it before of course, the column, and marked it, but there's always something else, something more, isn't there? Now, in the forty-watt light of the lone streetlamp, the plain whitewash glowed with the lustre of fine marble. The miserly illumination erased the surface flaws: the cracks and the pits, the scabs and the stains. And at this late hour, with none of the aggravations of traffic and people, you could see it, really *see* it. There was the signature capital—the transverse sections of a scroll, the slender fluted shaft...Without thinking, he began measuring its height with his eye—as reliable as callipers, he believed. It *was* nine diameters tall. Perfection!

Then the stench of urine hit him, and the anger surged back. '*Neanderthals*, the lot of you!'

The cheap spirit stung his throat. When the fumes subsided he walked through the arched entranceway, supported by the lately defiled column on one side and its twin on the other.

The large enclosed court he had entered had been designed on the lines of the great plazas of Renaissance Europe. Built in the second decade of the century, it was also proudly and emphatically Empire. Pediments, bow-fronts, medallions, friezes, quoins—froth and frippery that made the bulky masonry look like a playful bully. Even if you didn't care for this style you had to concede its lineage. It still ruled. With the old rod and the rood, although the rulers had long ceded and the empire gone to seed. Which was all jolly and fascinating, pondered in this shifty lighting, but turn on the floodlight of noon and the truth will out. And the truth was that the aristocratic quad was now a squat. A bloody refugee camp. A flourishing *township*. Shacks built slap-bang against the noble walls. Tarpaulins, tin sheets—in the colonnades, in the porticos, in the verandas... Cooking and washing—shitting on their doorstep, for heaven's sake! And filthy-ing the air with those chulas! He batted off the vestigial smoke and forced out a cough. Then he lit a cigarette.

If only one could bulldoze the place. If only one could bring back the original order. Not just demolish the shacks but rip out the *democratic* contraventions in the buildings.

The modifications made by the new colonists, the fucking *home improvements*. Aluminium glazing, air-conditioning units, electrical cables...

But given half a chance you'd also like to make some modifications of your own, wouldn't you? For example, you always felt that projection on the second floor was disproportionate to the mass. And the window flanking that balcony could have been higher—by a foot, perhaps? And the arch there... Stop it! You're no genius. Just a nitpicker and a bellyacher, a crank whose particular neurosis is he can never look at a building or enter any space, not even a cowshed, without going over it with a pencil and an eraser.

The cigarette was burning his fingers. He threw it down, ground it with his heel—and immediately picked it up, and pocketed it. Given the state of the street, his gesture would weigh as much as a fly on a barbell, but it was a habit. Smiling ruefully, he raised the paper bag to his mouth. The next instant, he lowered it. The old man was back, shrieking. 'Here! He's here!'

Biren became aware of voices, up and down the street, ringing like a cash register. *Ki? Ki hoyechhe, Dadu? Kothai?*

'He hit me!'

'*What*! Why, you bullshitting fossil, I didn't touch you! Well, hardly at all. I wish I had, though!' Biren controlled himself. Anything could happen at any time, and in Calcutta, things—unpleasant things—frequently did. To begin with the voices were converging on him.

'...he pushed me down!'

'A barefaced lie,' retorted Biren. He caught his breath. The crowd that had gathered around was some ten strong. 'Bloody hell,' he muttered. They were all men. And they looked as if they meant business. He backed into the shadow of the archway, but it was too late.

'Ei, what did you do to my uncle? Eh? You can torture him because he's a poor man and you are rich?'

'His fucking bank account is not relevant here—do you know what he was doing?'

'Capitalist bloodsucker!'

'Hein...he *attacked* me! With that bottle!'

Now that *is going too far,* Biren was thinking, when he was winkled out of his sanctuary, and frogmarched, he complained afterwards to Dr Murray, not quite truthfully. By a *mob*, he added, scaling up his modest escort. What he didn't tell Dr Murray, however, was that at that moment he was frightened.

'No, wait!' he cried. 'Stop!' A button popped. 'Easy!' He twisted away. There was an ominous sound of fabric ripping. 'Okay, okay! I admit I lost my temper! But,' he put the alleged weapon on the region of his heart (thankful none of his friends were in the assemblage), 'I swear I didn't attack him! However,' he opened out his arms, so that, in a reversal of roles, he appeared to be forgiving *them*, 'my humble apologies for the misunderstanding.'

The act didn't impress the crowd. An angry buzz began. Thinking quickly, he scanned the gaggle of heads, found the old man and, with a little bow, presented the bottle to him. His forfeiture was snatched by a brawny worthy in a singlet, who, without missing a beat uncapped it and swigged—and spluttered.

'Hey ma! This is *rum*! Why not whisky?'

'Because this is all I had, you ungrateful sod. Quite the nawab, aren't you?'

In the furore that followed—the old man claiming the bottle as his due, the others clamouring for their share—he slipped away.

His car was parked in Marquis Street. He unlocked it, fumbling, and, suddenly wobbly, fell on the seat and slumped over the steering wheel. Two blowtorches bored into his brain.

After a while, sensing movement outside, he lifted his head. A face was pressed to the window. Another face bobbed behind it, and another, and two more. The car was ringed with men. It was the crowd that had heckled him minutes ago. Seeing they had caught his attention they banged on the windows, and the bonnet. When he didn't react they began rocking the car.

He rolled down his window some four inches, thinking it might stop the onslaught. He couldn't hear for the pulse thudding in his ears. An arm snaked in through the crack. Something fell on his lap. With a gasp he flung off the object, which landed on the seat. Laughter broke out, loud and jeering.

He grabbed the window lever, and then let go of it. A hand was trapped in the four-inch gap. It waggled its fingers at the object lying on the seat. 'Take, take!'

He waited a few seconds, the sweat dripping off his chin. Then, he fumblingly undid the greasy newspaper wrapping. And extricated two samosas.

His throat constricted. Smiling with difficulty, his mouth a rictus, 'Thank you' he croaked.

'Thanku, thanku. Don't just say thanku, Dada, *eat!*'

He fingered a samosa queasily. Faces huffed on the windows. He smiled at them. They grinned at him. He waved their gift at them, hoping they would leave. They waved back—and stayed. His desperation grew.

The resolution, when it came, was unexpected, deafening and, as he related it to Dr Murray, quite Biblical.

It was a thunderclap. The crowd jumped back from the windows and dispersed. In seconds the wind swelled to a noisy gale, shaking the street out like a tablecloth after breakfast. Tarps flapped, shutters rattled, a dog yelped. Dried leaves scurried like roaches fleeing a fire. Fat boisterous drops of rain began flaying the dust. The street plunged into darkness. A nor'wester *and* load shedding.

He rolled down his window and stuck his head out. Spray stung his eyes. Cool rain laved his face. Bliss.

When the rain let up, he eased the car into Free School Street, already flooded because of debris blocking the drains. Post-storm, the city was eerily still. Only some power lines had been restored. The streetlights, few and far between, nibbled at the darkness like the last remaining teeth in a crone's mouth. Here and there, a hurricane lamp broke through the vaporous shadows, illuminating the most recent destruction: a tattered awning, broken glass, the wheel of an *Egg Bread-Toast Noodles* cart lying in a ditch. And direly, a tin sheet rearing up from the road, angled to slash his tyre. He braked hard, and hit his chest on the steering wheel. Cursing, he opened his door into a small landslide of putrefying food waste. Civilizations are destroyed by wars, he thought, and fire and water (and the lack of it), lava, sand, but *this* one will be wiped out by garbage. Shit, not to put too a fine point on it. It'll be a first, anyway. Whistling, he backed the car.

The glow of candlelight in the clinic's window told him Dr Murray was still there. He rattled the tin plate tacked on the door (*Free Clinic Open 10 a.m.—10 p.m.*), and pushed it open.

'Good evening, Biren. I was about to lock up. Is everything alright?'

Biren saluted with two fingers. 'Sorry, Doc. Got delayed. Waylaid, actually. Long story involving a fellow copping a pee on a column. An Ionic column, as it happened, and a damned good example of one too, although in a state of neglect. The upshot of it was I was forced to trade the grog for this.' He held out the packet of samosas, now soggy as well as greasy. 'Old lamps for new.'

The candle guttered. Dr Murray implored him to come in and shut the door, for pity's sake. Biren obliged. Thumping the frame of the shack, he said, 'This bearing up okay?'

'Oh yes. No leaks anywhere. You did a splendid job, Biren. I can't thank you enough.'

'That's alright, Doc,' Biren said, embarrassed. 'I wasn't fishing. Wait for the monsoon before the tributes.' He ran a thumb along the wall. 'I know you disapprove of this stuff but it's cheap and it's weatherproof, and anyway all that fuss about asbestos causing cancer is Western hysteria.'

'Really,' said Dr Murray, a little frostily. He began clearing a table crowded with bottles and tubes, strips of pills, cotton rolls and bandages, enamel dishes of sterilized equipment.

'Um, Doc, those crochet hooks. Could you please, um... Thanks.'

'They're ordinary surgical needles, you silly fellow,' said Dr Murray, thawing. He opened a drawer and drew out a bottle of whisky and two glasses.

'Thanks, Doc. Phew. Stiff. But salutary.'

'So how did you lose your bottle?'

Dr Murray wiped the sweat from his face with a towel. 'Peeing on a vandalized building here is like blacking a kettle, isn't it? If you see what I mean.' After a pause, 'Poor devil,' he said. 'He must have really needed to go.'

'There *are* public toilets, you know.'

'Have you used them? Exactly. So you had no call to go at him like that. You could have been beaten up, Biren. I'm surprised you weren't.'

'It relieved my frustration.'

Dr Murray put down the towel. 'Well, find a less heroic way to do it. Get on a citizen's committee instead. A civic body that addresses these problems.'

'It's what one would do in a civilized society.' Dr Murray started to say something and then shrugged. 'You've no idea how self-serving the politics of socialism is, Doc. How self-defeating. There *have* been proposals. The files are gathering dust. People have written to the newspapers too. That only opened a floodgate of complaints.'

The door blew open, rattling the tin plate. Biren rose and righted it, and then continued to stand in the doorway, looking at the huddles in other doorways. Pavement dwellers, sheltering from the rain. He rested his head on the jamb. 'It's just so soul-destroying,' he murmured. 'How do you even begin to...?' He lifted his head. 'I don't know if you saw a story in today's paper about a rickshaw-puller asking the court for permission to kill his paraplegic daughter because he couldn't feed her. I think he should get it. If only because he thought to ask. A modest request, wouldn't you say?'

'I don't want to discuss this, Biren, if you don't mind. And kindly shut that door.'

Biren pulled the door to. 'It is all very well for you to take a high moral stand. You're a visitor.'

Dr Murray peered at Biren over his glasses. 'What makes you think we don't see what you see, Biren? And I'm not exactly a *visitor*.'

'Of course,' said Biren. 'You're well acquainted with our mess by now. On really intimate terms with the filth. But you levitate over it.' Abashed, 'Sorry, Doc,' he muttered. 'I appreciate what you do, believe me.'

'You once told me denigrating Calcutta is a sign of shallowness.'

'If *you* did it I'd knock you down... I know! I know! One must reconcile with the realities. Learn to work the system— because that's what reality means here.'

'You have ideas, Biren. You don't have opportunities. I know they don't often go together, or come together, but that's not because the world's conspiring against you.'

'I hate ah, patronage. And compromise. Conciliation.'

'You want total submission.'

'Because people don't know what they want.'

'Pity they don't know help is at hand.'

Biren laughed.

Dr Murray didn't smile. 'If I were you...'

'If you were me you'd leave town,' Biren said. 'Because this city is finished. No, it's true. Populist ideology has killed industry. All enterprise. All *life*.'

Then, 'What would you do if you were me?' he asked meekly.

'Write. You mentioned the papers. Reach out to people who share your concerns. You might even change how people think. You're always complaining they don't think.'

'They don't and they won't. They're traditionalists. Regressives. Same thing.'

'Excuses, Biren.'

'Alvar Aalto famously said "God made paper to *draw* architecture."'

'Excuses.'

'Of course he wasn't thinking of kiosks and ice cream stalls.'

'Biren, you don't *draw* buildings like you draw pictures or write poetry...'

'It's okay, Doc, it'll happen.' Biren raised his glass. 'I am owed.' He caught Dr Murray's eye, and laughed. 'So. You think an article in *The Hoogly Times* will launch me.'

'It'll be cathartic.'

'Hmm... How's *your* work going, by the way?'

'Three more cases of cerebral malaria, thank you for asking. But there's no reason to panic, the Health Ministry says. Because ordinary malaria kills thousands. And more die of dysentery.'

'Of heartbreak, I thought.'

Dr Murray looked at him with affection. 'I don't know what I'd do without you, Biren. Annoying as you are at times.' He flapped his towel. 'Go home now. You've had enough, I think.'

Biren wiped his mouth with the back of his hand. 'Oh, I've

had enough—enough of this bloody city too. My tragedy is I can't have enough of it.'

2

On the morning of May 2nd 198_ at 6.30, give or take a minute, Pinaki Bose had a bad shock. After which he came to a sobering—and far-reaching—conclusion. He was nothing. He didn't matter—not to anybody, not to himself. He just didn't *exist*—not here, not in the world at large. He'd suffered this particular neurosis before—usually as a hallucination of wandering in a terrain of infinite vastness and desolation—but there was an epithetic quality to this one that made those others seem like trial runs.

The wise would have you believe that the feeling of nothingness is reached in a state of spiritual transcendence and, as such, is liberating. Pinaki felt crushed. Others might have seen stars orbiting their personal Black Hole, even have found comedy in the situation, but Pinaki wasn't given to such sightings, or to such humour. He brooded over how humiliating it was to have been null-and-voided by an ordinary young man he'd ordinarily have never noticed; a young man even more insignificant than himself (!), engaged in an activity that was neither elevating nor enlightening. And should such an ordinary incident have escalated to an existential crisis?

Yet it might never have happened. His morning had begun, as usual, with the noise of two crows tearing at each others' throats outside his window. The hands of the old-fashioned clock by his bed stood at 6.05—ten minutes before the alarm shrilled. He never had to set the alarm (although he always did), not just because the avian wake-up service was so reliable, but because his body clock, calibrated by the habit of years, worked with the precision of a Rolex. In the instant before the crows opened their beaks, a siren went off in his head.

The clank of a water pump outside his window completely cleared the mists of sleep. This was followed by—and this too was not unusual—a loud and self-adulating rendition of the theme song from the movie *Kya? Hua Kya?* Pushing down the alarm button before it could go off (and rouse his sleeping children), he threw off the sheet and stood up. All in one fluid movement. Well, not *that* fluid. He was getting stiffer with every year. In every way. Along with his muscles, his thoughts and reflexes, his passions were congealing. As if to endorse this doleful self-assessment, he tripped on a pair of slippers. That the slippers, which belonged to his wife, were flung on *his* side of the bed, while his grovelled under the bed, out of easy reach, ought to have given him pause. Up until this morning it hadn't.

He crossed the floor to the window with a dance-like gait—acquired dodging open manholes and dog shit—and studied the strip of sky allotted to him, the same dirty-white it always was at this hour and this time of year. He drank the entire water in his flask (another long-time habit), and then took several deep, bracing breaths, his belly working like bellows to inhale the collective aromas from a dozen kitchens. And the rich reek of garbage. Then, because it was there, right under his nose, and because he wanted to check, in an incurious way, the source of the singing (which *was* rather good), he looked down at the street.

What he saw was a bath in progress—unremarkable enough in these parts. The bather, who was also the songster, was a brawny, dark-skinned youth, of the type you see in their thousands in the streets and alleys of Calcutta. In other words it was too common a scene to attract even passing interest. And Pinaki wasn't a voyeur, not in the broadest sense of the word. But today an unseen agency had glued his elbows to the windowsill.

Stripped to maroon and green striped boxer shorts, the

youth was scooping water from a red plastic pail with a blue plastic mug, and pouring it over his head, enlivening the boring action with his song. After a minute or so of this he picked up a cake of soap wedged in the railing behind the water pump and rubbed it into his torso and under his arms and behind his neck, working up an exuberant lather. Then, his voice continuing to record the bliss of the experience, he scratched his right calf with his left foot, and his left with the right. *Like a fly sitting on sugar,* Pinaki thought. His smile changed to a frown when a soapy hand dipped into the back of the shorts and scrabbled around, as if searching for spare change—and deepened when the hand moved to the front of the shorts to forage *there*. An expression of dreamy concentration stole over the youth's face. The song trailed away into a pensive *o-o-o*.

Embarrassed, Pinaki turned his attention to the soapy water running along the curb. Rainbow colours played off its surface—an artistic effect he couldn't appreciate because he would have to jump over the nuisance when he left for work later. He stared moodily as the fellow wiped himself down, with a little shimmy. Why this should so fascinate him he could not say. Nor why he waited to see how the fellow dealt with his wet shorts: tying the towel, in this case a red-and-white rag, round his waist and hopping out of them. There was no call, either, to watch him retrieve his rubber flip-flops from under the railing, bending over at a precarious angle...

The towel fell off.

Pinaki's immediate reaction was to give the street a quick up-and-down to check if anyone had caught him staring. Then, struck by a new fear, he snapped his head towards the wall that separated his bedroom from his daughter's. Was she standing at her window too?

The youth had retied his towel. Lifting his head up, he caught Pinaki's eye and gave him a cheery wave.

Pinaki gave him a stony look. For no reason he could think

of then or after, he lifted his flask some six inches off the sill. When replaying the scene to himself he argued it could hardly be considered as offensive. However...

The youth turned, glanced over his shoulder to make sure Pinaki was watching, whipped the towel off and jiggled his buttocks.

Pinaki jumped back from the window, his cheeks flaming.

A minute later—he couldn't think why—he peeped out.

The towel was back in place. But the youth was waiting for him. Grinning, he made as if to remove it.

Pinaki's ears were on fire. All sorts of words came charging into his head, words he heard on the street, that he had never imagined he would have any use for, far less uttered. He didn't utter them now. He shook his fist. 'Shameless!'

The youth stuck his tongue out and made a rude noise.

'You...you *nonsense kothakar*!' cried Pinaki—and hurled the flask down.

The flask missed its target but hit the hydrant with a gratifyingly calamitous thump.

Pinaki clutched the sill to support himself. His legs had filled with water. He'd attacked the fellow. Worse. He'd called him a nonsense kothakar.

The youth was standing very still, his face devoid of expression.

Pinaki's heart banged away. What would happen now?

Nothing happened. Without a word or gesture the youth gathered up his clothes and toiletries. However, when he stepped on to the road, he looked up at Pinaki's window. As if he was marking the spot. Then he was gone.

Pinaki tottered to his bed, collapsed on it and covered his ears.

~

'I couldn't think, sir. Nothing came to me at that moment. Actually, I felt *I* was nothing.'

'And all because a fellow mooned you?'

Pinaki blinked. 'It was *morning*, sir, early morning.'

'Of course.'

'I saw my whole life in that moment. And it was a, a, blank.'

'I thought only drowning men saw their lives flash by.'

Pinaki shuddered. He *had* been drowning. In two inches of soapy water. 'I thought, for *this* I was born? To be insulted by such a fellow? To *live* among such fellows? What *meaning* is there in such a life?'

'Hmm. Rather an extreme reaction to a burst of youthful exuberance.'

'I am not only thinking of myself,' Pinaki said reproachfully. 'What if it had been my daughter looking out?'

'I shouldn't worry. She'd have laughed. Or cheered.'

And there was that figure of eight smile that evoked all manner of worldly experience, denied to Pinaki *because,* thought Pinaki, *I live in J. Mullick Road.* 'Well, *I* lost my temper,' he said a little crossly.

'You found your nerve though.' The smile gave way to a laugh.

'I shouldn't have thrown my flask at him.'

'No, that wasn't wise.'

But the words sounded as if they meant *good for you.*

Encouraged, 'It is not the first time I felt this way,' Pinaki said. 'Often I feel like an extra in a film. Someone in a crowd scene, you know, or in a party,' he added daringly, and was pleased by the interest this drew. 'You see, sir, nobody notices the extras. They are there only for the director's purpose.'

'How profound. An extra in a film illustrating a Zen principle.'

Pinaki didn't understand that, but in a strange way was comforted—and flattered—that his condition had a philosophical interpretation. Although he had often felt—and keenly—his insignificance, he had never spoken about it.

~

Pinaki's head was swimming. Slowly, he became aware of sounds—voices, clattering dishes, furniture scraping, footsteps...

'*Kiiiii*! Ki holo?' screeched a voice that could slam a door at four paces. 'I heard you shout at someone!'

His little bout of aggression was not going to go unheeded after all. His wife, for it was she who had screeched, burst in. Pausing for just the time it took to hear him stutter, 'Nothing, Rimi,' she ran to the window. 'Only my knee. Usual trouble.'

She didn't respond.

He gazed around him as if seeing the room for the first time. First the bed, on which he was sitting, hugging his arms. Orange and green checked sheet, frowsty with the humours of night. *I should have ignored him.* Sari, flung over the headboard. Trunk covered with a cloth embroidered by his grandmother (long-dead). His grandfather's floor desk... *But his behaviour was disgraceful!* The *Indian Chartered Accountant* (two years old), sewing machine (defunct), rush mat (torn in three places), macramé (half-finished) and what was an old camera case doing on the hat-stand? Whose cracked leather belt is that? *Maybe I shouldn't have thrown the flask.* Rimi's scent bottle— empty—and what a lot of glass bangles! *This road has become unliveable. Loafers, hooligans.* Cane bookrack, carom board...

Why was he looking at this rubbish? Because this rubbish, these old friends, soothed him. And then he saw with sudden clarity—what a morning this was turning out for *seeing* things—that the room, his refuge, was, in effect, a cage.

He put his head in his arms and whimpered softly.

The buzzing in his ear grew louder.

His wife was standing over him. 'There's nothing happening outside...are you feeling alright?'

He nodded, and massaged his knee with exaggerated care.

'Then why have you folded my sari?'

The sari on the headboard had indeed been folded. When had he...he couldn't remember! He passed a shaking hand over his face. To his relief he was spared an answer.

'Ki holo, Baba?' asked his daughter from the door.

'Dona! Coming in front of your father in that nightie! Go change! At *once!*'

His daughter bounced right in. 'Was it you shouting just now, then? At Baba?'

'You heard that? Now it's *me* who has been shouting!'

It usually is, Pinaki thought. He was wondering how to shoo them out when his mother entered.

'Ki holo, Bulbul? Did I heard you shout?'

'No, Ma.'

'*Yes,* Ma,' said Rimi.

'If he says he didn't then he didn't, Rimi,' said his mother. She put a hand on his forehead. 'You work too hard, Bulbul.'

Her daughter-in-law sniffed. 'It's not only *Bulbul* who works hard around here.'

Pinaki grimaced. He hated his nickname—courtesy the reedy voice he was born with. He had outgrown the voice but the name, of course, could not be changed. You were branded with it for life. When you were a dignified old man, presiding over your grandson's wedding, there would always be a fool cousin shouting across the hall, 'Bulbul, eh, *Bulbul*! Here, look here!'

Formal names are not *friendly*, his mother said. They are like going-out clothes. Starchy, uncomfortable, and just for 'show'. Why, Bulbul, don't you like your daaknam? *I* gave it to you! That was that. His worldview, unformed then, and lacking definition even now, had never lent itself to conflicts.

'I'm fine,' Pinaki said. 'Really, I'm alright.'

'Sometimes one just feels like shouting, taito?' said his mother.

'Anyone who lives here would, Dida,' said Dona. 'And not just sometimes.'

Rimi frowned. 'Nobody asked your opinion, madam, and nobody invited you here. Look at your nightie! Actually, *don't* look.'

Pinaki looked, and thought, how her skin glowed! And how pretty her hair was! The sun tipped the ends with gold—it was like a sunflower. She was fresh as a flower. He was tempted to pinch her plump cheek, chuck her under the chin... Recollecting himself, 'Dona,' he said. 'Were you standing by your window this morning?'

'No. Why, Baba?'

He was so relieved he wanted to give her a hug. He would have if his wife hadn't been in the way.

'I *told* you why!' she said. 'Your nightie...'

'It isn't so bad, Rimi.'

Dona took her grandmother's hand and kissed it. 'Thank you, Dida.' She pirouetted to the window and stacked her breasts on the ledge. It would drive Vinu mad if he was watching. He was always watching.

Pinaki leapt up. 'Get away from that window!'

'Hmm?' she said dreamily.

'Your father doesn't want the whole world to see you like this!'

'Why do you speak to her as if she's deaf, Rimi?' said his mother in a low voice.

Dona rolled her eyes. 'She always does, Dida, haven't you noticed?'

'That's enough,' snapped Rimi. 'Cholo, you're going to be late for class. *You* may have time to waste but I don't.' She turned to Pinaki. 'You're always cranky before your tea.'

A new charge, but he didn't debate it. He did feel strange today. But he preferred to avoid any problem by walking, rather than talking, around it. So, 'Can I have my tea now?' he asked, hoping this would clear the room. His wife didn't answer. She was glaring at Dona, now sashaying to the dresser mirror. And there the matter would have been dropped, for the time being at least, had not a new voice piped up from the doorway.

'*I* heard what you said, Baba!'

Tuli, fourteen years old, third batsman in the neighbourhood cricket team and acknowledged authority on fifty years of Test cricket scores, pushed past his mother and grandmother and ground to a halt in front of his father. Thrusting his chest out he said, 'You shouted *nonsense kothakar!*' Pinaki wanted to twist his ear.

When the commotion died down ('Who were you shouting at?' 'Nobody?' 'How can you say it *just like that*?'), Dona punched Pinaki's arm. 'You're crazy, Baba!'

Crazed with a need, Pinaki thought. But he couldn't spell it out. Not then.

Presently, drinking tea in the veranda, and reading *The Hoogly Times,* he called out to Rimi.

The clinking of glass bangles stopped. '*Ki?*'

'I asked if you're happy!'

She emerged from the kitchen. 'What, *now?*'

'No, *here.* In this house.'

'Well, I've lived here for twenty years. That's half my life.'

'Yes, but was it a happy twenty years?'

'The children were born here. Your father died here. And Ma wants to die here.' She paused. 'I expect I will too,' she said pensively.

'And I.' He smiled. 'But before those sad events, I hope Dona will be married here. Actually, Rimi, I was asking if you *liked* it here. With me.'

'Oof! I have no time for this now—are you going for the fish? It's getting late. The best will be gone.'

He had hoped she had forgotten the fish. This daily duty had just lost its innocent pleasure for him. The truth was he was afraid of going into the street.

'I'm a little tired this morning,' he said. 'Can you send Dona instead?'

She looked at him as if this was exactly the sort of thing that didn't make her happy.

Tuli presented himself to Pinaki to knot his school tie. 'Should we bat or bowl if we win the toss today, Baba?' he asked humbly.

Pinaki frowned, still cross with his son. Then, 'Bat,' he said, relenting. 'It's a fast pitch.'

'That's what I also thought.' Tuli leapt at the door lintel, smacked it. 'It's a *very* fast pitch!'

Later, while Pinaki was sluicing himself in the bathroom, the humiliation of the morning returned. He soaped his armpits with renewed vigour, and then emptied the bucket over his head to drown the din going on inside it. Through the blur of water he glimpsed an object on the windowsill he hadn't seen, or noticed, in a long while. A urine-bottle his father had used during his final illness, ten years ago. Was Rimi preserving it for *his* future use? Pensively he began drying himself.

He flung down the towel. It was a replica, to a stripe and tatter, of the one... Sweat spurted on his damp forehead and he ran out to stand under the fan in the bedroom.

Ten minutes later, dressed in his regulation teri-cot pants and a blue (much-washed) bush-shirt, handkerchief tucked in his pants pocket, spectacle case in his shirt pocket, wallet in his hip pocket, he sat at the dining table, set with his breakfast of two parathas, a fried egg and a banana. After eating he would brush his teeth again to rid his mouth of the taste of egg. He was strapping on his leather sandals—in urgent need of replacement—when the doorbell rang.

~

'And nobody was there when you opened the door. Although you heard footsteps clattering down.'

'Yes, but how did you guess that?'

'Oh, anyone can write this script.'

Anyone but you. And there was that smile that so churned Pinaki. Did it imply a sneer or sympathy?

~

Pinaki ran down the two flights of stairs to the lobby and rushed into the street. A figure detached itself from the left pillar and blocked his path. Before he could react he was pushed towards the wall and pinned there.'Vote for Rabin Paul,' said a flat voice into his ear. 'CPM candidate for Mominpur.'

~

'It was *him*, sir. The fellow at the water pump.'

'So I guessed.'

'He was fully dressed. Pant and shirt.'

'Really? You surprise me.' And again there was that figure of eight smile.

~

'I'll vote for whosoever I want,' Pinaki said in a shrill voice that unfortunately cracked.

'The name is Rabin Pal,' said the youth. The eyeballs didn't move. They seemed sewn to the skull. 'I will be at the polling booth.'

'So?' said Pinaki, although his heart was beating very fast.

The youth lifted a corner of his lip.

Now Pinaki was angry. 'Who do you think you are? Giving me the red eye!'

The youth wagged his finger at Pinaki's face. 'Do not forget.'
And he tapped Pinaki with his forefinger!

'Abhadro!' cried Pinaki, smacking away the finger. 'I will...
I will report you to the police! This is harassment!'

~

'That wasn't wise.'

But this time it didn't sound like *good for you*. You could
get away with telling people not to glare at you, and you could,
under extreme provocation, warn them to keep away, but to
threaten them with the *police* took the matter to another plane
altogether. Especially if they had anything to do with the CPM.

'He jumped on a bicycle, sir. Das Engineering Works had
laid it out on the pavement. He bent the spokes.

'Well, *he* lost no time in making his position clear. Kicking
the dog in the first reel.'

'It was a *cycle*, sir. And he didn't kick it, he...'

'So you said. So you said.'

3

At first Pinaki was too shocked to react. Then, without
thinking, he started after the youth. So intent was he on
keeping him in his sights he stepped right into the soapy
puddle—the legacy of the morning's incident—and then lost
a precious minute examining the damage to his pants. When
he resumed the chase, the youth was vaulting over a six-foot-
high wall halfway down the street.

The wall, decorated with peeling CPM election posters,
bordered an empty plot, the only formal ingress to which was
through a lean-to shed of galvanized iron sheets, built like a
house of cards. Pinaki darted into it. Diffused light from the
gaps in the sheeting illuminated husks of household appliances,

a floor splattered with tarry oil, the spilled guts of machinery. It took him ten seconds to ascertain there was nobody there. He ran into the yard.

The yard was overgrown with vegetation of the vengeful sort—nettles, buffalo grass, poison berries—and littered with glass splinters, used condoms and plastic bags. There was no place for even a cat to hide. Concluding that his quarry must have exited the way he came in—across the wall—he dashed back into the shed and out to the street.

'Eey, babu! Bosebabu! Catching a train or a thief?'

Pinaki stopped, turned around.

The proprietor of Aroma The People—already in position behind his wok, raised a dripping tea strainer in salutation. 'Ashun, cha kheye jaan.'

'No, no tea, thank you,' Pinaki said. 'I'm in a hurry.'

'Arre, babu, *that* I can see. Where are you hurrying?'

'I was following a young man...tall, not thin, not fat.'

Aroma raised his eyebrows. '*Following*? Why?'

'Have to talk to him,' Pinaki huffed. 'Black pants, blue shirt,' he gabbled. He pumped his arms. 'Healthy. Did you see him?'

Aroma laughed. 'Did I see an ant on an anthill?' He tossed two onions to a small boy in an oversized T-shirt, 'Cut,' he snapped. 'Taratari! See, Bosebabu also thinks you're a lazy bum!' Before Pinaki could protest Aroma aimed a bowl of slops into a pail, got the onions instead, and fell to cursing his assistant.

Pinaki seized the moment to flee, although he knew Aroma would be disappointed. He would have wanted Pinaki to tease him, as he usually did, 'What does it mean, Aroma The People?' So he could answer he didn't know, his son had suggested it, but wasn't it a good name since it made people stop to ask, and then stay to drink tea?

The sun was clawing his eyes. He made a visor with his

hands and surveyed the street. It was teeming with youths, but his man wasn't one of them. Not that it would be that easy to spot anyone here, in this jumble of handcarts, cycles, rickshaws, scooters. Perhaps he had ducked into one of the alleys? It didn't occur to him to wonder why anyone, especially *this* youth, would run from him. It just seemed to be in keeping with the bafflements of this morning that he, Pinaki, should frighten away a fellow half his age and twice his size.

Business enterprises were setting up shop on the pavement—barber, knife grinder, locksmith and shoe-repairer, and vendors of tea and food and produce, of maps, magnifying lenses and scissors... *But this is the* real *Calcutta*, he protested to unseen detractors. (As though the better areas were cunning simulations. Or movie sets.) *Every single thing we need is right* here. *Fresh fish, vegetables, fruit, morning and evening. Shirts, shoes, saris, noodles, egg-and-toast, all on our doorstep! And in the lanes there are plumbers, carpenters, electricians, tailors, painters, welders...*

~

'I get the picture. It's a drop of pond water under a microscope.'

Pinaki wasn't sure if he should take offence or nod in complicity. He compromised with a cough. 'We are lucky to be here,' he said. 'It is a caring neighbourhood. Everyone cares...'

'About everyone else's business.'

~

It used to be such a good street, he thought. Big, beautiful houses, big beautiful gardens. You could smell the jasmine all the way right up to Diamond Harbour Road! But now Sen Mansion is Mudra Dance Academy. Ray Villa? Sold to Ameena Maternity. (The Rays owned a button factory which was burned down by the union.) Mukherjee House? The women's hostel. Mrs Ghosh started Cambridge Montessori in her backyard... There was a huge palash tree outside—every March the pavement would be covered with flowers. We used to walk barefoot...

'You went barefoot in *this* street, Baba?'

'It was washed every single day, Dona.'

'When was this—before the Battle of Plassey?'

~

There was no sign of the youth. And, he suspected, he wouldn't find any. For, it occurred to him, he wasn't pursuing a quarry as much as exorcizing a demon. He had been driven by bravado, vexation, a misplaced sense of honour, and in any case what would he do with the fellow when, if, he found him? What *could* he do?

The probing yellow disc, which illuminated every square inch of the street, showed him, with painful clarity, how pitiful his position was. Its position, high in the sky, reminded him he had missed his bus. To add to his anxiety he remembered he had left his briefcase behind. With his lunch in it! Rimi would be so cross! But to go back now...the questions she would ask!

He wanted a cigarette. The situation craved this indulgence. And there, before him like divine consent, was the modi's shop. It had been in the same place for forty years but now he saw it as an omen.

He walked into the familiar clutter of household supplies, breathing in the nostalgic bouquet of scents—spice, rice, soap. Dust and mildew. The modi was attending to a customer 'Twenty-seven rupees. Sorry no discount.'

'But this tin is rusted!'

Pinaki started at the voice. Vinu! Dona's 'friend'! Who Rimi disapproved of!

'Don't buy it then,' said the modi, and smiling his lipless Buddha smile, 'Buy scent. All girls like it.'

Vinu frowned at the display shelf. 'What is this soap?'

'Luxury item. Very popular.'

Vinu picked it up and sniffed. 'Never heard of it.' He rubbed it on his nose.

'Don't finish it up... Ashun Bosebabu. What can I give you today?'

Vinu jerked around. 'Hello Uncle,' he said, looking a bit guilty.

Pinaki hesitated. Should he acknowledge the greeting? Rimi wouldn't like it. He nodded to the sack of rice, quickly made his purchase—lighting it from the smouldering tip of rope suspended from the ceiling—and took an inexpert puff. 'Have you seen,' he began, and then had a coughing fit. 'Have you seen a ...' He clutched the counter, his eyes streaming. '...a young man,' he gasped. 'Tall, thick hair with,' he sketched a quiff with his cigarette.

'Sounds like me, Uncle,' said Vinu, grinning.

Pinaki pretended not to hear. 'Black pants,' he said to the modi. 'Tight.'

'*I'm* wearing black pants,' Vinu said, giving his leg an affectionate pat.

'Yes,' said the modi. 'So tight that if I touch it with a razorblade it will go phhhrrrr!' He put his tongue between his teeth and shook with laughter.

'You just try,' growled Vinu. He slammed down the cake of soap and stalked out. Seconds later, his head popped round the door. 'Bye Uncle,' he said sheepishly to Pinaki.

The modi hadn't seen the youth. 'But since you are here, Bosebabu, a small matter...' He lowered his voice. 'Your good lady bought a kilo of rice last week. She has not yet, um-ah.'

Pinaki pulled out his wallet, making a mental note to tell Rimi never, ever, to do this to him again. He knew he would never, ever, tell her. It was a waste of breath anyway.

Outside the shop the Dignified Beggar waylaid him. Pinaki dropped some coins into his plate. 'I wonder if you saw a young man,' he said in the placatory voice he used for the less fortunate. 'Tall, strong...'

'That kind doesn't stop for *me*,' said the Beggar resentfully.

Pinaki sighed. It was so very hot. He was so very tired. And the Beggar was so desperately smelly.

A new paranoia gripped him. He was late! The next bus was due in ten minutes. Ten minutes! If he didn't catch it, Mr Sen would cut half a day from his leave allowance. He shouldn't stop now, not for man, not for God.

And then God's emissary was hailing from the Kali temple. 'Babu! You can't turn away from Devi!'

Pinaki put the rest of his change on the offerings plate. Then he hesitated. Should he? It could be an omen. 'Did a young man pass by here, Panditmoshai? Black pants, blue shirt?'

The priest gave him a batasa. 'Ki jaani, there are so many like that! What does he look like?'

Pinaki chewed the sweet. What *did* the fellow look like? 'Dark complexion, very dark...' The lips were the bitter black of coffee. 'White teeth.' That slow, horrible smile. He swallowed. 'Tall. Muscular.' He threw back his shoulders to make his point. He stopped chewing. Come to think of it, the fellow's chest was a little *too* fleshy. It looked like armour plates. In fact, it looked like... He shied away from the thought, embarrassed.

And now he had missed the second bus! He'd have to take a taxi...the expense of it! Should he take the day off, pleading sickness? But to stay home when he wasn't sick? He thought of the reassuring tedium of his office, the comforting gloom of his cell, the poignant smell of drains... Even Mr Sen was not so bad after lunch. So, should he go after lunch? He'd never done *that* before. The sentence 'life was never the same again' began taking a hold of him.

But life *would* be the same, wouldn't it? He would go to work, hear out Mr Sen on the subject of lateness and laziness, forget this incident, and tomorrow all would be as before. There was safety in sameness. But that was what was nagging him, wasn't it? When he died it would be remembered that he had walked down this street every single day of his working life. For forty years. That he had caught the same bus—Number 345—on Diamond Harbour Road. And he bought his one cigarette of the day in *that* shop. And *that* is the saloon where he cut his hair—every six weeks and always on a second Saturday. *There* is the teashop where he drank one cup of tea on his way home after work. *This* is the woman he bought fish from. (Her granddaughter now.)

For the third time that morning he wanted to howl.

When he reached St Teresa's Church in the corner of Diamond Harbour Road he was panicking. Late, so late! Resigning himself to the loss of half a day's leave, he leaned on the wicket gate to rest his aching legs.

Father John emerged on the porch.

Pinaki jumped back. 'Sorry,' he mumbled, and then was annoyed with himself. (Dona swore she'd seen him apologize to the doormat after wiping his feet.)

Father John waved to him. 'Hello! Beautiful morning, isn't it? Any chance of a shower this evening? We could do with a nor'wester.'

Pinaki glanced up at the sterile white clouds.

'You seem hot and bothered, sir. Can I do anything for you?'

Sir! Pinaki ducked his head, suddenly conscious of the oil stain on his pants where he had dropped his breakfast paratha.

And now Father John was walking towards him! And holding his hand out! 'I haven't had the pleasure of meeting you. I'm...'

'I know you,' Pinaki blurted out. 'I am Pinaki Bose. Father,' he added shyly.

Father John's hand was so cool and dry! And his own so...

In his confusion he had wiped his palm on his pants *after* shaking Father's instead of before. He suffered anew. Taking a deep breath, 'Actually I am looking for a young fellow,' he said. 'Tall, black pants, blue checked shirt, dark complexion and...' The whites of those eyes were yellow. 'Yellow eyes,' he said, and shuddered.

'What's his name?' asked Father John patiently.

'I don't know. I saw him for the first time this morning.'

Father John laughed. 'That presents a small difficulty. Why, what about this young man?'

'He was taking a bath at the water pump this morning. His towel fell off.'

'Ah. You want to return it to him.'

'No, no, that is not the case at all.' After a moment's hesitation Pinaki gave him an account of the morning's incident, edited, in deference to Father John's calling. 'He is a troublemaker.'

'You don't know that for sure, Mr Bose.'

Chastened, Pinaki slunk away.

~

At Daisy's Beauty Parlour Rimi sat back in a chair with her head on a cushion.

'What happened in your houth thith morning? People thay they heard noitheth.'

'Ouch,' said Rimi. 'Don't talk with the string in your mouth, Daisy. I've told you before.' She sat up to examine her eyebrows in the mirror. 'Too thin.'

'Latest fashion,' Daisy said in a bored voice, uncapping a tube of Boroline.

~

While Pinaki was getting into his taxi, Kalol Mondal was turning into a foetid alley off J. Mullick Road. Three youths loped up to circle him. *Pack dogs,* he thought, regarding them with a tolerant, if jaundiced, eye. He held up a pre-emptive hand. 'I can't talk now. I have things to do.'

Something about his face forbade the three to ask what he was so busy about. They drew back, disappointed. They had wanted to make plans for the evening.

4

Biren stood at the window, blowing smoke rings into the stinging brightness of the mid-morning sun. That eastern elevation needed relief. A rose window? A lancet? An arrowslit?

A small square grating. Such as you would find in the basement of a bank. Or a medieval prison.

He was drawing this when Manu brought the mail. There were the usual flyers and catalogues, a newsletter, all destined for the wastepaper basket. And one letter, with a logo that brought instant—and heart-stopping—recognition. Biren slit it open.

His stomach lurched. He felt a stinging on his neck, his arms, his back. It was a reject.

The thing about rejection is it doesn't kill you—although one died in that moment—it just cripples you. It diminishes you. Denatures you. You doubt, you hate, you envy, you grudge... No practice of detachment, no amount of cynicism, no attempt at indifference, and no experience of other rejects (an unedifying history), nothing can shield you from the jolt of *that moment*. You're never prepared for it. And yet you should be. You see failure, yes *failure*, everywhere you look. In the pitted floor at your feet, the eraser worn to a lump of dried snot, the table leg bandaged with a duster, the single person you employ... And at home, the side of your bed that's been cold for a decade.

Sorry, Mr Roy, your concept is interesting, and innovative, but regretfully, it is not for us. Apart from other considerations we don't have the means to construct such a building. We appreciate your intent to design something different but...

Different isn't the *intent* here, you blockheads! Different *happens*. And different isn't the word should use, *edgy* is. *Unique* if you must.

Vindicating the automated regret is the underlying resentment you've made a mockery of the project, their brief, their understanding, even.

There are other considerations. You know them only too well. Principally that a building is a brand too. If a *branded* architect screws up they won't get into trouble for picking him. And, face it. If *you* had to pick between a gold medallist and a contender who got knocked out in the heats, who would you go with?

Exactly.

~

'Just for the record, Biren, who, if anyone, has built anything you actually like? In recent times?'

'What you're saying, Doc, what you're *not* saying is that I can't afford to pass judgment. People who live in glass houses, that is, people who don't *build* glass houses or any houses...'

'Don't take it personally, Biren. And anyway you *have* built. And still do. For your Sethji.'

'*Now* you're mocking me.'

'Perhaps you could be a little more...compliant in your approach.'

'Every prophet was damned a heretic.'

'Indeed.'

'Beckett's first book sold three copies.'

'I've no doubt you check your facts.'

~

Manu was standing inside the door, his small, precise person taut with agonizing apprehension, his pale face etched with the memory of a long-inflicted hurt. Biren often wondered whether this was because of his personal misfortune—damaged and defunct vocal chords—or the dispiriting fortunes of his workplace. Whatever it was he bore it with a smile on standby.

Biren wanted to scotch the incipient smile. He folded the letter into a rocket, aimed and whizzed it across. (It hit its mark.) 'Save the cheers for another day,' he said shortly.

Manu rubbed his cheek and smoothed out the letter. When he finished reading it he made a small noise, like the backfiring of a toy motorcycle. Then, using the wall as a surface, he scribbled on it and held it up for Biren to read.

There may be a revaluation

'What's this—a class test?'

Miracles happen

'Miracles. Why don't we go to Lourdes?'

Judge is winner's uncle.

Biren jumped up. '*Stop* it, will you? Sorry, Sancho.' He sat down again. 'This is such crap. Such fucking...wait though. Perhaps we shouldn't be so hasty in rubbishing the verdict. Perhaps this is the masterwork the world is holding out for.'

The motorcycle sputtered.

'Yes, right. Enough of this nonsense. Let's look at the upside. We're never oversold—covertly or ignorantly. Never compromised. And we don't have to drudge for a living. If you keep commerce out of the equation it *is* a privileged life.' Manu gave him a doubtful look. Riled, Biren said, 'Anyway I have always maintained commerce undermines purpose.'

And your purpose is? Plotting an alternative destiny? That won't build you a portfolio.

He walked to his assistant and put his hands on his bony shoulders. 'You're a *fool*. A first-rate engineer should be working in a thriving, responsible practice, not for a deadbeat like me.

Go before it's too late.' Suddenly shaky, he dropped into his chair. 'I shouldn't have hired you. Now I can't do without you.'

When he opened his eyes Manu was holding out a mug of coffee.

'Thank you, Friday. But for you I would be lying in a ditch, my head pillowed on a dog.' He sat up, took the coffee. 'You know, there must have been times Belzoni doubted if there was anything in the desert. What if he had stopped believing? Then there's Van Gogh. Mad. Jeered at. What if *he* had given up?'

After a while he got up and filed the competition drawings in a folder that contained his stillborn projects. The folder, which he called *Unbuildings*, was discouragingly thick. On the same shelf was another prized possession—a box file of Frank Lloyd Wright's drawings for The Living City—that had cost him the entire fee of an early commission.

You wouldn't know discontent if you didn't know these. Weather isn't bothersome if the body cannot distinguish heat from cold. To discern is to feel. To feel is to suffer.

Frank never built his City. That was small comfort considering what Frank *had* built. Perhaps it would be apposite to rename *Unbuildings* The Dead City, and make it a companion volume, with the hope—unfounded, considering the dismal outcome of your hopes so far but still there was no premium for hope, only a high tax on disappointment (which you paid with more hope, throwing good money after bad, in the time-honoured practice of incurable gamblers)—that one day you would be up there.

He walked out to the studio, to a cage of steel in the far corner. 'Manu! You were right. This will not work for 120 km winds. We will need a heavier cross tie.'

Manu nodded glumly. Of what use was the experiment now that they had lost the project?

Biren looked at him for a long moment. 'Manu. Forget this project. Think of yourself being in a crusade—saving the world from getting savaged. Unsung but singing all the same. You don't seem convinced. Take the rest of the day off.' He pointed at the bandaged table leg. 'In heavier vein, as my Dadu would say, why hasn't this healed yet?'

An hour later he locked up and walked out. Free School Street, his favourite walk, began at the Park Street intersection, where the iconic and whimsical Park Mansion—cupolas, cusps, crenellations—takes up half a kilometre on both streets, a stark contrast to the square bulk of the Dunlop headquarters, which always put him in mind of the bullmastiff his father had once owned. Then comes a series of lightless and unequivocally shuttered doorways owned by companies that had fled the state's Communist regime, chased out by its ideology of idiosyncratic abnegation that had, in a decade, destroyed private enterprise, destabilized state institutions and demoralized civil society. After this, the street follows the trajectory of the city's economic decline. A straggle of hostelries populated by backpackers, and the inevitable support system of cheap eateries, dingy pharmacies, stalls of bottled drinks... As a postscript to this chapter of history it ends in a garbage pile where pigs and rodents root around. In the middle of this rebarbative stretch is the onion dome of the Madina Mosque, squashed between two faceless, genderless office blocks. *Arabian Nights in the Gulag,* Biren thought. It was the monotony that got you down. And *that* was a failure of imagination. After all, if an interesting solution costs the same as a boring one, and (for the sake of argument), requires the same resources, who but a hominid would pick the latter?

There was a fundamental flaw in this hypothesis, as you know only too well. It presumes people can distinguish between good and bad, or beautiful and ugly, on the strength of which they would make rational choices. It also argues a universal code for beauty. *There* you were on slippery ground. And, anyway, aesthetics was not an agenda here. Expedience was. If you need shelter and all you have is a couple of sticks and plastic sheet, then aesthetics becomes a luxury. Although, as with other inconsistencies, this too lacks rationale. Ugliness of any kind depresses the already depressed.

Rich, poor, rich, poor. It was a bloody refrain. And what about those in the middle? Virtue caught in a vice, poor sods. And in nostalgia.

Nostalgia! Nostalgia blurs the truth and counters reason. It subverts history, devalues the present, constricts the future. Nostalgists don't solve problems or make plans or set goals. They wander in the labyrinth of reminiscences and longing, and, in this city, in a self-congratulatory daze induced by past glories, that blinds them to its present mediocrity.

Yet how seductive is the idea of Calcutta as a memory! Liberated from the dreariness of *this* reality!

5

Pinaki's taxi dropped him in Dalhousie, where his work place was, in the street flanking the High Court. The district bustled with court-related businesses—cage-like shacks stacked with law books and college crammers, stamp paper and files, photocopying shops, typists sitting at small, collapsible tables under the trees. Knots of lawyers in greasy black coats stood around stalls selling fried noodles and omelettes. His eyes began watering from the fumes of the primus stoves on the pavement. Dodging the detritus—discarded carbon paper, cyclostyled forms, eggshells, shards of clay from the tea bowls, blackening bananas in a straw basket—he gained his destination, a red brick building that, according to a brass plaque, had been Warren Hastings' winter home circa 1781. It now housed, among other establishments, Jalan and Jalan, Chartered Accountants. Pinaki had had worked here since the time of his apprenticeship, twenty-five years ago.

The marble staircase to the lift lobby on the first floor began practically from the entranceway. The treads were precariously worn, but the central rail mooted every year had yet to be installed. Now Pinaki, like other wary long-term employees, clung to the balustrade.

He adopted a preoccupied expression as he entered the office hall, hoping it would be assumed he was returning from an errand. He slipped into his cubicle, and, after nodding to his colleague (already an hour into his work), buried his head in a file. Before he had read a page Mr Sen bustled in, brandishing the attendance register. 'I see you haven't signed, Bose.'

Pinaki mumbled he'd forgotten, he was in a bit of a hurry this morning...

'Late,' declared Mr Sen, and put a circle in the square next to Pinaki's name.

Pinaki didn't protest or try to explain. His colleague, though, was clearly expecting an explanation. They had shared their air space for too long, and their lunch and their concerns, to let the small matter of privacy come in the way of their friendship. Pinaki propped his elbows on the table, and made a screen for his face with his fingers.

A half-hour went by. Tea did the rounds. Pinaki's colleague slurped and got on Pinaki's nerves. How was it possible that three inches of tea could be made to last five minutes?

'Take.' His colleague was proffering a paper cone. A strong smell of mustard oil and raw onion tickled Pinaki's nose. His mouth filled but he shook his head, without lifting it, acutely conscious he was behaving badly, or at least uncharacteristically, which was as bad. He was thankful that Jalan and Jalan's seating plan discouraged communication between employees. Its furniture was designed for productivity. And underlined authority. Ultimate authority rested with the principals, Messrs B.K., H.K. and S.K. Jalan, who, when they came at all, occupied the entire window wall of the floor. Immediate authority wore the saturnine visage of Mr Sen, who played the role of a class monitor during the indefinite absence of the class teacher. He'd held this post for years but still retained the zeal of the newly promoted.

Pinaki waited for him to finish his morning inspection before making amends to his colleague. Holding up his empty tea glass, 'I've always felt this glass is too small for me,' he said. 'Twice this size would be better. Four times even better.'

His colleague brightened. 'A bucket would be best for *you*, Pinakibabu!'

Pinaki smiled although he didn't think it was much of a joke. 'Why is it that one glass always leaves you with a thirst but the second becomes an overdose?'

'It is psychology, Pinakibabu.'

'Ah. Tell me, are you happy?'

'Here? In this office? Sensaab says too-happy people are not efficient. So even if I am happy I should not show it, taito?' The silliness of this and of everything else made them laugh. 'Are *you* a happy man, Pinakibabu?'

And Pinaki, who believed he was one of the blessed few who had shoes *and* feet, now wondered if his contentment had been the bliss of ignorance.

On the way home in the evening he stopped at Aroma's for a samosa and tea.

'I have news for you, Bosebabu! I know who your young man is! The one who you were chasing this morning!'

'I wasn't *chasing* him. I only wanted to...to tell him something.'

Aroma slopped tea into a thick white cup and slid it across the counter. 'He's a regular. He was here just fifteen minutes ago, in fact. Imagine that!'

Pinaki hid his dismay behind his teacup.

Aroma was full of his triumph. A group of young men had come and he had had the brilliant idea to ask *them* if they'd seen the sort of young man such as Pinaki had described—although it wasn't much of a description—all young men look the same, taito? It could even be one of them! And it turned out it *was*! Wasn't that lucky, Bosebabu?

Pinaki gazed at him, speechless. Aroma talked too much. But then it wasn't his fault. He knew nothing about the incident, and Pinaki *had* been distraught. Still, this was going beyond the call of helpfulness. This was interference.

'Who is he?'

'Name of Kalol Mondal,' Aroma announced, as if he had been waiting for just this moment all his life. 'He works in Diamond Harbour Road.'

Of course, after this favour, Pinaki was obliged to relate his story, although he could tell within an inch of certainty that Aroma had already heard it—the bawdy version. New anxieties beset him as he stumbled along. The incident was street knowledge. It wouldn't be long before Rimi heard it. Should he tell her before someone else did?

Aroma burst out laughing. 'That Kalol!' He wiped his eyes with his towel. Catching Pinaki's eye, he sobered. 'You can meet him here tomorrow evening, Bosebabu. I told him you were looking for him.'

Pinaki clattered his cup. 'I may be working late tomorrow evening,' he said. Aroma gave him a smile, half-pitying, half-understanding.

The smile galled Pinaki. Looking into the distance, 'I'll *try* and fit it into my schedule,' he said.

The next evening something happened to precipitate matters.

When he returned from work he found a woman squatting on the pavement, right under his balcony, stirring a pot on a chula. The chula was billowing black smoke into the balcony. He hesitated, unwilling to enter into an altercation, and yet... The sudden appearance of Rimi in the balcony solved his problem. 'Eii!' she screeched at the woman. 'Ki korchish?'

The woman gave no indication she'd heard.

'Eijay!' cried Rimi. She had spotted Pinaki. 'Who is that woman? Why is she cooking *here*?'

'Why are you cooking here?' Pinaki asked the woman.

The woman spat a stream of paan juice.

'Tell her to go somewhere else!'

Come down and tell her yourself, he thought, annoyed. 'You heard,' he said jerking his head at the woman.

'She will stay where she is,' said a flat voice from behind him.

Pinaki turned around and looked into the yellow eyes of Kalol Mondal.

Pinaki had imagined him so often that at first he thought it was an apparition. Before he could collect his wits, Kalol Mondal spoke again. 'Why didn't you come to the voting booth if you wanted to meet me? Rabin Pal is not happy.'

At this juncture a bucketful of water cascaded from the balcony, dousing the stove—and splashing Kalol Mondal. The woman gave a howl of rage. Kalol Mondal leapt back with a curse.

~

For much of that night Pinaki lay awake, thinking. You would imagine the sky is free for you to roam in—except it isn't. The patch of grey trapped between the buildings is all you see. As for the air, it's used and reused so often you may as well live in a capped bottle. What *is* free is advice. *Go for a walk! Check your sugar! Take shark liver oil!* And opinions are free and plentiful too. *You're getting a paunch. You're going bald. You're becoming forgetful.*

That morning, again to his colleague's mystification—and frustration—he was more distracted than ever.

'What are you busy writing, Pinakibabu? Your will?'

Pinaki ducked his head and turned over the paper he was scribbling on.

There are two reasons for secrecy. When your life isn't going well and you fear pity (or ridicule) or when it is going all too well and you fear envy, and the evil eye. Curious to find out which it was in this instance, Pinaki's colleague tilted his chair towards him. 'Let me see...oh, it's a drawing. It looks like a *house.*'

Several things happened in a confused sequence. Mr Sen burst into the cubicle. The colleague lost his balance and crashed to the floor. The sheet floated down. Pinaki leapt up and snatched it. Mr Sen, concluding that the sheet of paper was the reason for the commotion, barked, 'What is that paper?'

Pinaki pushed it into a drawer. 'Personal letter,' he mumbled. His ears tingled.

'Electricity bill,' supplied the colleague, on the principle that details give credence to a lie.

Mr Sen sniffed. 'Where are the Kanoria tax papers? They are due today.' He yanked open a cupboard, picked three files at random and threw them on the desk. They were all marked CLOSED in red but Pinaki did not point out that this section of the cupboard was an archive. Instead he flung himself into the search.

The rotor blades of the fan cut endless strips of the damp, still air. Sweat gathered in his armpits, staining his shirt. He pressed his arms to his sides to keep impolite emanations from assailing Mr Sen's nose.

'What's the matter with your arms, Bose?'

Pinaki backed all the way to his table and lifted his arms and lowered them, to demonstrate they were in working order.

Mr Sen smiled sardonically. To Pinaki's relief, he merely said, 'I'll come back after lunch. Have them ready.'

But there was a warning note there that threw Pinaki in a new agony of apprehension. He had been marked for Mr Sen's disfavour. And, as surely as a stubbed toe is the one that *will* get stamped on, he was in Mr Sen's sights all morning. For someone who had a horror of being noticed (even for commendation), who liked the anonymity of crowds, who bought his clothes for their conformity to the dun-and-grey workforce of Calcutta, this was a heavy sentence.

Mr Sen returned fifteen minutes before lunch. 'The papers. Diye dao, diye dao, diye dao!' Observing Pinaki's panic, 'You haven't found them,' he said smugly.

Pinaki was too flustered to respond. Then he blanked out. He floated to his chair and sat down, leaning back and hands behind his head, uncaring of his armpits (which felt agreeably cool). 'Not yet,' he said dreamily.

Mr Sen's eyes bulged 'What do you mean by that?'

He looks like a bullfrog, Pinaki thought, stifling a laugh. 'You said *after* lunch, sir.'

'Hurry up,' said Mr Sen, in a sort of grumble.

When he'd left, Pinaki's colleague jumped up to shake Pinaki's hand. 'Wah, Pinakibabu, you were *great*! What a hero! And here I was worrying you're having some kind of breakdown! I mean, drawing houses...'

Pinaki smirked. 'I am sound of reason,' he said, tapping his head.

'Then why are you drawing houses like a six-year-old?' said the colleague, pretending to check his pen.

'Must you know everything?'

The colleague turned away.

Contrite, actually wretched, Pinaki said, 'You remember my grandfather's house I used to talk about?'

'What about it?' said the colleague gruffly.

'There were rice fields around it. Ponds filled with fish. And trees—mango, jackfruit, guava, coconut. You could see the sky—lots of sky.'

The colleague considered Pinaki for a long moment. 'So *that's* what you were drawing. Your grandfather's house. You're going to visit it.' His face sagged. *You could have told me.*

'I can't. We don't have it any more. We lost it. During that time. *You* remember.'

The colleague nodded. Everyone had a story to tell about *that* time. 'Did the Naxals destroy it completely?' When Pinaki didn't respond—the numbness was returning, in its previous debilitating avatar, 'Go for a holiday, Pinakibabu,' he said. 'Take your family to Digha for a few days.'

~

That evening, Pinaki found a piece of cloth stuffed into his letterbox. It turned out to be a pair of drawers, the kind of underwear worn by the lower classes of Calcutta. This one was ragged and looked as if it had been used to wipe mud. Or worse. He stood for a moment with the thing in his hands, frozen with revulsion, before flinging it out of the doorway into the street.

After a moment's hesitation he stepped out and walked very fast down J. Mullick Road. As if slowing down would reverse his resolve. He stopped once to ask the way, with the gratuitous information he had to see a friend 'near there'.

The lane he was directed to was lined with single and two-storey structures in varying stages of disrepair and incompletion. Electric cables and clothes lines festooned the flaking walls. Passageways, like capillaries, ran through the dense mass. A viscous black fluid seeped along the curb, the source of the unpleasant smell that trailed him. Children spilled everywhere. Several times he had to hop over a ball or duck one. He had been told to look for a red door, and that a proliferation of red sickle-and-hammer flags would indicate its approach. The door turned out to be more sepia than red. Set in a wall plastered with old election posters, it was shabby, even flimsy, for a Communist Party bastion. Three men lounged outside it. One leaned on the jamb, smoking, one squatted on a stool, chewing paan, and the third sat on a chair, whittling a toothpick with his teeth.

Pinaki's clothes were modest and his manner hesitant, but the stares made him feel as welcome as a rent collector. Without moving an inch they had encircled him. Without moving an inch he had backed away.

'Ki chai?' asked the pan-chewer.

'Who is the in-charge here?' Pinaki asked.

The toothpick-chewer took his time to move his toothpick to a corner of his mouth. 'I am. I'm the Chief. Why?'

'I have something to discuss.'

'Ki?'

'I want to make a complaint. I am a resident of J. Mullick Road.'

The toothpick-chewer nodded as if that was what he expected. Complaints were the norm here. He got up and beckoned Pinaki to follow him through the door.

A rectangular pinewood table and six rusting steel chairs filled most of the room. The Chief sat at its head and motioned Pinaki to an adjacent chair. The other two sat across from him. Three more men materialized to take the remaining chairs. The Chief worked his toothpick so it pointed at Pinaki. 'Bolun.'

Pinaki shifted on his chair—his neighbour was too close to him. 'A round table would be more comfortable,' he said.

The toothpick fell out. 'You came to tell us *that*?'

Pinaki gave a nervous laugh 'No, no. It was just an idea.'

'You can donate one if you like,' the Chief said. 'So. You have come to make a complaint.' As Pinaki hesitated, 'You can speak freely here,' he said, waving his hand.

'He means we are all friends,' murmured Pinaki's neighbour, nudging him with his thigh. Encased in polyester, it was uncomfortably warm.

'Do you know Rabin Pal?' Pinaki asked the Chief.

'Is your complaint about *him*?'

'Na, na,' said Pinaki. 'I don't know him at all. His name was mentioned by...' A wave of nausea silenced him. He patted his mouth with a handkerchief.

'Tell him the full facts,' whispered his neighbour, with an encouraging smile. His front teeth were missing. Pinaki did not find the gap disarming or endearing.

For the third time in two days Pinaki related the water hydrant incident, overplaying his concerns to amplify the gravity of it. The tactic failed. Pinaki had no talent for drama, no practice in oratory, and was a complete loss at persuasion. Plus, unfortunately, the incident was not without its comic aspects. Laughter broke out, loud, lewd, licentious. Pinaki chuckled sportingly.

The Chief held up his hand for silence. 'This rascal sounds quite a comedian. What did you say his name was?'

'I didn't...but it's Kalol Mondal.'

'Kalol Mondal?' The Chief pursed his lips. 'Olympic champion type?' He flexed his muscles. 'Gopal underwear body?' A titter went around the room. Pinaki's neighbour drummed his feet. They knew the story and were now having fun.

'Sit down, Dada!' said the Chief. 'I was only joking! I know Kalol. ('He is the nephew of his sister-in-law's cousin,' supplied Pinaki's neighbour, pointing his chin at the Chief.) What is your complaint?'

'He committed public nuisance!'

The toothpick snapped. '*We* are the public, Dada.'

'Hmm,' said Pinaki, smoothing his hair. There was a fallacy in this but he couldn't locate it.

'We are not asking to use *your* bathroom,' the Chief said, flipping a pencil between thumb and forefinger.

'Not yet,' murmured someone.

Pinaki shrunk into his chair. His neighbour gave his elbow a sympathetic pinch.

Faster and faster went the pencil. The room grew close with stale emanations. The thigh felt repulsively damp. How do you explain to these men the rules of acceptable behaviour?

They were waiting for him to speak. For night to fall. For the monsoon to break. 'Chhere dao,' he said. 'Let it be. I had hoped you would understand my problem.'

'But what *is* your problem? I do not see it. Do you?' The Chief consulted the table.

'No,' they chorused.

Pinaki's throat dried. At last, 'I am a law-abiding citizen,' he croaked. 'I pay my taxes. I...'

The Chief wagged his finger, 'If you didn't you'd be more of a parasite than you are. *Landlords*,' he spat.

Pinaki didn't see how his shabby (rented) flat merited him a landlord's status, or why he was a parasite, but it would serve no useful purpose to ask. 'We are a respectable family,' he said tremulously. 'I have a young daughter...'

'We *all* have daughters,' the Chief said, and winking at his cronies, 'You tell your daughter to shut her eyes, and we'll tell ours to do the same.'

Once more the room exploded. The thigh jiggled—it was enjoying the joke too. Now the arm snaked out and began exploring Pinaki's person. Fingers picked up his wrist to examine it, pressed lightly here and there, as if trying to locate Pinaki's pulse. Pinaki wriggled away. 'This is not a joke,' he shrilled.

'Cool yourself, Dada,' said the Chief. 'We are all brothers. Peaceful coexistence,' he wagged his finger, 'till we are all equal. That day will come.' His face darkened. 'Soon.'

The pressure eased on Pinaki's leg. His neighbour was distancing himself. It was a relief but also strangely disconcerting. He felt as if he had lost a friend.

The Chief stirred. 'Tell us about yourself,' he said in a let-bygones-be-bygones tone. 'Family background? Father, mother, brother, sister? How many children? Job? Income?'

Pinaki, anxious to cooperate, at least not to antagonize, spewed information like exhaust from an old truck. Unfortunately his every word amplified his otherness. Only a few hundred yards separated their homes but what a chasm it was! On his side a private school (although a modest one), a bank account (very modest), life insurance (more prudence than substance), but there was also *The Hoogly Times* instead of the *Bartaman* that Father John pasted on the church wall. And of course, the bathroom. His sensibilities spanned continents—theirs were lodged in this street. There were experiences he could aspire to and perhaps gratify during the remaining span of his life—a plane ride, a holiday in Goa... Then it struck him it was exactly these aspirations that made him the other, the enemy. He thought of saying his father was captured and traumatized—tortured—by the Naxals, and checked himself. His father had been targeted for his right-of-centre views expressed, with typical miscalculation, in a left-leaning newspaper.

The Chief was frowning, as if considering which of Pinaki's answers he would pick to score a point. Pinaki had no doubt he would score many points by the end of the meeting, which, he realized, had become all about scoring points. Rivulets of sweat ran down his face. He mopped his face. 'I hope this monsoon will be a good one.'

'Not *too* good,' frowned the Chief. 'This lane floods.'

Pinaki admitted that a good monsoon can also be bad, depending. But his audience was slipping away. He tried one last time. 'Who is Rabin Pal?'

Before anybody could answer there was a flurry of activity at the door. 'Ilish! Podda'r ilish!'

'Where?' The Chief half-rose from his chair. Two others leapt up, rocking the table. Pinaki's neighbour stepped on his toes. '*Podda'r* ilish? From Bangladesh?'

'Where else is the Podda, boka? *America*? *Hurry*!'

'*Where*?'

'Park Circus market! It's going fast!'

In seconds the room was empty. Pinaki walked out, thinking. Should he get some fish too—surprise the family? Ma could make her special shorshe ilish. He could buy fresh mustard oil from the modi...

He went home. The fish market would be swarming with the Chief and his cohorts.

6

Two days after his visit to the CPM office Pinaki stepped out of his front door at 6.30 a.m. to bring in the newspaper—and put his foot into something wet and squashy. It was a turd.

He hopped away with a yelp, and, his foot still raised, shouted, 'Rimi! Dona! Esho! Taratari! Bring some old newspaper! *Taratari!*'

Rimi was the first to arrive. Unheeding of his warning shout she jostled him from the doorway. '*Eeesh*!'

She returned with a bundle of newspapers. 'It's a dog's I think.'

'*Please*, Rimi.'

She followed him to the bathroom. 'How did it happen? Nobody's Dog has never done such a thing before. Has someone played a prank on us?'

The thought had occurred to him too. The mess was plumb in the centre of the doormat. That couldn't have been an accident... In fact, in fact...

'It is that woman downstairs,' she declared. 'I'll go talk to her.'

'No, don't! Leave it to me! I will...I will do something.'

'What? Look for the dog?' Which was funny, except it wasn't. 'You should go to the police,' she said. 'No point talking to these people.'

'No! I...I don't think we should bring the police into this.'

She put her hands on her hips.

The same evening, after work, he went to the local police station, a small, squat red-brick structure, unremarkable except for iron window grilles that Pinaki, in his present mood, found ominous.

Inside, jostled by its anxious and cringing custom, and ignored by its contemptuous custodians, he thought, if there was any hope to be found in this world it wouldn't be here.

At last he was sitting across the desk of the 'sergeant', on the edge of a wooden chair, with his knees pressed together, waiting for the great man to finish his phone conversation, apparently with his wife, placating her for not buying the right fish. We all have our troubles, he thought. Not that that was of any comfort now. He shouldn't have come here. He shouldn't have complained to the Party. He shouldn't have heeded Rimi. That wasn't an option, of course. He shouldn't have been so stupid in the first place. *That* wasn't an option either. His cubicle in the office would be a good place to be just now. Better still, his bathroom—with the door locked.

The 'sergeant' yawned and then laughed. 'Let me understand, Dada. This man took off towel on *purpose*, you are saying. Then he brought a woman to send smoke into your window on *purpose*. Tarpore, this morning he put dog shit on your doormat? Also on purpose?'

'Yes,' said Pinaki, mentally smiting his forehead.

'Shey ki? What did you do to deserve such treatment?'

'I don't know,' Pinaki said glumly, wishing he didn't.

The 'sergeant' thumped a bell. 'Someone will go with you to verify the complaint.'

'Eii, there's no need,' said Pinaki, alarmed. 'The mat has been washed. I don't think they will do anything again.' With a self-deprecatory smile he scraped back his chair.

The 'sergeant' looked irritated. 'Why did you come to us then? FIR has already been registered. Next step: verification. Esho!' A potbellied constable lounging in the doorway shot in and stood at attention.

Pinaki panicked. 'Jete dao, sergeant. You have more important cases. Don't waste your valuable time.'

'Go with him,' said the sergeant to the constable. He thwacked his bell. 'Next!'

The potbellied constable patted his belt. 'You will have to appear in court, babu.'

'No, I don't. This is not a police case. The court only deals with serious cases.'

'You have registered FIR,' said the constable reprovingly.

'*I* didn't...look at those iron rods on that cart! They are sticking out *four* feet! It is dangerous!'

The constable trotted to the handcart, shouted at the cart puller. Something passed hands—a banknote, Pinaki realized, feeling a little sick. The constable caught up with him. 'Where are you running off to?'

'It was *this* doormat,' Pinaki said, hoping that the lack of evidence—the mat was spotlessly clean—would persuade his escort to go away.

But when Tuli (as usual in the wrong place in the wrong time), answered the bell, the constable shoved his foot into the door, and was inside the flat in a trice, spurred, Pinaki thought, more by curiosity rather than duty. This was confirmed when Pinaki took him to the veranda where his eyes immediately went to the Ladies' Hostel across.

'As you can see nobody is there now,' Pinaki said, drawing his attention to the pavement. His relief was marred by the fear he would be indicted for bringing a fraudulent charge. 'But she was there this morning,' he said hastily. 'See that black spot? That was where the chula was.'

'Hmm,' said the constable, staring at a girl shaking out her hair, clad only in blouse and petticoat. Pinaki was wondering how to get rid of him when he turned and gave Pinaki a look that was part reproving and part expectation. Recalled to his obligations Pinaki dispatched Tuli to Bipinchandra Sweets.

Half an hour later, his visitor, with Pinaki in tow, was belching his way down the stairs. Kalol Mondal was sitting on a bollard, some thirty feet away. Shrinking back into the doorway, 'Eh, I will take your leave now,' muttered Pinaki. '*Please* tell the sergeant there is no need to pursue this case. The evidence is gone.' He sped up the stairs.

~

Next morning, when he left for work, he checked the doormat before stepping out. It was unsullied. He breathed a sigh of relief. What all we become thankful for, he thought morosely.

The gratitude was short-lived.

The lobby was awash with CPM flags. And bunting strung across the ceiling. And posters pasted on every available surface, including letterboxes and switchboards, the homemade glue still dripping. He clutched the newel post for support, and then turned and charged up the stairs.

'Ki hoyechhe?' said Rimi. 'You forgot your lunch box?'

'Bathroom,' he panted, grinding his teeth.

He reached it just in time. After he finished he splashed water on his face. Then he had to change his shirt. When he emerged, the household was a-buzz about the newly furbished lobby.

'What is going on?' Rimi asked. 'First the smoke, then the dog shit and now...'

'*You* said go to the police and you see the result?'

Dida plucked at his sleeve. 'I hope the old trouble has not come back, Bulbul. The police...'

'That happened almost twenty years ago, Ma. And because of the *Naxals*, not the Communists.' He had tried explaining the difference to his mother several times.

'Your father died after the police took him for questioning...'

'He died of old age, Ma. *Four* years after. And *I* went to the police—*they* didn't come for me.'

'Still.' Dida wiped her face with the end of her sari. 'You must never go to the police for anything.'

'They won't bother with this small thing anyway,' Pinaki said, more to convince himself.

'Go speak to *him* then,' Rimi said. 'The fellow who was with the woman. *He* is doing this mischief I think.'

'I don't think...' Pinaki began. And then his fears were up and running. A month ago, a housewife was roughed up by a youth for telling him not to jump the queue. Last Puja, a schoolteacher was shot for protesting against the loudspeakers. Every so often a young woman got acid thrown on her by a rejected suitor. The CPM encouraged its goons to run wild, and Kalol Mondal belonged to the Party. 'It is not a good idea...'

'I can speak to him, Baba,' said Dona from behind. 'I can give him a piece of my mind.'

Pinaki slewed around. '*No*! You keep out of this! Anyway, he isn't there.'

But he was. When Pinaki went downstairs he was standing at the bottom of the stairs, studying his artwork. He moved his torso, but not his legs, to allow Pinaki's passage, in a way calculated to give offence. But Pinaki was too agitated to reprimand him for his insolence.

And then Dona was doing it for him. Leaning over the railing on the landing above, 'Hey, you!' she called. 'Yes, I'm talking to *you*! Get away from the door! Don't you have anything better to do than make a nuisance of yourself?'

'Dona! What, why are you...' Pinaki pushed past Kalol Mondal and grabbed her arm. 'Go, go back!'

'But, Baba, *look* what he's...'

'Jete dao! Come, let's go!'

From the safety of the second floor landing he peeped down.

Kalol Mondal was looking up at them. He caught Pinaki's eye and his features eased into a smile. It was the first smile that didn't seem as if he was snapping his jaws but that only increased Pinaki's unease.

That evening, before dinner, Pinaki lay on his bed idling through *The Hoogly Times*. He didn't hear Dida call him to dinner. He ignored Rimi's exasperated summons. He waved Tuli away when he came in to fetch him.

Rimi flung open the door. 'Eijay, the rotis are getting cold.'

Without raising his eyes from the newspaper, 'Did you see this?' he said. He tapped the newspaper. 'I wonder...is it a coincidence that this should appear *today*?'

'Huh?'

'This article on Calcutta...' He got up. 'You must read it after dinner.'

'Too many big words,' said Rimi. 'Too many *words*. "A design rhetoric"—how to even *pronounce* it?—"of packing crates and egg cartons meta... metas..." oof.' She tossed back the newspaper.

'"metastasizing in the once spacious suburbs and expansive city centres, overwhelming urban scale, increasing urban blight, changing urban experience for the worse"...darao, Rimi. Don't go. It doesn't only say what the city has become. It goes on to explain what it must be. "A place that respects the individuality and sensibilities of citizens, heeding their rights but holding them to their responsibilities". He shook the newspaper. "'Dignity is an inalienable right. Preserving it is an unnegotiable responsibility." Space, light, air, peace and quiet, all that everyone knows, but respect? Dignity?' He looked up. 'He understands, Rimi!'

'Who? Understands what?'

But Pinaki had immersed himself again in the newspaper. 'Civilized discourse,' he murmured. 'And consensus...checks and balances...'

'Of course that makes everything clear. Enough of this nonsense...'

'No, wait, Rimi. It says here he's organized a clean-up operation at the Scottish cemetery in Wellesley Road. This Sunday at 10 o'clock. He invites concerned citizens to join him.'

'I've never even heard of it. How is cleaning a gorosthan going to make a difference to anybody? And who is *he*?'

'Biren Roy. He wrote this article.'

'Well, good luck to him. Nobody will go to clean a gorosthan.'

'I wonder. You know, I think this could be an opportunity...'

'For what?'

'Um? Oh, nothing.'

~

That Sunday Pinaki woke with a sense of anticipation. By 9 a.m. he was jingling the change in his pocket.

Rimi caught him at the front door. 'Where are you going?'

'Out.'

'Yes, but where?'

He shut the door firmly behind him.

The flags were still hanging in the lobby, but the street was free of Kalol Mondal. Pinaki had made sure of that from his bedroom window. Still, when he gained Diamond Harbour Road, he felt as if he'd safely crossed a field of landmines.

A small crowd was standing at the gateway of the Scottish Cemetery. Pinaki pushed his way to the front. A canopy of green met his eyes. Below it gravestones, in various stages of disrepair and decay, jostled for place. Plain slabs and ornate, sarcophaguses, cenotaphs, pergolas, obelisks... The roots of the trees twisted around them and knitted intricate patterns with the pathways.

Two men were scything the grass around a dilapidated pavilion. One of them wore a stained vest, a straw hat and pants rolled to the knees. The other wore a white shirt, translucent with sweat, and a handkerchief tied around his head. He straightened up, and, looking in Pinaki's direction, called to the other. 'We have more spectators than participants!'

'Typical,' said the straw hat. 'Perhaps we can lure them in to help. Drag some meat on a string or something. Manu!' he shouted, making Pinaki jump. 'Go and demonstrate what your sack is for!'

A third man, whom Pinaki had missed, emerged from behind a pillar and walked to the gateway, hefting a burlap sack. He mimed throwing a rusty tin into the sack, an empty carton, a bottle. The crowd booed. He twirled the sack in the air. The crowd cheered. He held it in front of him and wiggled his hips.

'I didn't ask you to entertain them, you clown!' cried the man in the hat.

His companion untied his handkerchief to wipe his forehead, revealing hair the colour of sand and a forehead as pink as the inside of a cat's mouth.

'Angrez!' exclaimed the crowd .

The pink turned a mottled red. The angrez held up his scythe. 'Would you like to join our effort?' he said, speaking as if he'd had trouble being understood. 'Ash-un. Bi-tho-re.'

An admiring murmur rippled through the crowd. The angrez spoke Bengali!

The angrez smiled. 'How about *you*, sir?' he said, suddenly addressing Pinaki.

'Me?' said Pinaki, shocked. 'I, I...don't know.'

The man with the hat came up. 'Are you trying to sway the masses, Doc?'

'Not with any success,' the angrez said. He gave Pinaki a rueful grin. Pinaki could have sunk into the earth.

'Allow me to intervene,' said the hat man. 'Here,' he said to the crowd. 'Either you come inside and help or get lost. This is not a fun fair. And it's not a fucking zoo either.'

'Easy, Biren,' the angrez said.

Biren? Did he say *Biren*? Pinaki strained his neck. The sun was in his eyes. Could *this* man be... Surely not! *His* man would be wearing a shirt-and-tie and shined-up shoes. *His* man had a big office and dozens of employees... This was an engine driver, whose workforce was a slight man who didn't say a word, and four street urchins, fighting over a mango.

'The animals are not on *this* side of the wall, you know,' he was telling the crowd now.

'Hush, Biren. Some of them must know English.'

It *was* him. Biren Roy.

'All the better,' said Biren Roy. 'They'll be under no misapprehension.' He made a shooing gesture. 'Bugger off, you lot. Go home and beat your wives or something.'

'You *can't* talk to them like that, Biren.'

'Why not? They don't care for me nor I don't care for them. Don't worry, Doc, they won't understand.'

'You don't know that for sure,' said the angrez, giving Pinaki such a warm smile that Pinaki felt quite overcome and stepped back—tripping over a stone. When he'd steadied himself, the three men were back at their task. Pinaki longed to go in and offer his services, at least bring them a cold drink—they looked so hot—but was too shy. The angrez might speak to him again and go and write up his answers in the notebook he was keeping on India. Pinaki imagined all white people who came here did that. This was the first he'd known they also came to clean it.

~

'Except I didn't understand why clean a cemetery, sir.'
'The folly, Bose, the folly.'
'Yes, that's what I thought too.'
'Beautiful, isn't it?'
'Beautiful? Foolishness is *beautiful*?'
'What... Oh. For a moment I thought you were admiring the pavilion.'

~

When the crowd dispersed, Pinaki found the courage to enter the enclosure. Skirting the pavilion where the angrez and Biren Roy were scraping the moss off the pillars, he joined Manu to scrub the flagstones. Quite soon he learned Manu couldn't speak, although he could hear.

At noon, a photographer from *The Hoogly Times* came, accompanied by a cub reporter. They wandered around, taking pictures. 'Mind you write *exactly* what I said,' Pinaki heard Biren Roy say.

After they left Biren Roy asked, 'Time for a lunch break, eh Doc? What are your views on Thai food?'

'Ambivalent. I prefer Chinese—your Calcutta Chinese.'

Biren Roy shuddered exaggeratedly. Pulling on a shirt (faded, crumpled), he said, 'And beer, of course. Primum prima.'

At least that's what it sounded like to Pinaki. It made the angrez laugh.

Biren Roy turned to the urchins poking around the gravestones. He gave them a severe look, and then pulled out his wallet. 'Manu! Get these monkeys something to eat. Puri, biryani, whatever junk they desire. We'll be back in,' he consulted his watch, 'one hour.' He and the angrez walked through the gate. 'This is too much for us to tackle, Doc. We'll have to get...hold on,' he said in a changed voice. 'I believe I'm having an epiphany.'

Pinaki's spirits, which had risen with Biren Roy's gesture towards the children, now dipped. *Epiphany*. What did it mean?

'Look at the street from this angle,' Biren Roy was saying. 'At *that* building. There's your salvation—just round the corner too.'

The angrez laughed. 'You don't give up, do you? By the way, I came across something the other day that might interest you. Let's see if I can remember. Restraint and freedom—free *will*—is the essence of good architecture.'

'Good recall, Doc. It was said by...'

Their voices faded.

They weren't there an hour later when Pinaki and Manu returned with the boys. Unsupervised, the boys began throwing litter at each other. They laughed at Manu's inarticulate noises and ignored Pinaki's feeble admonitions. After a while, tiring of their game, they ran away.

'Should we also leave?' said Pinaki.

Manu shaded his eyes at the street. He nodded.

Pinaki held out a scrap of paper and a pen. 'Will you write out your address—your office address? I would like to visit you.'

Manu obliged. In addition he drew a neat little map.

On his way home Pinaki realized that but for some

peripherals, principally an unshaven chin, he had no idea what Biren Roy looked like.

That evening when Dona brought him his tea, she said, 'You *have* to do something about that fellow, Baba—the one with the yellow eyes. Who decorated our lobby. And our doormat. He's been hanging around our building.'

The cup clattered in his saucer. 'Has he, did he do anything to *you*? Say anything?'

'N...o.' She scratched her calf with her big toe. 'He just stares.' She flicked her hair back and glanced at the mirror. 'They all do. But this one,' she paused. 'This one makes my skin crawl.'

7

Kalol Mondal clumped down J. Mullick Road, unaware of his effect on Dona, which would have shattered him. Whenever she floated into his consciousness, which was often, he was overcome with a flood of warmth. It lasted only for a few seconds. Afterwards, it was confusion and helplessness. What hope was there for him? His home was a kilometre from hers, but it could be on an alien planet. It was only in movies that someone like him attracted a girl like her. But movies were inspired by life. They were not all fairy tales. It must be so, else how do these stories get told again and again?

He turned into a lane, eight feet wide and crowded with mostly single-storied structures that formed a dense, homogenous wall. The alleys that cut through the mass, so narrow only two people could walk abreast, housed the lavatories, unlit stinking facilities shared by dozens like him. Women visited them in pairs at night. He knew the neighbourhood to every last ditch and open manhole. The

neighbourhood knew enough about him to keep out of his
way as far as possible. He believed there was no other city like
this one. Not in West Bengal, at least. It hardened you and
humbled you, expanded and reduced you, but it offered you
life in such abundant measure. And opportunities. It taught
you your place, but didn't fix you there. So he had believed.
But now everything that had seemed within reach was actually
not. The awareness was working overtime. Usually when he
thought about his life it was in plotting mode, not pensive.

The fact was that the city had taught him want. He wouldn't
have known want if he had been out of want's reach. She was
beyond his dreams and beyond his means. All those movies
of poor boy-getting-rich were made on another planet. He
had believed—fool that he was—that this was that planet.

For now all he could do was to keep her from the coarse
attentions of his colleagues. Fighting was his usual route to
get his way. Although that wouldn't help his case with her.
As for throwing himself in her path—he may as well throw
himself under the wheels of a train. No, fighting was not the
way forward here. Commitment was. Faith and sincerity were
eventually rewarded.

Halfway down the lane he stepped into a narrow veranda
and unlocked a scratched and splintered door. He was home.
A string bed took up half the floor in the room. Reaching it
in two easy strides he threw himself on it.

*Don't you have anything better to do than making a nuisance
of yourself here?* Her voice when she said that! The way she
had lifted her chin! If voice and chin were knives they'd have
cut him to pieces. What had she said that he didn't deserve?
Sending smoke into her flat! Hanging flags in her lobby! And
the dogshit...what were you *thinking*? Fool, accursed fool!

On the other hand, but for these wrongdoings he would
not have seen her. Seen her, properly, that is, not in the way he
(and his friends) looked at girls. Which was staring, teasing,
jeering... The very thought of it filled him with nausea now.

How come he hadn't noticed her before? But to be *so* noticed by her! Would it have been better not to be noticed at all? Perhaps not. At least now she knew of his existence. It was a beginning. Beginning of *what*?

Her sudden appearance on those stairs! *Don't you have anything better to do?*

In one jump he was at the window, clutching the bars. No prisoner had looked so yearningly at a world so unattainable.

When his agitation subsided he gave himself to the pleasure of going over her face, and, with unconfirmed data (though none the less pleasurable), her body.

He woke at 5 a.m. to the yipping of street dogs. Stripping to his underclothes, he washed his face in the tiny, stained washbasin in the veranda. In due course, his eyes went to the mirror, which, although mottled and lit by a flyblown bulb, could still tell an honest tale.

The tale might have discouraged nine out of ten young men but he was the tenth. In the reflection that gazed back at him he didn't see the permanently jaundiced eyes that woke idiopathic misgivings in most people—he saw the strong square jaw below. He didn't see the feeble fuzz on his chin that he scraped at each morning—he preened over his thick black hair. So it was a jaunty Kalol Mondal who wiped his manly face and calmed his ebullient hair, and Kalol Mondal the heart throb of the neighbourhood who went out to speak to Raja, its uncontested joker—and the cause of the present commotion on the street.

'Ki rey, Raja! You've woken up all the dogs!'

'Kalol!' cried Raja, as if it was a happy coincidence to find Kalol Mondal (of all people!) in his own home at five o'clock in the morning. He had come to borrow a bucket—his had sprung a leak.

'When will you give up this stupid job?' asked Kalol

Mondal, as he handed it to him. 'I've told you a thousand times to get a driving license.'

Raja raised his shoulders to his ears. 'Na rey, I can't pass the test. Washing cars is good enough for me.' He tapped his head. 'Nothing there, I keep telling you.'

'And I keep telling you I can get you a license without doing a test.'

'Na rey. I'm afraid of the police. And there's no fun in being a driver. It will be *Raja go, Raja come, Raja wait* all day long.'

Secretly Kalol Mondal agreed. 'You'll get a smart uniform, and shoes.'

None of the drivers they knew had either, but Raja didn't point this out. He gave Kalol Mondal his sloppy grin. 'Why don't *you* become a driver?'

'Because I have better plans,' retorted Kalol Mondal. 'Bokachod,' he growled, peeved. He had no plans. 'What will you do when you're too old to wash cars?'

'*You'll* be there to feed me.'

'I'll piss on your ass first.'

Raja clanked his bucket. 'Piss in *this*.'

Kalol Mondal told him where he could put his bucket.

Back on his bed, Kalol Mondal continued to be irritated by Raja, first for provoking him to make an empty boast, and then for his blind trust in him, that he called upon, like a genie, to get him out of trouble. And he would oblige the fellow too! The irritation subsided. It was more than gang loyalty. It was a debt—that he was happy to repay, but for how long?

After he had walked out of his uncle's home with just a change of clothes, and the family's ration card (because this one petty and pointless crime would punish more than if he had taken all the family possessions), Kalol Mondal lived on the streets for three days. On the third day, when he was drinking a glass of tea in lieu of dinner, a youth, about his age, offered to share his plate of rice and curry, forcing him to eat when he refused.

Fifteen minutes later, the youth offered to share his car-washing job—business whose turf was jealously guarded. He also invited Kalol Mondal to stay with him as long as he wished, omitting to mention he lived in a single room with his mother. Kalol Mondal was to discover that his saviour had a sixth sense for people's troubles. But no sense, he would scold him, when it came to acting on it. Still, he was very grateful that Raja had acted on his instincts this once.

Kalol Mondal had no reason to resent his uncle whose intentions were well-meant, or his aunt, who did her best in what could not have been an easy situation for her. He had every reason to thank them, in fact. When he was twelve years old, his uncle had visited his home in Midnapur. Finding his nephew in the mango tree at 11 a.m. on a school day, he hooked his umbrella to his leg and pulled him down. There was a family confabulation which ended in Kalol Mondal being marched off to the station to catch the last train to Calcutta, his mother's laments following them down the road. 'Laltu! Hey Ma! Laltu! When will I see you again?'

'*Laltu*,' scoffed the uncle, tightening his grip. '*Lal* means *red*, didn't they think of that when you popped out, black as shoe polish?' He thumped his terrified ward's head to knock out any other foolishness. 'Don't look back.' When they reached Calcutta, 'You'll be *Kalol* from now on. To *everybody*.'

For the next six years he lived with his uncle, aunt and their two daughters near the Kidderpore dock, attending the Kidderpore Academy for Boys. By the time he passed his matriculation examination—on the second attempt—he was eighteen years old and six feet tall, and his aunt was openly unhappy with his huge appetite and hulking presence. He could see his uncle tiring too. Finally there had been an unpleasant scene in which the aunt had remarked it was not a good thing to have a young man in a house with young girls. He walked out the very same morning.

Raja and he did get more cars to wash. Rather, Kalol Mondal did. His methods established him as a man it would be a mistake to refuse anything. Always a useful reputation to have, he told Raja, who had no desire, or talent, to acquire it.

The job had sustained him for two years. He augmented his income by selling petrol siphoned from the cars—another skill he initiated his faithful and fearful acolyte in. If he wasn't entirely satisfied with the way his life had turned out, he wasn't actively unhappy either. The very obscurity and lack of connections that bothered him had also given him the freedom to exploit the city for his ends. Having no family to account to, no home to protect, no job he absolutely needed, he had become one of the huge army of youths who lived by their wits—and their muscles.

Given his circumstances it was inevitable he should meet youths like him, that some of them should belong to the Communist Party, that lured by the promise of a better life and more than that, a new family, he would join the Party himself. He attracted the attention of the local MLA, the Chief, after his success at capturing a polling booth for the Party in the municipal election, and impressed him with his prowess at intimidation. His reward was the job at Rabin Pal's. It paid only a little more than car-washing but it was a step up the social ladder. And a step up the double helix staircases he saw on the silver screen. Although his new life still wouldn't get him the beautiful girls who floated on them.

He would find other ways to get them. Time was on his side. And the backing of his new-found friends in the Party.

Several times he urged Raja to join them. With no skills, education, connections, the Party was the way forward. He described to Raja the advantaged life that would be his. 'Everybody will be afraid of you, Raja! Even the police! The modi will charge you less, and Tip Top, Aroma... People will even pay to be left alone!'

Raja, scared rather than thrilled, declined the offer.

Kalol Mondal lay on the lumpy mattress, plotting his prospects, which, as usual, was a chart of peaks and valleys. Then, bored, he began to daydream. After a while, as is the way of daydreams, it popped.

The only girl he knew with any degree of intimacy was the one who smiled at him from the wall. You could balance an egg on her pout. Her flesh lapped at the edges of the poster. He had stripped off her swimsuit with a felt-tipped pen and enhanced her anatomy. She was now more a caricature than a celebrated beauty , but he liked his handiwork. Without shifting his gaze he reached into his pyjamas for the old dependable to ease his ache.

The day was well advanced when he got up, yawning and then recoiling at the animal fug of the room. The viscous light revealed a place that could pass for a gangsters' den in the movies he frequented. The cracked windowpane was mended with duct tape. The cane shelving unit looked as if it had been kicked. Cobwebs floated from the ceiling. Fungus furred the walls. Dirt coated the floor.

His eyes lit on the poster. The vulgarity of it shamed him. Consumed with self-loathing, he ripped it off. A chunk of plaster fell out, like the filling from a tooth. He tore down three others he had chosen with equal care.

Not enough.

He pulled out the contents of the cane shelves, cursing the junk that had accumulated behind his back. A mousetrap containing two dozen rusted nails! A dented talcum powder tin, a broken plastic mug, a disintegrating shoebox preserved because it was the one time he'd bought shoes in a box... He threw everything into the street.

On a rampage now, he picked up balled-up newspaper, sundry rags, broken clay cups, sticky with tea... The vortex caused by his frenzy sucked in the litter of his entire sojourn in the room.

Not enough. Not nearly enough.

Behind the door he found four paper plates, stained with orange oil. A cockroach fell out and lay stunned on the floor. He stamped on it and, his newly minted disgust mounting, dabbed the slime with one of the plates. Out, out, out!

Dust motes continued to swirl in the light slanting through the door and window. The sweat ran down his face and his legs. At this juncture, unluckily, he glanced at his naked torso. A greasy sheen highlighted the too-fleshy pectorals that he had not noticed till his young girl cousin, in all innocence, had pointed it out to the family. Teased by them, he had exercised madly to convert mass to muscle. It had seemed to him the condition had improved but in certain lights, such as this, he wasn't so sure. He draped a towel on his shoulder, put two clean shirts into a plastic bag, to give the dhobi to iron (for twenty paisa less than the going rate) and snatched his soapbox from the top shelf of the cane stand. He was halfway to his new bathing place—the hydrant behind the meat shop (where the dogs fought over entrails) when he remembered he had to retrieve his bucket from Raja.

Vinu wheeled his bike onto the street. With studied casualness he adjusted his helmet strap a fraction of an inch, slewing his neck to give any observers—specifically a certain someone in a certain balcony—an opportunity to admire the line of his jaw.

In the balcony above his audience (of one) sniffed. *What a dope.*

The backfire sent the crows into a frenzy of scolding. A hundred metres on, the showman executed a turn that brought his steed to its knees. He righted himself, bent double over the fender and roared off. A cascade of sonic explosions followed him. Das Engineering shook his fist at the receding tail-light.

Dona stretched over the balustrade to follow his progress. When he was no longer visible she glanced at the pavement below.

Her smile went out. Kalol Mondal was sitting on the culvert. Every ten seconds his head jerked up to look at her balcony. Her lip curled. Another dope.

Kalol Mondal got up, deep in thought. As an instrument for cutting people down to size, a 50hp bike was hard to beat. But hard to acquire!

'Bokachoda, esho!' he called out to Nobody's Dog. It ran up, wagging its tail hopefully. He held out a closed fist. 'Biscoot!' Nobody's Dog thrust its snout at the fist.

Kalol Mondal opened his empty fist. 'No biscoot!' He laughed in its face.

It whined and then, forgivingly, pushed its nose into his crotch. He gave the animal an expert kick—sending it yelping—and then set off down the street. As he passed Lucky Hairdressing Saloon, a cloud of black hair sailed out of the door. He was sidestepping the grisly heap when a happy idea struck him. He walked in.

Every square inch of the salon's walls not fitted with a mirror was tacked with pin-ups of popular film stars. Imtiaz, owner and chief hairstylist, came up. 'Ki holo, Kalol? Haircut?'

Kalol Mondal pointed to a blow-up of the star of stars, the one whose irresistible sneer every teenage boy had been practising in front of every reflecting surface.

'That costs double.'

'Just do it,' Kalol Mondal said tersely.

An hour later he emerged, jelled spikes standing in startled clumps on his scalp. Privately Imtiaz thought he looked like a lavatory brush. But Kalol Mondal was pleased. Running the tips of his fingers over his lips to mime a mouth organ, he swaggered to the peepul tree where his gang was arm-wrestling on a carrom board. He knocked down one of the arms and substituted his. Nobody protested. He was their leader, their champion. Besides, you don't argue with a ball-peen hammer.

8

The Monday after the abortive cemetery clean-up, Pinaki left at 5.30 p.m., which was the official closing time at Jalan's, except it never was. Snapping shut his briefcase, he told his colleague he had to buy mutton for dinner. But instead of taking the bus home he caught one to Park Street.

In the slender band of time between daylight going out and the lights coming on, Park Street is more than just a place. It's a mood, a charged atmosphere, like the hushed expectancy in an auditorium before the curtain goes up. Traffic is thin. In the restaurants, window shades have been lowered over extended office lunches and romantic assignations...

Pinaki stopped at the window of Oxford Bookshop, as he always did, to scan the titles, but not with his usual attention. Taking out a much-handled piece of paper from his pocket he read the pencilled notations for the nth time. The seventh cross. The *seventh*.

Someone tapped his shoulder. 'Arre, babu. Don't worry. She will be there.'

He recoiled, opened his mouth to protest, and then smiled weakly. After that he had an uneasy sense that his mission was clandestine. Even more curiously, that he had been lured into it. It didn't help that his side of the road was deeply shadowed.

Turning into Free School Street he suddenly thought of Daddy's Girls, the Dastur sisters, who taught piano in

J. Mullick Road. They said the city was once called the Paris of the East, that it was *the* place to be this side of the Suez, and this square mile was its epicentre. Smart restaurants, lively bars, glamorous nightclubs, tea dances at Firpo's, parties in Golden Slippers, polo at the Royal Turf Club... That was when Daddy was a covenanted officer with Williamson Magor. What would Daddy make of it today? Of the merchandise displayed on the pavement—bolts of netting, bales of cotton wool, foam, coir, old furniture and books and long-playing records...? Of the washing strung in the balconies, the air conditioners perched on window sills? The old men plucking at their pyjama strings, the women slumped in the doorways? And children, everywhere the children. He would have sniffed at the street food too—guavas smeared with chili paste, boiled eggs, fried rice and...hey ma! Pinaki stumbled over a green coconut that had strayed from the parent pile. In an unaccountable fit of aggression he kicked it into the street. Then, as atonement, he bought it. Sucking on the straw he thought how fortunate he was to sit behind a desk and not behind a pile of coconuts. Only the paper printed with his Bachelor of Commerce degree saved him from such a fate.

Darkness came hard on the heels of the first of the street lights. Neon signs began blinking on signs and hoardings—advertising products he had not heard of. More and more he was not in the know. There was a new hunger in the city, for material goods, for comfort, for ownership. The restlessness it engendered was straining its political manifesto. The old differences were showing through the tatters. Queues were getting longer, tempers shorter.

He stopped by the golden ingot thrown by the brightly lit glass door of the Monalisa Hotel (Air-conditioned Bar), lingering to enjoy the cooled air escaping from under the door till the receptionist sitting behind the glass caught his eye. Embarrassed, he raised his hand to wave, and then scratched his nose. The receptionist grinned and scratched *his* nose.

He tucked his head into his chin and walked away. In his hurry he almost fell over a figure crouching by the curb. It was a woman, holding her child, clucking encouragement as a thin yellow stream dribbled down its legs.

The image continued to haunt him for a long time.

At the fourth cross an old man was squatting on the curb, intoning 'Allah, Allah,' over and over. He threw him a coin, and, after a moment's hesitation, another one. *Pray for me too.*

~

'You know, sir, the first time I came to your office I felt I was doing a pilgrimage.'

'Via Dolorosa and the stations of the Cross? And salvation awaiting you?'

'You weren't *waiting* for me.'

'Perhaps I was, Bose. You weren't to know that and neither did I, but I must have been. Waiting for you.'

Pinaki shivered.

~

By the time he turned into Marquis Street, he was dry-mouthed with apprehension. But he also felt alert and ready.

The disappointment of arrival was so acute that every one of his senses rebelled. *This* building? Why, his own in J. Mullick Road was better than this! Black with soot and dirt, streaked with greenish slime where the water pipes had leaked, flaking, fungoid plaster, shrubs growing on the parapet. Perhaps there was some mistake? But the address scribbled on his scrap of paper echoed the legend inscribed on the pitted grey marble tablature. *Dinshaw Mansions Sinclair & Joyce 1920.*

The door was painted a glistening red. Who had thought of *that*? It stood out like a clown's nose. The stained-glass fanlight above was his mouth if you imagined the clown standing on his head. His chaotic thoughts didn't stop upon entering the lobby. Letterboxes in varying sizes and colours made a mural on one wall. Where the other walls were not spattered with paan juice, they were plastered with posters. Old torn posters calling workers to unite to protest, to strike, to close down... The grime would have to be chipped off the floor. In a daze he joined the queue for the lift.

After a longish wait, loops of hairy cables slithered down. The lift hove into view, swaying and creaking, and shuddered to a halt. A grizzled face peered out of the latticed metal door. The door opened with a crash. After the queue filed in, the cage shook like a dog with ague, and, swaying and creaking, rose. Pinaki, bound for the fifth floor, had ample time to take in the polished teak panelling and the mirror and the brass-trimmed wooden navigating wheel turned by the grizzled liftman, as if this was a pleasure boat on the Hoogly.

Passing the lightless lobbies, the apprehension returned. What was he doing in this place? *The Hoogly Times*, rolled tight in his briefcase, could do no more than swat a fly.

It took no clever guesswork to deduce that the door he stood before, panelled, scrubbed so the grains and knots in the wood were revealed, was the one he was looking for. The door number, cut out of steel, was four different shapes of four. A sculptural arabesque.

There was no bell. He waited a whole minute after knocking a third time to push the door open.

The room, although vast and lofty, was so like the main hall at Jalan's that his anxiety began subsiding. The same iron I-beams spanned the ceiling on which the same fans bloomed, and the electric wires veining the walls, thick as his wrist, furred with dirt, could have been transposed from there. Except this place was silent. Eerily silent. Jalan's on a Sunday. And

Jalan's in economic decline. Raw brickwork showed between the I-beams. The marble floor was so stained it was doubtful whether anything would restore it to approaching its original state. The motley furniture—no effete polish or cushions here—was clumped, not arranged. He made his way through the thicket, and stopped uncertainly at a clearing.

Glass-fronted book cupboards and pigeonhole shelves of dusty paper rolls took up most of one wall. Another was papered with drawings of buildings and blueprints. Coloured studies. A floor-to-ceiling window, cut into squares, took care of the third. One of the squares framed a cupola he recognized as belonging to Park Mansions. A section of the room was dedicated to what appeared to be junk. An old door frame and a window shutter. Lengths of rusted steel. Slabs of concrete soaking in a tin bathtub, the water covered with scum, which, he guessed, was the source of the dank smell in the room. Behind the tub was an object that looked like a large beehive. He drew closer to examine it—and froze.

Footsteps. They came from behind the door set in the wall of drawings.

The pace was quick but measured, pausing at regular intervals to, he supposed, turn. If he wanted exercise why didn't he walk in the corridor outside? This was *his* office, wasn't it?

After a while, reassured by the metronomic regularity of the steps, Pinaki moved to a table, high and large enough to bed an adult, to continue his investigations on the sheet of paper pinned on it.

'No, thank you. Don't bother, don't even try.'

Pinaki jumped back. The door was open. A man stood silhouetted against the light.

Pinaki recognized the voice. It was him. Biren Roy. Advancing as if he meant to tackle him to the floor.

Pinaki had the urge to drop the ball and flee. 'I, I... Pardon?'

The man, *Biren Roy*, wasn't tall, although much taller than Pinaki. Now, as he closed in on Pinaki, he grew two feet more. Pointing at Pinaki's briefcase, 'No bathroom tiles or bath fittings' he said. 'Or door handles, laminates, whatever you've got in there. And Firstlight Couriers is the second door to the right of the lift.'

Pinaki shifted his briefcase from one hand to the other. 'I'm not selling anything, sir.'

'Then why're you snooping around my studio?'

Pinaki's ears grew warm. 'I'm n-not...' he stammered.

'You're here to steal my ideas. And sell them to competition. Anyhow you're wasting your time. Because competition won't buy. And why? Because competition is a fool.'

'I came to meet *you*, sir,' quavered Pinaki. 'You are, I think so, Mr Biren Roy?'

Biren Roy gave a two-finger salute to acknowledge that this was indeed the case.

'The *architect*?'

Biren Roy admitted to this too. His mouth twisted into a figure of eight smile as if he guessed he hadn't fulfilled the minimum aesthetic standards of an artist—sunken cheeks, famished eyes—expected by Pinaki, schooled in the romantic tradition that he himself despised.

He walked to a table, switched on a conical green shade hanging over it and pulled up one of the stools mushrooming from the floor. 'What do you want to see me about? If it's a job you won't get that here.' He sounded tired.

Encouraged, Pinaki pulled up another stool, taking care to lift, not drag it, and placed his briefcase on it. 'Actually, I *have* come about a job, sir.' He gave a little trill of laughter. 'That is, not for me but for *you*.'

The glasses slipped down Biren Roy's nose and came to rest on a bump. Oval, narrow and somewhat feminine, they added a sinister touch, Pinaki thought, like the fluffy cat on the villain's lap. The villainous aspect was reinforced by a dark red mark that spread across the left side of the face. He averted his eyes from the damaged cheek. 'I want to build a house,' he said.

'You want to build a house.' Biren Roy took off his glasses and gave Pinaki a look of such intensity that Pinaki knocked over his briefcase.

Muttering an apology he set it straight. 'Yes,' he said. 'A simple house. Three bedrooms. A hall, dining and kitchen. And bathrooms—two.' He was smiling too much. He adjusted his features. 'Nothing more, nothing less,' he said with a firmness he would wonder at afterwards, suggesting as it did that there would be no nonsense about the project. With that he snapped open his briefcase, took out a newspaper cutting but shut it quickly—before Biren Roy could see it only contained his tiffin box. 'You see, I read your article in *The Hoogly*...'

'I knew no good would come of that,' Biren Roy said gloomily.

'It was as if you were speaking to *me*. I thought, here's someone who understands, who *feels* the way I do.'

Biren Roy's expression grew indignant at this unsolicited expression of solidarity.

Pinaki moistened his lips. 'You c-cleared up my confusions, sir.' (Biren Roy groaned.) 'It was an omen, a *good* omen that your article came out the same week something happened to me. Something very bad.' (Biren Roy's eyebrows went up.) He tapped the paper. 'You made a case for living in a house.'

'I made a case for reducing urban density. But not by exchanging inner-city congestion for suburban sprawl.'

'But...but you wrote...'

'I wrote about an ideal society,' Biren Roy said impatiently. 'Which this is not. It was a lament for what was, what should and cannot be.' His mouth twisted again. 'Nostalgia?' he murmured.

'But you also wrote about dignity, sir,' Pinaki said. 'Of ordinary existence. That impressed me.'

Biren Roy looked at him curiously. 'Living in a house isn't quite an ordinary existence in this city.'

Pinaki drooped.

Biren Roy huffed on his glasses. 'In any case building a house is not for everybody. Not in this city and certainly not,' he checked himself. Pinaki, guessing what he meant to say, flinched. 'How many individual houses do you see being constructed?'

It's not fair to ask me such questions, Pinaki thought. 'I don't go out much,' he said a little huffily.

'Take it from me, there aren't too many. And for good reason. Buying a plot and all that that entails—bribing the municipality, paying off the local thugs and the Party goons... are you a Party member?'

Pinaki shook his head. Biren Roy gave him a sardonic smile.

That annoyed Pinaki. He lifted his chin. 'It is not easy but not impossible.' Afraid he might have overstepped, 'That's why I have come to *you*, sir,' he gabbled.

'And that is reason enough for me to agree?'

Pinaki glanced around at the empty, ill-lit room in which, clearly, industry was not of the essence. Biren Roy's mouth tightened. 'I'm not in the business of disseminating happiness,' he said, and began making notations on a sheet of paper.

Pinaki sensed he'd transgressed somewhere. There was nothing he could think of to say now—even if he made bold to say it. He could creep away, but what would that accomplish? And he was sure he would precipitate a catastrophe if he as much as moved an inch. The creaking of his knees would set it off. He rested his hip on the edge of the table and covertly studied his inhospitable host.

Biren Roy, he guessed, must be in his mid-forties. His hair (set in rills) was iron-grey. The eyebrows, furry commas, were streaked with grey too. A shallow vertical nicked the high forehead. *That* pointed to a quick temper. That and the fiery mark on his face.

At this juncture he heard a gentle cough from the recesses of the room. Turning around he spotted a figure in the far corner, crouched under another coolie-hat lamp, his pale face glowing green like a ray fish. He was jolted into recognition. *Manu*. Had he been there all along? If so why hadn't he come forward? Hadn't he recognized Pinaki? Was everyone in this business so unfriendly? He craned his neck to see if anyone else was lurking in the shadows.

Biren Roy rustled a sheet. The commas came together to form a single wavering line. 'I do wish you would stop trying to be unobtrusive. It's worse than if you were shouting in my ear.'

'Sorry,' Pinaki said, in a small voice.

'Well, if there's nothing else you have to say, then...'

'There is, sir. You see, I was at the cemetery last Sunday.'

Biren Roy jammed on his glasses and peered at Pinaki. 'Really? I don't remember seeing *you*.'

Pinaki wasn't surprised or offended. Gesturing towards the silent figure, 'I was helping him,' he said. 'Manu. I cleared a patch of weeds.'

'Ah,' said Biren Roy, losing interest. 'Some kids showed up but did damn all. Not that it would've made any difference. The litter's worse than before,' he added morosely.

'We waited more than an hour for you to return,' Pinaki said.

'You should have been more impatient—we were back at six o'clock,' Biren Roy said with a straight face.

'I wanted to meet you and shake your hand, sir,' Pinaki said. What was he saying? He had wanted to do no such thing. He couldn't *imagine* it.

Biren Roy held out his hand. 'Here, shake it now. That at least is for free.'

Pinaki recoiled. 'I do not expect you to design the house for free!' Confused, he grabbed the proffered hand.

'Pleased to meet you too,' Biren Roy said gravely. 'You misunderstand me. I meant *I* don't want to pay the price of designing your house. Or any other house, for that matter.'

'I...I don't understand, sir.'

'*And* you won't,' said Biren Roy. 'Inscrutable me!' He bared his teeth in the smile that wasn't a smile.

His teeth were like the rest of him, Pinaki thought. They'd make quick work of you. He lifted his briefcase and then put it down.

'Alright,' said Biren Roy. 'What *is* your story? What set you on this, um, unorthodox quest? I can't believe it was just my modest literary effort.'

The ash grew long on Biren Roy's cigarette as, in fits and starts, Pinaki recounted the scene at the water pump and its aftermath. When he finished, 'Extraordinary,' Biren Roy said. (Pinaki smiled, flattered.) 'But you're overstating your case.' Biren Roy tossed his cigarette down, stubbed it with his toe, and *picked up the stub and pocketed it.* Pinaki stared at the dirty floor. As well inoculate a terminally ill patient against the flu.

Lighting another cigarette, 'You're afraid of this fellow,' said Biren Roy.

Pinaki was silent. Then, 'Yes,' he whispered.

'I wouldn't worry,' Biren Roy said. 'He's had his fun.' He picked a flake of tobacco from his lip. 'A house is an extreme and unnecessary solution. You don't kill a mosquito with a hammer.'

Pinaki chuckled feebly. 'I know. Just that the incident made me think differently, sir.'

'Well, think again,' said Biren Roy. 'Think why horses are made to wear blinkers.' He jammed on his glasses and picked up his pencil.

Pinaki understood this to mean he had overstayed his welcome in addition to overstating his case. Failure loomed over him. 'I had hoped you would understand my situation,' he said dejectedly.

'Oh, I understand. But in all conscience I cannot encourage it.'

'But...'

Biren Roy clicked his tongue. 'A house isn't the answer for you, and certainly not building one. My advice, for what it's worth, is, buy a flat. On the fifth floor, preferably. You need to rise above the chaos, not grub around in it.' His voice was gruff but not unkind. 'That's conventional wisdom.'

But it's not what I want, Pinaki cried silently. 'I want to be close to nature,' he said. 'Trees, grass, flowers, earth...'

'I know what nature is.'

'It's a primal need. Cultures across the world and through history...'

'Are you going to quote from that article?'

Pinaki thought hard. 'Built environments are transformational...'

'Quoting!'

'...shaping thought, beliefs, expanding our worldview...'

'Quoting, quoting!'

Pinaki fell silent.

Biren Roy exhaled two quills of smoke through his nostrils. 'All very instructive and I'm glad you got something out of it but don't get carried away. And now I must get back to work.' He rolled up the tracing sheet and got up.

He's dismissed me, Pinaki thought. *I've lost him. I've lost.* 'Excuse me,' he blurted out. 'Pri-mum prima.'

Biren Roy started. 'What the... Are you being funny? No. I see you're quite serious. I should take your advice then,' he said, inclining his head. 'So excuse *me.*' He tucked the drawing under his arm and began walking to the door he had emerged from.

'Wait!'

Pinaki spun around.

'Is your wife party to this scheme?'

'I haven't told her.'

'Do that. You'll change your mind soon enough.'

Pinaki smiled. 'You don't like ladies, I think.'

Biren Roy snorted. 'Oh, I like the ladies well enough. It's the wives. Those are bad news when you're building a house. Argue and interfere every step of the way.' He turned away.

Pinaki had reached the door when he heard Biren Roy call out again. 'What is your name?'

'Bose, sir. Pinaki Bose.'

All the way to his tram stop in Chandni Chowk, Pinaki thought about his visit. He wondered why Biren Roy had such a large office if, as it appeared, only he and Manu occupied it. He wondered why, if competition was stupid, it should so bother him. He wondered whether Biren Roy had meant what he had written or had Pinaki misunderstood it all? But that article seemed so heartfelt...

Something was missing in this man. Something vital. Sympathy? Sincerity? His manner, his voice, refuted both. His voice had an unfamiliar cadence, a nasal twang that one associated with English actors. Had he been educated abroad? But he was unshaven and dishevelled, as if it he'd spent the night on the floor. After a street fight... And the mark on his face—was it an accident or a birthmark? Misfortunes, both. Out of the blue, and out of context too, Pinaki recalled a bully from his school whose pious smear of sandalwood on the forehead somehow rendered his viciousness more vicious. How funny. He hadn't thought of that in years.

And yet Pinaki felt he could believe in Biren Roy. He believed in the way a teacher does that the most disruptive child in class was the most likely to win the Nobel Peace prize. Or die defending his country.

A dun-coloured cloud hung in the sky of smoke and dust fused by heat and humidity, and ghost-lit by the city lights.

Victoria Memorial's marble dome floated over it like a bubble on ditch water. Pinpoints of yellow picked out the roads criss-crossing the maidan, the thousand-acre breathing space of Calcutta. Pinaki's tram crawled through it, a glow-worm in the thicket of darkness. He rode in the first-class car, which had the luxury of a fan. He had a window seat too. These small pleasures quietened his spirits. He fell asleep.

He woke with a start. His neighbour was shaking him. 'Dada, engine-er tuning-ta thik karun!' Someone heard and passed on the witticism. It was repeated up and down the car. 'He said, "tune your engine!"' Laughter rose from all around. Pinaki grinned sheepishly and apologized for snoring.

His neighbour patted his shoulder and offered him a cigarette. 'It's alright, brother. Relax. It has been a long day for all of us.'

9

'Good heavens! It's you!'

'Finished work early, sir.'

'Whereabouts do you work?'

'Kiran Shanker Roy Road. I'm with Jalan and Jalan. Chartered Accountants.'

'Ah. And you do what—cook their books? Count the bales?'

'I am in taxation, sir.'

'What, playing hooky again?'

'I was passing by, sir.'

'Do me a favour. Use another route to go home. Or skip this stop next time.'

'This is too much! I've become a tourist attraction!'

'It's raining, sir.'

'Don't tell me your umbrella didn't open.'

'Actually it didn't. But that's not the reason I came...'

~

Dida sat in the Puja room, telling her beads. From time to time she fell asleep and had to begin a new count. Then the old familiar excitement would interrupt it, and she'd lose her place again. Durga Puja! In two months but still... The planning, the preparation, the food, the guests... All for only six days but what a six days! And of course *you'll* be there, Ma, she murmured to the Durga idol. Coming home again. What a welcome awaits you! Then she folded her hands and entreated the goddess, as she did most mornings, to grant her patience with her daughter-in-law. And for her daughter-in-law to make her son happy. She didn't hold out much hope for either prayer to be answered. Her second prayer was not entirely sincere. That is, she wanted her son's happiness, but she, not Rimi, had to be its provenance. Hastily she asked forgiveness for the uncharitable thought.

Pinaki, in fact, was quite happy at this moment. He was stretched out on the sagging rattan chair in the veranda, wiggling his toes, newly freed from his chappals. On the table by his elbow was a thick white china mug of tea and a saucer with four Marie biscuits. Some days the saucer held channa chur. Occasionally, on a rainy weekend, Rimi made onion bhajas. Once Dona had baked a vanilla cake in a tin box on a griddle.

He savoured this time as much as the tea. Today the house was unusually quiet. Everybody was out—Puja shopping. Still, when he went to take a bath, he knocked upon the bathroom door. It was swollen with the humidity and wouldn't shut, so you couldn't tell if it was occupied. He'd tried, without any success, to teach Dona and Tuli—and Rimi—not to barge in as if they were storming a fortress. Now, as he made his modest preparations, he hummed loudly to warn potential visitors.

With the first dipper of water he poured over himself he realized the tune he was humming was the theme song from *Kya? Hua Kya?* Icy needles pricked him all over.

Hastily he threw on some clothes and went to stretch out on the bed under the fan. He would lie there, watching the antics of a spider on the ceiling, till he was summoned to dinner. Or to help Tuli with his math. Or to arbitrate a dispute between Dona and Rimi...

The door squeaked. Through half-closed eyes he saw Dida hobbling across the room. She stood by the bed, hovering motionlessly, like a hummingbird over a petunia bush. He lay very still hoping she would think he was asleep.

When it was no longer possible to ignore her he sat up. She was wearing the expression he knew so well—and dreaded. He slid down again. Covering his face with his arm, he said, 'Let's avoid the Puja lunch this year, Ma.'

'You are tired, Bulbul,' she said in the gentle drone that he knew would be his undoing. 'You need a tonic. Shark liver oil.'

He swung his legs off the bed. 'I understand, Ma. It's a tradition. But just this once...' He stopped. Her glasses were flashing at him.

'When your Baba was alive,' her voice trembled, 'there was no question of not doing it. He loved that lunch. He *lived* for it.'

Pinaki ducked his head to hide his irritation.

She gave his arm a playful tap. She thought he had nodded! Undoing the knot on her sari she took out a small, worn notebook inscribed with names in minute handwriting and different inks, scratched out, rewritten, overwritten. The guest list.

'What is the matter, Bulbul? If it's the expense, don't worry. The money will come from somewhere.'

'From my bonus,' he said glumly.

She cackled. 'That's where you're wrong!' She took out a piece of paper from her blouse and waved it.

It was her pension statement. It had increased, and the arrears for the last two years had been credited as well. *A windfall! Enough to build a bathroom? Plaster how many walls? Perhaps all the woodwork...*

'Are you listening, Bulbul? I said for once we won't have to ask your stingy Bishukaka to contribute.'

When Dida left he popped his head into the dining room. 'It's working well, I see.'

'What?' said Tuli.

'Your new radio.'

'Yes, it is!' beamed Tuli.

'I could hear from two rooms away.'

Grinning sheepishly, Tuli lowered the volume. Pinaki shut the door behind him. He heard a gurgle. 'Well done, Baba. He drives everyone crazy with that transistor.'

Pinaki glanced at his watch. 'You're just back? Dona, you know the streets are not safe at this time!'

She eased the strap of her bag from her shoulder and leaned on the wall. 'Baba, it gets dark here at 5 o'clock. That's *afternoon*! Anyway, what you fear might happen in the dark can happen in the day.' She gurgled again. Catching his eye she pulled at her T-shirt. Which, he observed was too tight. Did she realize? Should he point it out?

He looked away. 'Don't you girls wear saris anymore? It is so graceful.' He mimed draping it across his chest and over his shoulder.

She burst out laughing. 'You're so funny, Baba!' She swung her bag so it hit him lightly. 'Don't *worry* so much! I can take care of myself. I'm old enough.'

You'll never be old *enough*, he thought. Not for me.

Rimi walked into their bedroom when he was folding the counterpane. Straightaway she said, 'I know what you're thinking.' Before he could answer, 'You are wishing you had another life,' she said. 'Away from here.'

This was so near the mark it took his breath away. He refolded the counterpane to collect his thoughts. 'What did Ma say to you now?'

'It is against her religion to be nice to me.'

'But what did she *say*?'

She stripped off her sari and threw it on the clotheshorse. It would lie there, he knew, till someone—he—folded it. He suspected her sloppiness was deliberate—it gave her some sort of hold over him because she knew how much order meant to him. 'She said your cousin Putul had been proposed for you before you married me.'

She was standing in her blouse and petticoat, hands on hips. Women with hips should undress in the bathroom, he thought. That wasn't fair. Women of a certain age shouldn't... That was downright unkind.

He averted his eyes. 'What does that matter *now*? There were other proposals for me—and for you too.'

She dropped her kaftan over her head and fumbled behind it to strip off her blouse. Her petticoat dropped to the floor. 'She hinted you'd have *preferred* Putul but Putul wanted to do her MA.'

'But Rimi, I really didn't consider... I mean, why think about it now? Once you are married you don't go back.' It's better not to, he could have added, but wisely didn't.

'Well, you don't think of me at all. You notice me as much as...*that*.'

He glanced at where she was pointing at the wall. Unhappily there was a damp patch right in the line of sight. He must speak to the landlord about it when he came next. In fact he should call him tomorrow. He nodded to make a note to himself—and heard an affronted hiss. She'd misunderstood the nod, and there was no point explaining, she wouldn't believe his explanation, and how absurd it all was!

'I'm sure Ma did not mean to criticize you, Rimi. What did she say anyway?'

'That Putul is a very good cook,' she said sulkily.

'That she is.' His cousin Putul's bapa doi was legendary! As for her bhetki paturi...And she was so happy to feed you! 'She's a good girl,' he said, without thinking.

'Then you *do* regret not marrying her,' Rimi said. 'I've been slapped twice.' She swatted her cheeks, first one and then the other. When he didn't react, 'Perhaps,' she said, with a sidelong glance, 'she's the lucky one.'

He flinched. Putul had married a doctor and lived in New York. Absurd, absurd! Yet, there was so much he could say to Rimi that he dared not. For instance, she wasn't beautiful any more than he was successful. That over the years her cooking—and her temper—had improved as little as his prospects. That they both lived with daily reminders of their disappointment, but that was the case of nine-tenths of the world. In the end, 'I married *you*, Rimi,' he said simply. 'I chose *you*.'

That wasn't true. Fate (and their parents) had conspired to bring them together. Although truly, it wouldn't have mattered who you marry because in time the girl becomes a wife. And a wife is well, a wife. And as he had recently learned, a liability if you're planning to build a house. At least that's what Biren Roy had insinuated.

Was he simply using it as an excuse to fob off Pinaki? A wife, after all, is an existing condition for most part. He wished he could be left alone to work this out.

She pulled her sheet up to her chin. 'You didn't choose me. Your mother did.'

Weariness engulfed him. 'I had no objection.'

He had blundered again. Dismayed, he retracted this lukewarm response. He had fully supported her choice, he said. That got him back to where they started—that there *was* no choice because Putul had opted out of the race.

'It's too late to think of all that, Rimi...' He gave up.

Honesty really was a problem with him. Plus he had no gift for evasion. It was true that since the time they'd met and married, the one happening on the heels of the other, he had been loyal to her, body *and* mind. But it was also true he couldn't remember when he'd last felt the frisson of excitement of the days when he came home to his 'wife'. He looked at her now with the eyes of a stranger. Hair the colour and texture of grass after a forest fire, lines parenthesizing her mouth—lines of discontent, the unnaturally thin eyebrows—the lack of, not beauty but *generosity*... Would he have married her, if he had foreseen this?

'Anyway,' he said brightly. 'Here we are, you and I, in this room we've shared for twenty years. *That* means something, doesn't it?'

She picked up her magazine.

It occurred to him then that she was punishing him. For *her* unhappiness. He had done all he could think of to make her happy. Perhaps...'I'm planning something special for you, Rimi.'

'What.'

'I'm going to build us a house.'

The magazine fluttered. 'A *house*? Shey ki? Where?'

'Here. In Calcutta.'

'In *Calcutta*?' The way she said *Calcutta* rendered the idea positively insane. '*Why?*'

'Where else,' he said weakly.

'Do you have the money?'

'No. But...'

'Why not buy a flat like everybody else?'

He gazed at the window, at a loss. Then, like an omen, a wet sari furled down from the balcony above, and flapped against the windowpane.

He pointed at it. 'Because of that!'

She stared at him. 'But you've never complained about that before. In any case that's no reason to build a house.'

That's when he saw, with dazzling clarity, what else the house meant to him. It was not just the escape he sought. It was a bid for immortality. 'A house has a past and a future. A house builds a tradition. It is a legacy for our children. Our children's children—it will become an ancestral property! Imagine that Rimi!'

'Where will this house be?'

'I was thinking of Narendrapur.'

'Narendrapur? Narendrapur is not *Calcutta*! There's *nothing* there!'

'There's peace and quiet. Fresh air. Trees...birds! The sparrows have disappeared from Calcutta.'

'I don't miss them.'

'Ei, you'll be close to nature, Rimi.'

'*I'd* like to be close to a cinema hall. And shops. My friends.'

'You'll have me,' he said, giving her leg a flirtatious tap. 'We'll have a house to grow old and foolish in.'

He ran his hand over his scanty hair. He had already shown himself to be foolish. As for deputing himself as a substitute for cinema and friends, he was flattering himself there, wasn't he? And how does one explain something that was not an escape, but an arrival? The idea of a homecoming? The sense of ownership?

'Doesn't having your own house mean something to you?'

'You once said that we come into the world with nothing and we'll go out with nothing. "Travel light", you said, when

I asked if we could buy a new sofa. A house is heavier than *that*.' He stared at her, astonished. 'People have to give up their possessions to become spiritual,' she continued. 'That's what the sages say. The first thing they do is leave their house.'

'What you're saying is you don't want to go away from here.'

'I might have—once.' Her voice was wistful. 'But it's the same wherever you go.'

He was speechless. Biren Roy had said something like that. There's no escaping the city, he had said. As if Calcutta was a fate.

'I'm alright here,' she said. 'This flat has been good for us.'

He was touched. So frugal was she with her appreciation that this was a precious gift. He could make it last for days, pulling it out and examining it, holding it to the light for rainbows.

Sensing victory, she became magnanimous. If he wanted escape he could go to the countryside on Sundays. Write poetry, paint. Although it was the only day in the week he was home.

He tried explaining the idea of the house was not to fulfil his artistic urges—but wait. Wasn't it though?

He took her hand. 'It is not just for *me*, Rimi.'

She snatched her hand away. 'It *is*. It always is. Everything is for the man. He does what he wants to and we have to suffer for it.'

That's not true for *you*, he cried silently. When did I ever treat you badly? Am *I* responsible for all the bride burning that happens, and female infanticide and rape? I only want to build a house! For you, us to be *happy* in! If you were me, he implored the new voice in his head, what would you do?

Look to your needs first, Bose. All else will follow. Or not. Put on your oxygen mask first before helping others, as they say in airplanes.

'Yes,' he murmured. 'That's what he would say.'

'Who?'

'Biren Roy. The man who wrote the article.'

'You *met* him?' She didn't wait for his reply. 'So he's the one,' she said. 'Putting ideas in your head. Well, you tell him your wife thinks this is a stupid idea.'

He swallowed as if to overcome the taste of something bitter.

A little chastened, 'You haven't said how you will pay for this house,' she said.

'I have some savings.' He hesitated. 'It will not be easy but we can do it.' And then, because he still held the moment, or so he thought because she hadn't protested, 'We have to make sacrifices, Rimi,' he said.

'Don't ask *me* to. I'm not the one who wants it.'

Disconsolately he walked to the window. The wet sari fluttered and smacked his face. Annoyed, he tugged at it. It came away in his hand.

'What are you *doing*?'

He didn't answer.

Kalol Mondal was standing by the electric transformer and looking up at their balcony.

He stumbled to the bed and sat down with a bump. 'I have made up my mind, Rimi. I'm going to build this house.'

She raised her magazine to cover her face.

'Rimi. Try to understand.'

She didn't reply.

It struck him then, the import of the unhappy exchange. If she didn't want the house, he didn't, in effect and to all intents and purposes—*this* intent and purpose, at least—have a wife. Which, it seemed, was Biren Roy's chief objection to the project.

It was all he could do to stop from cheering. Quickly, before she could sense his triumph, he walked out of the room.

He almost knocked over his mother. She was resting her cheek on the doorjamb as if she was easing a toothache.

She gave him a beatific smile. 'I was about to knock, ami kichu jigesh korthey chai... Should we have fish fry or the mutton biryani for the Puja lunch?'

He made a mental note to soundproof his new house.

10

Biren picked up the receiver. It was his old—and only—client.

'Good news for you, Mr Biren! I have become Spanish Consul for Calcutta!'

'Congratulations,' Biren said when he stopped laughing. 'But how's it good for *me*, Sethji? Do I get to be your footman?'

'Tch. Good news for friend is good news. Come this evening if you have nothing better to do.'

'I don't, actually.'

'Then this will be good enough for you. I will give you Spanish wine.'

Biren was ushered into the informal sitting room and led to the platform bed where the Seth was lounging, propped up by two bolsters. Velvet cushions succoured other parts of his slight frame. The air was thick with rose incense and day-old marigold. The household had vermilion smears on their foreheads, and coloured strings on their wrists or around their neck. The reason for all this piousness was, Biren knew, fear of losing money. It set his teeth on edge. He always wanted to crunch an apple after his visits. He had the same mixed-up feelings about his client that the manager of a rundown hotel would towards a loyal guest. Grateful for his custom but despising him for it too.

Biren toed the carpet. 'New doormat, Sethji? Where did you pick it up?'

'The *carpet* is from *Persia*, Mr Biren.'

'Of course.'

After the Spanish wine was poured, and the Spanish cheese sampled, 'Business now, Mr Biren,' said the Seth. He put down his untouched wineglass, settled the folds of his diaphanous dhoti, and called for a sherbet—something he had clearly been dying to do. 'I want new look for my house. A different get-up. Something,' he moved his arms as if he was parting a curtain, 'Smart.' He gave Biren a sharp look. 'You don't like the idea, it seems.'

'I should take away your picture books, Sethji. I have to point out, since I am honest and have your interests at heart, that we did extensive—and expensive—alterations last year.'

'It's because of this consul business,' said the Seth, suddenly unsure. He punched a cushion and settled it behind his back. 'I need a cultural context.'

'What context are you thinking of?' Biren asked, with a straight face. 'Modernista?'

'Spanish of course. Parthenon.'

'That's Greek.'

The Seth crumbled cheese and glared at it, willing it to morph into a paneer pakora. 'There is no good Spanish building,' he huffed.

'Isn't that a bit unpatriotic? The Alhambra is very popular, I believe.'

'It is not as famous as Parthenon. Also Parthenon is holy. It's a *temple*. Of goddess Diana.'

'Athena, as I remember. But I could be wrong. After all, I'm not the Greek Consul. And its Mammon you want to build a temple to.'

The Seth blinked. Then he gave Biren a roguish tap with his glass, anointing him with drops of sherbet. 'Always joking, Mr Biren. But you see scientific angle too. I appreciate that. Okay here's a challenge for you. Use local traditions for this.'

'It *will* be a challenge—reconciling Gaudi with haystacks.'

The Seth held his yellow topaz ring to the light and admired it. Without taking his eyes off it, 'I have more good news for you,' he said. 'My son is going to Harvard, for Senior Managers Business Program.'

'With all respect, Sethji, your son has just started working. In fact, he's only recently graduated to long pants.'

The Seth frowned. 'They gave him admission.'

'Money opens doors, as they say.'

'Are you saying I bribed?'

'Not at all. Just that Harvard is a capitalist institution and capitalism is built on opportunism. Anyway Sethji, since you have the money for Harvard there is the small matter of my bill...'

'Not today. I'm busy.' The Seth swung his legs off the platform. His dhoti rode up, exposing his calves, pale and hairless, and a little creepy.

'We haven't finished the wine!'

'Take it with you,' said the Seth, groping for the floor with his feet. A minion shot out and pushed his chappals under them. Bending with difficulty, he bundled the cheese in its wrapping and thrust it at Biren. 'Take this also. No-one will eat. It smells of goats.' Unexpectedly, he winked. 'I may have another project for you, Mr Biren.'

'A power plant for one of your factories?'

The Seth shook his head. 'This is different.'

'Let me guess. Spanish steps?'

The Seth slid a finger along the side of his nose. 'It is very much Indian. And it's not steps. There'll be lifts. *Elevators*.'

Biren's heart skipped a beat. 'Will it buy me a new car or a new drafting table?' The Seth smiled. He wouldn't be caught out so easily. Biren looked at the Seth from under half-closed lids. 'It's the office annexe you mentioned once.'

'Oh, *that*,' said the Seth, flicking his fingers dismissively. 'No.' He gathered up the end of his dhoti and hopped to the floor. 'All good things must wait, Mr Biren. Come, I will walk with you to car.'

Biren's car had trouble starting.

'Tut. You *do* need a new car, Mr Biren.'

'I can't get a new *bicycle* with what you pay me, Sethji.'

'Tut. *Always* thinking of money, Mr Biren. But you are a good fellow, my dear. Your time will come. In life everything has a time and a place.'

'I hope you're clairvoyant...is something the matter?'

The Seth was frowning. 'We failed to qualify for the quarter-final, Mr Biren. By just one goal. Tcha! Don't you read the papers? World football championship.'

'But we don't even play... Oh, I get it. *Spain.*'

The Seth smiled, displaying childishly small teeth. 'Correct.' He gave Biren a speculative look. 'Maybe I *should* tell you about the project.' After a short pause, 'It is a hotel,' he said. 'Five-star.'

Biren gripped the gear shift. 'Where?'

'No more now, Mr Biren. It is not public knowledge.'

'Right. Um, Sethji. The bill for your factory canteen. You said you'd clear it after the roof was cast. It's been two months since...'

The Seth frowned. 'That roof leaks, Mr Biren. From the beginning I told you it would.'

'Okay, let's forget the bill. Pay instead for my new prototype portable hut for construction labour.'

The Seth's Adam's apple bobbed like a life buoy at high tide. 'No more experiments, Mr Biren. Last time you made prototype, all the asbestos sheets were stolen. What will you gain by it anyway? A few huts will not change the world.' He leaned into the window, fanning Biren with his cardamom-scented breath. 'You cannot save these people from their fate. Practise my philosophy of karma. It is a forgiving one.' He drew back, his eyes narrowed. 'You are not a communist, are you?'

Biren laughed.

11

From the coveted corner banquette Biren watched his father enter the bar-room. For a whole minute Mr Roy Sr stood at the door, marking down the room, his expression conveying he was used to better and bigger. As always, he gave the impression of being borne in on a palanquin, hefted by four bodybuilders. *Club ties on the naked torsos would be a nice touch,* Biren thought.

Without any preamble, 'What's the joke?' Mr Roy asked Biren. He held out his hand, the fingers drooping. Did he expect Biren to kiss them? Biren gathered them as if they were the straying strands of a rope, and tugged twice.

'The air conditioning doesn't work in this corner,' said Mr Roy.

'I've been alright with it, actually, these past twenty minutes.'

Mr Roy looked at Biren's glass. 'You've used your time well, I see. And if you're hinting I'm late, I was button-holed downstairs by Sam Dinshaw. Come on, let's sit over there.' He beckoned a bearer. 'Boy!'

Biren winced. He'd tried telling his father not to use this form of address, forty years after India repossessed her self-respect. Picking up his glass, he followed the little cortege to the banquette in the opposite corner.

Mr Roy sat down with a thud. 'Scotch and soda. Small.'

'Another of this, please,' Biren said, tapping his near-empty glass, and to his father, 'Save him the bother of going back.'

Mr Roy grunted. 'Two smalls are *my* quota for an evening. You're drinking *gin*?'

'Yes. It's fashionably recherché, I believe. But I hope I'm not embarrassing you? It's not a social gaffe or anything?'

Mr Roy pushed the bowl of nuts across the polished surface of the table. 'I shouldn't be eating these. I recently learned I'm

an endomorphic type. Water, vegetables, fibre—*that's* the way
to kill the toxins.'

Biren helped himself. 'It's a toss-up which produces more
toxins,' he said slyly. 'Self-denial or self-indulgence.' He pushed
the bowl back. 'So I wouldn't hold back.'

'*You'd* do well to hold back. You're already looking raddled.'

Biren touched his cheek. 'This is nature's doing, not mine.'

'You know very well I didn't mean *that*.'

The room was long and high-ceilinged, with tall windows from
which heavy drapes were looped back with knotted cords. The
glass was mottled with condensation. Russell Street floated in a
misty haze, through which Biren could see the dissolving neon
sign over a liquor store across the road, and the faded painted
signs over a plant nursery, an auction house. His skin puckered
with preternatural chill, but outside, he knew, the temperature
was 38 degrees centigrade, with 80 percent humidity. Weather
is a class divider, he thought, not for the first time.

'Well? Which are you plotting to rebuild—Queen's
Mansion or the Turf Club?'

Biren turned from the window. 'Sorry, Baba. You were
saying something.'

Mr Roy waved his glass at a noisy foursome three tables
away. 'I was wondering if I should complain. Bangladeshis.
God knows why they come here. They hate us.' He scrabbled
in the bowl of nuts, tossed four into his mouth, and chewed
as if he was grinding his teeth.

Biren was about to remind him he was from Bangladesh—
when it used to be East Bengal—when an unexpected pang of
nostalgia overcame him. Time was—roll back forty years—
when he would toss the nuts into that mouth, one at a time,
moving further and further back for each try, his father egging
him on. Time was—roll back thirty years—when he brought
the nuts in a silver bowl, the rear guard in the parade of glasses,

bottle, ice pail. And a few years after that, he was taking part in the ritual. It was their moment of truth, the truth of what they were to each other, and what he would become one day. With what implicit trust had the father saluted his future and the son embraced it!

Mr Roy swallowed. 'So. Any new commissions? Anything got off that drawing board of yours?'

Biren tasted something dark and viscous. Like engine oil. He sluiced his mouth with gin. We've outlasted the trust, he thought. We're no longer each other's habit even. 'I should go easy on those nuts, Baba. You'll endomorph into peanut butter.'

'If you were less of a smart aleck you'd be more of an architect.'

Biren put his glass down. The ice cubes imploded, catching the light.

'I should avoid these,' muttered Mr Roy, pushing the bowl away. Then, 'Think seriously of an alternative career, Biren,' he said. 'There's no logic to sticking with a profession plagued by economic uncertainties...wasting a first-class education, connections, every advantage...sales, marketing, corporate affairs...my contacts still work. Jardine's, Dunlop, Braithwaite...'

The words rose and fell in chaotic waves. His father had a quota of them for these evenings. Biren sat back, only half-listening. What it must be to have no self-doubts, and no regrets. And to live a life of privileges, unperturbed by ideas. It was ironical that another privileged life, his dead grandfather's, should keep him in ideas now, and pay his rent, his ex-wife's alimony...

'...regular hours, a cheque every month, increments and bonus...'

'And a watch-and-handshake on my sixtieth birthday. No. Not for me, Baba.'

'Of course not. After all, what are primitive survival needs when there's a whole world out there waiting to be set fire to?'

Biren picked up his glass. He felt cramped and suffocated. His father could make even this room seem like a broom cupboard. Too late he remembered gin gave him a terrible hangover. In the desperation of the moment, 'I wrote something for *The Hoogly Times* last week,' he blurted out.

'Oh yes. I read it. Some interesting ideas.'

'I had hoped people would find it interesting enough to respond.' *Damn* the gin.

'Did anyone...?'

'One.'

'That's it?'

'That's it. I would've got a better response with a poem— preferably about rain.'

'*Philistines.*'

Biren started. It was the closest his father had come to a compliment. He mopped the spilled drink with a paper napkin. 'It's isn't a dead loss. The fellow wants me to build a house. A very modest one.'

'You have potential, Biren. Don't think I don't see it. But potential can be a placebo. You have to *find* clients. *Court* them. Market your skills. Ambition is all very well, but it needs an out. Channelled properly, it can build a Rome.'

'Overreach, and it can destroy it.'

'Why are you so *cynical*? At your age you should be thinking more, well, constructively. No pun intended.'

True, thought Biren, running a finger around the rim of his glass. Hitler was my age when he was redrawing the map of Germany.

Mr Roy was looking a little lost. 'Biren,' he began, when a bearer materialized at his elbow.

'Another drink, sahib?'

'No, thank you.'

'Yes, please,' said Biren.

Mr Roy frowned at the bearer. 'There's no call to *ply* us...

oh, alright, bring me one too.' He gave Biren a dour smile. 'Since we're making a night of it.' He coughed and spat into his paper napkin, chucked it into the ashtray. 'It's all very well to be anti-establishment when you're young, Biren, but now you *are* the establishment. The flower children have seeded over,' he said with heavy jocularity.

'Some of them may even be standing for President here.'

'And you can't imagine a more humiliating end.'

'I think it's a pretty good thing actually. Access to this bar for one, any number of *boys* jumping at your bidding, thousands of people lobbying to get in...'

'*You* don't have to. You know that.'

'Yes, I know. Thanks but no thanks, Baba. Get my Sethji in. He's asked me only about fifty times.'

Mr Roy flicked his nose with a very white handkerchief. 'We don't admit traders. As it is, this place looks like a third-rate hostelry. We weren't consulted on the renovation.'

'Hemingway used to talk like that,' Biren said idly.

'Like what?'

'In the royal plural. He's an entrepreneur actually—my Sethji.'

'Well, he can't get in. Not even if he owns all of Park Street... I need to go to the bathroom. No, sit, sit. I can manage. I'll see you in the dining room.'

Biren massaged his eyes with his fingertips. The things a man had to do to keep alive. Gutting a pig. Quarrying stone. Pulling a rickshaw. Enduring evenings like this.

What idea of self could you explore in a cage? In a chain gang?

Mr Roy put down the menu. 'What do you recommend?'

The bearer murmured the roast mutton was very good today.

'We'll have the fish,' declared Mr Roy. 'Grilled. Never eat

what they recommend,' he said to Biren. 'They always push the old stuff.'

Biren smiled at the bearer. 'I'll have mine fried. Thanks.'

After the man left Mr Roy leaned into the table, looking a little furtive. 'Hmm, Biren. I was just wondering... I hope you aren't depressed or anything. Your divorce, well.'

Biren hid his surprise behind his water glass. 'It happened long ago, Baba. And the marriage was short-lived.'

'Then why this, this—I don't know the psychological term for it. Reluctance to engage with the world? Inability to reconcile with, with reality?'

Biren pretended to consider. 'Schizophrenia, probably.' He put his glass down. 'Quit trying to analyze me, Baba. It frustrates you and it bores me.'

'What I would like to understand is why you, anyone would do this to themselves.'

'Do what exactly?'

'Well, swim against the tide, I suppose. It's such a struggle. And for what?'

'I suppose for the same reason there are elections. There has to be an opposing view, else people will get away with murder. They do anyway, but why make it easier for them?'

Mr Roy clamped his mouth over a breadstick. 'How, pray, can you oppose anyone if you don't get out there and fight? See, you can't answer. You're just hiding behind...'

'Columns?'

'Delusions,' said Mr Roy. His features wavered. 'Hiding from the bogeyman is acknowledging him, Biren. And you're no coward.'

Perhaps this evening wasn't going to be a complete write-off, Biren thought. 'I must confess I *was* scared last evening. Imran Khan was bowling and we needed ten runs off six balls to win.'

Mr Roy chuckled. 'So are you going to build this house?'

'No. Not worth my while.'

'Suit yourself. Carry on building cloud castles. You need no bidding to do *that*. Although I don't see much happiness there either.'

Biren bit back a retort. Why bother? Why would a pauper insure his home? Against what—the birds? Let them in, he thought fiercely, let them all in! And shit upon our heads!

'It keeps civilization afloat,' he said woodenly.

'I see. Making a living is vulgar now.'

Biren's jaw ached. The anger was moving through him like poison. 'I *have* a project actually,' he said. He could have kicked himself.

'Really? What is it?'

'It's not public knowledge yet.'

Mr Roy raised his eyebrows.

'Yes, it must be hard for you to believe that,' Biren said.

The soup—mushroom—was put before them. Mr Roy poked at the black specks in his bowl. 'What are these singularities?'

Biren laughed.

'I forgot to bring your cheque,' continued his father, looking a little sheepish. 'I only realized that in the bathroom. I'll send it around to your studio tomorrow.'

'I've told you before, Baba, to just transfer the capital. Save bother.' And we could dispense with this unedifying ritual.

'I don't have to remind you this is your single source of income—steady income. I don't wish it jeopardized by some foolhardy scheme.'

The bread knife trembled in Biren's fingers. 'I don't have to remind *you* that Dadu left the money to *me*.'

'I *will* remind you it's in a trust and I manage it. Till I see fit.' Mr Roy waved his spoon, consecrating the tablecloth with drops of soup, 'There's been nothing to inspire that confidence till now. A barn of a studio, and you're paying Quasimodo, what, two thousand, for making paper chains?'

'He has a speech impairment,' Biren said, through barely moving lips. 'And what I pay him is nobody's...'

'Ah, but it *is* my business is the point.'

Biren gripped the knife.

The main course came. The bearer proffered a platter of boiled beans, peas, carrots and roast potatoes. Mr Roy asked for asparagus, which, naturally, would be tinned at this time of year. Biren had seen far too many displays of such affectation to be impressed by them. Without disturbing his fish, he entombed it with the peas. Then he built a retaining wall of carrots and beans. It would annoy his father, he thought, observing with satisfaction that he had abandoned two limp worms of asparagus, and was eating the spurned carrots-and-peas.

Mr Roy clattered his fork. '*Bones!*' He removed a shard from his mouth and placed it on the side of his plate. 'Preposterous!' He called the bearer. 'You call this carcass, this *carrion*, fish?' After terrorizing him for five minutes he said, 'You have to make amends, my friend. Replace it with another dish.'

Predictably he picked jumbo prawn—the most expensive item listed. 'The same for you?'

'I'm fine with this, thanks.'

His father gave him a disgusted look. 'I thought thinking too *big* was your problem.'

If someone started a cult of patricide, Biren thought, I would be first to join up. Perhaps I should show some enterprise and *start* one.

A white-sleeved arm insinuated itself politely between them. 'Mango mousse?'

Mr Roy dragged the ladle through it, raking it as if it was mulch, before waving it away. 'This is too fancy for me.'

Biren didn't react. It was another of his father's conceits, to reiterate his ordinariness in this way. He took a huge helping of the mousse, to recompense the bearer for his trouble.

'...so kindly acknowledge the remittances, Biren. Last month I had to call my bank *twice* to check. I'm getting a bit tired of...'

'It's called donor fatigue, I believe.'

'Your mousse has dripped on your trousers. In a rather awkward spot, I may add.'

That made your day, Biren thought but didn't say.

They walked together to the car park. Mr Roy held out his hand. 'Prove you're ready for it and I'll do the transfer.'

Biren touched the proffered hand. 'That's about as redeemable as a deathbed promise.'

Mr Roy looked at him expressionlessly. Then he nodded. 'Take a shot at real work some time. You may even find you enjoy it.'

Biren made himself walk away slowly. The loosely packed gravel moved like ball bearings under his shoes. Saunter, he muttered under his breath. Don't let him think you're fleeing his bloody coruscating humour.

12

All that week it rained. Every morning, the city woke to twilight and mouldy towels, traffic snarls, the suspension of essential services, shortages of all kinds. It's baffling, Biren thought, re-reading yesterday's paper as he drank his black coffee. The merest sprinkle and the city seizes up. The monsoon was a good time to hibernate, to postpone all but vital activities, such as dying. The permanent dusk had one advantage though. He could drink his rum-and-water any time he chose instead of his usual moral flag-off—the moment he could no longer read his wristwatch by the light from the window. There were times when the sun popped out just as he was getting down to it. Manu was careful to keep out of his way during those times.

For Manu, the humidity brought a different vexation. The smoky vapour made stubborn smudges on his tracing sheets. He rubbed them with day-old bread. Grey crumbs were always scattered around his table.

Pinaki wondered, as he battled the flooded roads, why there should be a traffic jam in the relatively dry High Court area when it was raining in Park Street, three kilometres away. Or why, on less critical days, with only six millimetres of rain, his bus should be delayed by half an hour. It's a psychological problem, not logistical, he concluded vaguely. Still, it had been a good week. Mr Sen had reported sick with a viral fever. With luck it would last till the weekend. Five days without Mr Sen!

Finding the door ajar, he pushed it open and stood decanting water on the floor. Biren Roy put his novel-face down on the writing desk and picked up his cigarette. 'Look, Bose, this must stop. I haven't exactly encouraged you, you know.' In a rare gesture of consideration, he turned his neck away to exhale smoke.

Interpreting this as an invitation, or at least not outright expulsion, Pinaki came into the room and sat on the less shaky of the two chairs.

This was his first time inside the sanctum. It ran the entire length of the studio and ended at the window. To the right of the desk was a table fitted with a drawing board. Bookshelves lined the wall opposite the window. A rusted Remington sat amid the books, steel wire twisted into shapes, a papier-mache ball made of newsprint and a foot-high edifice of irregular blocks in different colours, glued together. On a tall bench sat half-a-dozen dusty building models in cardboard and thermocol. On the desk was an object like a bird's nest, made, it appeared, of fused steel strips. Pinaki craned his neck to look inside it. It contained eggshells. He caught Biren Roy's eye and sat back.

'You appear somewhat excited, Bose. Won a lottery?'

'My wife, sir. She doesn't want this house.'

'I'm glad someone is thinking straight. But why are *you* so happy?'

'Because you said you would take on the project if there was no interference from...'

'I never said anything of the sort. Don't extrapolate and impute.'

Pinaki's skin puckered with sudden chill. 'I—I thought...' He swallowed. 'I thought because she would not interfere we could...you could... I myself am a simple man, sir. I don't have many needs.'

'Well, you seem to need a house to accommodate them.'

Trying to keep his eyes from straying to the birthmark, 'A small house,' Pinaki said. 'I'm a simple man.'

Biren Roy gave a short laugh. 'You keep saying that and people will think you're stupid.'

'I understand you work on big projects, sir. But you would be able to design this house in a day. *You* would.'

Biren Roy frowned. 'Please don't try to flatter me.' In a milder tone he said, 'Size, or simplicity for that matter, is not a factor of time.' He sneezed and wiped his nose on his sleeve.

'But, but, this is only a house!'

'What, it's only a house now? I thought it was a parking place for your soul.'

Biren Roy was teasing him! Cheered, Pinaki pulled out a piece of paper from his briefcase and proffered it shyly. 'I drew this, sir.'

'Very pretty—what is that row of teeth? And that waffle cone?'

'It's a railing. That's the roof.'

'Hmm...Look Bose, give up this idea. Just buy a flat.'

'But...'

'You could be contained in a nutshell, and still feel a king of infinite space. You don't have to believe me—a philosopher said that.'

'Yes, I also think a house is infinite space.'

Biren Roy sighed. Picking up his cigarettes, he walked out into the studio. After a minute Pinaki went out too. Biren Roy was standing by a contraption made of tin sheets. A pedestal fan was blowing on it. Something sounded loose, like a belt that's slipped off, Pinaki thought. Should he point it out? He tripped over a stool.

'For heaven's sake, Bose! Walk round the edge of the room!'

Pinaki retreated inch by inch—in the quiet you'd be able to hear a worm chewing a leaf—backing up all the way to the wall of drawings.

The wall was striated like sedimentary rock with pale blue, sepia and white paper, tracing sheets. They were buildings—just about. They were as nothing he had encountered before—except in photographs and movies. What did he know, anyway, outside the eight square kilometres of his office–home beat?

'I didn't know you are building the Hoogly Township, sir,' he said respectfully.

'I'm not.'

'The Lake Market Centre?'

'Nor that.'

Pinaki peered at the drawings, puzzled. 'I don't understand, sir.'

'And you never will.'

Crushed, Pinaki sidled towards the door.

'Hold on! Do you have a site?'

Pinaki turned around. 'No sir.'

Biren Roy snorted. 'You're hopeless, Bose. Just a waste of time.'

I inspire bad manners in people, Pinaki thought, as he climbed down the stairs. But what did he mean, do I have a site? Should I, dare I...

He felt like a well digger who has turned up the first damp clod.

'Put away that smirk, Friday,' Biren said sourly. 'It's not going to happen.'

Manu held up a piece of paper. *Can't you make an exception? We don't have work*!

'No,' snapped Biren. 'It'll be an unedifying job with no returns. And for your information, we do have work. The State Transport Terminal. Only a proposal and only for dismissal—probably—and certain disdain, but at least it has substance.'

~

Late that evening there was a lull in the rain and he went out for a walk.

The light was on in the clinic. Dr Murray was crouched on the floor, peering into a sieve. 'It's an Oleander Hawk Moth,' he explained. 'A rare sighting and a beautiful specimen. I wish I had my camera.'

'I didn't know you were interested in moths, Doc. I should take you to the Tolly—the Tollyganj Club, I mean. I believe they have the most species of butterflies there in Calcutta. More than the Botanic Gardens.'

Dr Murray smiled. 'I'd enjoy that, thank you Biren.' He stood up and put away a bundle of antibiotic tablets. 'What have you been doing? The little man's house?'

'I can't build on a cloud. That's where his present site is.'

'Ah.'

'The fellow's such a romantic he makes *me* feel like a bricklayer. He's the kind who will force fate to do its worst. The kind who forgets to switch off the bathroom light and returns to find the house burned down.'

'I didn't know architects required character certification from their clients.'

Biren laughed. 'It's not worth my while, Doc. And *he* doesn't need me to knock together his four rooms.'

'You could explore your ideas there as much as in a skyscraper. It isn't only,' Dr Murray paused, 'size that gives a building its significance.'

Biren was silent.

'And it isn't only significant buildings that give a city legitimacy.'

'Secular reasoning for a religious fanatic, Doc.'

'Biren... Oh, never mind.'

'Go on, say it. Say I'm living beyond my dreams.'

'Don't be childish, Biren.'

'Great cities aren't built by proliferating huts, you know.'

'This isn't a great city, Biren, and it never will be. Not in the tradition of great cities.'

'That is so patronizing. The zero was discovered here, in this country, in the third century BC. The Pantheon hadn't been built then.' After an awkward silence, 'You think my grand vision is a grand delusion.'

'I mean that there isn't going to be the renaissance you imagine. Not in your time. I wish you'd accept that. And settle for something less, well, ambitious. For your, um, peace of mind.'

'My peace of mind. Is that even relevant?'

'What is relevant for you then?'

'Buildings.'

'Fantasies,' Dr Murray said shortly.

'The truth comes out,' murmured Biren. He shook out a cigarette. '*Unbuildings* weighs in at fifty pages. Indications are it will go to another fifty. Not exactly the Wasmuth Portfolio, but still.'

Dr Murray's glasses flashed. 'Biren, you're a hypocrite. You say you want to change the face of the city. Yet you won't make a start with the one chance you've been given! Why are you so perverse?'

Biren bit into his cigarette. Every nerve was straining to rush out of the shack. 'For your information I *do* have a new commission,' he said, through clenched teeth. 'A *significant* one.'

Dr Murray smiled. 'Congratulations. What is it?'

'I can't talk about it yet, sorry.'

Dr Murray raised his eyebrows. 'All in good time, eh? Here. I have something that might interest you.' He pulled out a sheet of paper from a drawer. 'It's by an architect called Kazuo Shinohara—heard of him? He says—I'll read out—"if architecture can change the world at all, it would do so not by promoting radical social visions but by creating small, modest spaces to nurture and protect the individual spirit".'

'Small. Modest. Inconsequential.'

'Not quite. It seems he built powerful concrete pillars—ostensibly to resist the pressures of a corrupting society. *That* should appeal to you.'

~

The rain resumed in the night, continued into the morning. When Biren turned into Free School Street the water was waist-high and rising. Abandoned cars bobbed like whalebacks. Bare-chested youths splashed about, offering to tow their occupants to safety.

His car coughed, sputtered and breathed its last. After ten minutes of contemplating the inevitable, he pushed open his door and jumped out.

Warm water nuzzled his crotch—a sensation not unlike the sneaky childhood thrill of peeing in the swimming pool. But this water was murky. There were things floating in it, and things dissolved in it, and open manholes. He closed his eyes and waded on. The current—quite a strong one—pulled at him.

Manu was squatting under an umbrella on the compound wall of Dinshaw Mansions, holding a bamboo pole over the water. As Biren neared, he jerked up the line. A small fish wriggled on the hook.

'Not enough for lunch,' Biren commented. 'Throw it back and get back to the studio.'

'I have news for you, Manu,' he said when they reached the studio. 'Change is here at last. The Left is thinking of reintroducing English in government schools. Haha! Okay, I won't tease you. Our Seth is building a five-star hotel.'

There was a roll of thunder. Biren looked up. 'I'm glad I'm not superstitious...what's that you're scribbling?'

Manu gave him the piece of paper. *Dry the notes in your wallet.*

Six kilometres away in J. Mullick Road it had stopped raining, but a school holiday had already been declared and schoolchildren were flying kites on their terraces.

Vinu rappelled down a water pipe, holding a kite in his teeth. Landing with a thump, he made a smart about-turn, put the kite to his chest, and bowed.

Idiot, murmured Dona. But she smiled.

The smile went out. Kalol Mondal was sitting on the culvert. He wasn't looking at her but she knew by the way he held his head that he had been, an instant ago, and was calculating the right moment—when she wasn't looking—to look again.

Come on, she muttered, *come on, come on, come on, come on...*

His neck snapped up and then dropped. Wincing, he began massaging it.

She snorted. Another idiot.

13

Pinaki's colleague was annoyed with him. Three times he'd asked if Pinaki was going to Ustad Amjad Ali's sarod recital—historic, because he was coming to Calcutta after eleven years—and all three times Pinaki had answered, no, he didn't want to go out for tea.

'You are again thinking about that house of yours.'

'I never stop thinking about it,' Pinaki said simply. He hesitated. 'In fact, I have found someone to build it.' He allowed a whole minute for his colleague's stupefaction. 'The man who wrote the newspaper article I showed you. In fact,' he paused, enjoying himself now, 'I visited his office many times.' Then, since this was a friend of thirty years, 'He hasn't been too um, helpful,' he confessed. 'Actually he is a strange man. Very intelligent, but,' he paused again, thinking how Biren Roy could be described in one word. 'Complicated'.

'Have you seen anything he's built?'

'I've seen drawings of his projects,' Pinaki said, and, since honesty was a problem with him, added, 'They are not built.'

His colleague gave him a pitying smile. 'So. He doesn't build on land and you don't have land to build on.'

'You can tell he knows his subject,' Pinaki retorted. He snatched up a file. There were limits to a friendship. It doesn't allow for mocking that which is sacred to you. It struck him that the concern hid disapproval. His colleague was making it clear Pinaki was getting ideas above his station. Here he was again, with that deceptively solicitous drone.

'I hope you know land is controlled by CPM thugs, Pinakibabu. Remember that murder last year in Salt Lake? It was a land deal. And what happened to the farmer who refused to sell his field? Also land deal. And the girl who was kidnapped? Again...'

'It is not surprising. My architect says land is a prime resource and so prime motive for crime. Wars are fought for land, he says.'

'It is my impression your architect says too much and does too little. And by the way, he isn't *your* architect, Pinakibabu. Not yet.'

'That is because I don't have land—yet.'

~

Pinaki had shortlisted two land brokers from the personals page in *The Hoogly Times*. In the last week of August, he set about hunting for his plot. It wasn't going to be easy, he discovered.

In Shyambazar—squashed between a marriage hall and a garment factory. 'Very central, babu!'

'To what?'

In Garia—next to a new cancer hospital. 'Very convenient, babu.'

'For whom?'

In Chinatown—flanking the lake. 'Very beautiful view, babu.'

'Of the tanneries?'

In Behala—behind a stinking gutter. 'Not toilet—only bath water.'

'How do you know?'

'There's a flat for sale in this very same road, Bosebabu!'

Pinaki wondered why, if his stated objective was to get away from where he lived, he should be interested in a place that was next door. 'No, not a flat. *Land*. How about Narendrapur?' he asked hopefully, as after an old love.

'No plots available at the moment, babu. Also prices have gone up because of the new township. But if you want a flat there, booking is going on now...'

'No, thank you.'

Within two days Pinaki's quest became public knowledge. Within the week it became a matter of public concern.

'Oi, Bosebabu! Is it true—you are going away? Why do you want to go from here?'

'We heard you had some, ah, problem, here, babu. But problems can be solved!'

'So, Mr Bose, I heard a rumour you may be leaving us soon. A sad loss, indeed. Although our interactions have been few and you aren't a church-goer, I feel we are somehow connected.'

Pinaki began to wonder whether he had, after all, been a little too hasty. A little too adventurous. But haste and adventures are short-lived. This itch had outlasted his wife's tantrums, endured his colleague's forebodings (which still blighted his lunch hour every day), quelled his own uncertainties, and most of all, weathered, and continued to weather, Biren Roy's snubs.

Patience, he told himself. If every salesman gives up after the first door slammed in his face, there would be no production of the *Encyclopaedia Britannica*.

He had to acknowledge, though, that it was Kalol Mondal who hardened his resolve every time he wavered. Whenever Pinaki thought of him, which was far too often for his peace of mind, any incipient doubt disappeared. That Kalol Mondal should be his inspiration! And give him courage! In principle, of course, not in person. Each time Pinaki sighted the fellow, again too frequently for comfort, he changed direction or darted into a shop. And before stepping out, he always checked the street. Nothing had happened after the incident of the flags, but Kalol Mondal's presence seemed to hover around. In that he was not far wrong. As Dona complained, the fellow haunted J. Mullick Road. Admittedly he was corporeally present only in the early mornings and late evenings, but those hours seemed to cast their gloom over the rest of the day.

As was inevitable, Pinaki let down his guard one evening when he went to buy sugar at the modi's. Kalol Mondal stepped out from behind a lamppost and right into his path. It appeared to be a planned manoeuvre because Pinaki found himself penned by an ice cream cart and a pile of garbage, with no means of escape—except to retreat. His self-respect, such as it was, wouldn't allow that. He stood, waiting for Kalol

Mondal to do his worst. Kalol Mondal did what he was best at. Radiating tension.

After a few seconds of this, 'I hear you are looking for land,' he said.

'Who told you?' croaked Pinaki.

Kalol Mondal smiled and leaned against the lamppost, legs crossed at the ankles. The lamppost was Nobody's Dog's favourite peeing spot. Pinaki chortled inwardly. For a blissful moment, he forgot to be frightened.

Kalol Mondal whipped out a pack of cigarettes, shook one out, and flipped it into his mouth with one hand. The other was busy adjusting the death's head buckle on his belt. It occurred to Pinaki that buckle and cigarette parodied Hindi cinema, which parodied life, which parodied art. He was so pleased with this observation that he wished he could share it with Biren Roy. It was the kind of thing he might think of.

The euphoria evaporated. The yellow eyes were raking him over. 'Contact Rabin Pal,' Kalol Mondal said in his flat voice.

'Why should I?'

'He will get you land. He is an estate agent.'

'But you said he is standing for the municipal election.'

Kalol Mondal stretched his cindery mouth. 'Side business.'

The smile reinforced Pinaki's qualms about Kalol Mondal. Fight or flee? A spurt of adrenalin activated his legs. He pushed past the enemy post, and, and he was out!

His back prickled with the arrows of Kalol Mondal's ire. The muscles of his calves ached with the strain of walking slowly, which he had to do to show he wasn't running away. The street began to take on the unreal aspect of a cinema. In a weird shift of perspective, he felt he was crawling, antlike, on the lens of the camera.

When he had gone a safe distance—although he'd have to burrow into the centre of the earth to feel really safe—he turned his head, as if to check it for traffic before he crossed.

From the corner of his eye he saw that Kalol Mondal was indeed
following him. 'Don't follow,' he began in an unnaturally high
voice, when he glimpsed something that made him forget the
rest of his words.

Kalol Mondal was looking at him with a very odd
expression. He's upset, Pinaki thought, astonished. His hands
were convulsing on the cigarette pack as if it was a ball he had
allowed past the goal line. And was he trying to say something?
His mouth was moving... Pinaki wasn't going stay to find out.

Late that evening, Dona was walking along the ill-lit stretch
of road by the municipal school when a figure detached itself
from the shadows.

'Madam, what is time?' he asked, in English.

She walked on, pretending not to have heard. It was an
old ploy that she was adept at dodging. Never stop for them.
Never make eye contact with them. Never ever speak to them.

'Excuse, Madam, Didi! What is time please?'

She clutched her purse to her chest and, keeping her head
down, shoulders hunched, walked faster.

The tap-tapping of the footsteps behind her synchronized
with hers. A shiver ran down her spine. She darted across the
road, ran all the way to her building, only to find the doorway
blocked.

'You!' she exclaimed.

Kalol Mondal bobbed his head but otherwise didn't stir.
In fact, he seemed unsure what to do except stare at her.

Irritation defused her fear. 'Move,' she said tersely.

'Dhorun,' he stuttered. 'Sister. Didi. One moment. Excuse
please.'

'*No*,' she said, her eyes flickering over the deserted lobby.

'Apni eta niyenin.' He passed a very pink tongue over very
brown lips. 'Please you take.' He thrust a small white package
at her. 'I buy for you.'

'No, no. I can't...'

Before he could renew his suit she pushed past him and gained the staircase.

'Excuse! Please! Respected Madam, sister, apni... you are very nice.'

She raced up the staircase, two, three steps at a time, her heart bounding ahead of her. Through a tidal roar in her ears she heard him cry, 'I only wanted to give you present!'

She kept her finger on the doorbell, and almost knocked Tuli down when he opened the door.

'Ki holo, Didi? Bathroom jabe?'

'Get out of my way!'

He scampered to Pinaki's room and burst in. 'Baba, I think something has happened to Didi.'

Pinaki jumped out of his bed. 'What? Where is she?'

'In her room. She's locked herself in.' Tuli trotted behind him as he hurried out of the room. 'Maybe she fought with Vinu.' Pinaki told him sharply to get on with his homework.

There was no sound from Dona's room. After some pleading she let Pinaki in. Without a word she went to her bed, and buried her face in the pillow. He sat beside her and stroked her arm. She lifted her head. 'Stop that, Baba. It gives me goose pimples.'

He began patting her hair. Her hand shot out and swatted his.

'Shall I bring you a samosa from Aroma, shona? An ice cream?'

She made a curious noise, a snort or a laugh, and turned her head on the pillow. 'No, but maybe you could get rid of that man for me.'

'Which man?' He felt cold, sick. His mouth filled with sour saliva. *Panic has a taste*, he thought distractedly. 'Why... what did he...'

She flopped back into her pillow. He rose, too agitated to sit, to stand, to act, and yet what could he do? *I am to blame! I am to blame!*

After pacing the veranda for five minutes he ran down the stairs and out into the street. Motorcycles screeched by. Vendors and customers shouted at each other. A taxi rattled past, backfiring as it went. Shaking his fist, 'Bodmash!' he cried into the noise. 'Loafer! You bad, bad fellow!' He turned and ran back into the building.

His imprecations went unheard. Kalol Mondal, after his unsuccessful and humiliating courtship, had stomped off. They were unnecessary too, because Kalol Mondal was cursing himself, and his miserable lot and his miserable room where he was kicking off his miserable new shoes, which were pinching him for his presumption.

His gift had been 250 grammes of a savoury, spicy snack from the famous Ujjala Chanchur's, freshly made and custom-mixed, with cashews instead of peanuts. And he had unprotestingly put up with a reprimand from the shop assistant for jumping the queue, and the indignity of being sent back to wait his turn.

He stood by his bed, feinting punch after punch at the shop assistant. When he tired of that he flung himself on the cane shelves, dug into his clothes—the washed and unwashed in an incestuous tangle, including a pair of balled-up socks smelling so bad that even he recoiled.

The item he was looking for was under a framed photo (of a film star) that Raja had given him. Lost in its lurid pages, he was, at last, back in the world that was kind to him. By and by, his hunger satiated—after a fashion—he wiped himself with a sweat-stained singlet, and sank into sleep. His last image, ungratefully, was not that of the girl who had so good-naturedly stepped out of the magazine to succour him, but of the heartless one who had rejected his heartfelt overtures.

In the evening, when he stopped to look in on Aroma's for his usual glass of tea and, today, to ponder his next move after his aborted attempt at finding love, he heard a familiar voice at the counter.

It was her father. He was debating what to do—had she told him about last night?—when Pinaki, groping for a stool, straightened up and looked straight at him. His expression was stern and aloof and quite unlike the feeble fool Kalol Mondal was familiar with.

'Ey, nomoshkar,' Kalol Mondal blurted out, folding his palms. Who knew but that his courteous greeting might effect a thaw, followed by a chat, and perhaps, dare he hope, an invitation to her home.

Pinaki turned his shoulder.

Vexed, Kalol Mondal was about to tell him off when, *this is her father,* he remembered. He shuffled off to the other end of the counter and, with bluff joviality, called for a glass of tea.

Pinaki's legs began to vibrate, a nervous up and down jerking. He couldn't help it—they seemed to have a will of their own. In his agitation he snatched a half-biscuit left by a customer and threw it to Nobody's Dog.

It flung itself on the largesse. After that, with a contrariness that was more cat than dog, it ignored its benefactor and wiggled its rear at Kalol Mondal.

'Chol hut!' hissed Kalol Mondal, and meted his routine punishment. The creature backed off, yelping. Then, to Pinaki's disbelief, it crawled back to the foot that had kicked it and licked it.

Kalol Mondal pulled in his foot and was about to kick again, when, to Pinaki's surprise, he bent down and stroked his head. 'Bokachod,' he murmured, and in English, 'You stupid fokka.' Catching Pinaki's eye he smiled sheepishly.

~

'That was when I felt differently about him, sir. Not actually good, but not so bad.'

'But whatever gave you the idea you could trust him?'

'My mother says dogs can sense a man's character.'

'Well, I suppose Mother knows best. Of course, Bullseye was devoted to Bill Sykes. You might want to consider that.'

Pinaki thought he would need his entire life to consider all that Biren Roy said.

~

After Pinaki paid up he turned to Kalol Mondal. 'Ei, about this Rabin Pal. Where can I find him?'

~

That evening, Pinaki caught his usual bus home but got a ticket for a stop a couple of kilometres after his usual one on Diamond Harbour Road.

As soon as he stepped off, a sudden downpour ambushed him. Dozens of black umbrellas bloomed on the street. Unfurling his, he joined the funereal parade. Grey clouds had closed over the grey buildings, turning the evening into a dingy night. Lights glimmered in the darkness, but the rain obscured the signboards. He plodded down the battered pavement, tilting his umbrella to peer through the fringe of water. And at last he saw what he was instructed to look for: *Ganguli and Grandson, Bengali Sweets since 1940.* There was the doorway almost hidden by a signboard which said: *Pal Enterprises Estate Agent Bus Tours Train Tickets.* An arrow pointed to the sky.

He dithered, wondering if he should indulge in a samosa and a sandesh to fill the hollow pit in his stomach when someone jostled him and his umbrella collapsed on his head. Shaking the raindrops from its folds, he began climbing the vertiginous, paan-stained staircase.

The short flight ended at a door. He had to stand two steps below and lean on it to turn the handle. The lintel was not only lower than usual, there was a doorstep to further cut its height. However, the lintel was padded with vinyl-covered foam to protect your head. Although he had no need to Pinaki ducked as he entered.

The room's single occupant was penned behind a table and further barricaded in by a newspaper. Only his big bald head was visible. When Pinaki clattered in, the newspaper was lowered to indicate that the office was open to business.

'Bolun.'

'Rabin Pal achhe?'

The man nodded and pushed his chair back, hitting the wall. 'Hein, ami Rabin Pal.'

Rabin Pal had a walleye that wouldn't stay still and had large teeth that splayed out like a Japanese fan when he smiled. He wore a very yellow gold ring with a red stone. 'Bolun. What can I do for you?' The eye found temporary refuge in Pinaki's face, and began rooting around in it.

Pinaki introduced himself. He didn't need to state his business. Rabin Pal knew all about it. Briskly, and with an impressive economy of words, he told Pinaki he had the perfect plot for him. For immediate sale.

'Good size, good location, good breeze. South facing.'

Pinaki didn't point out that all plots had four sides so one would have to face south anyway. 'Where is it?' he asked. 'How big? How much?'

'First you see, Bosebabu,' Rabin Pal said. His tone was indulgent, as was his smile, but his eye skittered, giving the lie to both.

The eye, both the eyes, presented an unfamiliar challenge. Pinaki was unable to decide which one he should address. He settled for a point in-between. Then, worried this would make him look shifty, he lowered his gaze—and was confronted with another disturbing sight. The torn linoleum (lime green and brown) revealed wooden planks pocked with wormholes.

The floor could give way any moment. Anything was possible in this place.

He raised his head and immediately encountered one of the eyes, peering at him as through a peephole in a freak show. 'Ei,' he said feebly. 'If you recommend it so highly then...'

'Don't believe me, Bosebabu. Always see before you buy— anything. This is my sincere advice to you.'

Pinaki, who did not buy a toothbrush without subjecting it to a close inspection, nodded gratefully.

Rabin Pal hunted through an impressive pile of papers. From behind a cretonne-curtained doorway faint strains of Rabindra Sangeet wafted in, and the sentimental smell of fish frying. The smell made Pinaki feel he was far away from home and safety. It also made him feel hungry.

The curtain parted, and a woman emerged with tea and sandesh, which she put on the table. It would take extraordinary willpower not to fall on the food. Pinaki's failed him. He dispatched the sandesh in a single swallow and finished the tea in a gulp.

'So. When do you want to see this plot?' The eye hit the wall, ricocheted, hit Pinaki. Pinaki had a crazy vision of himself chucking it back to its owner. Alternately, of telling him he should do something about it—wear an eyepatch, or mining goggles...

Rabin Pal rapped his ring on the table to bring him to order. They fixed a time for the coming Saturday.

As Pinaki was leaving, his host jumped up, sending the swivel chair crashing into the wall. 'Eta dhorun, Bosebabu.' He put his head through the curtain. 'Ejey! Kathal ni esho!' He sat down again and beamed at Pinaki. 'Wait one second, Bosebabu.'

After a minute a hand, holding a plastic bag, appeared through the curtain. A sickly but powerful smell filled the room. Rabin Pal slid his chair across the floor to take the bag, skidded back, and presented it to Pinaki. It was half a jackfruit.

~

'And that, for you, was a pledge of good faith?'

'Well, he need not have given it to me,' Pinaki retorted. In fact, he had deemed the jackfruit a good omen, although it had stirred such envy in his taxi driver that he had been tempted to give it to him.

'Pity you don't have a suspicious nature, Bose. That might have tempered the foolishness.'

14

On Saturday afternoon Rabin Pal picked Pinaki up from Jalan & Jalan in a Fiat car. Although old, the car reassured Pinaki he must have a substantial, reliable, business. 'You were the Left candidate for Mominpur in the municipal elections, I believe,' he said.

Rabin Pal waved a conciliatory hand. 'They forced me to stand. Actually I am too busy to do the post justice. My business leaves me with no time, you know.'

Pinaki did not press him about who 'they' were, lest that lead to the disclosure he had met the Chief. He was content to know that Rabin Pal was a busy man. Possibly the busyness was on account of many successful land deals.

They took Lower Circular Road to Park Circus, and headed out for the Eastern Metropolitan Bypass.

Topsia loomed up. 'Is it here?' asked Pinaki.

Rabin Pal smiled and drove on.

Beliaghata, Pinaki hazarded.

Rabin Pal's smile grew broader as he breezed past the turning to Beliaghata. It became a sly chuckle as he slowed down, and then revved up, at Kakurgacchi. The moue he made as they speeded through Lake Town—turning his head so Pinaki got the full benefit of it—was positively flirtatious. In the end, Pinaki sat back and let the breeze dry the sweat on his forehead.

The city gave way to an unconvincing suburbia of makeshift settlements interspersed with indeterminate fields. The famous football stadium went by. A roundabout, corded with cycles. Hotel Blue Dreams, boringly respectable under the schoolmistress-y glare of the 3 o'clock sun. On and on, past unruly vegetation and rickety tea-shacks. Just when Pinaki began to worry that they were heading for Barasat after all, Rabin Pal turned off the main motorway. They rattled along on a narrow stone-paved road that soon petered into a dirt track. It was open country now, and flat, the land receding swiftly towards the sky. Endless flats—paddy fields in the main, divided by narrow mud bunds and dotted with bamboo lookout towers. Tender green shoots floated in the watery maze, like herbs in gravy. Silvery, feathery kaash bobbed up here and there. The air was soft, friendly and smelled of wood smoke.

The track ended abruptly at a large body of water. Lily pads floated on its blue-black depths, egrets waded in the reeds, ducks paddled… 'Isn't that an ibis?' asked Pinaki.

Rabin Pal placed a hand on his chest and closed his eyes. 'It's the land of Tagore, Bosebabu! And Satyajit Ray!'

Pinaki marvelled that Rabin Pal had something like a soul. For some reason it made him think of a charging tiger stopping to sniff at a rose. 'Where is the plot?' he said.

Rabin Pal, switched off the engine and got out of the car, easing his pants from his crotch as he walked. 'Oidhike dekhon,' he said with a spacious wave.

'But that is a lake.'

'Exactly,' said Rabin Pal. He cupped his ear. 'Listen, Bosebabu, to the music of nature.'

'I can hear frogs,' Pinaki said, nodding. 'Can we see the plot now?'

'There is swamp antelope also. I myself have seen.'

'But the plot...?' Pinaki asked, a little desperate now.

Rabin Pal's fugitive eye swivelled to a tangle of barbed wire Pinaki hadn't noticed. 'Nine kathas. 6,500 square feet.' He moved his torso right and left to semaphore the approximation. Then, squelching through the wet grass, he hopped over the wire, pirouetted around, and threw his arms out. 'So, what do you think?'

Pinaki was lost. There had been another occasion in his life when he was asked the same loaded question—*so what do you think?* And he had been out of answers there too. His non-response hadn't quite changed the course of his life but, he had to admit, it had consequences. That occasion was his first meeting with Rimi at the formal tea arranged by their families with a view to his marrying her. After they came home, his mother had said, 'So what do you think?' And he hadn't been able to think beyond how she, Rimi, would feel if he said, 'I don't know, I'm not sure, I need time...'

A gust of wind pulled at his shirt. He looked at the ground for answers. It appeared very marshy. *It is also very isolated,* whispered a lone voice, just as it had whispered, on that other significant occasion, that Rimi's mouth was a little hard.

He looked at Rabin Pal. 'This is the plot?'

The eye was skittering about like a ball in a pinball machine. 'Yes. This is your plot.'

Pinaki thrilled to the *your*. 'Hmm,' he said, pretending to consider. Then, 'Shops?' he asked sternly. 'Provisions, vegetables, milk?'

Rabin Pal indicated the lake. 'Fish.' With his other hand he essayed a more general wave in the direction of the fields. 'Vegetables.' And more vaguely, at a cluster of huts just visible in the distance. 'Other things.' He stamped on the spongy earth. 'Very good property, babu. Virgin soil.'

The soil did look untouched. Excepting for a mango tree in the middle and a line of bushes along the boundary it was all rough grass. 'There's a lot of water,' Pinaki said, lifting his foot with a sucking sound.

'That is the beauty of the place.'

'There will be flooding.'

'Only in the monsoon,' said Rabin Pal, and with a hint of reproof, 'Whole of Calcutta floods. This is a unique place, Bosebabu! Many people come from all over world to study it. Do research...you don't know?'

'There is a lot to learn from nature,' equivocated Pinaki, who didn't know.

Rabin Pal regarded Pinaki with a tolerant gravity that he tried to enhance by closing his wayward eye. This had the effect on Pinaki of being enjoined in a private joke. He was wondering whether the joke was on the crazy foreigners who came all the way to this forsaken place, or the ignorant locals unmoved by its wonders, when Rabin Pal suddenly pursed his mouth and frowned. Now Pinaki felt he had offended him by doubting his assertions that it was world famous. That it flooded only in the monsoon. That swamp antelope had been sighted here. 'There is nothing like it in this hemisphere,' declared Rabin Pal.

Pinaki was impressed with this specificity. 'It is nice,' he admitted. And feeling he had to make a more intelligent contribution added, 'But it is also very far.'

'Far from where?'

'Everywhere.'

Rabin Pal made a noise suspiciously like a snort. 'Any place will be far from somewhere and near somewhere else. That is logic, na? Bosebabu, with your budget, you will get twenty square feet in Ballygunge.' (Pinaki cringed.) 'Maybe 400 square feet in Budge Budge. But do you want to live next to a slum? No. Will you settle for Anwar Shah Road—the azaan blaring five times a day, extra on Fridays? You see Bosebabu, in life you can't have everything.'

Pinaki was silent. *That* he understood only too well.

A buttery luminosity filled the sky. Like ice-cream, Pinaki thought. More fancies followed, as the poet in him stirred. This was a vast amphitheatre echoing with soundless applause. He was a drop in the stream of existence, invisible, weightless, but also, gloriously, alive. All the hours stolen from him in the city would be returned to him here. His throat constricted. A wonderful lassitude crept over him.

Rabin Pal, who had beaten a tactical retreat, now came forward. He coughed. 'Ready to leave, Bosebabu?'

'What? Yes...no. No. Give me five minutes.' Rabin Pal withdrew discreetly behind a little rise.

The sun made a dramatic exit. Cerise and purple clouds streaked across the sky. Wavy gules appeared on the water. A cormorant took off, neck stretched towards its destination. The hush was broken by a thin wailing, floating towards them on the breeze. Presently two boats hove into view. Canoes, with bonnets like a baby's pram. The plaint separated into words, rising and falling with the slap-slap of paddles.

His village is surrounded
by deep boundless waters,
and I have no boat
to cross over.
I long to see Him,
but how can I reach
His village?

The boats slipped away, leaving in their wake a mournful silence and a landscape bleak as a vault.

On the journey back Rabin Pal told Pinaki there were two other buyers for the plot. One in Hong Kong and the other in Dubai.

It would have occurred to anybody to ask why anybody from Hong Kong or Dubai would be interested in an isolated, mosquito-infested plot of land in Calcutta—actually, not even in Calcutta. And to wonder why anybody in Calcutta hadn't snapped it up if it was so desirable. Pinaki asked, 'When do I have to let you know?'

'Yesterday. These are serious parties, Bosebabu.'

For the first time the rogue eyeball and its hapless twin converged on Pinaki's face. It was a momentous collision.

Pinaki took a deep breath. 'I will take it,' he said.

~

'You said you'd take it? Just like that? Not, you'll think about it?'

'If one thinks too much one never will do anything. Destiny is a matter of chance.'

'Wah, wah, Pinakibabu. This house is already making a philosopher of you. My advice is get a lawyer—a registered lawyer—to check the papers.'

Pinaki prickled at the rider *registered* for his prospective lawyer, insinuating he was too cheap to get a bona fide lawyer. On the other hand he was embarking on a project requiring a lawyer. This necessity, curiously, lent *more* rather than less credence to it. A serious purpose. So might a business tycoon be advised before an important venture.

So, to find a lawyer. An affordable one he could depend upon to give him correct advice. Ideally there should not be any correlation between their reliability and their fee. Logically, an expensive lawyer would be more reliable because his practice would have prospered on his superior abilities. Although, of course, not everybody is fortunate enough to get rewarded for their brilliance. Look at Biren Roy...

Did everything have to come round to Biren Roy?

~

As it happened, it was Rabin Pal who solved his dilemma, by calling him. 'Bosebabu, Hong Kong party phoned twice already. Dubai party expected any day. What should I tell them?'

'Can you wait a few more days? I have been advised to get a legal opinion. To, you know, verify that the land is, the land is...'

'Land is what?' The line crackled. 'What is there to verify Bosebabu? You saw the plot for yourself.'

Pinaki ran his tongue over his lips. 'I require the papers. Allotment deed, proof of ownership... Who is the owner? Who will stand guarantee? And bank details...'

'Durgama! So many doubts! I will provide everything. You will be buying it from one Govind Dutta, whose family had it for hundred years. The sale deed will be made *on stamp paper* during purchase. Registration at the village panchayat. I will be present.'

Pinaki gripped the receiver. Given the circumstances of their association, he had every reason to doubt Rabin Pal. There was, too, his complete ignorance about land transactions. But would a better understanding take him closer to his goal? Now he remembered how he'd felt about Rimi after that first meeting. He had to marry, that was a given, and he wanted to get the business over with the minimum of fuss. He felt the same disinclination now to engage in tedious inner debates. Unconditional surrender to fate *was* reckless but it did make life easier!

'Are you there Bosebabu? I was asking...'

'I will come tomorrow to sign.'

'You won't regret it, Bosebabu.'

Wise people know that the 'you won't regret it' assurance is given when the likelihood of regret is strongest. But Pinaki was a man in love. And he was being rushed off his feet too — Rabin Pal was up and away and talking about signing papers, power of attorney, registration, payment...

'The security deposit is 10,000 rupees, Bosebabu. In cash.'

'C-c-cash?'

'It is always cash in this business.'

Pinaki wiped his upper lip with the back of his hand. 'Can you make it five thousand?'

'I can't, Bosebabu. Sorry. In this business one needs working capital. So...tomorrow six o'clock?'

'Eh, I have to, to take my mother to the doctor tomorrow. She suffers from gastric.'

He heard a distinct snort.

In the end, Rabin Pal graciously allowed an extra day. 'Deadline five o'clock.'

'Seven,' said Pinaki, feeling as if he was pleading for his life. But Rabin Pal had rung off.

Pinaki replaced the receiver on its hook. This was how, he imagined, people might feel after they've been told they'd been exposed to low-level nuclear radiation. You would only know its effects later. Years later. Meanwhile you believed you would be spared.

Spared what?

'Eesh,' said Dona. 'Who's been using the phone? It's *sticky!*'

~

The bank manager was sympathetic but not encouraging. The bank didn't lend money to buy land—it didn't give unsecured loans. He could, however, give Pinaki a loan for a house with the land as collateral.

Mr Sen was neither kind nor helpful—he seemed outraged by the request. He looked at Pinaki from over his glasses, and then from under them, *as if,* thought Pinaki, *I'm the tail part of a very bony fish.*

'We are not in the habit of loaning money for real estate speculation, Bose.'

Pinaki explained it wasn't for speculating. He said, with modest pride, he planned to build a house.

For some reason this seemed to irritate Mr Sen even more. 'It is a large sum to ask for in your position. I will have to speak to Mr Jalan. He *might* make an exception since you're an old and valued employee.'

Pinaki felt he'd been put in his place. As an old employee he was entitled to more consideration than this. After all, he was not asking for an advance on the next month's salary because he was behind on the rent. On the other hand he was valued. But not valued enough to be trusted to pay back a loan...

'...anyway, I can't do anything till next week. I hope you know what you're doing. If I were you I would get a lawyer.'

Pinaki wished he was as generous with money as with advice. Mr Jalan wasn't known to be generous with anything. He was famous for attending his employees' weddings bearing just a bouquet of flowers.

The next day, Pinaki withdrew all his post-office savings. Giving a daughter in marriage would be like this, he thought. You waited for the event, with every expectation of joy and fulfilment, and, in all honesty, relief too, but when the time came it was all too soon and all too late and all too right and all too wrong. That's the best and worst of such undertakings.

When he handed over the cash, Rabin Pal's wilful eye clung moistly to his. The sensation was like a sweaty handshake after a transaction in a dark alley.

The receipt was succinct or sketchy, depending on your point of view. It received with thanks from Pinaki Bose, son of Kunal Bose, a sum of Rs 10,000 as security deposit for a plot of land measuring nine kathas in Mukundapur. The sale deed would be made out upon balance payment of Rs 15,000.

That is reasonable enough, Pinaki thought. He was

heartened by the letterhead: *Rabin Pal, Estate Agent, 50A, Diamond Harbour Road, Calcutta, 700034*

~

'That paper means nothing, Pinakibabu. Did you sign a sale agreement? A memorandum of understanding? Did you ask about municipal clearance? Land tax receipts?'

'Please. Why can't you say a single positive thing? Why does everybody keep discouraging me?'

'Relax, Pinakibabu! Don't get so tense! It is not good for digestion!'

15

'It's me, sir.'

'No, Bose, please. No more of this. I'm in no mood to...'

'But I've come to tell you I've found a plot.'

Biren Roy put his novel down and peered at him over his half-glasses.

'It is nine kathas, sir. That is 6,500 square feet.'

'I know what a katha is. Have you bought this plot?'

'I've given an advance. Ten thousand rupees. I have to pay the rest after Puja. I have asked my office for a loan. I plan take a loan on my life insurance policy also. And the bank has said...'

'No personal details, Bose.'

'Yes, sir. I was going to say the bank will only give a loan for house building, not buying land.'

'With reason... Naturally you've factored your neighbours in this grand plan.'

'Pardon?'

'The ones who'll demand a king's ransom to vacate your prospective lawn.'

'Pardon?'

'Oh lord, man. Don't you read the papers? There was a story today about a family fighting to get back its land from unauthorized shacks. Put up overnight—when they were away.'

'Yes, but...'

'It won't happen to you? You'll mount guard round the clock? This is *Calcutta*, Bose.' Biren Roy sounded more bored than irritated. He picked up his novel, tilted back his chair and began to read.

'But my plot is not in Calcutta. At least not exactly in the city.'

Biren Roy raised his eyebrows over the novel.

Provoked, Pinaki said, 'It's off the E.M. Bypass.' Biren Roy continued to regard him with that smile of his which made Pinaki feel ridiculous—in this case an illiterate who didn't know his geography. 'It's the countryside,' he said, raising his voice. 'There're ponds, paddy fields, coconut trees...'

'What?' Biren Roy brought his chair down with a bump.

Pleased he had made an impact, 'It is a unique place,' Pinaki said. 'I believe it is world famous.' He was peeved by Biren Roy's look of disbelief. 'People come from all over to study it.'

To his astonishment Biren Roy clutched his head and groaned. 'Those are the wetlands, man! The East Calcutta Wetlands!' He lowered his elbows on the table. 'You fool, you fool. How *did* you get into this?'

Pinaki clasped the back of a chair to steady himself. 'I...I what do you mean, sir?'

'The wetlands are a protected area, Bose, surely even you must know that. You can't go about building houses there. And transacting land there is illegal.'

Pinaki swallowed, swallowed again. Small unidentifiable creatures pattered up and down his spine. 'But there are villages there.'

'Of course there would be—the place supports a traditional rural economy.'

Pinaki's bewilderment grew. 'But all of Bengal is like that.'

'No, Bose. All of Bengal isn't an internationally recognized heritage site. All of Bengal doesn't have special zoning regulations—specifically building regulations. And all of Bengal isn't a natural sewage system for Calcutta, but for which the city would be choking on its shit.'

Pinaki's heart was banging away. From far away he heard Biren Roy ask, 'How did you come by this plot?'

'Through an agent. He...he has all the papers,' he said. 'There were many buyers for it. He said I would have lost it if I hadn't paid the advance. I didn't know it was illegal! He didn't tell me.'

Biren Roy snorted. 'Of course he wouldn't. Who is he by the way?'

Pinaki told him. Biren Roy rubbed his stained cheek. 'So he's the Lord of Misrule,' he murmured bafflingly.

'What shall I do now?' asked Pinaki. His face was stinging.

'I don't know, Bose. Grow watermelons on it—*if* you get it.'

Pinaki clutched the edge of the table. 'One must have faith in God,' he murmured, rocking to and fro. 'He will answer your prayers...'

Biren Roy made an impatient noise. 'You sound like a Catholic priest. Try praying to Saint Jude.' He pushed back his chair. 'Look Bose, I really don't want to get involved. I mean, what can I advise? I only hope, for your sake, that it's on the edge of the wetlands, at the city limits, so you might just scrape through.'

Pinaki thought of the journey he had made with Rabin Pal. It had seemed to go on forever, away from the city and into the countryside. Into the wetlands.

The lights went out. After a few self-deprecating clicks the fan stopped. The hum and whir of the city receded. In the silence, the drone of the generator next door sounded as loud as a fighter jet. Pinaki stumbled to the window, illuminated by the lighter blackness of the sky. Candlelight wavered in the windows of the building across the street. In one of them he saw a woman, holding a spill like a wand, touching one wick after another. A tableau sprang to life—table, tablecloth, chairs, a china cabinet, gilt-framed pictures, a globe, a mirror... The colours were as rich and subtle as an oil painting.

The candles guttered, a telephone shrilled, the spell broke. Pinaki turned away. It was just a dismal, desolate room—all those empty chairs and dusty cups—tenanted by a thin-haired woman in a shapeless shift.

'Here, Bose, take this,' Biren Roy said, waving a stub of a candle. 'It should last till you reach the lobby. Stay on if you prefer,' he added kindly.

Pinaki decided to take his chances with the candle.

Pinaki's presence continued to flap around the studio, like a sparrow ambushed by a ceiling fan. *It's not your concern,* Biren told himself. *You didn't instigate it. You didn't encourage him.* Yet the more he tried to distance himself, the closer he was being drawn in, it seemed.

Using his cigarette tip to see by, he locked up, went down to the lobby, and into the street. Smoke from power generators muddled the darkness. Isolated flickers of light stuttered in the gloom—candles, bicycle lamps, shorting wires, sparks from a tandoor outside an eatery... The smell of singed meat and spiced oil cut through the diesel fumes. He felt suddenly ravenous. Closely spaced steel rods, like the strings of a harp, were suspended over red-hot coals. The perspiring harpist plucked at a rod strung with fiery orange chunks of meat and smiled at him. 'Ki khabe, babu?'

He asked for a double chicken roll, with onion and chillies. He was putting away his wallet when he heard a crash. A man charged out of the eatery, chased by a stream of slops. Dal dripped down the steps. A screaming altercation started. Biren snatched up his roll and crossed the street to the doorway of the shuttered Fenner's showroom.

'Ladies,' spoke a voice in his ear. 'You want? I get special rate.'

He moved away. 'No, thank you.'

'Khoob bhalo, babu. Beautiful, virgin, fourteen-years-old... No? Okay, no ladies. Boys? Okay, no boys. You want to find out if your wife is cheating? I'm a private detective.'

He laughed. 'And I'm the Nawab of Oudh.'

'I once caught a Hindu girl running away with a Muslim boy. In Howrah station just before the train left.'

'To think our war of independence was fought for scum like you! Bugger off.'

In the eatery, the fight had wound down to an inventory of complaints. The table that had been knocked down was still kneeling but the steps were being mopped. Like a thunderclap the electricity came back. Shouts of relief rang out.

In Peace on Earth, the air was redolent with the sweet scent of a newly mown lawn. The proprietor, his old schoolmate, emerged from behind a stack of defaced paperbacks, his hand behind his back. When he saw Biren he brought his hand out, waved a damp, ragged cigarette and grinned sheepishly. 'You're the first customer today,' he said. 'The till's rattling like a Red Cross tin.'

Biren picked up a book from the display table of second-hand books, holding it with a thumb and forefinger. 'Where do you get these—the Salvation Army Guesthouse?'

His friend bent over the table and blew a jet of pungent smoke. 'That's how I fumigate them.'

Biren chuckled. 'How much for this one?'

'It's for free. I'm doing a literacy drive.'

'You're stoned, you clown. Here, put this in your tin. Use it to get a haircut.'

'Thanks, man. You're a prince. Have a drag. This is a fresh stash.'

An hour later Biren got up, swaying a little.

16

Rabin Pal wasn't there, but Kalol Mondal was. He was sitting in his boss' chair, resting his feet on his boss' table and reading his boss's newspaper. He jumped up when the door opened and sat down again with a bump. His chair slid from under him.

I have given him a shock, Pinaki thought, sitting down. He was too tense, however, for the elation to last. He had rehearsed his speech many times on his way here and he was anxious to get it off. 'I want to talk to Rabin Pal.'

'Gone to Burdwan on business. I am in charge.' Kalol Mondal's disquieting gaze was alleviated by an amiable smile. The smile unnerved Pinaki. *The brightest berries are the poisonous ones,* he remembered Dida saying. Cyanide smells of almonds...

He pulled himself together. 'You tell him, you tell him from me, the land he sold is bogus. It is an illegal sale. Because it is a wet land. No, no, don't make an objection. I have proof. My architect said so.'

'So? He doesn't know everything. Rabin Pal is the expert. He has sold other land there.'

Pinaki was momentarily thrown. 'So? Two wrongs don't make a right. Building there is not allowed.'

'Yes, it is.'

Kalol Mondal's manner was actually helpful, but to Pinaki it seemed as if he was playing a new game, of the cat-and-mouse variety. 'You tell Rabin Pal I don't want this land. And I want my money back!'

'That will not be possible, Dada. In this business transactions are final.'

He has been well tutored, Pinaki thought bitterly. 'In this business nothing is straight,' he said. His heart gave a warning thump. Ignoring it, 'I will complain to the police,' he said.

'Police will not help,' Kalol Mondal said. 'Police are...' Giving Pinaki a meaningful look he rubbed a thumb and forefinger.

Pinaki rose from his chair. 'Then I will go to the municipal authority! To the local MLA! To Writer's Building!' He sat down with a bump. 'I will file a case in court.'

Kalol Mondal shook his head. 'It won't be any use, Dada.' He rolled a pencil across the table to jolly Pinaki out of his mood.

Pinaki would not be humoured. 'I have been cheated!'

Kalol Mondal started from his chair. 'You are calling us cheats?'

Pinaki's heart gave another, harder, thump. Strangely, despite the thumping, a part of him was actually relieved that Kalol Mondal was reverting to his old self. It reassured him that his unnatural affability was not another sinister scheme. 'I am saying you did not reveal this is a wet land.'

Kalol Mondal used a finger to smooth his frown. 'You can't do anything about it.'

'Are you threatening me?'

'I am advising you, Dada.'

This was too much. 'You are advising me? *You?* Nonsense kothakar!'

Kalol Mondal leapt up (sending his chair spinning), but by the time he extricated himself from it Pinaki was clattering down the stairs. He didn't slow down till he reached his bus stop half a kilometre away.

Kalol Mondal returned to his chair. His breath was coming in snorts. After a while he calmed down, and inevitably, drifted into his favourite dream.

Dona is walking down a dark road. Alone. A hoodlum, with a face like Vinu's, except uglier, jeers a lewd remark. She ignores him, but you could see (at least Kalol Mondal could), she is frightened. The fellow grabs her arm. At this point, he was always undecided whether there should be any further outrage. To stop there would be too tame, but to go beyond excited him in a shameful way. Anyhow, she screams, and that settles the matter. Kalol Mondal shoots out of the shadows and, with one mighty blow, knocks the ruffian senseless.

Anyone watching Kalol Mondal would conclude he was having a spiritual experience, not pounding out the brains of a fellow human being. Of course, a tearfully grateful Dona, holding his bloodied hands in her soft ones, was as close to a spiritual experience as he was likely to get.

He rubbed his eyes. None of this was going to happen. She wouldn't touch you the way you are now. The smartly dressed hero in your story, yes, but the village yokel sitting in your chair? Out of the question. And who could blame her? Just look at your shabby pants, your unfashionable shirt...

He locked up and took a bus to Chowringhee.

The newly opened 'exclusive one-stop shop for discerning men' in Lindsay Street occupied the entire ground floor of the Globe Theatre building. When he walked in through the revolving door, the confidence of his stride and the set of his mouth belied the paltry contents of his wallet—hundred and fifty rupees—all that Rabin Pal's petty cash box had yielded.

The chilled air, the bright lights, the merchandise, increased his confidence rather than the reverse. It reinforced his belief anything was possible in the city.

When he read the price tags on the shirts scattered on the counter, his bravado flailed. Still, he persevered, picking them up, one at a time, weighing them in his hand, mouth pursed in deliberation, for the benefit of a hovering salesman.

Catching the man's eye, he made a face to convey his dissatisfaction.

The salesman gave him a look that skirted a sneer. It questioned his presence here, his motives, his character even. Kalol Mondal glowered back and turned to scan the rack of ties strategically next to the shirts. He pulled out one or two, turning them over as if to check the make but again to read the price tags. Who bought these? And then he saw a large woman carrying two bulging bags with the shop's insignia. His resentment swelled. He stumbled off, and almost collided with a display of sunglasses on a rotating stand. They were each chained to the slots. Were they afraid they'd escape? Snickering, he moved on.

Could even socks cost as much as this? He was examining a pair, curling his lip to convey his disdain, when he became aware he was being watched. By a salesman. The same one who'd been at the shirt counter, and whose reflection he'd caught in the mirror above the sunglasses. The man was following him.

He dropped the socks into the bin. Furious with himself, he immediately pulled out another pair. From the corner of his eye he saw the salesman coming at him. As if he *meant* business, not to *do* business. Sure enough, 'What you are looking for?' he asked, jerking his chin at the bin.

Kalol Mondal said that he was looking for his lost dog. Wasn't it obvious?

The salesman glared. Before he could reply, a loud grumble came from behind them. 'You were going to show me some more brands.'

The speaker, a long-haired youth, wearing scruffy jeans and an ear stud, was holding a clutch of watches. A hippie type, Kalol Mondal thought, but the salesman had left him unattended. While *he* was not to be trusted with a pair of socks. Or sunglasses. For of course the sunglasses had been chained with him in mind.

'Ekuni ashchi, sir,' said the salesman to the hippie. 'I am just bringing. Well?' he said to Kalol Mondal. There was an edge to his voice.

Kalol Mondal wanted to push his teeth in. Holding out the socks, 'I'm buying this,' he said. 'How much?'

The salesman pointed to the cash window. 'Over there.' The icy dismissal made Kalol Mondal long to knock his head off.

The long-haired one, irritated at this continuing antiphonal exchange, snapped, 'I can't wait all day!'

Kalol Mondal threw the socks into the bin and marched out. He wished he could have flung a lit match in with them and watched the shop go up in smoke!

He burst through the red door. 'I want to, I want to...' He ground his fists into his stomach. His face contorted. 'I want to *kill* him!'

'Is that all?' said the Chief. 'I thought you wanted to pee!'

Laughter erupted.

Kalol Mondal wheeled around. 'Shut up!'

'Cool down, little boy,' said the Chief. 'What happened? Who do you want to kill?'

Then Kalol Mondal knew what he wanted. Not to kill the fellow but beat him—at his own game. So he could go back, buy up half the shop, and look the fellow in the eye. Look and look and look...

He turned to the Chief. 'Get me a job, Dada. Sales assistant. In a *company*,' he qualified, in case the Chief should think to send him to another Rabin Pal, to sell weekend packages in the Sunderbans.

'No problem. Plenty of companies in Calcutta, and all of them are looking for assistants like you.'

The sarcasm was lost on Kalol Mondal. 'Really? Where?' The Chief frowned. This rejection of his munificence—he had fixed Kalol Mondal with Rabin Pal—was more insulting than ingratitude.

Kalol Mondal hastened to correct this impression. 'Please don't misunderstand, Dada. I have never forgotten how you helped me. You saved my life.' He stretched his lips in an ingratiating smile. 'I am happy there but I want to do more. I don't have,' his brow furrowed, 'job satisfaction.' He'd heard the term once in a movie dialogue and it had stuck. It had the weary, self-indulgent overtone of a rich man's predicament.

'Hmmm,' said the Chief, scratching his belly. 'So why come to me? Why does everyone come to me?'

Kalol Mondal folded his hands. 'Because you are a father to all of us, Dada. You are our God.'

He reached home in high spirits. The Chief would definitely find him something. He walked on water! And he liked him. There's something about me, he thought, preening at his image in a windowpane. I make an impression.

Something hard pushed into his crotch. It was Nobody's Dog.

A scream of laughter came from across the road. 'He smelled something interesting there, Kalol!' More laughter ensued.

Kalol Mondal aimed a kick at the dog, missed, swiped air. His chappal went flying. The laughter got louder. The dog capered, barking hysterically.

Kalol Mondal dashed into his room, snatched up the spray gun he used on roaches and aimed it at the luckless creature's face...

It ran howling. Kalol Mondal followed him with the gun, not stopping till the end of the street where it disappeared into a cloud of dust and traffic smoke.

'A brave man,' commented someone.

'Hein! Puro hero. Ki rey Tarzan!'

Kalol Mondal stalked into his room and slammed the door behind him.

17

Rabin Pal's expression was one of unfocussed hostility. 'I cannot return your money, Bosebabu. A deposit is a guarantee, you understand. It protects both parties.'

'But you didn't mention it was non-refundable.'

'If everybody asked for refund I would be out of business. I have lost other opportunities because of your word.'

'In one week?'

'In this business, time is money.'

Pinaki thought the better of challenging this. The knave eye had proved as effective in nailing a point as evading it. 'Are you are saying nobody can change their mind?' he said.

'Not in this business. Why, what happened, Bosebabu? You were very sure as I remember.'

Pinaki ran his tongue over cracked lips. 'Well you see, the problem is that...'

The problem was that, thanks to Kalol Mondal, Rabin Pal was briefed and ready with his defence. Now Pinaki's only resort was begging.

'I, I don't have the money. My loan didn't get approved. Please make an...exception.'

The walleye rapped him on the knuckles. 'I turned down very good parties because of you, Bosebabu. If I go back to them they will bargain. Also they will not trust me. In this business trust is everything.'

'Exactly! I trusted you.'

'What does that mean?'

'You didn't tell me the plot is a wet land. That is concealing information. It is...' *Cheating*, he was about to say and stopped himself in time. 'It is not right. Not at all right.'

A guffaw greeted this. 'You are really very funny, Bosebabu,' said Rabin Pal. Making a show of wiping his eyes, he said, 'Don't say anything you will regret.'

Pinaki felt himself trembling. He visualized clinging a telegraph pole in a storm, a recourse that had often helped him. It steadied him now. He would take Rabin Pal to court.

And then it dawned on him that he had nothing—no paper, no proof of the advance paid, no bank stub even. He had paid in cash. *In this business trust is everything, Bosebabu.* He rubbed the gooseflesh on his arms. In hindsight, there had been nothing about Rabin Pal that inspired trust.

The curtain parted and the woman put her head in to ask if they required tea. Rabin Pal sent her back with one eye. The other continued to needle Pinaki.

'I want to see the papers again,' Pinaki said, feeling as if he was flying into a headwind. 'And the land records. Title deeds, sale deed, tax receipts.'

Rabin Pal pulled out a file from a drawer and threw it on the table.

Pinaki could make nothing of the minute writing—Bengali and English. 'I will have this checked by my lawyer,' he said.

Rabin Pal tucked his teeth behind his mouth and made a snorting noise. He was laughing. He knew Pinaki didn't have a lawyer.

Pinaki wished he had a lawyer. He wished he had a friend. He wished he could drink some water but feared that asking for it would, in some way, weaken his case.

He wished he had a case.

Rabin Pal's expression underwent a subtle change. The new one, of paternal indulgence, was more worrisome. It warned you of the consequences of straining the indulgence. A lawyer's notice would push Rabin Pal over the edge.

Pinaki didn't want to think of what could be there.

Rabin Pal waved his hand to and fro across Pinaki's face. 'Bosebabu. Shuno. Lawyer-shawyer bhuley jao. Lawyers will just complicate the issue. Don't get into their hands. Lawyers, police, doctors—all worst case,' he added in English. 'As your younger brother I am advising you.' He eased the file from Pinaki's hands. 'You have already spent ten thousand rupees. Just another fifteen and you will be the proud owner of property.' He stuffed the file into a drawer and began shuffling through the litter of papers on his desk. 'So I can expect the balance next week?'

'I don't know, I, let me think...' Pinaki dried up.

He had no excuse. He had no choice—or the will to exercise choice. He had no plan.

He had no plan either to visit Ganguli & Grandson, but he found himself sitting at one of their four tables, ordering their special peas puris, which he ate with the stealthy, feverish anxiety of a hyena at a lion's kill. He finished his repast with the house speciality—ginger-cardamom tea and tottered out. The nervous flutters in his stomach became a churning.

While he had been inside a traffic accident had occurred. All the components of a disaster were in place. Abandoned minibus, stranded passengers, shrieking ambulance, battered police van and in the epicentre, the mangled remains of a cycle.

Spot dead. Spot dead. Spot dead. Ooohhhh.

In the scramble to escape the confusion, he slipped on a patch of slush and cracked his knee on the curb. He opened his mouth and unleashed a long wail. Rainwater entered his mouth, flavoured with smoke, soot, mud...

Panic had this taste too.

~

'Oh, Pinakibabu, I don't want to remind you but I advised you to check the papers.'

Pinaki thought, it is funny how people who say they didn't want to do something do it anyway.

Bugger the advance, Bose. Don't throw good money after

bad. The idea of writing off so much money was grand even if frightening. I had to write off some money, he practised saying into the mirror. He tried it with a careless smile—and looked as if he had toothache. He tried it with a shrug. It looked as if he was writhing.

He couldn't do it. If he wasn't cut out to take risks, he was less attuned to losing money. And he knew he would not look for another plot if he let this one go. He could not start all over again. He would never build a house. He may not now, but there was always the hope rules may change. Or that Biren Roy could be wrong just this once...

After four days of reeling between dizzying optimism and abject despair, he called Rabin Pal. He would pay the balance money after the Pujas.

~

The Puja frenzy provided a welcome distraction. For weeks, every advertisement and every hoarding had featured the face of Durga. Now the finishing touches were being put to thousands of Durga idols and the pandals where they would be worshipped. Such artistry, such imagination, and such rivalry! Pandals like Aladdin's cave, like a Chinese pagoda, the Kremlin, the Library of Congress... The buzz on the streets, the crowds in the shops—the drummers had arrived in the city!

We don't need *four* drummers, Ma. Oh, alright. I forgot they have to be hired as a group. Three saris, Rimi! But why... oh, alright. Please, Dona, you're too young for that... Oh, alright. It's the fashion.

~

'This Puja business is such a nuisance, Pinakibabu! Traffic jams, litter, choked drains...'

'Biren Roy says it is a good thing for the city. It keeps the lid on, he says, or else the pot will boil over.'

'That man now lives in your head, Pinakibabu. Did you think to tell him that if the lid is on, the pot can explode?'

~

On Mahalaya, the day flagging off the festival, Pinaki went to Biren Roy's studio. A blast of cricket commentary greeted him. Pinaki bellowed over the static.

'What?'

The static exploded in a volley of gunshots. Biren Roy snapped off the transistor radio. 'Now tell me.'

'We're having a mahabhog on Ashtami. Please come, sir. With your family of course.'

'Thank you. Very kind of you.' Biren Roy unscrewed a bottle containing a brown liquid (Pinaki thought queasily of rat poison), slopped some into a glass and filled it with water from a dented and discoloured plastic bottle. He drank half of it before he said, 'I'm afraid I don't celebrate Puja, Bose.'

Something in his face prevented Pinaki from asking why. He shifted on his seat. A nail had popped up and was digging into his flesh. 'Come at lunchtime, sir,' he said. 'And to see our pandal. It is an igloo this year.'

'Ah. Durga as an Eskimo or Santa Claus?'

'Eskimo. In a fur hat. We have a real harpoon.'

Biren Roy laughed.

'Last year we did a Rubik's cube. Unfortunately it rained and the colours ran. Everyone thought it was a Holi theme.'

Biren Roy laughed again and tossed the rest of his drink into his mouth.

Giddy with success Pinaki said, 'Five years ago we had a pyramid.' But Biren Roy had lost interest.

Pinaki thought hard. 'We are getting the Durga from Kumartoli. Those sculptors are world famous.'

'That's another bit of Bengali mythology.'

After a short silence, Pinaki said, 'I was hoping to celebrate next year's Puja in my new house.'

'Everything comes back to your house, Bose. We begin and end with it. It's like the national anthem. Anyway, what's the latest about your land?'

Pinaki eased his thigh, but the nail just dug him in a new place. His happy mood had quite gone. 'I have decided to buy it.'

'Ah. Belief is born in ignorance, and arguably, fostered by need. And underwritten by stupidity.'

Pinaki closed his mouth. Then, 'I believe it's all written here,' he said, drawing a line on his forehead. 'I will get my house if I am destined to.'

Biren Roy refilled his glass. 'Come on, Bose, don't be such a fatalist. If a door shuts find a window! Although it's usually barred,' he said glumly.

Pinaki wondered if he had understood right. He decided he had. 'You are right, sir. We should find a window.'

'Excuse me? We?'

Pinaki said, less surely, 'I thought, you meant you would help me to...' His voice trailed off.

'No, Bose, I did not mean that at all. That's your extrapolation. I'm not party to your foolish enterprise. Now, if you'll excuse me, I have work to do.'

Pinaki sat on, confused and upset, fighting a shameful urge to put his head on the table and weep.

And then he was doing it. Putting his head down, that is. The cool, smooth wood, its familiar scent of classrooms and childhood, the steady hum of sounds transmitted through the wooden partition—voices, footfalls, telephones, fans whirring, furniture scraping the floor—calmed him.

He rose and went into the studio.

Biren Roy was bending over one of the tables. A cigarette rested on its edge, dripping ash on the floor. The cigarette fell and he bent down to retrieve it. 'Damn,' he panted.

Pinaki started. 'Sir?'

Biren Roy stubbed out the cigarette. He rested his forehead on his hand, sitting so still Pinaki grew afraid.

'Sir? Are you alright?'

Biren Roy jerked up. 'Don't ask me if I'm alright. You're the one in a mess.'

Pinaki got a whiff of the cheap spirit. He drew back, sickened. The stench lodged in his nasal passage. *The smell of panic*, he thought. Tears started in his eyes. He turned his head to the window to hide them.

A silvery light filled his vision. The moon had broken free of the clouds. Biren Roy was gazing out of the window too.

'Perhaps one *could* get away with a small house,' he murmured. 'Considering all the violations committed in the city this would be small change...' He walked to the window. 'A form that doesn't ride roughshod over the land. Something hugging the ground. Low-slung—like a sports car.' He pressed his cheek to the windowpane. 'Curves are too obvious, too formulaic. Something with more, more spirit. A rock is contoured by water but a cliff stands up to the wind. Angles, then. On the horizontal *and* vertical axis...'

A spear of lightning struck the windowpane. He started back. Pinaki had been listening, hardly daring to breathe. 'Build it,' he said eagerly.

'What?'

'This house you are describing, sir. Build it.'

Biren Roy smiled. In the greenish illumination of the coolie-lampshade his eyes were skeletal hollows. 'You know, I'm almost tempted to. It would make a change from the endless chasing after hope...' Then his expression changed. First there was the shock of recognition, as if he had seen somebody—or something—unexpected. Then it hardened. Finally it blanked out. 'I can't, Bose. No, it's nothing to do with you. It's...it's a longstanding pact—with myself. Too personal, so I can't explain.'

'I understand,' said Pinaki, who didn't.

'I'm sorry, Bose. I got carried away. I suffer from flights of fantasy. In that I am like you, I suppose. Unfortunately that dooms us to the same fate. Extinction.'

Pinaki's heart leapt. 'We both think the same way, sir?'

Biren Roy smiled again. 'You're a literalist, Bose.'

The smile clinched it for Pinaki. Biren Roy had had said he was like him. At least he hadn't denied it. Although the caution, the rider, was disturbing. He hastened to reassure Biren Roy on this point. 'This house will not be doomed to extinction, sir. Because it will be a real project for you. Not like those.' He pointed to the wall behind him and, with timorous jocularity, 'It won't end up there,' he said.

Biren Roy put down his glass with a sharp crack. 'Alright, Bose, end of meeting.'

Pinaki rocked on his stool. 'Pa...ar...don?'

'I don't want you to come here anymore.'

Pinaki lifted a trembling hand to his mouth. 'I'm sorry, sir. I didn't mean to, to upset you. I just...'

'I don't care what you meant, even if it was that you were kissing my ass. Just leave.'

Pinaki's ears were ringing. 'Please don't mistake me, sir. I'm sorry. A hundred times I am sorry.'

Biren Roy folded his arms over his chest and looked at him over his small, mean glasses. 'I want this space to myself and you're filling it like a fucking gas leak.'

Pinaki crumpled. 'I know I'm not good enough for you,' he said bitterly.

Biren Roy made an impatient noise, but Pinaki decided he would have his say. It was going to be his last anyway. You have nothing to lose if you have nothing to gain. 'Nothing and nobody is good enough for you,' he said. 'Nor for your buildings. That is what you believe, and you are punishing me for that. You are punishing yourself also—but you will not see that. Till it's too late. You will never be happy because you think only stupid people can be happy—and you are not one of them.' Appalled, he covered his mouth with his hand.

'Thank you for the precious insight,' Biren Roy said coldly. 'Now get out.' He went into his room and slammed the door.

18

Drumbeats and music, car horns, police whistles, speeches... The city was resonating like a singing bowl. Fantastic structures—the hallucinations of an entire lunatic asylum—had sprung up between grimy blocks of flats, at road intersections and in the city squares. Biren swerved around a small but feisty reproduction of the tower of Pisa leaning into his path, and swerved again to avoid a group of schoolgirls. Crowds attract crowds, he thought. They clump together like magnetized iron filings. Perhaps it's a law of gravity. People gravitate to people.

The fretful chords of a sitar on loudspeakers along the road informed him he was nearing his destination. The crowds had so slowed his progress that his car was crawling alongside them. Then there was the problem of parking. It was usually impossible to get parking within two kilometres of any pandal. And there was more than one Puja on this road—the music had become cacophonous. If he didn't find a spot he would turn back. He applied himself, not too zealously, to looking for one. And then the miracle (the inevitable?) happened. A parking attendant chased off a motorbike sneaking into a car space, and waved him in.

The familiar scent of flowers and incense greeted him as he entered the Cambridge School playground. Freshly watered earth. Cigarette smoke and camphor. Mothballs from storage trunks... Stirring up memories of Pujas gone by, of carefree, optimistic, confident youth. With every step he took over the bumpy, pale blue plastic sheet, ostensibly a snow field, his desire to flee grew stronger. But he stumbled on, towards his objective, a white half-dome scored with pale grey lines to simulate ice blocks. Only to find its entrance blocked by two electricians fixing a wire.

A crowd stood waiting to get in—men in identical cream crimped dhuti–kurtas, women in the plumage of lorikeets, everyone in shop-creased finery, and their children darting in and out like needles through tapestry. In his dun cotton pants and white shirt he felt as conspicuous as a lion wearing a tutu. But nobody knew him—he could be another electrician.

When the igloo opened for business, the crowd charged into the maw, he with them. Eight heads short of the doorway, a guard on duty put a cord across it.

It was going to be a long wait, he knew from experience. Boredom began creeping up on him, like desert stealing into pastureland. He had made the effort, hadn't he? He had come, he had stayed for ten, well, almost ten minutes, and his host was nowhere to be seen. He could leave with a good conscience. Walk away. *Now.*

'Dadababu! Welcome, welcome!' Pinaki was coming towards him, full tilt, beaming, tripping over his dhuti in his excitement.

Biren saluted, puzzled. *Dadababu*? And the exuberance? Was it Puja spirit? Just overcome, perhaps, and making the best of it. Well, it hadn't been easy for him either, to come here today.

~

'Who is the winner in a clash of egos, Biren, the one who yields or the one who prevails?'

'There was no clash of egos, Doc.'

'The fight with yourself, then. The eternal fight, I may add.'

'Strange. That's what the little man said. More or less.'

'Perhaps he's not so little after all? Just *go*, you tiresome fellow.'

~

Now here he was, saying (with poor grace), 'My pleasure entirely, Bose.'

Pinaki bounced on his toes. 'Come this way, Dadababu—see the puja first! Lunch will be ready soon.'

He couldn't stop smiling. His teeth, at close range, were small and crowded, the enamel peeling like poor quality pearls. The pitiless light showed up his tired skin—tenderized by heat and humidity, and muddied by endless cups of tea. A forehead trammelled with the petty computations his life must entail. Eyes worn to the colourlessness of pebbles under a fast-flowing stream. A mouth that had uttered so many conciliating words it kept puckering even when not in use. Biren rubbed his damaged cheek. 'I'll peep in on the puja, Bose, happy to, but I'm afraid I can't stay for lunch.'

Pinaki looked disappointed.

Biren hastily waved at the igloo. 'It's very authentic. It won't melt—even if your visitors do.'

Pinaki laughed, a little too heartily. 'Good joke, sir! Oh, there is Rimi!' Cupping his mouth with his hands, 'Rimi!' he called. 'Esho! Dakhon, who is here!'

A figure detached itself from a cluster of women and made its way towards them. She was a person of some authority here, Biren thought, the one you paid obeisance to—before Durga. You saw that in her bearing, her expression and in the knife-edge pleats in her sari. There was a hardness about her that made him think of scratch-resistant paint. She was the kind of woman who sized up this year's Puja gifts to work out hers for the next. Her eyes went to his empty hands, his shabby clothes. She'd formed her opinion about him.

'My wife,' Pinaki said unnecessarily. 'Mrinalini. Rimi, eta Biren Roy.'

Biren folded his hands. 'Nomoshkar. Shubho Puja.'

'Welcome eeyou to awer Puja,' she said, pushing out her lips like a trumpet. 'Have you had sherbet?'

'I've just come. But don't...'

'Dona had the tray,' Pinaki said, and peering around, 'Where is she?'

'Jani na. She is not staying for lunch.' She frowned. Plainly there had been an altercation. 'From the morning she's been arguing. Sheta, that blouse is too bold, I told her. It is not decent...'

'Chhere dao,' Pinaki said hastily. 'Dona is our daughter,' he explained to Biren. 'She finds our Puja boring.'

'*I* don't, Baba!' An eager-faced boy, all elbows and knees, shot forward. 'I like our Puja best of all!'

Pinaki smiled sheepishly. 'Our son, Tuli. I mean, Shantanu.'

'Nomoshkar, Uncle!' The boy dived for Biren's feet.

'Hey! There's no need for that! Bless you, long life, whatever. Which class are you in?'

Before Tuli could reply, an elderly gentleman swooped. 'Ask him how many rosogollas he has eaten! How many, you rascal? He's a havoc eater, sir!'

Biren laughed. Then he felt rather than saw Rimi's eyes on him. Sure enough, 'Do you have children, um-ah?' she asked. 'A son in Presidency College, maybe? Doing PhD? Or working in London?'

'Alas, I'm not so blessed.'

'Ki durbhaggo.' She gave him an arch look. 'Bad luck for us too. I am always on the lookout for good boys of marriageable age for awer Dona.'

'Ki bolcho, Rimi! What will Dadababu think?' Pinaki clasped his hands in apology for her forwardness. Her obviousness. Her supernaturally black hair. 'I will bring you sherbet, Dadababu.' Gathering up his dhuti, he fled.

'Eijay! The drinks are in the shed! Oof-o, he didn't hear. I will get it.'

Abandoned by his hosts, Biren walked to the igloo. The crowd had dispersed, leaving him free to enter the arched doorway to the short tunnel that preceded the dome. It was so narrow, he could barely see the mishmash of Bengali folk art decorating the tunnel walls. It was uncomfortably low too—he had to bend to keep from knocking his head. The bluish illumination, however, was a coup. It effectively melded Hindu inscrutability and Icelandic chill, so the result was eternal as well as elemental.

The igloo was stifling with smoke from the puja, heat from the chandelier, the exhalations of the visitors and the exertions of two charged, perspiring drummers. On the platform, the Puja tableau showed Durga in fur hat and boots astride a polar bear and brandishing a harpoon, and her children, Ganesha and Kartikeya, wearing deer skin. Under the tableau sat the priest, surrounded by the paraphernalia of his profession, including the smoking incense burner. An elderly lady was reading from a prayer book.

After five minutes, Biren decided he'd adequately discharged his social responsibilities. It was not going to be easy to leave. The place was swarming with a new wave of visitors. He began backing away to the entrance. Immediately there was a yelp. He received a hard, retaliatory jab in the small of his back.

'Pata to puro istri korey dilen!' said an indignant voice. 'You are ironing my toes, sir!'

Muttering an apology, he twisted around, coming face-to-face, that is, nose-to-nose (almost), with a girl.

He stepped back and drew another protest. This time it was a male voice. 'Dekhte parcho na? Look where you are going!'

'I'm sorry,' he said, 'but the eyes behind my head don't see too well.'

A trill of laughter acknowledged his feeble wit. It was the

girl. She was still too close for him to see anything of her, except her eyes, which shone with a wicked light. They were enlisting him in some sadistic enterprise. Urging him to stamp on some more feet behind him, perhaps? Cause a little stampede? He smiled to himself. He would oblige her.

Unsurprisingly he drew a chorus of protests. Ignoring it, he continued to press back. He knew he was behaving badly but he wanted to buy himself more viewing distance. He had liked the look of those eyes.

She was enjoying the fracas. He caught a sporting gap in her front teeth, which made her look game for, well, anything. Her eyes, still sparkling wickedly, had been pulled out at the corners with kohl. Her skin was moist, luminous. She looked freshly peeled. There was a tiny pink bump on her chin. An abomination.

There was an indignant murmuring from behind him but he stood his ground.

Her hair had been pulled back tight, leaving short bangs on her wide forehead. It was a style sported by cinema actresses portraying saucy schoolgirls—although in this instance the aim was obviously the opposite. She had made herself up to look older than she was. In this, she had spectacularly failed. The inexpertly applied rouge highlighted baby fat. The lipstick looked as if she'd been sucking on an ice-lolly. She was what, seventeen? Eighteen?

A bell began ringing. The drummers set to with renewed vigour. The rituals were reaching a climax. She turned her head towards the tableau, leaving him free to stare. Through the flimsy stuff of her leaf-green sari her belly—a sausage roll of a belly—was visible. The sleeveless blouse had pinched the flesh under her arms into little loops, and squeezed out an exclamation mark between her breasts, which had been pushed up—touchingly—too high. There was some glittery hardware on her ears.

The pleasure resurfaced, tinged by nostalgia and something else. A pull? An ache? Regret? All those, but there was also a warm rush to his head, as after a hastily downed drink. Sight and sound intensified. He was not middle-aged or jaded or spent. He wasn't spent at all! He was ready to start over again. Begin his life unmarked as a new day. That joyous commotion in his body—what was it but life?

He had a crazy desire to secrete her away somewhere on his person—in the crook of his elbow, say, or buttoned into his shirt. Out of sight of everyone else. So he could, at will, take her out and enjoy her, bury himself in that riotous flesh... unconscionable fantasies. Galloping away with him. A long-ago girlfriend called him a satyr. The Satyr Rides Again.

What are you thinking? You're a goat as well as a satyr. These are impossible fantasies. The conceit of them! What are you? A choleric walled into his studio, shrivelled of mind and soul—and body. Toad of Toad Hall.

But it is not a sin to want to live! You're only responding to a call. Easier to defy gravity than resist this pull. Or stem the surge of neurons.

She caught his eye—caught him off guard—and raised her eyebrows, as if she'd guessed his thoughts. She knew she was having an effect.

Then someone came in-between and she was lost to view. As swiftly as it had risen, the elation died. A plug had been pulled on the neurons. The pulsations of life ceased.

She was so young. So...uncooked. An egg broken on a cold griddle. She was young enough to be... He was old enough to be...

She was making hectic conversation with a friend. '...but this week was the limit. I mean, on Monday I lost my ring—yes, that one. On Tuesday a bee stung me. And yesterday I chipped a nail!'

He cleared his throat. 'Were my misfortunes so light!'

Her head jerked up. A frown dented the plump forehead. 'Excuse me?' She lifted her shoulder. The sari slipped off. She flipped it back, adjusted it, and resumed her monologue in a low mutter.

What would she be like out of her Puja finery? In baggy T-shirt and tight jeans? Feet dyed reddish brown by the flimsy, raw-leather chappals favoured by her generation? She would participate in experimental plays in halls packed with sweaty young bodies, and, afterwards, tryst with one of them in a disused storeroom. Off with the tees, the belt, the pants, the...

'Excuse me! The Durga is over *there*, you know.'

He grinned. 'Pawky miss, aren't you?'

She looked puzzled. Then, tossing her head, 'Let's go, rey,' she said to her friend. 'It's too stuffy here.'

But he was closer to the entrance and was out before them. He emerged into the vivid air, dazed and disoriented. So must animals feel when they come out of hibernation. The world is the same and yet not. Spring has arrived.

Spring didn't last long.

'Dadababu!' cried Pinaki. 'There you are! I was looking for...Dona! Tumi kothai chheelay?'

'Bithorey, Baba. I was helping Dida with the puja.'

His pulse leapt. It was the girl in green. She was wobbling on her ridiculous sandals, clutching her sari and biting her lip in concentration.

'Slowly, Dona!' Pinaki cried. 'You will break your ankle!' He turned to Biren, his face runny with pride. 'My daughter, Antara,' he said. 'Dona, that is. Dona, this is Mr Biren Roy. Architect.'

She looked up obediently but with a touch of impatience. Parents' friends! And then, when she recognized him, her eyes widened.

When he could breathe again, 'We just met in the igloo,' he said. 'Rubbed noses, actually.'

Pinaki was chuckling as if he knew better than to believe this. Recalled to his duties, 'This is Nini,' he said, indicating the friend, who was hanging back. 'I mean, Indrani. Dona's best friend.'

He put two fingers to his forehead and saluted. 'Hello. Can I rub noses with you too? Since we're all Eskimos today?'

The two girls looked at each other and giggled.

Dona turned to Pinaki. 'Baba, please tell Ma I *have* to go to this other...'

'Did you hear what I said, shona? This is Mr Biren Roy! The architect!'

'Don't stuff her head with useless information,' Biren said.

She laughed. Her teeth were like a mesh of cleanly picked hilsa bones. He ran his tongue over his own dingy incisors.

'Shubho Puja, Uncle,' Dona said, folding her hands. Her black eyes danced. 'I hope you enjoyed our Puja.'

'I did indeed. Very much.'

After a short silence, 'We have to leave now,' she said firmly. 'Excuse us.'

Biren nodded after them. 'Are they in college?'

'First year. I only wish Dona was a little more serious about her studies.'

'Ah.'

'She's taken Sociology and History but she likes painting. She's good at drawing.'

'Ah.'

'Maybe she could do something with that.' Pinaki glanced at Biren. 'Someone like you would know, sir.'

Biren's eyes narrowed. What was the fellow driving at?

'Perhaps,' said Pinaki, watching him, 'you can see her sketches one day?'

'Perhaps.'

'And could you...speak to her? Give her advice, that is. If I brought her to meet you.'

A truck hit him broadside. 'What?'

'At your convenience of course...are you feeling sick, sir? Sir?'

'Concussed, actually. Just joking, Bose. A touch of the sun, perhaps.'

Pinaki looked relieved. 'You see, her mother and I do not understand these things. And she won't listen to us.' He bunched his dhuti. 'But she will to *you*. You know a lot about... everything.'

'Not about young people. In fact, I would be quite... unsuitable.'

'No, I am sure you would be the right person, sir.'

Is he serious? Does he actually believe you have something useful to contribute? (To a college girl?) Or is he sneaking in a little détente here? Well, if he's sincerely seeking your help, you have to oblige. Especially after the disgraceful way you have treated him.

Are you arguing your case to a higher tribunal or a corruptible earthly one?

'Well, I'm in my studio most Saturday afternoons, Bose. *As* you know.'

As they left the enclosure they passed Rimi, in shrill altercation with the drummers.

Pinaki heaved a sigh. 'Sometimes I wonder why we marry.'

'I take it that's just rhetoric.'

'It is our duty, I believe.'

'To whom, pray?'

Pinaki considered. 'To our parents,' he said, and, less surely, 'To society. Marriage protects women.'

Biren laughed. 'What a mediaeval take, Bose. What do your contractual obligations as husband include?' He took out his car keys. 'This Saturday, then. Take a chance,' he added quickly.

Gold and silver challenged the afternoon sun. The clear bright air stuttered with balloons, toy windmills, gewgaws, gizmos of all kinds. Multicoloured bunting fluttered across shop fronts. Saris, scarves, kurtas swung on display on the pavement. Crowds swarmed around hawkers' stalls, sharks in a feeding frenzy. Blocked by a roistering throng he eased the car to the curb and got out to stretch his legs. Without thinking what he was doing he walked into a shop.

Half a dozen women sat at the counter, harrying a heap of coloured silk. Two salesmen were attending to them, ferrying boxes and bolts, alert to the slightest flicker of interest to amplify their sales pitch. After a minute of watching them, he pulled out a length of turquoise from the heap. Absently he stroked it and then held it to his face. It felt like skin—and was blessedly cool. He pressed it to his burning eyelids.

'Apnar ki chai, Dada?'

Startled, he put down the silk. The customer behind whom he was standing edged her chair away.

'You want to buy that sari, Dada?' asked the salesman. 'It's very good quality. South silk.' His manner implied Biren was morally obliged to buy it. Since he'd been on such intimate terms with it, it was as good as used.

Biren shook his head. 'Sorry. Another time, perhaps.'

19

He had been sitting at his desk all afternoon, 'reading' a novel. A preliminary—premature—drawing for the Seth's hotel, a scribble in effect, lay on his drafting table. From time to time he glanced at it. At last he heard Pinaki's cheerful bellow in the studio. 'Kemon achho, Manu? Bhalo? Good, good!'

He smiled to himself. Pinaki knew Manu wasn't deaf.

In a further show of familiarity he waved his briefcase at Biren as he entered. 'Good evening, sir!'

He'd got her down so accurately he thought he was looking at a caricature. The jeans were on target—they were straining their seams. (Her figure would be described as bell-shaped in the beauty magazines she consulted.) One sleeve of her T-shirt was scrunched up by the strap of her satchel—slung shoulder to hip—and the other was hanging like a dishcloth from a hook. His eyes slid down. Spot on! She was wearing chappals of reddish, uncured leather. He raised his head—and stopped smiling.

She looked absolutely mortified. She was, in fact, close to tears. Puzzled, he glanced down again.

She was scrunching her toes, trying to hide them under the narrow straps. The second toe, he now observed, was disproportionately long, dwarfing the big. The others were runts. The graceless family gave the foot character, even piquancy, but to her they must be a leper's stumps.

A wave of compassion swept through him. *It's alright,* he wanted to tell her. *I hadn't even noticed them.* She continued to brood while Pinaki bustled, fussing with his briefcase, putting it now on the table, now on the floor. In the end he stowed it on his lap, hugging it.

Biren blew a stream of smoke from the side of his mouth. 'Now tell me what I can do for you.'

She gave her father a sidelong look. *You* brought me here, *you* speak.

Pinaki cleared his throat. 'As I mentioned, sir, she is doing BA in Sociology and History. She isn't, that is, she says she isn't interested in pursuing those subjects... Tell Uncle what you want to do, Dona!'

She tossed her head, jangling her earrings. Cheap, glittery, they were as redundant as the moons of Jupiter. The face reflected the restlessness of adolescence—discontent fostered by the romantic novels and trashy movies that must colour her daydreams.

'Kichu bol na, Dona.'

She hooked her thumbs to the edge of the table. 'There's

nothing to say. Those subjects bore everyone. Even our teachers. He won't be interested.' Her voice was high, a treble, with a curious inflexion at the end of some words like the bending of a twig under a weight.

'*Uncle*, Dona, not *he*. Show Uncle your drawings, at least. Hurry up. He's a busy man.'

'They're no good,' she muttered. Her thumbs, still pressed on the table, were bitten to the quick.

'Let Uncle decide that, shona.'

She took out a file from her satchel, and pushed it towards Biren, eased it along, the way a parent would a first-born towards the school door.

It took him only a few seconds to see the sketches for what they were. Or, in this case, what they were not. He couldn't think of anything encouraging to say about the childish renderings of lurid sunsets and bug-eyed women.

She was biting a thumbnail with furious concentration. *I know, I know,* he commiserated. *I understand exactly how it feels when a jury sees your Picasso as an idiot's doodle.*

He took a steadying pull at his cigarette and nodded at her through the smoke. 'They have a certain, um, an unpretentious charm. Fresh, um, use of colours.' Which was tantamount to telling a chef you liked the bread best.

'See?' exclaimed Pinaki. 'What did I tell you? Uncle likes your work!'

'He hasn't actually said anything.'

She had more intelligence than he thought.

'He said they were *fresh*, shona,' Pinaki said in a pleading voice. 'That is positive, taito?' Unmindful of her frown, 'She won second prize in the Brooke Bond sit-and-draw competition, sir,' he said.

'Ten years ago. I never won anything after that.' She slid the strap of her satchel off the chair. She was readying to leave!

Hastily he stubbed out his cigarette. 'Let's see how best you can use your, um, talent, Dona.'

'No. It's no good.'

He didn't contradict her.

Pinaki smiled as if his shoe was pinching him. 'I thought, perhaps she can try for...architecture?'

He studied Pinaki over his cigarette tip. *Don't. Don't even try. I shan't fall for it.*

'It requires drawing so...' Pinaki looked at him helplessly.

Desisting from pointing out it wouldn't exactly be a sit-and-draw, 'It's a thought,' he murmured. How white were the whites of her eyes! How black the irises! 'If she's interested.'

Interested. His mouth twisted. What a travesty. It had to be nothing short of a passion, an all-consuming passion for him to be interested in even discussing the subject.

'She has read *The Fountainhead*,' Pinaki offered.

He clapped a hand to his forehead. 'Oh lord. That hoary fairy tale.'

Her face fell. 'I liked Howard Roark,' she said bravely.

'Of course you did. Just don't go looking for him. He doesn't exist.'

She was standing up! Picking up her bag!

'Would you like tea?' he said, jumping up. 'Or coffee, if you prefer.' *What about this magnifying glass? That drafting pencil? The picture you were looking at—I could take it down for you...*

Pinaki was staring at him. 'Tea,' he said in a bewildered way. 'Thank you.' He shot Dona a triumphant glance. 'Sit, shona. Uncle is making *tea* for us.'

She sat down, mindful of her manners but not caring to hide her impatience to leave. The interview, as far as she was concerned, was over.

Declining Pinaki's offer to help, he went to a small, stained table in the corner that accommodated his rudimentary tea making equipment—an electric kettle, a box of tea bags, a jar of instant coffee, a bottle of sugar, two ceramic mugs and a glass.

He looked out of the window as he waited for the water

to heat. The evening sky was suffused with a post-coital glow. A constellation of lights picked out Park Street. Green fluorescence seeped out of the crack between two tallish blocks of offices. The city was readying itself for the night. Except, where was the party?

Slewing his neck around he asked, 'How murky do you like your brew?' Smiling at their incomprehension, 'A tea bag only makes coloured water,' he explained. 'Not tea. The longer it's left in the murkier it gets. Like Marxist politics in West Bengal.' He deposited the drowned bags on a saucer where they oozed like squashed roaches. 'Bad analogy. Bad tea too, I suspect. There's no milk.'

Pinaki accepted his mug with a show of gratitude, Dona with the contempt it deserved.

He returned to his chair. 'So Dona, tell me. Have you ever thought of architecture school? No? Do you notice buildings at all? Which one? Let me think... (*Pick a card, any card.*) The Bishop's House on Chowringhee? Esplanade Mansion?'

Her face was blank—not bewildered blank but unheeding blank. His spirits sank. Is it possible to live in Calcutta for as long as she had and not be struck by the beauty of its architectural gems? (But what could one expect from the superficial understanding imparted by the crib notes that formed the bedrock of her education?) He would try her with one of its horrors. 'How about Chatterjee International?'

That should be easy enough, even for her. Everyone in Calcutta, even those who had no interest in buildings, far less discernment, had heaped scorn on it.

'It's alright,' she muttered.

Irritation flared. 'That it's far from alright is the point.'

'What point?'

Of everything, you little fool. Everything that matters, which is everything that defines civilization. He had a violent urge to shake her out of her ignorance. Her apathy. Her ill humour.

Her indifference to him.

'The point is I don't really care,' she said, raising her chin.

I wouldn't say that here if I were you, he thought, grinding his cigarette into the bird's nest. 'It would sharpen your sensibilities if you did,' he said. *At least make you less vapid.* 'So you would be part of the thinking minority in this city, and one day, who knows, contribute to reshaping it. Make it what it should be. What it deserves to be.' *Dream on.*

'You would like that wouldn't you, shona?' Pinaki said brightly. She gave him an old-fashioned look. Pinaki squirmed and nipped at his mug. 'Calcutta is not what it was,' he said. Glancing at her—she was rolling her eyes up at the ceiling, 'It has been spoilt,' he muttered.

Biren felt sorry for him. 'Your father has a point, you know,' he said. 'Despising Chatterjee International may not seem relevant but building it was a crime. And locating it on Chowringhee, with the Indian Museum, the Arts College, the Asiatic Society, makes it an unforgivable one.'

She had leaned forward, her mug cupped in both her hands. He decided to interpret that as a sign she was taking something in. 'Buildings affect us, Dona. More profoundly than you can imagine. If I had my way everybody would do an architecture appreciation course. We might be less like savages.' He smiled to take the edge off his words. 'Enough of me. Let's hear *your* views.'

She had switched her attention to a moth spread-eagled on the windowpane, watching it with concentration. Her little paunch had popped its moorings. He had a disgraceful wish to poke it. He lit a fresh cigarette. 'So, Dona,' he said. 'What *do* you make of your city? Don't be inhibited by the fact it's people like me who have contributed to its present state.'

'I haven't thought about it.'

He gritted his teeth. 'Think, then. Always a first time.'

Her eyes grew stormy. She hadn't wanted to come here.

Now she was being shown up—in a way incomprehensible to her. She scratched her arm and inspected her nails for crud. She no longer cared what he thought—if she had cared at all.

A tarpaulin descended on him.

And then she spoke. 'I wish we had malls,' she said in a high, brittle voice. 'Like they do abroad. Not that it would make any difference. I never buy anything.'

He laughed. 'Good news for Daddy, bad news for business.'

'I like looking at interior design magazines,' she said, watching him to gauge his reaction. 'They have buildings too,' she added, uncertainly.

'That's a start,' he said, getting up to switch on the overhead. The lamplight moulded her face in greenish gold metal. Its warm liveliness reminded him of what had drawn him to it in the first place.

Pinaki stirred. 'Architecture is not just nice pictures, shona.'

She brushed the side of her neck as if flicking off a fly. Then, looking straight at Biren, 'Baba says you're building a house for us,' she said.

He frowned. Why was Pinaki persisting with his delusion? And dispensing false information about it? The fellow's confidence in his ultimate capitulation had become a religious belief.

'Is that so? First I'm hearing it.'

Pinaki's smile went out like a damp match.

She was biting her lip. Clearly one of them was lying. His ire increased. 'But we haven't settled your future yet, Dona,' he said effortfully. 'You haven't said what you want to do.'

'What I *don't* want is waste my time studying. I want experiences.'

'A worthy ambition,' he said, ignoring Pinaki, who had started out of his chair. He was suddenly bored. It was no fun baiting people who weren't aware they were bait. 'Your daughter seems to know her mind, Bose.'

'It *might* change,' she said. 'Without my knowing it.' She giggled.

The tarpaulin lifted. A parodist! Potentially.

Pinaki was drooping over his briefcase, like, Biren thought, a defeated player packing up his gear. He raised his head to acknowledge the sympathetic cheers of the last spectators. 'Thank you for giving us your time, sir.'

Biren stood up. 'You're welcome. 'I'm afraid I wasn't much help.'

She smiled, surprising him. 'I would like to borrow a book on architecture,' she said 'An easy one.' The caveat included both of them.

She is sparing her father's feelings, he thought. A little late in the day. And there's no need to appease mine. But wait. If she borrowed a book she would have to come to return it! He went to the cupboard and slid out *Visionary Architects of the 20th Century* from a shelf. Hardly a beginner's guide and guaranteed to discourage any but the most diligent (and keen) scholar. Which she was most certainly wasn't. After a moment's hesitation he picked *Post Modern Architecture*—a choice even harder to justify. Was he flattering her with his confidence in her intelligence, or showing off his own?

'Start with these favourites of mine. Treat them well— they're precious.'

It said much for her composure that she didn't push them back at him. In her place he certainly would have.

'I'll bring them back on Tuesday evening,' she said.

'But you'll get nothing from them in three days!' *Not even thirty days,* but that was not why you're lending them to her, are you?

'I have exams this month, Uncle,' she said, looking him full in the face.

The silence resonated like a stadium after a game.

But she had smiled at him. And she had laughed. She would be back on Tuesday. And surely her discourtesy must presume his tolerance of it?

20

On Tuesday evening, Biren's state of alertness was that of a border patrol after a skirmish. Every rustle was amplified, every scuffle and thud, every creak and crackle in the building's ancient joints...

At 4.30 p.m. he got up and shut the windows. He wouldn't be able to hear the knock when the infernal azaan sounded. A little after 5 p.m. he heard a muffled sound in the studio. He had just enough time to jam on his glasses and snatch up his pencil.

She was wearing a skirt today, and rather plucky of her, a pair of open-toed sandals, from which the toes tumbled, higgledy-piggledy, like children let out of school. The toes tensed. Hastily he looked up.

'I brought your books back,' she said stiffly. 'Thank you for lending them.'

'Did you, could you,' he began, when there was a small stir at the door.

'Hello, Uncle!'

Nini walked in.

'Hello!' he said, not a little put out.

'I was looking at your office, Uncle.' She gave him an arch smile, as if the contraband she'd found would be their secret.

'Studio,' he corrected without thinking. She snapped gum at him.

He smiled at her. 'How do you keep so neat and fresh in this weather?' Although why he had to mollify the girl he couldn't say. 'I could be tending a steel furnace. Feel like it anyway.'

She rolled her eyes at her friend. Her friend ignored her (hurrah!) and put the books on the table. 'Thank you. They were interesting.'

'But not interesting enough to keep longer to read? Ah, well. I suppose that was a bit much to expect.' He didn't say *of you* but the words hovered.

The lights went out.

'Well, that puts paid to that.' Whatever did he mean? The book or the visit? His chances, such as they were? The silence was certainly discouraging.

Heat dropped over their heads like burlap sacking. The single candle drew them into a circle that was awkward rather than intimate. The place was jumpy with shadows. He offered them a candle to light their way out but they decided to wait for the lights. So then, small talk. Brutal weather, wasn't it? Yes. Had they come straight from college? Yes. Did they take the Metro? No. What did they usually do after class gave over? Nothing much.

The exchange, sagging with pauses as he lurched from one platitude to another, reminded him of one of his ex-wife's less successful dinner parties. Like her, he had an obligation to keep pouring the wine till something gave. Seeking a breather, he went into the studio to fetch his cigarettes.

When he returned they were engaged in a whispered argument. Dona stood up 'We decided not to wait for the lights,' she announced.

'Do you live anywhere near Elgin Road, Uncle?' Nini asked. Dona nudged her. 'We were hoping you could give us a lift,' she continued.

'Where do you have to go?'

'The Hazra crossing,' Nini said promptly. 'I live there and Dona has her music class near... *aii*!'

Dona had nudged her again. 'We'll take a bus,' she said in a tense voice. 'There are lots going from Chowringhee.'

'Sheta, I'm telling you they'll all be full at this time!'

'I can drive you there,' he said, taking care to keep his tone casual. 'It won't be much of a detour.'

'The traffic's bad in Elgin Road just now,' Dona said.

'Not if you take Allenby,' Nini said. 'There's a lane that connects.'

That girl will go far, he thought. She was sexier than Dona, by the established index for sexiness, but to him she had no charm. Her eyes had a gleam—a counter-intelligence that had intuited whom he did find appealing. He had a sudden wish to protect Dona from her. He picked up his car keys. 'Alright girls. You make up your minds while I lock up.'

'We'll come with you, Uncle,' Nini said firmly.

A short distance from the Lansdowne Road crossing, Nini announced this was as far as she needed to go. Dona said, 'But Nini, your house is further on!'

Nini sighed theatrically. 'You know Ma, rey. If she sees me coming in a strange car...'

'Your mother's a wise woman,' he said. 'Strange cars are dangerous.'

She gurgled. 'It's not the car!' She scrambled out of the car. Bending to look into his window, 'Thank you for the lift, Uncle,' she said. The knowing eyes glinted. 'Good evening.'

Dona turned to him. 'I'll also get down here.'

'But you said your class is near the Samaritan Clinic!'

'It's too late for it,' she said, intent on the handle. 'I can get a bus from here.'

He thought fast. 'I need to go to the stationer at the end of the road. I'll drop you at the next stop. Save you ten minutes.' Before she could answer he put his car into gear.

The evening traffic was moving like the sewage-choked Tolly canal. It saved him from pretending his car couldn't go faster.

Beside him Dona was fidgeting. Catching his eye, she said, 'Only friends are allowed to call her Nini.'

'Uncles can claim the privilege,' he said amiably.

She hugged her arms. Against the achromatic shabbiness of the car, she glowed. Her black hair crackled. He could smell her pubescent scent—sweat, sweet talc, shampoo, potent as a drug. She was so alive, so palpably *there*. She turned her head to the window, straining the tendons in her neck.

They were halted by, and how predictable this, how fortuitous, a roadblock. A van had broken down and pedestrians and cyclists, other drivers, were milling around the stricken vehicle.

On the curb was a small, grimy Kali temple, wedged in by makeshift huts. Thinking he would break the silence (why is it we feel so threatened by silence?), to distract her from leaving him (which she must be plotting), he drew her attention to it. 'Om, shanty, shanty, eh?'

She bridled. 'That's so *mean*. To make fun of people who are poor.'

'Lighten up, Dona.'

'I have a conscience.'

'Very laudable. But don't get lumbered with it. And don't jump out—not just yet. There's a bus coming behind.'

The bus edged past, with inches to spare. She shrank back.

They were moving again.

'Why did you come to our Puja?'

Surprised, he replied, 'Your father invited me.'

'Yes, but why did you *come*?'

'How do you mean?'

She pushed out her bottom lip. 'You looked so bored. And irritated.'

'Really?' So she'd noticed him!

'Yes. As if you disapproved of everything.' She gave him a

sidelong glance. 'I suppose you thought you were doing us a favour by coming?'

'Is that what *you* thought?'

'Well, you seemed so, *imperial*.'

'I think the word you want is imperious.' She didn't like that. 'If you must know, I was feeling a bit out of it,' he said.

He was feeling a bit out of it now. He was going nowhere with her. And his back ached—he could feel every bone through the worn-out padding of his seat. He could do with a drink. Plus he needed the bathroom, and it was a long ride home. 'Oh, get a move on,' he muttered. Thankfully they did.

She was adjusting something on her neck—a bit of metalwork that twisted around to a snakehead resting in the hollow of her throat. He reached over and touched it. 'This thing must feel cold in the winter.' His fingers brushed her neck. The snake writhed. 'So, who's the lucky boyfriend who keeps it warm?'

Her mouth flew open. 'Let me out.' She fumbled with her door handle.

He braked sharply, and, ploughing through a chorus of curses, pulled up at the pavement.

When she was scrambling out he leaned over to murmur in her ear.

'*What?*'

~

'He said he liked my toes!'

'Eeeyooo! Creepy! A pervert, Dona. Tell your father.'

'Na rey, I can't. Baba believes this man is God.'

~

'Say hello to Daddy and Mummy from me,' he called after her.

She didn't turn around. He stuck his head out of the window. 'You're welcome!'

~

The bathroom became a pressing need. If he didn't do something soon...there would be...unpleasant consequences. He cast about for a restaurant, a snack bar. A hole in the floor would do, this was no time to be picky.

He pulled over, leapt out—and almost fell over a bundle of filthy rags.

A head of hair, like the pelt of a very dusty sheep, poked out of it. Flies foraged on its blackened mask.

He extracted a note from his wallet. 'Here. Don't drink that up. Oh, hell, drink. I would if I were you.'

A swarm of urchins sprang up from the pavement, blocked his path. He sighed and took out his wallet again. 'Do you brats grow out of spores?' In the end he had to show them the single banknote that he was left with before they would let him go.

He emerged from the lavatory, his face damp and his undershirt clinging to his back. Feeling obliged to consume something he sat down at a table.

'Uncle!'

She was standing in front of him.

'I forgot my books in the car.'

'Well, I'm going to drink coffee, since I used the um, facilities here. If you'd like to join me...' To his surprise she pulled out a chair.

She touched her hair self-consciously. 'You were joking, weren't you? About not having a conscience. I saw what you did outside.' She tried to look cross—and failed.

'In my defence I don't often do that.' The waiter arrived. 'Coffee for you too?'

She nodded. Hooking a wisp of hair behind her ears she said, 'There was an egg in your car. Near my feet.'

'So that's where it went!'

'You carry eggs around?'

'They're useful. Except these aren't much fun because they're boiled.'

After a few seconds she laughed.

'I eat them, actually. They make boring pets.'

She laughed again. 'You say such funny things.' She chewed her finger. 'You do funny things too. You stamped that old man's foot in the igloo. On purpose.'

'He was in my way.' *Old man? The fellow had been younger than him!*

'Do you do that to everyone who gets in your way?' The black eyes sparkled. She was enjoying herself!

The coffee arrived at that moment. Chiefly beige froth. But she appeared pleased with it. *Doesn't know better,* and with a surge of tenderness, *doesn't know much.*

'You only pretend to be mean,' she said, stirring away. 'Actually you're impatient—with people who're not like you. I think they have to prove their worth before you will have anything to do with them.'

This was so near the mark, he laughed. 'So. If I'm to understand you, I'm an intolerant phoney. And I need proof—unspecified yet—before I will have anything to do with you.'

She bit her lip. Was he pulling her leg?

He smiled at her. 'Let's talk about *you.* How do you propose to get Daddy out of your hair?'

She got to her feet. 'Thank you for the coffee. I'd like my books now, please.'

He retrieved her books. 'Here you go. Perchance we'll find each other under the same palm tree someday.'

She shaded her eyes at a non-existent sun. 'My music class is on Wednesdays and Saturdays. I usually finish at 5.30.'

He followed her gaze. 'I usually replenish my stationery on Wednesday.'

She dropped her hand and walked away quickly.

In a happy daze, he took a wrong turning at the racecourse, and landed in a clutter of road construction. It was the flyover leading to the new bridge across the Hoogly and the Bombay highway. When he broke free from the maze he found himself in a tunnel of trees edging the maidan.

A glimmer of silver between the trees alerted him. The river! He was driving on the Strand. Drawing aside, he parked and crossed the narrow railway tracks to the promenade.

Flickers of blue, like live current, darted through the water. A docked ship rocked gently in the middle of the river. The lights of Howrah City plotted an erratic graph in the chalky sky. Black smoke from factory chimneys drifted across the grey. To his left was the skeleton of the new bridge. A couple of kilometres upstream was Howrah Bridge, the cat's cradle of steel that had excited the imagination of the country for half a century.

He could smell jasmine. The thicket behind him was starred with bloom. A fresh breeze lifted the hair from his forehead. He opened his arms out. Sham, drudgery, broken dreams... Not especially a beautiful world but how liberating to know, and without a shred of doubt, that there was nowhere else you'd rather be than here.

It began to rain. Warm drops fell, pocking the surface of the river. In the hush he could hear the slap-slap of the water. It was calming but it also made him want to pee. 'What the hell,' he said aloud. Finding a gap where the balustrade had caved in, he unzipped.

21

Four days after the Puja, when Calcutta was still in a post-festival daze, Mr Sen summoned Pinaki to take a phone call in his office.

Pinaki's heart began thumping. The last time he'd received a phone call at work was two years ago when Tuli had fallen off his school bus. Who was sick now, what had happened? The additional anxiety that Mr Sen might think he was sneaking his outside life into the office, that he should even have a life outside the office, made him so nervous he tripped and fell on to a chair.

Mr Sen had the grace to leave the cabin—but his displeasure was written on his back. The tightness grew in Pinaki's chest.

'Shubho Bijoya, Bosebabu.'

'Shubho Bijoya,' croaked Pinaki.

'I had a very good Puja. In Burdwan. Family get-together—relatives from Midnapur, Assansol, Dibrugarh... How about yourself? Rained on Navami, but full sun on other days.'

Pinaki held the receiver away from his ear. It didn't interrupt the flow of gratuitous information or diminish the anxiety, but it helped him breathe. 'Is it something urgent? Why are you calling me here?'

'You gave me this contact number, Bosebabu.'

That was true. Pinaki had had to make a heads-I-lose, tails-I-lose choice between Mr Sen's ire and Rimi's inquisitiveness. He heard a crackling as of paper being ripped. The caller was blowing his nose.

'Your final instalment is due Bosebabu.'

'But we agreed...you said after Puja!'

'This *is* after Puja. The last day was last week. You are due—overdue.'

The ceiling was pressing down on Pinaki. 'I need...some more time.'

The phone crackled. 'I'm sorry, brother, we have an agreement.'

The ceiling crashed on Pinaki's head. 'But I haven't got the money yet!' The murmuring outside the cabin had stopped. Cupping the receiver, he muttered, 'Okay, alright.'

'Friday. With the money, brother. Okay, Saturday. Only because you are my brother.'

Pinaki received curious looks on the way back to his cubicle. He smiled, he nodded, he waved, but the response was lukewarm. That became cause for a new unease. They suspected he was in trouble. And in the mysterious way these things get about, by the end of the day everybody knew Pinaki Bose had a money crisis.

'O Pinakibabu, now you are really in soup,' said his colleague, looking at Pinaki like a teacher who has just heard that his favourite student got a second in the finals. It was hard to bear.

Before leaving the office that evening Pinaki went to Mr Sen. Before he started to speak Mr Sen lifted his hand. 'End of the month, Bose. We have a cash crunch just now.'

Pinaki had no reason to either believe or disbelieve him.

'No,' said Rimi. 'Ask your mother to sell her jewellery.'

'She hardly has any, Rimi. Even if she did I can't ask her to do that... It's alright. I will find some other way.'

Dida removed her ear from the door. Absently she fingered her cupboard keys, knotted into her sari end. He would come to her. They always did. A son is a son, no matter how foolish he is. Smiling to herself, she swung the weighted knot. It hit the door with a crack.

The door suddenly opened. She drew back, but wasn't quick enough to hide her guilt.

'Did you want something, Ma?' Rimi asked, all innocence.

Dida put her head inside and peered all around the room. 'Are my glasses here?'

Rimi sucked an invisible lemon. Taking pity on his mother, 'Come in and check, Ma,' Pinaki said.

Dida limped in, patted the bedspread, lifted a newspaper here, a towel there. 'Hmm. Must be in the kitchen then.' But she didn't leave. Pulling a chair to the bed she set to getting the knots out of her knuckles.

It set his teeth on edge. 'Is something bothering you, Ma?'

Dida laughed an artificial laugh. 'I was going to ask *you* that, Bulbul!'

Rimi laughed shortly. 'I can tell you. It's money. To buy some land.'

Dida gave her a brief stare. 'Your eyebrows don't match,' she said.

Rimi left, banging the door behind her.

'Now tell me, Bulbul,' his mother said. 'How much do you need?'

Pinaki's face grew hot. 'It's alright,' he muttered.

She gave Pinaki's big toe a playful tug. 'Shothi? God promise?'

Pinaki had to clench his jaw to keep from snapping at her.

Rimi held a pencil to her nose in the bathroom mirror. The wretched Daisy!

~

At dinner, when Tuli helped himself to a third piece of fish Pinaki looked hard at Tuli's plate. 'Vegetarians live a long life,' he commented.

'We are not vegetarians,' Rimi said flatly.

'Tuli needs fish for his brains, Baba,' Dona said. 'He is going to win the Nobel, remember? Baba thinks you eat too much,' she said to Tuli.

Pinaki's protestations were a little too forced. He turned to Dona. 'So, Dona, are you going to be an architect?'

'No, Baba, I am not.'

'So what will you do after college?'

'I haven't thought.'

'Better think. Or you'll be selling jhal muri on the road.' The words were out before he formed them.

Dona got up. 'Just because I don't wish to be an architect doesn't mean I have to sell jhal muri.'

The unpleasantness didn't end there. He couldn't, it seemed, stop himself. Late at night, spotting light under the dining room door, 'Who switched on the lights here?' he barked. 'Wasting electricity?'

'I'm doing my homework, Baba,' Tuli called out.

Pinaki walked into the room. 'Don't lie to me!' he thundered. 'You're reading comics! Don't think I don't know you hide them inside your books!'

'I'm not, Baba! See for yourself!'

Pinaki picked up a book. 'What is this then? Eh? It's a storybook!'

'It's *Tale of Two Cities*, Baba! It's on my reading list!'

Pinaki thwacked his son's head. 'Why are you not doing maths? Eh?'

'Ki holo?' Rimi ran in. 'Eijay, why is he crying? What did you do to him?'

Pinaki stormed out.

Back in his room, he continued to rail at the ceiling. Later, unable to sleep and hungry, he got up and padded into the kitchen. Scavenging in the alien territory he found the remains of the fish curry they'd had at dinner and ate a chunk straight from the bowl. Waves of nausea rose. Rimi would notice the missing fish and blame the maid. He bent over the kitchen sink waiting for the nausea to do its worst. Then he washed his fingers, scrubbing his fingers raw with a plastic brush.

In the morning he skulked in his bedroom, too ashamed to face Tuli and yet longing for some sign—a smile, a word, a gesture. He would take anything.

Tuli didn't ask him to knot his school tie.

Dona didn't come to say goodbye.

Das Engineering Works didn't wish him. Perhaps he was too preoccupied?

The Dignified Beggar didn't ask him for baksheesh. Too drugged?

The modi's back was turned. Taking stock?

Was there to be no forgiveness for him? From any quarter?

'Bosebabu!' called Aroma. 'Cha khabe?'

'Of course! You make the best tea in Calcutta!'

But he had to make peace at home.

In the evening, 'How was cricket practice today, Tuli?' he asked.

Tuli ducked his head. 'Fine.'

'Did you bowl or bat?'

'Both,' muttered Tuli.

The next day was better, but only because he was getting used to his pariah status, even taking a gloomy relish in it.

On the way home that evening he had a crisis that pushed this self-destructive mood to the brink. It started with remembering he needed shaving blades, of a brand not available at the modi's. Also a stick of shaving soap. So he went into a general store en route to his bus stop.

The salesgirl left a modest selection of his requirements on the counter and went off to argue with a customer who apparently had found wormholes in a slab of chocolate bought from here. While they were arguing he prodded the toiletries, brooding over his situation. Then—he could never explain what hideous impulse prompted him—he slid a stick of shaving soap into the pocket of his pants. In a trance, he pocketed a Dairy Milk too, from the tray, and walked out.

He looked over his shoulder once or twice, half-hoping the girl would call him back, ask him why he was leaving in such a hurry. Then he could smuggle the stuff back on to the counter.

Or, he could own his mistake and offer horrified apologies, pleading absent-mindedness. And then buy expensive, pointless items to prove his sincerity. And solvency. But she was too preoccupied to notice his departure.

He bumped into people, stumbled on pavement wares. His pocket grew heavier and heavier. The entire inventory of the wretched grocery store seemed to be contained in it. He transferred the loot—of course that's what it was—from his pocket to his briefcase. It didn't get any better. His briefcase was full of bricks now.

Why did he do it? Did he imagine such acts would help make up the balance money he needed for his land? Sticks and bars in their hundreds—a lifetime's supply of them—would not add up to that terrifying amount. They wouldn't buy his passage to freedom from Rabin Pal, from Kalol Mondal, from Rimi. In the arithmetic of crime the zeros come after, not before, the decimal point.

He would give the chocolate to the first crying child he saw. (And the blades?) But the children he saw were all tethered to their mothers. He lingered by a policeman, in fearful thrall to the law, ready to fling himself under the wheels of justice.

The policeman winked at him.

What strange manner of punishment was this? He crossed the road. There was no going back now. He had crossed over in every sense.

Bus after bus sailed by, all of them packed. As time wore on, he began viewing his crime in a different light. It was a prank—the exploit of a schoolboy stoning mangoes in the neighbour's garden. Its magnitude was so insignificant as to be ludicrous. He had done it! He hadn't been caught! Light-headed with triumph, he swung his briefcase in the air. When an elderly woman tried to jump the queue he ordered her back curtly.

And in the bus he ate the chocolate, all of it, and didn't feel one bit sick.

As soon as he reached home, he scuttled into the bathroom, locked himself in, and put his trophy on the shelf over the basin. It stood for *something*. Defiance, he decided. He'd shaken a fist at years of being under the yoke of Jalan & Jalan. He had accumulated so much virtue during that time that this would hardly dent the bank.

He opened the packet and counted out the blades. Sighing deeply, he put it back on the shelf. The only self-knowledge he'd gained from the experience was that he would never have given the chocolate to his children.

Which didn't necessarily make him a good father.

~

On Thursday afternoon, Dona, hunched over the telephone in the hall, saw her mother approach with the duster. She covered the receiver with one hand and batted the air with the other. 'Not now, Ma!'

Rimi took a swipe at the telephone. 'Where has your Dida gone?'

'Oof, I don't know! I'm talking to someone, Ma!'

'She's gone out alone.'

'As if you ever cared before...okay, she's gone to the bank. Ekhon jao.'

'Don't *you* order me about...how do you know where she went?'

'Because she took her fixed deposit certificate file! Leave the wire alone, Ma!'

Rimi stood still. 'But she just renewed it. Ki korey janle?'

Dona rolled her eyes. 'Because we share a room!' The guilt of the betrayal stung her. She dug the receiver into her chest. 'Maybe she had to check something. Now please will you go?'

Rimi stared into the distance. 'She must be cashing it. I think I know why,' she said grimly, and swished off.

Dona took her hand off the receiver. 'I think I've got my grandmother into trouble,' she said dismally. 'And my father.'

Returning home that evening, Pinaki bumped into his landlord. 'Nomoshkar, Bosebabu! Kemon achen? Good, good!' He swept up the end of his dhuti. 'Off to a wedding,' he puffed. 'I just came to check the water tank.'

'Check the wiring too, Sarkarbabu. The other day there was a shorting.'

The landlord, a scrawny peppery man given to hopping when excited, jumped nimbly on to the curb. 'Yes, yes! I will fix it one day.'

'One day someone will be electrocuted.'

The landlord bared jagged little teeth. 'Hundred years ago they predicted a major earthquake in California, Bosebabu. But people are still living there. Safely.'

'Anything can happen anytime, Sarkarbabu. You need to rewire the building.'

The landlord's features gathered to a point. 'I would if I got more rent. But will you agree to *that*? You all want to pay me what your fathers, your *grandfathers* did!'

'I'm sure you would like to get your flats back, Sarkarbabu. So you can let them out for more rent.'

'Who wouldn't like more rent?' retorted the landlord. 'But nobody leaves!' His nose twitched. He looked, Pinaki thought, like his Class 5 schoolteacher whose sole reason for setting tests was to catch cheaters. 'Why, are you thinking of leaving?'

'Not at all, Sarkarbabu. Unless...how much would you give me if I left?' Pinaki's laugh was a little too forced.

'I know what is going on,' said the landlord heavily. 'I am not a fool. You are building a house and you need money. So you are asking for money to vacate my flat. Isn't that so?'

'No, Sarkarbabu. That is not so at all...'

'I'm not asking you to stay, sir, and I'm not asking you to go. And I am not giving you money to go!'

'It is what all landlords do if they want their flat back.'

'If they want. But I don't want. *You* want. You want to go, so go! Go tomorrow!' Spit flew in the air.

Pinaki surreptitiously wiped the spit. 'No, no, Sarkarbabu, please don't misunderstand. I wanted to ascertain...it is the law so I thought...'

'It is *not* the law,' said the landlord, hopping from one foot to the other. 'It is the practice of our corrupt country!' He shook a finger in Pinaki's face. 'One day I will sell my building. But I will choose that day. And I will choose how to do it also. Don't threaten me with the law. I will cut your electricity.' He swooped and snipped the air so close to Pinaki's nose that Pinaki jumped back. Then he called out to Das Engineering Works. 'Listen to this! *He* wants to leave my flat and he is making *me*...!'

Pinaki walked away, looking neither left nor right.

Kalol Mondal, sitting on the culvert outside Pinaki's building, got to his feet as Pinaki hurried past. 'Shubho Bijoya!' he cried. Before Pinaki knew it, his shoulders were being gripped and Kalol Mondal was touching his chest three times to Pinaki's. First right, then left, then right again. Then, with his hands still on Pinaki's shoulders, he laughed into his face. 'What is the matter, Dada? You don't like doing kolakoli? Arre, Dada, it is only a Puja greeting!' Insensible to Pinaki's fury, 'I am still doing my Puja visits,' he said. 'I have to pay my respects to an uncle.'

Pinaki had a disconcerting vision of Kalol Mondal bending to touch his uncle's feet and grabbing his neck.

The moment Pinaki shut the front door behind him Dona shot out of her room. 'Baba, did you see...'

'Yes. He spoke to me.'

'He tried to speak to me too.'

'So?'

'Never mind.'

'Sorry, sorry, shona! I wasn't paying attention. I was thinking...what did he want? I hope he didn't...'

'He wished me shubho Bijoya. It's alright, Baba,' she said in an altered voice. 'I can handle him.' She touched his arm. 'You don't worry.'

Tears came to his eyes. It was the first consideration he had received in a long, long while. And she, dear child, had forgotten his bad-tempered outburst of two days ago.

Then he was pouring out his unhappy story, taking care, even in his pain, to project Rabin Pal as a villain rather than himself as a fool. It was wrong to burden one's children with one's troubles, but he had had such a day.

He patted her cheek. 'Never mind, shona. It is my problem, not *yours*.'

'Okay.' She turned to go back to her room.

Stung by this ready acceptance of his situation—he would have liked some understanding of his anguish, some appreciation of his efforts, because, after all, they were for *her* too, 'If only Biren Roy would cooperate,' he cried. 'If only he agrees to build the house!'

That got through. She spun around.

'I started the project because of him,' he said mournfully. 'He made me believe he was interested.' Which was skirting the truth by a mile but he was tired of being honest and getting it wrong.

He got it right this time. She pushed her fingers into her mouth.

'Ki korchho, Bulbul?'

He started, almost dropping the sheaf of papers in his hands. Dida was standing in the doorway.

His heart back-pedalled. 'I...I was just going to check the date on your fixed deposits, Ma. For...for renewal. I thought they were about to mature.' He replaced the papers in their folder and put them back, fussing around on the shelf. 'Don't leave your keys here and there. You can get burgled. Or I might forge your signature.' He gurgled weakly.

'Oof, Bulbul. The things you say!' She limped to the cupboard and rummaged under a pile of clothes. 'Foolish boy,' she murmured as she took out a bundle of bank notes, 'You are right. They had matured but I didn't renew them. I cashed them.' She removed her glasses, wiped them on her sari. 'Here. You have more use for this than I do.'

22

'When a fellow's asked a girl to tea four times in a fortnight it isn't the tea he's interested in. Especially if the tea's sugared engine oil.'

She giggled. The black eyes danced. 'You know something? Nini is known as the Staircase. On account of her, um, you know. They're one-up and one-down.'

'What a good friend you are. Are those louts blowing kisses to you or me?'

She giggled again. 'Me! Let's go to the new coffeehouse in Pretoria Street. It was in the *Roundup* on Sunday.'

'As long as it's under the radar. Not on the regular beat of your coevals—your pals.'

She chewed her thumbnail. 'It's expensive, Biren.' (She'd been persuaded to drop the 'uncle', and he loved to hear her hesitant *Bi-ren*.)

'Just the place then!'

His mood changed when she pointed out the newly constructed office tower where the coffeehouse was located. It was another of his phantom projects. The city was a graveyard for them. He was filled with gut-wrenching envy. What he could have done with this site!

He reversed the car with a fearsome grinding of gears. 'I can't go in there.'

'Why not?'

Her simple question needled him. It brought to the fore the very frustrations he sought to escape through outings such as this.

'Because, look at it.'

'What's wrong with it?'

'It's an assault on the senses. A physical version of *it's a dark and stormy night.*'

'What are you talking about?'

'Keep your head inside. Ugliness is catching.'

'You're the only one who thinks it's ugly. The *Roundup* said...'

'I'm the only one who matters.'

'Why?'

'Because I'm the only one with reason in this city.'

'So you think.'

'So I know.'

'So everyone must listen to you?'

Yes. Because I'm the arbiter of aesthetics in this city. *As it happens.*

'...you're just jealous because it isn't your building.'

'I wouldn't build something like that if you held a gun to my head. Bang! Bang, bang, bang!'

'You're crazy!'

She was still in battle mode as he swung into Lower Circular Road. 'How do you know your ideas of what is ugly and what is beautiful are right?'

'I hear voices.'

'In other words, you don't know.'

'As a matter of fact there are rules.' *Oh, Vitruvius! Oh, Gropius! Mies, Frank, Eero, Louis, where are your rules now? There are no rules but that they must be broken! Again and again.*

'What are they? What? Huh? See, you don't know. The only rule is people must agree with *you*.'

'They don't have to agree with *me*, Dona. They have to discover the truth for themselves. If they care to.'

'Then you'll say they've got it all wrong. And squash them.'

He had the unhinged sensation he was opening and shutting his mouth with no sound coming out.

'They're indestructible, alas,' he murmured.

They made peace soon after that—the peace initiative, as always, coming from him. He persuaded her that an ice-cream at the Hobby Centre in Park Street would be a very good substitute for the coffee. She was easily fooled by the manoeuvre. Ice cream, she prattled, was her second favourite thing. And if it was coffee ice cream, well that was the first and second together! What fun. He would order her a triple sundae just to hear her shocked delight. 'You must share it, Biren! I couldn't eat it on my own.'

Of course she could.

As usual, because it was more likely there was someone she knew in a place like this, she went in first.

'You're like the aggey-wallah on the golf course,' he told her. 'The caddy who goes ahead to clear other golfers off the green. Like a minesweeper.'

She laughed. 'Where could one see that?'

'At the Tolly Club, for one.'

'Can you take me there?'

He cursed himself for the slip. 'Not a good idea, Dona. The Tolly's a minefield—of public-spirited souls. Who'll compete to report the news of my new, um, companion.'

'To whom?'

'Well, my father for one.'

'You're afraid of your father?'

He cursed himself again. Before he could respond—and what possible response was there—the sundae arrived.

'It has strawberry too,' she said happily. 'Look.'

He looked at the gloop, beige and pink, flecked with maroon. 'All yours,' he said faintly.

What was he doing, what had he become? A schoolboy turning cartwheels in the playground. This wasn't where he should be! He should be drawing, preparing for the seminar on the Rabindra Lake Park. He hadn't gone to his yoga class for a month now. He hadn't played tennis for weeks—his Tolly and South Club partners had stopped calling him. Dozens of greasy meals, gallons of poisonous brews, hours of aimless drives wouldn't let him have his way with the little vestal. Time's relativity put even more years between them. Death, which for him crouched under the bed, was for her the moon in the window. But a broken promise, a broken nail, could end her life in a moment.

Once, driving aimlessly, he spotted a signboard *Fashion Design & Ballroom Dancing* in a muddle of signage. Pointing it to her, 'How about we learn dancing, Dona?' he asked 'Or, if you prefer, fashion design?'

'Oof!' She made a face. It was so unselfconsciously grotesque he found it endearing. She could get away with it now, but he could imagine the years changing the artless contortions to awkward twitches. It didn't bear thinking about.

'Is *that* why you won't take me to the Tolly? Because I can't dance?'

He burst out laughing. 'No, girl, taking *you* to the Tolly would be like taking out a newspaper ad about us.'

'What do you mean, *us*?'

He looked at her with new respect. And fear. She knew there was no *us*. No future to their game.

Once, when he braked for a handcart and she was flung against him, 'Did you do that on purpose?' she asked. 'You didn't have to stop for him.' He saw the wizened arms through the windscreen, trembling with the strain of holding the cart steady—and wanted to tip her out of the car. But he could no more do that than he could bomb the Victoria Memorial.

The driver of the car alongside was staring at them. What did *he* see? A middle-aged father taking his daughter to the dentist? Or an elderly fool shoring up his youth?

'You could be more gracious, you know,' he said. *Keep it light.*

'You could be less arrogant. And stop acting as if you're better than everybody else.'

He gave her a meaningless smile. 'Wright, Frank Lloyd, said that early in life he decided he would choose honest arrogance over hypocritical humility.' *That's keeping it light?*

'So how did his honest arrogance help him?'

He laughed. He had to. If he didn't, he would burst into tears. What was he doing with her? His world was both too big and too small to share with her. She would never understand it, much less want to explore it. And, who knows, be happier for her ignorance. Her world was emptier than his—and fuller.

He was jealous of her world.

Once, to understand her world, he stood outside the ticket booth at Nandan Cinema in a motley queue of down-at-heel men and housewives—who else would see a movie in the middle of the day but idlers and fugitives from tedium? At 1 p.m., when it was scheduled to open, there was no sign of activity. At 1:15 p.m. a murmur rippled through the queue. At 1:25 the window flap went up to reveal a bored-looking man who, whatever else, hadn't used the delay to shave.

After all that, he fell asleep during the movie and had to be shaken awake twice.

They were walking by the fountain outside, she briefing him on the plot which he had missed altogether, when, mid-sentence, she broke off and ran forward.

He started after her. 'Hey! Where're you go—'

Tilting her head, 'Please don't bother me,' she said coldly, and in the same breath, 'Hello!' she cried, waving. Her face assumed the hectic enthusiasm of a socialite who sees the camera lens swinging towards her.

It was a trio of girls coming towards them, not a camera. 'Dona! Have you come for this show? You didn't tell us!'

'No, rey, I saw the matinee with my aunty. I've lost her I think. Have to go—talk to you soon!'

'Aunty, eh?' he said, when she joined him outside the gate.

She giggled.

'Twice more you'll deny me. Grim thought.'

He refused to explain.

His curiosity about her was insatiable although the pickings were thin. More chaff than grain. Yet he picked and sorted. Which was strange, considering other people's journeys had never interested him.

'What are your expectations from life, Dona?'

'You don't *expect* if you live in J. Mullick Road, you *accept*.'

He laughed.

'In any case you can't have expectations if you aren't beautiful.'

'So what do you plan to do—crawl into a hole and die?'

She gave him a half-hearted smile. She'd expected him to reassure her she was eligible for expectations.

'Beautiful people tend to be selfish, Dona. (That wasn't just beautiful people, was it?) That's not so attractive is it? And they're usually discontented. Always reaching out for bigger and better. (He should know!) Also they attract the um, wrong sort of people. Positively have a gift for it.'

She gave him a look he read straight off the bat. Any girl could find herself in *that* particular situation.

Once, for the meagre pleasure of an extra half-hour with her, he took her all the way to J. Mullick Road. She was about to open the door when, with an exclamation, she asked him to reverse the car a little.

The reason turned out to be a loose-limbed youth with a scraggly beard.

He glanced at her. 'The boyfriend?'

She tossed her head but didn't deny it.

'I bet he drools on his pillow.'

'He does not! I mean I don't know...oof! You're *mean*.' She gave him a sidelong look. 'Good-looking, isn't he?'

He tasted bile. She was teasing him, of course. She couldn't be serious about the oaf.

'What does he do—besides gawping at your window? It is your window, I suppose?'

'He's doing Economics at St Xavier's,' she said, with dignity. 'But he wants to be a painter.'

'How modern. Does he have a head for heights?'

'Why?'

'To climb ladders. Sit on scaffoldings.'

'What do you...oof. I meant an *artist*.'

'How clichéd.'

She told him she'd broken off with a boyfriend when she discovered a keloid on his shoulder. He hadn't a hope in heaven, he thought, rubbing his stained cheek. Still he tried—resorting to unprincipled means sometimes.

'I'd like to buy you a present, Dona. Something small and

shiny—how greedy you look! But don't get carried away. I'm not a rich man.' She pinched his arm—she didn't believe him. 'Stick to silver.' He patted the bracelet she wore.

She twisted the bracelet. 'This is not silver, you know. I wouldn't have bought it if it were.'

He picked up her wrist and kissed it. ('Hey!') She was so without artifice. He should be warning her against himself. And arming her, instead of the opposite.

'It *is* my birthday next month,' she said chewing her lip. 'So I suppose it's okay.'

'Of course it is. And advance greetings. I hope this will be a very good year to look back to—to paraphrase Frank Sinatra. You are seventeen, after all.'

'I don't know what you say half the time! Can we get it now?'

'No, this you must do on your own.' Her face fell. 'You'll dive into every shop we pass.'

She giggled. 'I don't know why I do that!'

'Perhaps for the same reason people climb the Everest. To get a high.'

'That's quite funny,' she said politely.

Often, when talking to her, he felt as if he was trying to make a bonfire with (damp) grass. But each time they parted, he felt bereft. He could raid entire granaries and still raven. He was not one to live from moment to moment—that would be as satisfying as sipping beer through a straw—but she had shown him the merits of such a format. Now he felt like those miracle weight-losing machines that you just strapped on. So what if the promised results didn't happen? Caveat emptor.

He was under no delusion that she shared his feelings. She probably looked at him, at all male interest, through the prism of self-love. And she was consumed by curiosity too.

She wanted to know what he did in the evenings, where he

went for his vacations, who his friends were, what happened at the parties he attended. She wouldn't believe there were no parties, no vacations, no glamorous friends. She thought he kept this other life from her because she wouldn't fit in. She said he could afford to dress badly and behave badly because he was rich. His bored contempt of the privileges he pretended to shun was just a façade. Underneath it was a damaged psyche, which, for some mysterious reason, she had been chosen to nurse back to health.

He gave up trying to disabuse her. Instead, he tried to elevate their inane banter to something instructive (as much as he could), and so mitigate the guilt of fooling around with a girl—here it was again—young enough to be his daughter. To his credit he never touched her. Well, hardly at all. Kissing her wrist didn't count. He usually contented himself with watching her. Sniffing at a flower didn't harm it, did it?

He loved the way she tugged at her hair when she knew he was watching. And the way she rolled her eyes when he said something she didn't understand. The way she walked towards him became a reliable indicator of her mood. Her mouth was a live thing, her skin so heartbreakingly innocent. Once she had a pimple on her face, a fiery eruption around which her cheek glowed as if some trace radioactive element was embedded in it.

~

Another time he dropped her at J. Mullick Road, he paid for the indulgence with a flat outside St Teresa's. Cursing under his breath he hauled out the spare tyre and the jack and spanner from the boot. Two youths were lounging by the gate of the church, following his progress. They didn't offer to help and he didn't ask them. It wasn't easy though, to work under their scornful scrutiny.

'Hello,' said Father John, appearing at the gate. 'Tough luck,' he said to Biren, now wiping his hands on a rag. 'Would you like to come in and wash?'

'That's very kind of you,' Biren said. 'But I managed with this,' he held up the rag, 'and my trousers. They're interchangeable as you can see.'

Father John laughed. He waved Biren off, latched the gate and went on his way.

Kalol Mondal turned to Bhola. 'The padre didn't say hello to *us*,' he said resentfully.

'Because he doesn't see us. None of them do. Know the fucker in the car?'

Kalol Mondal shrugged. 'No, and I don't care. Probably a professor,' he said, and didn't know why he did.

'*Professor*?' Bhola laughed, holding his sides to exaggerate his mirth. 'Uni kichu professor noi! Which respectable professor would put his hand on his student's cheek and keep it there?'

'What do you mean?'

'I've seen him do that with the Bose girl. Three, four times.'

Kalol Mondal felt his heart shoved rudely aside.

'He drops her here,' continued Bhola, watching him from under his eyelids. 'Late in the evening. Never at her doorstep, though. A professor, a *respectable* one would go up and have tea with her parents.'

Kalol Mondal was silent. His mind was racing.

'I can find out who he is,' Bhola said, with another sly glance. 'What will you give me if I do?'

Kalol Mondal bared his teeth in a semblance of a grin. 'A promise not to beat you into a pulp.' He gave Bhola's head a powerful whack as a token incentive.

'Late again, Dona! Where do you go?'

'Oh, here and there, Baba.'

'That's not an answer. What do you do at this time?'

'Oh this and that.'

'Of course, I am only your father so I should not be asking at all.'

'Oof! Stop it, Baba!' She bounded across and hugged him.

Naturally he hugged her back. 'I worry about you, shona.'

'I know, Baba. Ummm, Baba. About the lipstick I want—remember? Cherry Brandy?'

'Your mother needs a new saucepan, Dona. Remind me next month.'

'Oof, I have to ask you twenty times for anything!'

'Good. Otherwise you will never talk to me.' He smiled and took out his wallet. 'Alright, how much?'

'Thirty. I won't worry you again, I promise.' She huffed on his ear. 'Not for lipstick,' she murmured, and smothered a giggle.

His heart lurched. Sometimes he was so flooded with love he felt he would drown. He feared *she* would drown. In his love. Why is it he always feared for her and not for Tuli? As if his love made her more vulnerable to the world, while his relative indifference to his son protected him. He sighed. It was so wrong, so unnatural.

'She takes advantage of you,' Rimi grumbled.

'I'm here for that only,' he said simply.

23

Kalol Mondal stood in the door of the smoky kitchen, watching his sister knead dough. 'If you were a girl what would you think of me?'

'*If* I were a girl?'

'If you weren't my sister.'

'I'd think you were a fool.' His sister's head jerked up. 'Are you—you're interested in a girl!'

'No, I'm not.'

'*Ma*! Laltu has a girlfriend!'

Snatching up the rolling pin he muttered that if she didn't shut up... She burst out laughing. 'You want to get married! *Ma*! Laltu wants to...'

He leapt across, pressed a hand on her mouth, and pushed hard. 'Stop screeching, you, or I'll...' She went limp. He let go of her.

She resumed slapping the dough, grinning all over her face in that horrid way she had. 'So who's the girl who's won my handsome brother's heart?'

'Chup re!' He lunged at her again. She balled herself, hiding her face behind her arm.

Without thinking, or because she was faceless, he lowered his guard. 'There's no one in this dump anyway.'

The unsavoury glint was back in her eyes. 'Oho, so it's a *city* girl! *That's* why I heard you practising your English in the mirror. *Hellooo! What eez your name?*'

His hands itched to strangle her. He controlled himself. He would just be squeezing a balloon—she would pop up in another place. 'There's a reason for that,' he said, with chilly dignity. '*You* won't understand. You understand nothing but how to make chapattis.'

Thankfully that distracted her. She gave the dough a powerful whack—and kept whacking it as she spoke. 'Go eat somewhere else. I'm not making these. For *you*.'

'I've come all the way *only* to eat them,' he wheedled.

'You think I enjoy this, hanh? I also want to go to the city. But will I be allowed to?'

'I'm moving to a bigger place soon. Then you can come and stay with me.' He didn't mean it of course, and she knew that, but it served to deflate the tension. 'I'm getting a new job,' he continued. 'In a big showroom. As a salesman. That's why I need English.'

'Oh? What has that got to do with *girls*?'

He cursed under his breath. He would have to lie if she asked what he was selling. Even she wouldn't believe that women, far less girls, frequented paint showrooms. He was told at the interview, in fact, that he would be dealing with tough contractors negotiating kickbacks for large orders.

She sprang up and siezed his face. 'You're lying. People come to buy, not talk to you.'

'That's all *you* know.' He swept his hand around the tiny, smoky kitchen, knocking down one of the pots responsible for her ignorance. 'You have to talk to sell.'

After she had screamed at him, she said, 'I'll tell Ma to get ready for a bohu. Or won't *she* come here?'

Laughter pursued him all the way to the front door. 'Arrey, dharao! Tell us her name at least!'

He walked down the road, ignoring his mother's shrill pleas. Come back, Laltu! Your sister says sorry! I have made you dhokar dalna! And mangsho...! Laltu!

*Eat this, Laltu, drink that. And, when will you come again? Can you give me some money? I need, your father needs...*All his visits home were the same. If not for the food... He quickened his step to overcome the temptation to go back. (Grand gestures have a disproportionately short time span.) He could imagine what would follow. 'Do you remember Mithu, Laltu? She's grown into such a pretty girl. Just see her—that's all I ask! You don't have to say yes or no.'

He railed again at his stupidity. He'd also provided free entertainment to the town. The publicity agent he'd unwittingly engaged, his fool sister, would be at it even now—announcing her news up and down the streets, gathering friends and family around her. Cousins, aunts, grandmothers!

He got into the waiting train, found a compartment that was comparatively less full, told the passengers to move up, move, can't you hear? After one look at him, they complied.

They pulled out, undisturbed by any last-minute remorse from his family, expressed in the form of a tiffin box thrust into the window. He sank back, a disillusioned man.

The train crawled over the sun-baked land, stopping at every shack and signpost that passed for a station. Every rock and bush too, he thought. A dog could keep pace with it. Yet the carriage shook and swayed, throwing its passengers into a state of intimacy enjoyed only by lovers and the parents of small wriggly children. Lulled by the vacant landscape, the high unchanging skies, and the rhythm of the wheels grinding down the ancient tracks, he fell asleep.

A fly feeding on his nose woke him and alerted him to the cessation of airflow. The train was suspended over an expanse of cowpats. It was a dried riverbed. White heat shimmered over the seamed flats and the browning fields in the distance. What a place! But for the chance visit of his uncle, he would have been stuck here forever. But for chance he would never have seen *her*. How crucial, how capricious, chance was! What were his chances now that he had directed that foolish little man—her *father*—to Rabin Pal? Rabin Pal's land deals were far from straight. The one with her father was no exception. He slapped at the fly that had returned, surprising a baby into a thin wail.

He scowled at the baby. If her family was paupered by the deal they would have to move from J. Mullick Road to a cheaper place. If all went well, they would go away to their new place. Either way it would end badly. He had engineered his own downfall! Fool, fool, fool, that he was! He sprang up, hit his head on the plank above, and flopped down, cursing.

Perhaps he wasn't the fool here. *People who trust so*

blindly have only themselves to blame. A sensible man would have checked his facts. As for getting scared of me, that was a sign of weakness, wasn't it? Although there may not have been a choice there. Most people fear me. (He smirked.) *Maybe he's afraid his daughter will run away with me.* (He smirked some more.)

The train was pulling into Howrah station when he had a stroke of inspiration.

She didn't have to move from J Mullick Road at all! *He* could move in when the family left. (Rents for those old flats were very low.) *That* was the twist in this plot. *That* was the destiny he would write for them.

He jumped down lightly and ran to the exit.

~

Vinu was working at his motorbike, testing the brakes.

'Ki brand, tomar machine-r?' asked Kalol Mondal, rolling his shoulders under his tight T-shirt.

Vinu adjusted the side view mirror—a quarter inch, tightened the cap of the petrol tank—an eight of a turn. *He's nervous,* thought Kalol Mondal, his lip curling.

Vinu flung himself over the seat and gave the starter a mighty kick. Jerking a thumb at the lettering emblazoned on the belly of his bike, 'Read,' he said, and roared off.

A black cloud of exhaust settled on Kalol Mondal. Cursing, he stomped off.

Nobody's Dog charged into his path. It rolled over, and, in a further gesture of goodwill, displayed its splendidly engorged gonads.

Kalol Mondal lashed out with his foot. 'DDT,' he hissed, pumping an imaginary spray gun at it. The dog got to its feet and wagged its tail. Either it had forgotten its recent punishment or was philosophical about the realities of street life.

Stamping his foot on the ground, '*Get out* you fokker,' snarled Kalol Mondal.

The gang was gathered as usual around the carrom board under the old peepul tree. As usual, they swooped on him as if they hadn't seen him in years. He looked at them with exasperated affection. It had been exactly twenty-four hours since they'd met.

'I haven't won the World Cup,' he said.

They reset the board to accommodate him, even giving him the first strike. After all that fuss, he annoyed them with some very erratic shots, compounding the offence by overturning the board when they cursed him out.

Dipu understood what the problem was. Drawing Kalol Mondal aside, 'Malancho Talkies jabe?' he whispered. '*Naughty Neeta*, night show.'

Kalol Mondal shook his head. The thought of watching a pornographic movie made him feel slightly ill.

'Let's go eat dinner then,' said Bhola craftily, 'Mutton biryani khabe?'

Kalol Mondal's stomach rumbled. 'Well...'

'At Aminia's. Kababs, Kalol. Tandoori chicken.'

'Thik achhe. Chol.'

Raja jumped. The others pumped their fists in the air. They had got their man.

Zakharia Street was iridescent after a recent downpour, and buzzing in the run-up to Eid. Merchandise for the festival overflowed into the pavement—embroidered kurtas, sequinned slippers, velvet skullcaps, lengths of satin and silk and gauze... The dome of the great Nakhoda Mosque rose over the muddle, shops clinging to the building's sides like barnacles to a rock. Charred kababs spiced the warm, humid air. There were queues outside every restaurant and crowds around the dozens of pavement food stalls. Every one of them would be sold out within the hour. Anyone with a tandoor and a saucepan would make a killing that evening.

Kalol Mondal picked up a piece of seviyyan from a tray and chewed it moodily. Rainwater dripped down his neck from the awning. Should he have come here? He wanted to, so very much, but should such want, that is, desire, direct one's actions? Shouldn't it be a higher purpose? Such as improving himself, becoming more her kind? To sacrifice one's miserable wants to such an ideal would be a fine thing.

His dilemma was that any sacrifice he made was pointless if she wasn't there to appreciate it. And if she didn't share his life one day. Yet if he *didn't,* there was no hope for him at all. Like anyone who's had a hard life, he hated waste of any kind. He also hated making a wrong decision, even if it was as trivial as picking a bad movie.

There was a large, disorderly crowd at Aminia's entrance. His friends hung back, intimidated, but Kalol Mondal elbowed his way through it, ignoring angry protests and retaliatory shoves. Marching straight to the pay desk he got a table—and plenty of ill will from Aminia.

The biryani was better than last year's—a unanimous declaration they made every year. But his enjoyment of it was marred by his doubts. The Chief had promised him a new job. Would that achieve his present purpose? Or would it turn out to be a cruel awakening—that nothing changed for people like him?

Spectacles! They made you look scholarly and somehow, respectable. Plain lenses of course, his eyesight was perfect. But she was a spirited girl. He wanted to attract her, not bore her.

Moustache! A dashing moustache could offset the spectacles. He had to go away, though, to grow it. How long would it take—a month?

He couldn't leave her unattended for a month! He had to keep her in his sights, else something terrible might happen in his absence. An accident—or she might run away with that Vinu fellow! Of course there was no logic to this, except that a watched pot never boils. And even that wasn't entirely logical because the pot will eventually boil—he had verified this as a boy. It only seemed longer. *That* he could believe. The wait for his goal was already feeling like eternity. He looked gloomily around him as if it was all already a thing of the past.

A scooter! A scooter was the very vehicle of change he needed. A scooter was status, image, convenience, and ways and means, all rolled in one. He would 'accidentally' pass her bus stop—picking a really hot day, and she was alone—and offer her a lift. Naturally, she would refuse. He would be surprised and disappointed if she didn't. That was not the way of 'good' girls. He would have to try a few times before, with extreme reluctance, she accepted. The plot was scripted by those who knew how such stories should end. In every movie, the brave boy got the beautiful girl. But a new employer would not loan him money for a scooter. Neither would a bank. He would have to borrow. From a moneylender? It wasn't a happy proposition. That lot had nasty ways to deal with people who reneged. The bloodied face, the broken legs. The body in the ditch... And once the word was out about the scooter, it was only a matter of days before the letters from home would start. *The house needs repairs, Laltu. Your father has pain in his knees. I am getting old, Laltu. A maid to help me...Your sister has to be married and they are asking for a refrigerator, a television, a scooter...*

He bit into a chilli. It bit back with surprising vindictiveness.

'Ki holo, Kalol? Not liking the food? Too spicy?'

'Na, rey,' Kalol Mondal said, wiping his nose with the back of his hand. 'It's very good.'

'Bhery good. What, you've become angrez now? Forgotten your language?'

Kalol Mondal dealt the offender a rebuke that made him cough up a partially masticated potato.

His friends had long abandoned the useless aluminium spoons supplied by Aminia's and were delving into the food, dripping it on each other. Raja was twitching a leg from the chicken carcass—with his left hand!

And now he was leaning towards Kalol Mondal and offering it to him, the oil running down his wrist.

Kalol Mondal shook his head, gesturing *he* should eat it, but Raja pushed the leg into his mouth. The fool would pay for the meal too, he thought, exasperated. Blowing up two days' earnings on it.

He would have to give him up. All of them. They, the only ones he didn't have to chase, and with whom he could be himself!

He flung an arm around Raja's shoulder. 'Cholo, order ice-cream! My treat!'

'Fully happy, eh, Kalol?'

She wouldn't be taken in by the spectacles and moustache. Even if she was, you would live in constant fear she would tire of you and leave you.

So it came to this: luck overlooking you, or luck running out on you (literally). Not to have tried at all would doom you to a lifetime of regret, and to have enjoyed it briefly would damn you to a lifetime of longing. It says much about you , though, that you are willing to punish yourself so. In effect, you're too worthy of her in spirit, and not in the material sense. What a riddle.

'Ki holo, Kalol? Stomach ache?'

'Na, rey. I'm alright.'

'Arre, he is in another world today. Where, Kalol?'

'He's dreaming of girls, taito?'

'*One* girl. Forget her, rey! She has eyes only for that Vinu fellow!'

'That puppy,' said Kalol Mondal contemptuously. 'I can beat him to a pulp with one hand.' He leaned back, locking his arms behind his chair. His pectoral muscles stretched his T-shirt.

Raja patted the globular chest. 'Eta ki, Kalol? This looks like a *girl's*!'

Kalol Mondal quivered as if touched with an electric needle. Bhola made a snorting noise into his glass. Dipu guffawed.

'Where is that ice-cream?' said Kalol Mondal, smiling with his teeth. Then he put his arm on the table and waggled his fingers at Raja. 'Chol, Raja. Ekta match kheli.'

'Okay,' said Raja readily.

The others cheered. Kalol Mondal was their champion arm wrestler. Raja was next best.

After a minute Raja's eyes began bulging. After another minute he looked ready to pass out.

'Chhede din, Kalol,' murmured Bhola. 'You win.'

'Tui champion rey, Kalol,' Raja said, massaging his arm.

Just as he was beginning to relax, Kalol Mondal dashed the ice cream cup from his hand, seized his wrist, and twisted it.

Raja screamed.

Kalol Mondal slammed some money on the table and left.

An hour later, when Dona got home, Kalol Mondal was lounging on the bollard outside her entrance. She hesitated only for a few seconds before going up to him.

~

'You're a crazy one, rey,' Nini scolded. 'Which girl would say, "No more presents for me?" to a guy like that?' She proceeded to enumerate all the dangers her friend had opened herself to.

'Something just got into me,' Dona said dismally.

'*Everyone* says that when they do something stupid.' There was a smug note in her voice that made Dona bang down the receiver.

What she didn't tell Nini was that she had compounded her crime by kicking up a heel in the flirtatious way that Biren told her was provocative.

~

Kalol Mondal stared at Dona's retreating back. Did she really want another present? Had she smiled at him? He walked to Aroma to ponder it over cream toast and tea. Cream and sugar having a naturally calming effect—hallucinatory when consumed with strong tea—he fell into a happy daydream. He wasn't a bit riled when Aroma asked who the girl was. Because being teased about 'a girl' made her more of a reality.

Later, when he passed her building a faint, unfamiliar strain of music wafted down to him from her balcony. English music. In another world, another age, he would have scoffed at it as he did at anything he didn't understand. But now the cacophony seemed sophisticated—and unfathomable.

What more would he have to learn to like? To *learn* first?

English. He needed to learn it properly, not in the incompetent way his teachers had taught them, *not* taught them, in fact, because it was the master's language, that no self-respecting, free-thinking Bengali should adopt. We have been fooled, he thought now bitterly. We are still slaves—to those who know English.

He had walked all the way up to Diamond Harbour Road. And there, in the corner, he found his solution. Above the horseshoe entrance to St Teresa's porch hung the message for the week: *I am the way and the truth and the life.* The illuminated notice board invited everyone to the special evening mass at 7.30 on Sunday. Pencilled below that was a postscript in Bengali, announcing free English classes in the parish hall. Anyone interested was to enquire at the office for details, or to speak to Father John before 10 any morning.

Months later, Father John was to tell him what he had seen was a sign, not just a signboard.

Next day, Father John glimpsed a youth walking into the church from the window of his office. A prospective student of English? Or a putative soul to be saved? ABC or C of E? Technically it was C of NI (for Church of North India) but C of NI didn't have rhythm. Poetry over piety, he thought. In a rare gesture of flippancy he tossed a coin

Before he could see which it was, Kalol Mondal was knocking on the door.

24

On Tuesday evening, Biren returned to the studio after yoga to find his room had been invaded. Violated. Defiled. How would you feel, he asked a crow perched on the window ledge, if a fly had drowned in your beer while you had gone for a pee?

He threw his keys on the desk and continued gathering proof.

His pencil studies of the National Museum had been moved to the right of the desk. The shoelace that marked the page in his novel was gone. So was the ancient Fevicol tube—which still had two squeezes. But a defunct marking pen, a windshield wiper and a paperknife were lined up with the precision of a surgical tray. Curiously, the four porcelain tiles that served as paperweights, usually stacked on his table, were tumbled on the windowsill.

They weren't tumbled. They were *arranged*. In an asymmetric spiral. It was an attempt at artistry.

Manu would never move anything in his room. Much less make forays into art. He knew he would be courting dismissal if he touched Biren's desk—and Manu valued his job.

He tapped out a cigarette and yanked open the top drawer for the matches. It fell out. Someone had freed it from jamming. Now he was seriously angry.

He rifled through bills, bank statements, tax receipts, and found the letter. It had been refolded.

Taking long, deep breaths, he smoothed it out on his desk.

My dear Biren,

Hey and howdy!

At last I've managed to put pen to paper—a formidable feat at my age. For want of time—dinner's nigh—I am obliged to make this letter shorter than I would wish. I write chiefly to enclose a piece of communication from yr cricket coaching camp, meant for speedy action. So hurry and respond if you wish to out-bat the Nawab of Pataudi. Unless you aim to be the new Charles Atlas. Bodes ill for my biceps when we spar! How is your tennis? I hope you're getting your first serves in. I heard from your mother that you are becoming an expert with Maggi noodles. Wish I were there to partake of the feasts cooked by you! Huzzah Anatole!

Exit the lighter vein. Are you keeping up with your grades in Physics and Math? How about Chemistry? Your last letter was excellently drafted. I'm glad they're teaching you some English.

I too missed you at my 75th. Friends and relatives have deluged me with—among other things—books that they would have me read. Not a single gun or a veiled lady in the lot! Hardly fit for your poor old grandfather's addling brains! I will keep them for YOU to read one day.

Do write me a letter—a long one—after you finish your

homework, of course. Good luck in your term tests. Needless to say I'm rooting for you. Courage friend, the devil is dead!
    With love and good wishes,
    Yours affly,
    Dadu

~

The knock came at 5 p.m.

He didn't return her smile when he waved her into a chair.

'It's very dark in here,' she faltered.

He reached behind himself to switch on a light.

'And hot.'

He turned up the fan's speed.

'Say something!'

'What did you expect to find, Dona? Secrets? There *are* none.'

She drew back, a little frightened.

He blew a smoke ring and watched till it vapourized, writhing, before sending up another dervish.

'Don't you think I'm entitled to some privacy?'

'I just wanted to know you better!'

'And do you now?'

'No...o. Except that you're very untidy. This is a,' she cast about, 'a junkyard!'

'It's a studio, not an ice-cream parlour.'

She got up but not, as he expected, to leave.

She had stopped at the typewriter. 'This is rusted.' It was a complaint, not an observation. 'There's not a single pretty thing,' she continued. 'I suppose your home is also filled with junk.'

'My home is quite empty actually. I decided long ago I wasn't going to be a curator.'

'Obviously. You're an *architect*, not a doctor.'

He chuckled.

'You know something? Howard Roark's office would have been like this.'

He groaned.

The childish cheeks drooped. 'I don't understand what you have against him.'

'He's a caricature, not a person. Plus I find overweening ambition insufferable.' Would she recognize him in this malediction? 'I suppose you imagine yourself as his love interest—whatshername, the striptease artist with a fetish for unwashed men...hey, where are you going?'

He was out of his chair in a flash but she was already out of the door.

Unfortunately for her, the furniture prevented a dignified exit. She had to wriggle through it, and her wiggle was too gauche for art. Her hips were not art either, but they were receding—and fast.

He didn't want her to leave. In fact, he was frantic at the prospect.

'Dona! Come back! I was joking!' He dashed back to his desk, rummaged in a drawer, found what he wanted and charged out again. 'Look, I have something for you!'

She faltered. After a heart-stopping moment she retraced her steps, dedicating each one to an imaginary ramp, her expression aping a fashion model's vacuous disdain, but, again, her body let her down.

He grinned to himself. She was so easily lured. And with such modest bait! He kept a stock of gewgaws for her in his desk the way a horse trainer keeps sugar in his pocket. Enamelled mirror, papier-mâché box, jewelled hairpin...

'Come skipping down the path next time,' he said. 'Scattering roses.'

She was busy examining her new keychain. 'It's pretty.'

'Good. Now sit down.'

She pouted. 'Give me *one* reason why I should.'

'Because I'm an old man who hasn't got much to cheer about. And you're a kind-hearted girl who spares the time to amuse him.'

'You're not old. Although you have grey hair. And you have wrinkles.'

He laughed, although the merciless scrutiny made him want to run for cover.

She leaned over—her collar yawning helplessly. Allowing him a peek down her blouse.

Oh, my enfeebled heart!

She was touching the stain on his cheek with a fingertip. 'Does this hurt? Itch? Is it...infectious?'

'It's a discoloration, not a disease.'

'I'm sorry,' she said in a small voice. 'I didn't mean to upset you.' She brightened. 'You could grow a beard over it.'

He smiled at her. 'It's okay, Dona. I don't mind. I've lived with it all my life.'

'*I* don't mind either. In fact, it makes you look...' She narrowed her eyes. 'Distinguished,' she said a little breathlessly. 'Wait, let me take these off.' She reached for his glasses. His nose was inches from her breasts—*oh, my heart*!

'That's better. You look younger.' She wagged her finger at him. 'You have to *think* young, you know.'

'My memory would have to be recalibrated.' He retrieved his glasses. 'Have you seen soda bottles with marble stoppers? Cigarettes sold in a tin? Have you drunk a Coke? Ridden in a Pullman coach—do you *know* what a Pullman is? Or a bioscope?'

'No!' she cried, laughing. 'I don't know what you're talking about. Those things don't exist!'

'True. Most things exist only at an experiential level.'

'That's intense,' she said, her eyes swimming up at him. 'I like intensity in people. It's a sign of intelligence.' She twisted a lock of hair round her finger. 'My Dida says too-intelligent people get burnt. I'm in no danger, fortunately.'

She was quoting him! His mouth twitched. 'That established, can you get your bottom off my drawing?'

She jumped down, crumpling the drawing. Wincing, he retrieved and smoothed it out.

'Oof,' she said, and, 'Baap rey! Look at the *time*!'

'Daddy waiting for you with a stopwatch, eh?'

She giggled.

'Post adolescence, parents *are* a bit of a joke, aren't they?'

He stopped smiling. She wasn't a post-adolescent yet.

'He's been worse since this Kalol Mondal business.' A shadow crossed her face.

'I thought that's now in the family archives.'

She twisted the shoulder strap of her bag. 'He still hangs around our building. He scares me.'

'*Scares* you? How?'

'He has this horrible stare. And he follows me. At least he seems to be wherever I am. He thinks I don't notice but I do. He asked me *twice* for the time. And he has a watch too.'

He stifled a laugh. 'The poor mutt has a crush on you. All those romantic poor-boy-meets-rich-girl movies have given him ideas. Be warned. They all have a happily-ever-after ending.'

'It's not funny.'

'No, I agree it's annoying. But hardly scary. Come on, Dona, you're a spunky girl.'

'It's nothing to do with what *I* am. It's how *they* are. Men.' She passed a limp wrist over her forehead.

'What, it's *men* now, is it? Why, you cruel little coquette, you!'

No sooner did the words leave his mouth than he regretted them. He caught her waistband. 'No, don't go Dona...'

She jerked away. Her satchel slammed him in the ribs. He doubled up.

When he straightened up he saw she had buried her face in her hands.

His head was behaving in a most unpleasant way. 'Dona. I'm sorry. I truly am.'

'You aren't sorry,' she said in a muffled voice.

'Try me.' Her chest was rising and falling. It was agreeably, dizzyingly distracting.

'If you have to *try* you're not.'

'Believe me, then.'

'Why would I?'

The absurd exchange could carry on all evening if he allowed it. 'Well, have it your way,' he was saying when she dropped her hands.

'You make fun of people. People not as clever as you. Me, my father. We're a joke for you.' Moisture dotted her forehead, beading the filaments of down like dew on grass. 'Our house is too.'

He came to with a start of disappointment. Was this what it was all about?

'You made Baba believe you would build it.'

Irritation flared in him. It was gone in an instant—replaced by a powerful desire to wipe off the dew. 'Then I have much to answer for, haven't I? You see, Dona, it isn't that simple...' He stopped.

She was smiling, a sardonic smile. *His* smile. 'No, *you* see, Biren, *I'm* not that simple, although you think I am. That's why you like being with me, isn't it? I make you feel bigger, better, smarter. No, put away your keys. I'll take a bus home.'

This time her exit was stately, even elegiac. The furniture made way for her.

At the door she made a partial turn. 'Grow a beard,' she said. 'It will give you something to do.'

He chuckled hollowly.

He knew, with the same sense of inevitability that had shadowed their every meeting, that she would not return. His certitude was established by the lack of artifice in those hips.

Upon her departure the studio felt lightless, purposeless. Bleak as a nightclub at noon. He returned to his desk, stopping on the way to collect a glass and bottle from the tea-making table. The fierce rush of warmth made him dizzy. He put down his glass and staggered to his drafting table.

There was the drawing on which her pert little bottom had rested. And there your glasses, that she'd tugged off. And here (he touched his cheek) is where she touched you. And this, your hand that...

You have no right to, no business to, no call to...

But you didn't! You won't! You can't...

You lie loudest when you lie to yourself. Which begs the question: Can anyone ever take control of their destiny? I mean, does destiny come with a rudder?

Three-fourths into his third drink, he peeled and ate an egg. Her cheeks, her neck, the underside of her arms. *Stop.* The yolky, yeasty, secret scent of her when she... *Stop. Stop right there. Don't beat yourself. Ask not for whom her heart beats, it's not for thee.*

Paranoia, delusion, obsession...it's all there. You certainly have come into your own. You're so lost you can't find your bearings in a matchbox. The only meaningful relationship you're capable of is with a *brick*. Your closest friends are a draughtsman stricken by his tongue and a doctor stricken by his conscience.

The rum clawed his throat. He staggered to the window and rested his head on the windowpane. The city was blurred, like a page held too close to the eyes. It was unnaturally silent too. Rothko said silence is so accurate. Perhaps, but this silence is Hell's sabbath.

When he opened his eyes, he was arcing across the sky, hooked to a crane. The landscape changed from burnt hulls and tar pits to shining steel, radiant glass. Now he was going backwards in time, high, not on a crane, but the magic weed. He was back in his college canteen, changing the world.

An architect is as good as the buildings he builds. Not what he doodles. You don't draw to relieve an itch or fill a void or get something off your back. Writers, painters do that. You have to *build*.

You don't have much time left, you know. Only from now until you dement. Or moult. Or degenerate. Or die. And time moves like a cat in the dark. Soon you'll not even have dreams to salvage.

He tilted his throat back to finish his drink, and felt his neck click. Groaning, he slid to the floor.

The marble, like the cheek of a faithless mistress, offered cold comfort. Black and white squares sped away, vanishing to a pinpoint. A one-point perspective. Funnel vision. That's what you have.

You want a foxhole. The little man wants a house. And she? What does *she* want? A glass palace?

But in the *wetlands*? Going against every grain of your beliefs, your principles?

You've already gone back on them. She's *seventeen*, you degenerate bastard.

So it's not *morality* we're talking about here.

What is it then? *Charity*?

At 1 a.m. he heaved himself up, stumbled to his desk and dragged the telephone to him. He spun the dial. Nothing happened. He spun it again, thinking, I'm just the croupier anyway.

The rings went on and on, enclosing the silent room in tighter and tighter circles.

At last the phone was answered. The voice at the other end was hesitant, fearful of some disaster, at this hour.

'Bose! Is that you, Bose? *BOSE*! I'll do it, Bose! I'll do it, damn you!'

25

The dial tone shrilled in Pinaki's ear. He continued to stand in the semi-dark, holding the receiver.

'Is anything wrong, Baba?'

It was Tuli's voice, but it was Dona who stood at the door, looking so anxious he wanted to hug her.

He replaced the receiver on the cradle. 'It was a wrong number, shona. Wrong number,' he told his mother, peeping over his daughter's shoulder. 'Wrong number, wrong number!' he sang as he walked back to his room.

'Some drunk,' he mumbled, pulling the sheet over his head.

'Oof,' said Rimi. She yanked the sheet back. 'I hope you gave him a piece of your mind.'

'Oh, yes. He won't call again.'

He lay motionless, although a hundred birds were flapping in his chest. *Yes, I'm building a house. I have commissioned an architect to design it. He doesn't do houses—too small for him—but he made an exception for me. Yes, he will be expensive but it is once in a lifetime, so one should go for the best.*

'Eijey! You hit my *nose*! And you are talking in your sleep!'

He sprang down from the bus and trod air all the way to his office. He was still floating when he made his way down Free School Street at the end of the day. So euphoric was he that he forgot to knock on Biren Roy's door.

He leapt across the room and grabbed Biren Roy's hand with both his. 'I don't know how to thank you, sir!'

'Don't attempt to then, Bose. If you must, then with banknotes.'

'It is a miracle!'

'Let's not overdo it, alright? And you can stop waving that briefcase at me. I know it only contains your lunchbox. Now go away, if you don't mind.'

'I thought you would like to meet me, sir.'

'No, I do not. I have a hangover.'

'Oh. I thought we could discuss...'

'No discussions. I want to repine.'

'No problem, sir. I can wait till you finish your prayers.'

Biren Roy chuckled, and then groaned.

'Can I ask what made you change your mind, sir?'

'No, Bose, you may not. And if you continue to sit there like a praying mantis I will swat you.'

'Haha. I had given up hope! Now thanks to you I can...'

'Please.' Biren Roy covered his ears. 'The trumpets are deafening me.'

'What? Where...?'

'Angels' trumpets, Bose.'

Pinaki smiled indulgently. 'You aren't feeling well, I think so.'

Biren Roy had covered his eyes with his hand. 'The light, Bose. It's blinding mine eyes.'

'Oh?' Pinaki glanced at the twilit window.

'Divine light.' Biren Roy sighed. 'It blinds men to the truth about themselves.'

'I knew that from the beginning, sir. I knew you're a god-fearing man.'

Biren Roy raised his head. 'I always wondered what that meant.'

'It means you will never harm anybody.'

'Except myself. So I must be possessed by the devil.'

Pinaki laughed. 'Good joke, sir.'

Biren Roy went to the tea table. Without consulting Pinaki he spooned Nescafe and sugar into two mugs, poured lukewarm water from the kettle, and handed Pinaki one of them.

Pinaki looked at the cloudy liquid. 'Thank you sir,' he muttered. Holding it to his chest he followed Biren Roy to the window. Together they contemplated the single flaccid cloud that hung in the parchment yellow sky.

Pinaki brought the mug to his mouth, lost heart, lowered it. 'Can you...is it possible to do the design by next week, sir?'

'No, Bose, it's not.'

'But it is a small house!'

'Small spaces are harder to work with. You can't let yourself *go*. Have you tried fucking...making love on a bunk bed?'

'Dona wanted a bunk bed,' gabbled Pinaki. 'With a ladder. When she was a little girl.' He hurried to the tea table, put down the mug. 'Mustn't miss my bus!'

Halfway down the stairs he ground to a halt. He hadn't arranged with Biren Roy to visit his plot! He retraced his steps.

'You scuttled off,' Biren Roy said accusingly.

Slender ropes of steel lashed sky to earth. Lightning ripped the sky. *Abnormal weather,* reported the Alipore Met Dept. (Although abnormality was the norm at this time of year.) *Cyclones are pounding the Coromandel Coast all the way up to the Bay of Bengal. Expect the storms to continue for two more days.* Meanwhile enjoy the thrills, muttered Biren, as he negotiated the car through the water-logged streets. Rain and the traffic had slowed their journey out of the city. The last stretch looked like a garbage bag burst open and dragged along. Lean-to sheds, dilapidated shacks, strafed walls, sagging fencing... Stretches of faceless structures interspersed with straggles of grassland. Everything that could break—railings, culverts, signposts—was broken. Grime impartially coated everything. Now and then, sizzling blue arcs from welder's torches gave artistic expression to the city's substratum industry.

'How is it possible there isn't a single exception to this parade of horrors, Bose? Not even by accident?'

'Don't you like Calcutta, sir?'

'I want to screw it out of existence so I must do, I suppose. Just think. A dozen Calcutta monsoons and even Paris would become Angkor Wat. But we haven't gone under. That's something, isn't it? We are the ones who make the city, Bose. A sad truth and an ironical boast.'

An undifferentiated greyness prevailed over the landscape. Only the lookout shelters were visible. Pinaki was staring at the road as if, Biren thought, keeping it in his sights would keep them on it. In a funk as usual and as much fun as a rock. Probably wishing he was home and dry. Biren debated pointing out this *was* home, or would be some day, and decided he wouldn't tease him. Fortunately there were no traces of him in the daughter. And fortunately too she had none of the awful mother. There was no accounting for how nature metes out rewards and punishments.

A gargantuan wave spattered the windscreen with mud. The car stalled, bucked. Ferocious revving dug the tyres deeper into the mud. 'Stuck in a rut,' Biren said, switching off the engine. 'There's a message there for me, I expect. *Someone* is always sending me a message. I ignore them all, of course. Only way.'

The rain continued to batter the metal carapace. Water had seeped in and was lapping at their feet. Far from the life-affirming element it had become a threat. At least a nuisance.

'You might have to think house*boat*, not house, Bose.'

In that moment sheet lightning swept across the sky, unveiling the countryside. Pinaki pointed through the window. 'I think it's over there, sir! My land! There were trees just like those.'

Four trees were bobbing on the horizon, like heads over a wall.

'We passed many trees *just like those*, Bose.'

'There was that electric pole also, I think so.'

'You're such a poor liar.'

Mist rose from the doused earth. Heat wrapped them like a poultice. The car reeked of decaying rubber.

Pinaki stared at the single light blinking on the dashboard, as if it was his only assurance they might, after all, survive this 'I'm sorry about your car,' he said in a small voice.

'Well, it would help if you cheered up a little. Your sighs are fogging up the windshield.'

Pinaki cleared his throat. 'There wasn't so much water last time.'

'There you go again, Bose. Water is what defines this place.'

Pinaki looked sheepish. 'Rabin Pal says there is fox and antelope,' he said tentatively.

'As far as I know there's only monkey and mongoose. Grass snakes.'

'He says it is virgin soil.'

'Well, rice has been planted here since time immemorial. But what do I know? *I* don't own land here...what the... hey!'

Ignoring Biren's warning Pinaki opened the door. 'That's the lake!' He sounded both strangled and exalted, like the first note of a violin in a concert. Then he was off, shielding his head with his hands.

It was hard to tell with so much water around. But a duck and two geese were floating on it and an egret was standing in a stricken pose in the middle of the expanse. Also they could hear the synchronized croaking of frogs, sounding like the diseased lungs of an entire sanatorium.

Pinaki began stamping around as if trying out new shoes. 'This is it! My land! I remember that tree!'

'Don't start that again,' Biren groaned.

'That's the village!' In the far distance four tiled roofs pitched and tossed in the wind.

'Right. I believe you. That established, can we leave?'

Pinaki stood on, swaying like a windsock.

'Let's *go*, Bose! Help me get the car out of this.'

A querulous grumble rose as they heaved at it. Underneath, a cat was dismembering a field rat.

'At least someone's having a good day,' Biren commented.

The sky was still sputtering but there was a luminous cloud to mark the sun. The landscape reflected the runny monsoon light. Somehow they retraced their way back to the bypass.

Biren thought he'd never been so glad in his life to see a chai stall. 'I had hoped your plot would be on the edge of wetlands,' he said, after they ordered tea. 'Where the city ends. It would have sidestepped the moral dilemma—literally. This, alas, is well inside. I don't know what you were thinking of, Bose.' *I don't know what I am either.*

'A bagan badi. Maane, a garden house.'

'*Country* house.'

'Yes. People build those for weekends. Holidays.'

'You mean you'll spend all your savings on a place for Sunday picnics? You do have grand ideas!'

'It is also for my retirement, sir. Transportation won't matter.'

26

At 11 a.m. the next day Biren parked his car in the lane outside the Calcutta Club. As expected, he found Mr Deb in the reading room, behind an old copy of *Punch*.

'How's the heart doing, sir?'

Mr Deb smote his chest. 'All tickety-boo!'

Biren grinned. All his father's friends spoke as if popping corn in their mouths. Mr Deb reached for his stick. 'If you want to chat, Biren, let's get out of here. That old codger is already giving us the eye.'

The view from the long veranda had stayed unchanged

since Biren had ran around in it in rompers. Outside it was a lawn like a billiard table, edged with canna lilies and a tangle of bougainvillea. Gardeners squatted on the grass, tweezing out invisible weeds. From behind the bougainvillea came the pock-pock sound of ball-on-racquet.

'This isn't anything to do with your father's um, political ambitions? I hear he has expansionist plans—wants to be President here too...sandwich? There's Marmite—they keep a jar especially for me. No? Right, then, ham it is. And tea, bearer. Darjeeling, please. So then, young fellow, what did you want to see me about?'

Mr Deb's cloudy old eyes had lost none of the power that had once sent his juniors scuttling. 'I don't understand how land was transacted there in the first place, Biren,' he said. 'It's highly irregular. Even if, as you suggest, the villagers were coerced to sell by the land mafia. And no, no concessions have been made in the area. The water treatment plant was a hasty, ill-conceived proposal by the kind of people who think a shopping mall in the Taj Mahal is a great idea. There's a stay on it from the High Court. *You* should know—you were quite vocal in your objections to the fishbone fertilizer facility. And *that* was a development initiative.'

Biren poked at the abject slice of lemon clinging to the side of his teacup. He wished the teacup contained something stronger than the tepid brew, or that there was a flowerpot nearby for its discreet disposal. He looked up. 'If the city is to expand, then planned growth is better than encroachment with the messy aftermath of court cases. And fait accompli by the government—mutatis mutandis. For example, the Watermark Apartments was built on a pond and then passed as *reclaimed* land.'

Mr Deb was looking askance at him. Realizing his gaffe—Mr Deb had briefly been the Environment Secretary—Biren apologized. 'I meant nothing personal, sir. I do understand bureaucrats are powerless against the machinations of politicians...' Another gaffe! 'I imagine there are exigencies, um, mitigating circumstances.' He was floundering now. 'I mean, outside your control.'

Mr Deb looked as if only decency prevented him from telling him what he thought of his comments. 'You seem quite au fait with the functioning of the state,' he said dryly. He brushed the crumbs from his chest and called for the bill book. Scribbling in it, he said, 'For a while you had me thinking you were lobbying for change. Not looking for an exemption to build this house.'

'I wanted to check if the guidelines had changed, sir,' Biren said, wooden-faced.

'They haven't and they won't. I am disappointed, Biren. I didn't think you'd put self-interest before professional ethics.'

Biren thought of all the rejoinders he would never make. Such as, self-interest was the defining principle of all existence, and the working principle of all institutions. And that Mr Deb's concern for the wetlands was also, in part, self-interest. The wetlands, like the rainforests, were an internationally recognized phenomenon and Mr Deb would like to be on the side of the gods. You couldn't suggest to him that it was time we developed our own sensibilities, based on our realities and needs. You couldn't appeal to his nationalism. He loved Marmite! What else did he cling to—*Gentleman's Relish*? The politics of Mr Deb and his kind was traditionally colonial with a tint of socialism, like the angostura in their gin-and-tonic.

'...in any case I can't help you. I'm toothless now. Hardly visit Writers'. Nobody there I know.' There was a noticeable tinge of resentment in the words. Mr Deb had experienced the hard seat of a waiting room.

'I would never ask you to go out of your way, sir.'

Mr Deb's features softened. He patted Biren's hand. 'You're

one of us, Biren. And I know you'll do the right thing.' Winding his scarf around his neck, he said, 'You know the depressing thing about getting old? Besides sneezing with every draught? There is nothing you can do about it.'

'I thought it was realizing you can't dodge the law of averages.'

Mr Deb laughed, and adjusted the scarf. 'Of course the upside is that nothing matters as it used to.' Biren went round to pull out his chair. 'Thanks. We go back such a long way, Biren.' His eyes glazed. 'Your dear mother used to be the toast of the 300. And Firpo's. We were all quite smitten. She'd sit at the bar and smoke Sobranies.' A triangle of his tongue showed between his teeth.

Biren looked away.

~

Dr Murray folded his arms and studied him over his glasses. 'I don't know what to say, Biren. I had you down as a maverick whose worldview is informed by um, unswerving self-belief...'

'Thanks!'

'Underpinned by pig-headedness ...'

'Oh, come on!'

'But I thought it was anchored in principles.'

'It's a small house, Doc. It won't dent the landscape.'

'I didn't realize how easy it is to shift a moral centre.'

~

Dona called Biren in the evening. '...that is, if you would *like* to,' she said, breathily. It was the first time she had initiated a date. The reason was obvious, of course, so he wouldn't deceive himself there. Pinaki had told her his news.

He pretended to consider. 'Let me see... I *could* be free after six o'clock.' Really, he was too old to be playing these games.

As reward for taking the initiative (motivated by self-interest, but still), he suggested the coffee shop on Pretoria Street that they had never gone back to after that first aborted attempt.

She was delighted. 'They have twelve kinds of coffee now. Including one with chocolate chips.'

He shuddered. No doubt the infernal Nini had recommended it.

Sure enough, 'Nini said it's very good,' she said. 'Can you pick me up from home today? I'm not going to music class.'

Did he have a choice?

Her nose was nuzzling his neck. She was going to kiss him!

It took all his willpower to keep his hands on the steering wheel.

He was under no illusion it would be but a short reprieve. Sooner or later he would have to do something else—learn a new trick—before she grew bored with him. Ironically it was what she had accused *him* of on their first meeting. Boredom. She was an attentive pupil. He understood why Pinaki feared for her.

'I was telling Nini about it,' she said, tucking her skirt under her legs. 'I'm so...o excited! Baba said it's going to be a garden house!'

'Country house,' Biren corrected. 'Unless you're thinking of a tool shed at the bottom of the garden.'

'*Country* house.' She bounced up. 'That sounds grand.'

The café was one of those places that pass off shoddy finishes as chic. Misaligned column and beam, cracks in the plaster, wires draped like entrails in a slaughter house... A ham trying to do character, he thought. The act had evidently found its target market.

'Someone should tell them the hippie trail's gone cold,' he remarked. She smiled obligingly but didn't look up from her menu.

The lighting was bright and intense, but flat and chilling like the visitors' room in a prison.

'Do you suppose they'll sound a siren at closing time?' he murmured. All at once he felt depressed. His instinctive—and confrontational—engagement with his surroundings, his inability to ignore them, diminished him. In the way garrulity is a symptom of loneliness and insecurity, this habit was a symptom of his frustration with his practice. It is a devious conceit, he thought morosely, to think that the minutiae and the mundane trivialize lesser people but *your* eye for detail saves planes from crashing.

'Tropical Spice,' she announced. 'It's sweetened with grape molasses.'

'How odd. It was exactly what I thought you would like.'

How she glowed! She was a natural for light while he stalked darkness. She was gazed at her coffee—cinnamon and cocoa riding the foam in thick, misshapen earthenware cups—as if she couldn't believe her luck.

'Lovely,' she sighed. 'Have a bite?' She proffered a cutlet on a fork.

He looked at its heavy, arctic coat of breadcrumbs and its corsage of sauce—orange, glutinous, of doubtful origin. To eat it struck him as an absurd idea. 'I'm not hungry, Dona.' He lit a cigarette and sat back. And bumped heads with the person behind him. He drew his chair in. The clinking and clatter, the smell of coffee and frying, evoked the dining cars on the train journeys to and from boarding school.

She was watching him over her cup. 'I feel sorry for you, Biren. You always seem so preoccupied. And restless. As if you want to do *something*—but can't.'

'Do something about what?'

She dunked her nose in the cup, giving herself a beige moustache. Wiping it off she said, 'About things not being, or going the way you would wish, I suppose.'

'Do they ever?'

'You can't fight everything and everybody, Biren. You'll be the loser.'

He caught a glimpse of the mother she would be one day— and was amused and dismayed at the ache that caused him.

'Biren! Don't *stare* at me like that.' She wriggled and tugged at her shirt (pale blue spotted voile), which reminded him of the terrifyingly self-possessed little girls who came to his childhood birthday parties.

'You look very nice, Dona.'

'You look very surprised, Biren.' She put out her tongue to show him the sugar cube she was sucking on.

'Lovely... Tell me, Dona. Where would you have gone this evening if not for me?'

She crunched up the sugar (he winced). 'My friends are seeing *Aaj Kal* at Roxy.'

'Would you have liked to go too?'

Two slow, very slow, heartbeats went by before she shook her head. Her *no* was a little too emphatic.

He blew out smoke to hide his disappointment. Then he smiled. 'There's a Persian word—I forget it—which means refusing something you wish for. A sort of formal politeness, you might call it.'

'Like a lie? A white lie?'

'Hiding behind the truth is closer,' he said, through a fug of gathering depression. 'The truth in this instance is you would have preferred to go to Roxy.'

'No, the truth is I would have liked to go to the Tolly.' There was an edge to her voice. When he didn't reply she said, 'That's the problem with this relationship, isn't it?'

The problem with this relationship, Dona, is that there's sand in its foundation.

His throat constricted. Was she tiring of him?

She was looking at him. 'We won't ever go there, will we?'

When he didn't answer, 'I'll tell you why,' she said, in a tight voice. 'Because I'm not your type.'

Thankfully not, he thought. Actually, you're not any type— not yet. Or as much of a type as a blob of protoplasm. And that's fine too. Protoplasm is not a bird of prey.

'No, you're not,' he said—fatally.

Her face blanked out. 'I've changed my mind about the movie,' she said, sliding the strap of her bag off the chair. 'I want to join my friends.'

He lost his temper. Pushing away his half-finished cup, 'Next time think twice before dragging me to places like this,' he said.

'*If* there's a next time.'

'What the hell do you mean by that, Dona? You want to end this?'

She drew back, frightened. 'Yes!'

Yes? After all you've exacted from me, you little ingrate! Time, emotion, principles, my *regard*...

'Would you like to go to the Tolly?' he asked, in desperation. 'Pancakes? Mushroom toast?' He would rue the offer, but it was his only trump card.

'No.' She scrambled up. Before he could stop her she was gone, ingested by the crowd.

He motioned to the waiter for the bill. Forget her, he muttered. But he could sooner do that than forget Calcutta. She *was* Calcutta. Difficult and frustrating, *impossible*, but dreadfully addictive.

~

'Biren Roy, isn't it?' A car door slammed and a man was walking up to him, holding out his hand. 'What an unexpected pleasure! Do you remember me? We met at the IIA seminar on the Hoogly Riverfront Development about, um, six years ago.'

'Sorry. I have no recollection at all.'

'Manosh Dey,' said Manosh Dey, smiling with his lips pressed together. 'You disappeared after the second session. Before my talk.'

'Ah. I hope you don't hold that against me.'

'You spoke to some of us during the coffee break. We got late going back.'

'I hope you don't hold that against me as well.'

'No, no! It was the most memorable part of the evening!' Manosh Dey smiled his closed-mouth smile again.

The man had something to hide, Biren thought. His teeth? A forked tongue?

'Where have you been?'

'Around,' said Biren, restive now. 'Now if you'll excuse me...'

'Practicing your theory of enoughness, no doubt! You brought it up remember? As a design philosophy.'

Biren looked at him hard. He appeared quite sincere.

'You made a pun about drawing the line. I often quote it. You also spoke about minimalism—the danger of minimizing to the point of vacuity. You wanted to write a book, *More on Less...* Did you?'

'No,' said Biren shortly.

'Then you spoke about introducing the concept of essentialism as a rider to minimalism. And then I asked,' he gave a self-conscious cough, 'since truth is the essence of design isn't it an essential too? And you said yes, but unfortunately truth is not incorruptible. Because truth is subjective.'

Biren frowned. What was the fellow talking about? And why had he bought into it? 'I really must...'

'No, don't go please! Not before I tell you how much I admire the staff quarters you designed for the Silver Cloud Tea Estate. I think it is your best work, sir.'

Biren smiled bleakly. There's nothing more demoralizing than to be told that your best work was done twenty years ago. Especially if whatever you've done since is unrecorded history.

But Manosh Dey was brimming with friendliness. He meant it as a compliment. '...fractals, the floating roof, the composite walls!' Biren was beginning to feel like the proverbial wedding guest. He shifted his feet. Manosh Dey moved in swiftly. 'You were quite famous for it!'

'A fame with the product lifecycle of a strawberry flavoured detergent,' Biren said dryly.

Manosh Dey was delighted. 'Good to find your humour is intact, Mr Roy! I saw you coming out of there,' he continued, tipping his chin at the building. 'I wonder if you know I designed it?'

'No. But I'm not surprised.'

'I would so appreciate a critique. Your honest opinion.'

That translates to *your approval*, Biren thought. Actually, *your high praise*. Well, here is my *honest* opinion. Your building is, in effect, a vertical extension—and horizontal spread—of the dismal post-independence walk-ups built for low-ranking government employees. Flanked by two of the few great houses left in Calcutta. Where is your context, man? Where are your sensibilities?

Of course your opinion doesn't count. Because you have not built a project of this significance. The sorry truth is you had competed for it, a fact that will not be mentioned of course, although it is buzzing around your head like an angry bee.

Manosh Dey was ravishing his work with his eyes.

'It's quite a display of musculature,' Biren said. 'A jock pumping iron.'

'Amazing you should say that! I consider it my most masculine building.'

'Excuse me, but I really must run now.'

'Can I give you a lift?' Manosh Dey indicated a brand-new Contessa, looking, among the shabby Fiats and Ambassadors, like a lady in crinoline.

Enough. *Enough*. 'Thank you, but I have a car,' Biren said.

27

Just as suddenly as it had blown in, the cyclone blew out. There was a quickening in the air, as of a refrigerator door opened in a steamy kitchen, a hopeful blue seeped into the grey-white sky, the first chrysanthemums appeared in florists' windows, and one morning the city woke to winter. That is, the cool season. Winter, more a concept and a promise here, just meant you didn't have to engage with the weather in battle mode.

Biren celebrated the change with a detour through Southern Avenue. A longer route into town, but it was a pleasure to drive at least one kilometre without having to change gears, even if the labyrinth of lanes that was his regular route offered more interesting sights. The biodiversity of a tide pool, say, compared to that of a fast-moving stream. Pleased with this analogy, he whistled a bar of song.

Pollarded bauhinia trees stood in the narrow park dividing the avenue, frail and wraithlike in the weak sunshine. Whorls of gold—recently shed leaves—wheeled along the curb in the slipstream of the car. He wanted to reach out to the trees. Gather them in his arms, ravish them, and, well, *enter* them. So beauty did that as well. It fomented lust. At which, and how inevitable this was, she inveigled herself into his consciousness. She was always there anyway—a subcutaneous insert. Her olive eyes, her glassy skin, her giggle, her wiggle. Her predilections... the coffee houses, the gewgaws...

A fearsome honking woke him from his daydream.

The sign on the gatepost said: *Seth Kamal Singhania is pre-occupied.*

The Seth was in a bad mood. 'This Harvard business is costing too much. My son requires a new slide rule every month! He eats them or what? Anything particular you came for, Mr Biren?'

'Well, yes. I was wondering about the hotel project. It's been a longish um, caesura.' When the Seth didn't answer he said (fiddling with a penknife to keep the anxiety from showing), 'Not having second thoughts, I hope?'

'No, no! In fact I was about to send you the brief. Now you can take it yourself. Here.'

'A sealed package? But why?'

The Seth shifted on his chair. 'Actually, Mr Biren, I'm holding a competition for it.' He looked at Biren. 'What do you say to the idea?' he said a little too loudly.

Biren extricated a cigarette to hide his dismay. 'It doesn't always get the best results. You'd be wasting a lot of time and money.'

'No smoking.'

Biren put away the cigarette. 'And you thought of a competition for what reason?'

'Ah, reason.' The Seth twisted his ring. 'You see, Mr Biren, I want the hotel to be showpiece, so...' He cleared his throat unnecessarily and turned his palms up.

'You can't trust me to design it.'

'Not like that, my dear,' said the Seth, wriggling in his chair. 'You see, I felt we are too used to each other.' He paused for a nervous giggle. 'In fact, I think I can read your mind. Just as you can read mine.'

'We could make a pile as fortune tellers if we expanded our custom.' Witter, witter. It's a nervous twitch. 'So the familiarity has bred contempt—yours for me.'

'No, no, Mr Biren. I respect you. You are a very good architect.'

'But not good enough for this project.'

'No, *no*! It is that...' The Seth contorted his body to reach the glass of water on a side table. 'This is a big project, Mr Biren. I have investors for it. I have to consult their wishes also. You understand how it is with such people. They wear Gucci-shuchi, Armani...'

'And I am Bata shoes. I would imagine that you, as the promoter, would have the final say.'

The Seth made an elaborate show of doing up a kurta button near his throat, and then undoing it.

It dawned on Biren that the idea of the competition had not originated with the investors. The Seth had 'arrived' and he wanted it acknowledged in the accepted way. A 'name-brand' architect. Biren wondered who had been commissioned to write his biography, for of course there would be that too. And which hospital would get a new wing named after him.

The Seth had regained his equanimity. 'I am thinking of a different kind of building this time. You see, Mr Biren, you are too modern. Nothing wrong with that, mind you, except it does not have *show*, my dear.'

'Not true, Sethji. What about your porch? It's obscenely showy.'

'*I* designed that.'

'*What*?'

The Seth's mouth turned down. 'I guided you. Otherwise you would have produced a factory-type box. I want something outside the box now.' He chuckled at his witticism. 'This building has to be more...'

'Sexy?'

The Seth drew in his shoulders. 'It seems you are not serious, Mr Biren.'

'Oh, I am. I was just trying to read your mind and kind of lost my way.'

'Not serious.'

'I feel a bit let down, Sethji. Perhaps I presumed too much on our long association and mutual respect, and, I daresay, your appreciation of my work—a misguided conceit, I'm beginning to realize now.'

The Seth shifted uneasily. 'It is because of long association that I am doing this.' He adjusted his shawl. 'You see, Mr Biren, I am also finding it a bit difficult to work with you. You are very good, very clever, but you are a little bit...rigid. A little bit intolerant also. A little bit,' he hesitated, 'arrogant. Sometimes.'

'And all the little bits add up.'

'You always want your own way, my dear.'

Biren rubbed his cheek. Was it his paranoia or was the Seth actually easing him out of the project? He felt an overpowering need for a walk. A swim. Something brisk and bracing—far, far away from this room.

'You've seen the work of these others, I suppose? Assuming you didn't pull the names out of a hat. Which you may as well have done.'

The Seth gave Biren a beaky stare. 'I have seen.'

Biren began to feel as if a part of him had detached from the main body. He recognized the curious symptom. It didn't augur well. It usually preceded a bout of meanness. Some bad emotion, typically self-destructive.

'That means nothing actually,' he said. (The Seth's face hardened.) Indicating a painting behind the Seth's desk, 'I haven't seen that before,' he said. 'Who's the jungle queen?'

'You know very well she is Durga,' the Seth said stiffly. 'It is a Hussein.'

'She must be worth the GDP of a medium-sized African country then. Since you are feeling rich...'

'I settled your bill.'

'...we could build my prototype cabin for migrant labour...'

'I am not running charity.'

'What *do* they do to you people? Remove your conscience with your tonsils?'

The Seth stared Biren down. 'Having conscience will not change the world,'

'Useful philosophy, Sethji. The image of starving children won't give you indigestion.'

The Seth got up and walked out.

Biren sat at his desk, massaging his forehead. Behind it, a knot of worms coiled and uncoiled. For years you had waited for something like this. For *decades*... It was in danger of becoming a bloody refrain. He spun around on his chair and hit the wall with his fist. '*Aaarghh*!'

'Imagine the poor fool who believes he's won the lottery only to find he read the three as an eight.' His lips twisted in a smile. 'You don't have to imagine him, Manu. You're looking at him.'

Manu made a small clicking noise, as if a baby chick was lodged in the back of his throat.

'The Seth's project is a competition. Given our success rate in winning competitions...'

The chick began drowning in saliva.

'Exactly. We should hold off ordering the foundation stone. It's a dream brief, by the way.'

The site was an audacious (inspired!) pick. It was a row of abandoned warehouses, in a state of picturesque—spectacular—disrepair, on the Strand, an arterial road along the east bank of the Hoogly pounded all day long by trucks and state transport buses. A scenic site was rewarding, a historic one was challenging but this concurrence of scenic, historic, idiosyncratic, was as rare as a murder in a cathedral.

He had always wanted to work with those warehouses. That raw brickwork! The fallen arches! The cast-iron columns! As sexy projects went, this was a bodice ripper!

Later that evening his father called. Without any preliminaries, he said. 'Well, Biren. I've done it. Transferred the capital to your account.'

After a brief silence, 'Are you sure?' Biren asked stupidly.

'Well, I spent five days thinking about it.'

'And sleepless nights too?'

'...my last few medical tests weren't too encouraging.'

'I'm sorry to hear that.'

'Happens. Life. Have to sign off sometime. Well. Anyway. Perhaps this is as good a moment as any to tell you the one quality I appreciate about you. You won't stand down.'

Biren's cigarette had burned down to the tip. In the scramble to put it out he missed some of his father's speech, coming in when he said, '...the courage of your convictions. Pride. And integrity. You get that from me, I daresay.'

'Isn't that a bit selfish? To appropriate so much of me? Leave something for Ma.'

His father laughed sadly. 'I'll leave that for you to decide.'

28

Saturday afternoon Pinaki found Biren Roy on Free School Street, buying cigarettes. 'I went to check my land again, sir.'

'In case Rabin Pal has rolled it up and sold it as carpeting?'

Pinaki laughed dutifully. Then it occurred to him Biren Roy may not have been entirely joking. He appeared anxious—he was smoking a cigarette in rapid little puffs. Touched by this concern and also to reassure himself (by now Pinaki was quite confused who he was defending), he said, 'It is as before.'

But Biren Roy's attention had wandered off to a pavement stall. 'Cellophane butterflies. That's a new one.'

Pinaki picked up a small motorcycle made of coloured wire. 'Nice for my son, no?'

'Well, for all of the two minutes that I saw him, he didn't strike me as retarded.'

A lengthy haggling followed before Pinaki and the vendor agreed on a price. 'Now something for Dona,' he said, diving down again. After much deliberation he chose a small wine glass filled with a jelly-like substance. He held up a red one and a green, unable to decide.

'Oh, buy the red—if you must. She would prefer it to green.'

'That is correct...but how do *you* know?'

Biren Roy shrugged. 'What on earth would she do with it anyway?'

'Put it on her desk,' Pinaki said. 'For fun. She is still a child, you see.' He began a second involved negotiation. After he finished, he straightened up. 'We can go now, sir.'

But Biren Roy had gone. Pinaki stood there for a while longer hugging his packages and wondering at the sudden desertion, and trying not to feel hurt by it. Then he set off for his bus stop.

Aroma was arranging biscuits in a glass bottle, in an artistic spiral. Flanking the bottle was a tray of bright orange jalebis, attracting flies and the sticky gaze of urchins. A straw basket of samosas sat on the floor. Tea steamed away on a primus stove in the corner. Pinaki sighed. How foolishly he'd thrown away this uncomplicated life! How impossible to get it back! He bolted his tea in a single despairing gulp.

'Have a sandesh with your tea, Bosebabu,' Aroma said. 'You look weak these days... No, no,' he waved away Pinaki's purse.

Pinaki was deeply moved. How kind people were! Good days like this were hard to come by. Most days the tram broke down, or there was a long queue at the fish stall, or the milk was burnt in the office tea. Sometimes these misfortunes struck together. On those days it didn't help to remind himself he had shoes *and* feet. Even his two perfect children weren't a comfort. He needed something more substantial. A house to build his dreams on.

'Good evening, Mr Bose! How is every little thing with you?'

'Fine, thank you, Father. I hope you are also fine?'

Father John turned on his serviceable smile. 'Yes, indeed! By the way your young man is coming along nicely. He's a quick learner.'

'Who is that, please?'

'Oh, I'm sorry. I was referring to the youth who gave you that bit of bother. He comes to my English class.'

It took Pinaki a few seconds to understand whom Father John meant. Then, 'He's not my young man,' he stammered. 'He's a...he is nothing to me. He's a loafer.'

Father John clicked his tongue. '*All* human beings are unique in God's eyes, Mr Bose. And created for a divine purpose. Every Saul is a potential Paul. This young man is not bad. Just a little...high-spirited.'

Pinaki ducked his head. I don't care if he's Saul or Paul, he thought, or learning English or French, as long as he doesn't practise it on my daughter.

'You don't look convinced,' said Father John. 'He's striving to better himself, Mr Bose! He has a new job. And he wants to buy a scooter!' He turned to pat a child. 'Hello, little man!'

Pinaki walked away quickly. As if I care what Kalol Mondal does or buys. What was Father John doing anyway, listening to such stories?

Father John wasn't particular whom he talked to. He just liked a cosy chat over tea. Kalol Mondal believed he needed some distraction to drink the horrible stuff.

'What is your life's goal, Mondal?'

'To live in a flat. Like the ones in No 63.' He ducked his head, in case his face should give away his secret. Father John had second sight. *And* he knew the road well.

Sure enough, 'Isn't that where the Boses live?' asked Father John.

Kalol Mondal began gathering the papers scattered on the table. 'Das Engineering Works is on the ground floor,' he muttered.

Fortunately Father John got distracted. 'Leave those alone, Mondal. To live in a flat, *any* flat, is not exactly a *goal*, my friend.'

But for Kalol Mondal it *was*. To get on, one had to get out.

Vinu, standing on the street, lifted his head to the sky, ostensibly to adjust his helmet. Dona, sitting in her balcony, ostensibly studying for a test, was quite aware of his ploy. *Idiot*, she thought. The fat chess pawns made the balustrade as effective as a screen in a harem. She pushed her feet into the gap between two of them. It would kill him to see just her feet, she thought. That restored her good humour—history was *not* her favourite thing, despite what she had told Biren.

Biren. She put down her file of notes and picked up an enamelled vanity mirror (that he'd given her) and gazed into it, turning her chin this way and that. There were two tiny spots on it but they had taken over her entire face.

'Baba, shall I make you tea?'

'No, thank you, shona. But go look on your desk. I have left a surprise for you.'

She picked up the wine glass, turned it around, and then held it up to the light, biting her thumbnail. *What does Baba think I'm going to do with this?*

She returned to Pinaki's room. 'It looks exactly like wine!' She pretended to drink it, throwing her head back, and reeling afterwards. He laughed with her. Red had been the right choice, he thought contentedly.

~

'So what is the great man's daaknam? Your friend, philosopher and guide?'

'He doesn't have one, Rimi.'

'Of course he wouldn't. Gods don't.'

'He doesn't because he refused to answer to it. When he was *two* years old! Defied his mother, imagine!'

'Tatey ki?'

'Well, it just goes to show, doesn't it?'

'What? That he was arrogant even then? Oof. What you see in that man I don't know.'

What *he* makes me see, Rimi. The moon moving the boats on the Hoogly. The sun speared on St Andrew's steeple. Lightning stitching the clouds. (Stitching, not splitting, Rimi!) *Light is drama, Bose. Light is a live thing!*

'He makes you think, Rimi.' *You think space is emptiness, Bose? A void, right? Wrong. Space is a shape. An entity. Space is the subtext in a building. A building decodes space. Space defines shape just as silence defines music.*

'The things he says, Rimi.' *Shelter is not just a house, Bose. It is a cave, a nest, a mousehole, an anthill. A beehive, mollusc, hell, a sewer pipe, an oil drum... A house is just a formal delineation of spaces, with the conceits of civilization, a cultural context, and rules made over time. And continued without question. Think now: Why should a door be 3 feet wide? And the lintel 7 feet high? What are these standards when we don't come in standard sizes? Is everyone a Vitruvian man?*

Pinaki couldn't answer that. But he was pleased to be asked. It meant he had, in some way, qualified.

'That man makes me believe, Rimi. Believe that things will happen—good things. That he'll make them happen.'

Of course she paid no attention to any of this. The feelings and opinions of a cytoplasm in a paramecium are not of consequence to the host body.

~

Dona went back to the balcony. Before resuming her homework, she peeped out. Vinu & Bike had gone but Kalol Mondal & Book were there. Perched on the culvert, he was moving a finger over the page. Her lip curled. He was pretending to read, of course. He was doing that a lot these days.

She grinned to herself. Pulling her hair out of its clip, she leaned over the balustrade. 'Ei, shono! Uparey dekho! Over here!'

His head jerked up. A slow joy spread over his face. He jumped up, spilling his book, and waved to her.

She swallowed her laughter. 'Make me a special,' she cried. 'Double chillies, double onions! Extra mustard oil, okay?'

He spun around. The muriwala was standing behind him.

When she went down to get her cone of muri, Kalol Mondal was frowning at his book.

~

'He offered to pay for my muri, can you believe it?' she reported to Nini. 'Who does he think he is? I said, excuse me, I don't accept things from all and sundry!'

'Well, you did ask him why he didn't buy you any more presents.'

~

What did she mean, thought Kalol Mondal, by all and *sundry*? Was sundry a type of person? A *good-for-nothing* maybe? Aroma's incendiary chutney brought the sweat spurting on his brow. He drank a glass of water, threw a coin on the counter and staggered out. Father John would know what it meant.

Halfway to St Teresa's he changed his mind. Father John would probe him for the context of the word, and winkle out his secret. Father John had a way of getting you to talk. Why, the other day he found himself confessing to him that he liked to read *those* magazines, which Father John, surprisingly, knew all about. You'd think his profession would have shielded him from the coarser aspects of life.

Thoughtfully he made his way to Saraswati Books & Stationers.

It wasn't exactly *good-for-nothing* but the inference wasn't any better. As he replaced the dictionary on the shelf, it occurred to him the term could find an application in the larger context of his life. His friends were all and sundry. So were his neighbours. The Party members. Rabin Pal's clients definitely qualified as all and sundry. *She* was the only one outside this sordid circle.

29

Biren was on his way to show the Seth the preliminary design. It wasn't ethical, of course—this was a competition—but *this is wartime,* he thought, clenching his jaw. It was hard to forgive his perfidious client.

The lobby, an atrium, he had called the Agora as a nod to the Seth's Eurocentricity. The facilities—shops, bar, lounge, banquet and spa—were stacked along the parabolic whorl around the Agora in an adaptation of his favourite Archimedean spiral. A tower for the guestrooms broke through the old roof, topped by a glass dome with the roof sliced transversely. The bar and restaurant. From here the city lights, river life, the shifting mood of the sky would be experienced as through a kaleidoscope.

How much of architecture is viewed in metaphors! Egg crate, cliffs, dunes, sails... Mediaeval man, standing in a forest, observing the sun slanting through latticed branches, thought of a celestial heaven, and sought to describe it in stone. Now, when you visit York Minster—soaring stone trees, lacy fan vaulting, the sun streaming through clerestory windows—you think *forest.*

The Seth was not pleased to see him. 'You didn't phone you were coming, Mr Biren.'

'I was just passing by,' Biren said, borrowing a line from Pinaki.

The Seth raised his eyebrows. His mansion was in a

cul-de-sac that required six complicated moves to park. 'Sherbet?'

Biren felt it would be imprudent to refuse. Without thinking, he lifted a Lladro horse from the table.

'Careful, Mr Biren, I paid a lot for that.'

Biren put the horse down and reached for his hip pocket. 'No smoking.'

Biren pushed down the cigarette packet and took out his handkerchief—a greyish rag that had been recently commissioned to wipe rubber solution. He used it now to polish his glasses. Without effect.

'You come for specific purpose, Mr Biren?'

'Actually, yes. I want to show you the sketches I've done for your hotel.'

'It's against competition rules.'

'Yes, I know.' Biren opened the folder he had brought. 'But I thought I'd take the liberty with you. Anyway since when have *you* been so worried by rules?' He heard a sharp intake of breath. Filling his own lungs, he traced a line on the blueprint with his finger. 'Now, if you just orient yourself to the Strand...'

'Not just now, Mr Biren...'

'...retain the original brickwork and pop the new floors through the roof in a three-sided shaft. That would give the guestrooms a view of the river and one of the city...'

'Another day, Mr...'

'...shops, offices and gymnasium contained within...'

'There you are! Come in, come in!'

Biren looked up, annoyed.

The Seth was waving at the door. Glancing at Biren he said, 'I think so you know each other?'

'We are old friends!' said Manosh Dey in a cheerful shout. He bounded up and shook hands—pumping, thought Biren, fit to fill a tanker. His thoughts were whirling. Extricating his hand, he murmured, 'I don't know whether I'm coming in or going out.'

'A nice surprise, Mr Roy,' said Manosh Dey, beaming.

Biren caught the gleam of teeth and felt he had been let into a secret. 'It certainly is a surprise. I didn't know you were one of the competitors.'

'Competitors?' faltered Manosh Dey. He looked at the Seth. Biren looked at the Seth.

The Seth looked at the door. 'Ah! You've brought the model!' Biren turned. Two minions were staggering in with a building model, which they deposited on a table.

He made certain disagreeable calculations. 'I see,' he said, through stiff lips. 'There is no competition.'

'I changed my mind,' said the Seth. He had assumed a nonchalant expression, but his eyes were darting all over the room.

Biren had a peculiar sense of being outnumbered. 'I suppose it isn't unreasonable to ask you why?'

The Seth lifted his arm to summon a minion. His white kurta sleeve fluttered like a truce flag. Accepting the glass of green liquid rushed to him, he said, 'Mr Manosh will be a refreshing change.'

'You speak as though he's a seaside,' said Biren. His self-control snapped. 'I suppose it didn't occur to you to inform me of your decision before I wasted my...'

The Seth put down his drink with an exaggerated twist of his torso. Patting his upper lip, he said, 'I will compensate you for your time, Mr Biren. Of course, they're not *finished* drawings.'

Biren smiled through his pain. Some things never changed.

'...you enjoy designing. You always said that is what gave you most pleasure. In fact, you are collecting your projects to publish like an art book.'

'I say a damn sight too much,' muttered Biren. Then, since Manosh Dey was fidgeting with his collar, and the Seth had dunked his nose into his glass, he turned to examine the model.

'Let me explain,' Manosh Dey said, starting forward. He tapped a block that dominated the layout. 'This houses the facilities—bar, gym, sauna. And this is the restaurant and food court...'

Biren only half-heard the rest of it. He was flipping through a folder of drawings. It was dawning on him why he was eased out of the project. 'It's a sleight of hand,' he murmured. 'But easy enough to decode.'

Manosh Dey stared. 'Decode what?'

'The project's ultimate objective.'

'Ultimate...?'

Biren regarded him with dislike. Surely the fellow wasn't so thick that he didn't realize reading drawings for him was like reading Mother Goose for kindergarten teachers. He shook out a cigarette. 'A lobby big enough—and ugly enough, I daresay—to park a fleet of tankers, and with north lighting, a ridiculously large restaurant—an indoor badminton court— why? It looks like a factory. It *is* a factory. Potentially. In a commercial zone.'

'Excuse me?'

The Seth stopped kissing his glass. '*No* smoking, Mr Biren.'

'This is less poisonous than agarbattis.'

'Kindly respect the rules in my house, Mr Biren.'

Biren studied the tip of his cigarette for a moment before grinding it on the floor with his shoe.

'Coitus interruptus. It's the story of my life.'

Manosh Dey chuckled uneasily. 'Mr Singhania said you would be the project advisor, Mr Roy. It would be a privilege for me to...'

'Mr Singhania takes too much upon himself.'

'Your inputs would be invaluable, sir.'

'You don't need them, Dey.'

Manosh Dey gave him a feeble smile. Looking at the Seth he said, 'I will take your leave, Mr Singhania. We will meet again—at a more convenient time.'

'Tomorrow,' said the Seth, in no uncertain tone.

Manosh Dey turned to Biren. His handshake fervent with relief. 'I'm counting on you, Mr Roy.'

But he didn't specify for what, and Biren didn't ask. His thoughts were spiralling. Telescoped into the moment were the long years of his association with the Seth, the exasperations, the frustrations, the arguments, the *fun*. For all his idiosyncrasies and bullying and stinginess and craftiness, the old man was a sport. There was also his trust. His simple, tacit trust. ('It appears quite scientific, Mr Biren.') His willingness to experiment. ('Do it, Mr Biren. *Someone* has to be guinea pig.') And to forgive. ('Don't worry, Mr Biren. There is next time.') We were a team! We were an act!

The Seth was staring at him. His eyes were two holes in a sheet of parchment.

'Alright, I admit I overstepped,' said Biren. But penitence was not in his lexicon. Nor in his psyche.

From his expression the Seth thought so too. 'You made a serious allegation, Mr Biren.' He began slamming papers on his desk as if he was attacking a jumpy fly.

'Come on, Sethji, you know I don't mean half what I say.' But I did mean this. I believe it, in the way Creationism is believed even if God is not an established truth—at least not an indefensible fact.

The Seth banged down a paperweight. 'You sounded very sure.'

'I was upset. I was a little...surprised.' I was devastated.

'Even so,' said the Seth. His face was tight with anger. 'You insulted me. And Mr Manosh's design...'

'Don't build it.'

'What?'

'Save your project.'

'From Manosh Dey?'

This so exactly echoed Biren's thought he almost said yes. 'From the city, if you will.' It was a cool evening but his skin felt clammy. 'Sethji,' he said hoarsely. 'Please. Listen to me.'

'Let go of my arm!'

Biren sank back. 'You said think out of the box. That building *is* a box. A vertical coffin with a façade like, like mattress ticking. A waffle iron. There's no...clear concept, no originality.' To his horror he was choking. 'No...vision.'

'I suppose yours is unique?'

'I won't pretend it's not.'

'You mean I will have no choice but to agree that it is.'

'Yes,' Biren said simply. 'It is interesting and it is beautiful. It is...' He thought hard. 'It is a building I can see in design journals.'

'You won't,' said the Seth. 'Because you won't be building it.' He drank the rest of his poisonous brew.

In a fair and just world, Biren thought, the Seth would keel over, writhing. The Seth seemed rejuvenated. In fact his face looked like a raisin plumping up in water. He sat back, patting his stomach. 'Mr Manosh's Semco Tower won first prize in Asian Paints contest. It has been compared to Windsor Castle.'

'You know what, Sethji? You're the worst kind of snob. An ignorant one. Your cultural pretensions wouldn't impress a middle-school dropout.'

'You're a bad loser, Mr Biren.'

Biren smiled with his teeth. 'On the contrary. I land on a trampoline every time I fall.'

The silence was pushing him out of his chair but he was too numbed to move. At last, 'You said you'd compensate me for my time,' he said. His face grew hot. It was the kind of thing a child would say after throwing a tantrum—with the childish notion that a fresh outrage would divert a parent into forgetting and forgiving the original offence.

To his astonishment the Seth took out his cheque book.

30

Dona couldn't (wouldn't?) meet Biren. She was busy. She was tired. She had homework. She would call him when she was free (willing?) to meet him.

She didn't call. He did—every day and twice a day, when he knew she would be at home, and answer the phone because her friends called at that hour. What a man will do to appease his, well, to assuage his, to relieve his... Humiliating himself is the least of it. It's the organizing principle of life, isn't it?

If he were thinking straight, he would know this was a sure way to frighten her off. He should intrigue her, not wear her down because, wasn't *intrigue* the mainstay of their affair?

But he wasn't thinking. The scene with the Seth continued to trouble him. Whenever it came back to him he would clap his transistor to his ears with the volume turned up to the maximum.

Then, one day, she did call. To tell him her father had taken to shutting himself up in his room. He wouldn't speak, hardly ate, and, she believed, hardly slept too. 'I'm sure it's something to do with *you*,' she said, in a tone that conveyed that it almost always was. 'Have you said designed our house? Have you *begun* it?'

'I think you should keep out of things you know nothing about.'

She disconnected at once.

For three days that month the city came to a halt. The first shutdown was called by the Left to protest a hike in petroleum prices, the second by the Congress party to protest the Left's burning of a Congress member's shop that had defied the shutdown, and the third was with the connivance of both parties because it was the final day of the third and crucial Test match between India and Pakistan. With the backlog of work after the strikes, Pinaki didn't have time to think of his house, and so was taken by surprise when Biren called him.

It was a short conversation, with none of the baffling banter and elliptical loops and sarcastic undertone that, in a general way, Pinaki had come to expect of Biren Roy. All he said was, 'Come over this evening, Bose.'

To Pinaki it had the ominous significance of a police summons. By the end of the morning his nerves were jangling. Pleading an upset stomach, he left work early.

He stood outside the door, wiping the sweat from his face.

'Don't let I dare not wait upon I would,' Biren Roy said courteously. 'In other words, it might facilitate communication if you,' he mimed shutting the door, 'and,' he indicated the chair across him, 'availed the modest comforts of my little establishment.'

'You wanted to see me, sir?'

'That was the idea. To check if, interim, you have been visited by doubts.'

'I don't understand, sir.'

'Well, I find myself in the awkward situation of having bent my conscience, insofar as I possess one, for what has given me lower returns than junk bonds, and I'm naturally averse to committing another moral transgression, albeit minor in comparison, without the reassurance it will be worth compromising my reputation for. So far,' he sounded bitter, 'I have no reason to be optimistic.'

This only served to establish that Biren Roy was immutably and infuriatingly Biren Roy. Pinaki was annoyed. Why couldn't Biren Roy talk as normal people did? It was so, so rude. Now the furry eyebrows, like an extra pair of eyes, were considering what else to mock him with.

What Biren Roy said next, however, was chillingly comprehensible. 'Are you absolutely sure you want to go ahead with your house?'

'Of course, sir. Why do you ask?'

Biren Roy tapped out a cigarette. 'What about your family?'

Pinaki was puzzled. The family had never been of interest to Biren Roy. In fact, he had implied they posed a hurdle best circumvented. Now he was searching Pinaki's face. What did he expect to find there? And what was Pinaki supposed to answer? 'My family is part of me,' he said.

Biren Roy laughed and struck a match. 'Ah, but are they one with you?' Looking at Pinaki over the flame, 'what do they feel about it?' he asked. And again there was that tension, as if he was waiting to hear—what?

My resolve is being tested, Pinaki thought. If I tell him Rimi is hostile, Ma is worried, Dona is indifferent, he will conclude *I* am wavering. Squeezing his hands between his thighs, 'They are keen, sir,' he said.

Biren Roy blew out the match.

That was the end of the interview.

~

'Been a while since I saw you, Biren. Dare I presume you've been busy with your little man's house?'

Biren propped himself on a support and lit a cigarette, ignoring Dr Murray's disapproval. He thumped the wall. 'We could substitute fibreglass sheets for the asbestos if you wish.'

'That would be nice, Biren. When you have the time.'

Biren twined his fingers through a stethoscope. 'Oh, I have the time, Doc. All the time in the world.' After a pause he said, 'The hotel is off.'

'I'm sorry to hear that. You can devote yourself to the house then. Are you?'

Biren took a long pull at his cigarette, trying not to let his irritation show. 'I'm not sitting with the mice flirting with my toes, you know. I'm rationalizing the design parameters. There are,' he blew a smoke ring, 'some, um, existential conflicts to resolve first.'

'I'm sure there are,' Dr Murray said dryly. 'Philosophers have been doing that for centuries.'

Biren emptied a bottle of pills on the table.

'Leave those pills alone, Biren... So what's your excuse really? It doesn't fit in with your grand plan?'

Biren began popping the pills back into the bottle. 'I'm beginning to question the relevance of my work. Because what difference will it make to the milkman doing his rounds?'

'You know the answer to that better than me, Biren.'

'I don't actually. I thought I did—once.'

'What was its relevance to you—once?'

'*This*. I didn't want to be living in the most dismal place on the map during the most unedifying period of its architectural history—and doing nothing about it.'

'And now you find you're alright with that? Doing nothing?'

Biren slammed the lid on the bottle. 'Yes! *Yes*! And you know why? Because nothing is going to change!'

'You're designing a house, not attempting a new world order.'

'A little house in the sticks, some idiot's delusion...it's *irrelevant*, I tell you!'

'So it *is* the insignificance of the *project* that's getting in your way. Not *your* insignificance in the world order. Biren, you're such a hypocrite.'

'I wish I was,' Biren muttered, turning away. 'It wouldn't be so...hard for me.'

Dr Murray took the bottle from him. 'I wish you weren't so hard on yourself.' He looked at Biren. 'A fellow I knew would only make seven letter words when we played Scrabble. He would keep changing his tiles—missing his turn—waiting for one. By which time the game would be over.' He tossed the pills into a tray. 'After a while nobody would play with him.'

'This is such useful advice.'

'Well, that's your excuse, isn't it? This house is not your seven-letter word.'

'I can't think, I can't *draw*! I'm just doodling! I keep asking myself, *why*? When it gives me no pleasure?'

'You should be asking yourself why you can't draw. Because that's what's causing this crisis, isn't it?'

'Round and round, eh, Doc? I *told* you why not.'

'Please, Biren. You're wearing me down.'

'Don't give up on me, Doc. If you also do...you don't understand how wretched it is to be so, so obsessed.'

'My dear man, isn't wretchedness the fate of all obsessions? When they're not fatal?'

~

'May I come in, sir?'

'Well, you won't be crowding me out.'

'I was hoping...'

'There is no hope for this world, Bose. None at all.'

'Oh. You are alright sir?'

'Going to wrack and ruin, if you must know.'

Pinaki took a sidelong look at the drawing board. He felt suddenly queasy. The sheet pinned on it was the same one he had seen three days ago. He recognized the bearded imp doodled in the corner.

'There's not a lot going on there, but yes, that is more or less your house.'

Pinaki's heart jangled like a Calcutta bus on a Calcutta road.

~

'So will he build you a functional house, Pinakibabu? It will be no consolation to you that your house is beautiful if it lets the rain in. In my experience these *artistic* types are not practical.'

'Well, he knows a lot about buildings. And he is always drawing—something.'

'What does that matter if he will not build your house?'

'He will.'
'When?'

~

Pinaki lay awake that night (again!) thinking the unthinkable. Could it be that Biren Roy was actually incompetent? Perhaps the mocking manner was to make you believe he was what he wasn't? (Or he wasn't what he was?) Anybody who absented himself as frequently as Biren Roy did must have a locked room somewhere.

Pinaki had to unlock it.

'I bought this for you, sir.' Pinaki put an *Inside Outside* magazine on the table. 'Special issue on houses.'

'Very thoughtful of you.' Biren Roy made no move towards the magazine.

'It says a house takes less than a year to build—start to finish.'

'Believe too that Rome was built in a day.'

'But this is not a city.'

'True.' Biren Roy scratched his chin. 'You know Bose, design should have the complexity and elegance of a quadratic equation, the power and purity of a Vedic chant...'

He continued to weave through the thickening mist of Pinaki's comprehension. Their interactions always made Pinaki think of a road roller ironing out a hair ribbon.

'...the hardest part is committing it to the ground. Because then you are tormented by the thought of all the possibilities you haven't explored.'

Pinaki thought the hardest part—inasmuch as there were parts to this enterprise, which seemed to be a single unscalable mountain—was getting Biren Roy to commit his ideas to paper. 'You are a philosopher,' he said, not meaning it as a compliment and not caring it didn't sound like one either.

Biren Roy laughed.

Then Pinaki was angry. He pushed back his chair, roughly, again not caring if it disturbed Biren Roy. In fact, he hoped it did. However, the great man was leaning back in his chair, eyes closed. Philosophizing, Pinaki thought, turning on his heel.

He developed an angry headache, which raged at him all the way to J. Mullick Road, exploding when Aroma offered him a free sandesh again.

'This is the *third* free sandesh you're giving me! First is friendly. Second is kindness. Third is *charity*. Ki bhebecho—you think I am a *poor* man?'

Aroma was so offended he ignored the money Pinaki held out for his tea.

The headache kept him awake all night, easing only slightly with his morning tea. The sight of his colleague's orange Hajj beard brought a fresh—and unreasonable—spell of anger.

'The azaan is getting louder and louder these days!' he exclaimed, flinging down a file. 'These mullahs are out of control!' Oblivious of the chill in his colleague's manner, 'The faithful must be stone deaf,' he continued. 'Or in a coma. That's what my architect says.'

'A word of advice, Pinakibabu,' said the colleague heavily. 'No man, not even a god, should have so much influence over you.' He looked at Pinaki from under his eyelids. 'So how far has the *castle* come?' When Pinaki didn't answer he smiled. 'It is as I suspected. Your architect is befooling you.'

'Pity you didn't come back from your Hajj with faith instead of an orange beard.'

Things weren't better at home either that week. He longed for a chat, pleasantries, for someone to say *something* to him, even if boring, but his family seemed to be cutting an ever-widening circle around him. Admittedly his bad mood was to blame, but if a man can't depend on his family for support where else could he go? Biren Roy?

'I hope I'm not disturbing you, sir.'
    'Not at all. How are you?'
    'Temperature-wise okay, sir. Otherwise, not so good.'
    'Oh dear. Anything I can do?'
    'Design my house?'
    'Give over nagging, Bose. I've started on your house.'
    Pinaki walked to the drawing board. '*This* is my house?'
    'In some circles it would be considered a rather original one.'
    'But it's like a yantra!' Pinaki's hand flew to his mouth.
    But Biren Roy was smiling. 'Why, thank you, Bose!'
    Pinaki turned away. If he remained a moment longer he would, he would ...

'Just a minute, Bose!' Before he knew it Biren Roy was sitting him down and, to his extreme discomfiture, *kneading* his shoulders. 'Perhaps I *do* need something to get the juices flowing. Some stimulus.'
    'Yes, I also think so.'
    'Good! And it seems to me the crucial input I'm missing is your family.'
    'My...family?'
    'Yes. I should meet them.'
    'Why?'
    'To get their um, views, first-hand. You see, Bose, any design, and especially as individualistic as a house, needs a comprehensive understanding of the um, end users. It would speed the process if I didn't have to guess their requirements or rely on your understanding of them.'
    'I see,' Pinaki said faintly, although he didn't. 'When do you want me to bring Rimi here?'
    Biren Roy shuddered. 'Actually, I would like to meet

everyone—and in your home. That way I would get a first-hand idea of, um, their views.' He smiled. 'Don't worry, I don't expect a free run of your house. Just ah, um, a peek.'

Pinaki stared. Why would he want to come all the way for a peek?

'You don't seem too happy, Bose. Don't you want me to come?'

'No, sir, it isn't that...'

But it was. To have Biren Roy see a Puja pandal you were proud of was one thing, but to expose him to the very place you sought to escape? Would you invite a minister of sanitation, assuming there was such a person, to visit your lavatory with its broken toilet seat?

Waiting for the lift, Pinaki wondered how and at what point he'd invited Biren Roy to lunch. He put down this inability to reconstruct that part of the conversation to his routine confusion in his presence.

He trudged down Free School Street, wondering how he'd break the news to Rimi.

As it happened, the opportunity presented itself when he entered his flat. His family was sitting at the dining table over a late tea. From the snatches of conversation he could hear, he gathered they were discussing the new house. At last they were taking an interest in his project!

'*Pink* marble for the thakurghar,' Dida was saying. 'After all, I am there half the day.'

'A *big* kitchen,' Rimi said. 'I'm there *all* day.'

'I spend more time in *my* room than you do in the kitchen,' Dona said.

'Because you sleep all the time. A bed anywhere is enough for *you*.'

'As long as I don't have to share it,' Dona said. 'And it doesn't smell of pee.'

Dida looked stricken.

'I'm going to tell Baba I want a dressing room,' Dona said in the belligerent tone she used when she knew she had transgressed. 'And a bathroom to myself, because Tuli has constipation. All geniuses do.'

'I *read* in the bathroom! It has the best light. All *I* want is a window beside my study table.'

Pinaki had a premonition Tuli's one modest request would cause more trouble than all the others. First, it would be lost in the stampede of demands. Then Biren Roy would forget it (if and when he got round to designing the house), and when he remembered it would be too late.

'...an observatory! With a telescope!'

'You can't have your stupid observatory because *I'm* going to have a dressing room.'

'Dona! Tuli! Your poor Baba doesn't have unlimited funds.'

'Ma can save a lot of money if she didn't go to Daisy every second day.'

'Nobody asked for your advice, Miss.'

'I can give up cricket coaching, Ma.'

'*Sweet* boy.'

'Yow!'

'Ki korcho! Dekhao how red his nose has become!'

'He's your *brother*, Dona!'

'That's not *my* fault.'

Pinaki chose this moment to step in and tell them they could communicate their requirements directly to Biren Roy when he came to lunch on Sunday.

After the furore died down, 'I invited him,' Pinaki said.

'Why? Is he homeless as well as jobless?'

'Don't be silly, Dona,' Pinaki began. Where *did* Biren Roy live? In a forest? Over a garage? With a lopsided balcony and a steep wooden staircase, missing treads? (Pinaki's imagination occasionally took flight, sometimes making it as far as the treetops.) 'He wants to understand your requirements first-hand,' he went on, preening a little.

Dona snorted. 'Of course he will oblige us.'

'Tuli, have you finished packing?' Dida asked hastily.

'Packing for what?' said Pinaki.

Rimi got up. 'Oof! He's only said a hundred times he's going to Bankura tomorrow!'

'It's a field trip, Baba,' Tuli explained. 'I can't decide what to take.'

Dona reached out to pull his ear. 'Take an opium pipe and a toothbrush. That way you won't care if you've forgotten anything, and your friends will still talk to you.'

Pinaki stared at her. Since when had she started talking like this? She sounded like, like *Biren Roy*. The man had an astral reach, it would seem.

31

That same evening, Kalol Mondal let himself into his new home located at the far end of J. Mullick Road, away from his old haunts. The ground floor, occupied by Toppers Coaching Centre (*Efficacious Maths and Accounting Tuition*), lent it dignity. 'I live above the Coaching Centre,' he imagined saying. It implied there was only one coaching centre that counted, and if you didn't know *that* you weren't very educated, were you?

It was a family-type accommodation (as his landlord described it), of three small rooms including a poky kitchen, on the second floor of a three-storied building, canary yellow, green shutters, fanlight over the front door, wrought iron spiral staircase. The last two features he was particularly proud of. He stood on the top rung of the staircase to take in his new surroundings—a patch of scraggly grass, a path of mossy stones and six pots of sickly ferns. Not exactly a place to bring a fair bride to, but perhaps love would thrive here even if the ferns did not?

When you looked out of the windows you were smacked in the face by the unpainted cement wall of a printmaking facility. The cliff-like plainness was unrelieved by graffiti or posters. The silent grey was a perfect background for contemplation, and, as now, a projection screen for his fantasies.

He was indulging his fantasy, though not in the old way that disgusted him now. This one involved touching parts of his body—throat, lips, a cheek, the inside of an arm—feeling his way around, pretending to be a stranger. Pretending to be *her*. Even if the voyage of self-discovery left him somewhat unfulfilled, it was the clean, uplifting hunger of a religious fast. Absently he slid his hand into his pyjamas.

He whipped out his hand. The sacrifices one had to make!

The Chief had told him he had fixed him up as a sales assistant. So far he had filed catalogues (second day) brought coffee for a client (third day), counted paint tins in the warehouse (fourth and fifth days), fixed a broken shelf (sixth day)...

In the second week, when ordered to unload a truck, 'I am a sales trainee,' he said to the supervisor.

'Yes, yes! Now you unload this! Taratari, no time to lose!'

It is funny how you can get swept up in someone's urgency even when you're rebelling against it. To Kalol Mondal, the supervisor's request became a command to lower the lifeboats from a sinking ship. He grabbed a crate that two loaders were struggling with and carried it across the storeroom. He set it down and kicked it for the last couple of feet to show he was only being obliging, only this once. Then he became aware of the hush in the room. Work had stopped. Everybody was gaping at him. Flattered by the attention, he lifted the crate again and, without losing a beat, placed it on the stack.

The supervisor said nothing. But the next morning, he introduced him to the showroom's owner.

The owner had the abstracted air people assume with their inferiors—for fear of being applied to for favours that were, in the general course, irksome. While he spoke he kept twirling his stylish sunglasses. Whether it was to draw attention to them or to his preoccupation with weightier matters than the present, Kalol Mondal couldn't say. But a feeling of resentment swept through him, the origin of which was only partly the sunglasses (which he keenly coveted) and the questions he was asking—silly questions, Kalol Mondal thought, refusing to be impressed. Where was Kalol Mondal's family home? Did he play football? Was he a Party member? How long had he lived in Calcutta? Did he like the city? How well did he know the MLA who had come here on his behalf? They were arbitrary, but Kalol Mondal was not fooled. He had to tread carefully. His new employer shouldn't think that his old links would threaten his interests, but he must also know they were there...

No, it wasn't just the questions or the sunglasses (which were now grooming the smartly creased pants) or the face that glowed with an expensive shave. The owner reminded him of *somebody*. Somebody who bothered him. That tilt of neck was familiar. And the amused twist to the mouth, which made it plain it was no use sharing ideas with you because you would never understand, the polite mask of interest behind which the seconds were being counted to get away from you...

Memory has unsettling markers.

The bogus professor! That was who he looked like! Bhola had found out his name. Biren Roy. This man was another Biren Roy. The way he spoke. As if he owned the entire city not just the shop. The way he looked. As if he lived in a place where it was always springtime, eating mutton and ilish maach every day, drinking foreign liquor (you could hear the clinking of ice in that accent), emerging for short periods into the hot, dirty world to torment the people who toiled for them...

All men are created equal, Father John said. You want to believe that but experience says you can kick at a wall all you will, but it won't bring it down.

'Sir is waiting for your answer, Mondal,' snapped the supervisor. 'How well do you know this MLA?'

Kalol Mondal beamed his yellow eyes at Sir...scorching him with his sincerity. 'Quite well, sir.'

He panicked. Should he have said the Chief was a *close* friend? Or not a friend at all?

Now they were murmuring together, their backs to him. The supervisor's chin retracted into the folds of his neck. He looks like a turtle, Kalol Mondal thought, cheered by the image.

'Ah-um,' he said to get their attention, and eased his mouth into a smile. His smile went unacknowledged. Its intended beneficiaries were walking away.

He returned to his corner with his customary scowl. One day he would look into their eyes, look and look and look, till they crumbled.

The showroom kept late hours, and it was nearing 8 p.m. when he entered J. Mullick Road. He looked in on Aroma's as usual, and then loitered around. When the probability of Dona's appearance became next to nil, he thought of his friends—realizing, with a start, that he hadn't seen them for more than a week. His new job and house had occupied him completely. Besides he hadn't wanted to meet them, the accursed bunch of them, after the Aminia evening, but now it struck him that their non-attempt to contact him for seven days was more than discourtesy. It was disloyalty.

The peepul tree was deserted. No carrom board, no light. He stood for a minute, jiggling the change in his pocket, and then set off for Raja's house, muttering *sneaky bastard* but without rancour.

Raja's mother shut the door on him before he said a word.

Fuming, he stomped off.

Dipu's room was locked. Bhola's was crowded with fellows playing cards, none of them Bhola, and none knowing—perhaps not telling him—his whereabouts.

In the end Kalol Mondal ate a solitary dinner of rotis and vegetable curry at a nearby pavement stall, sitting between two brawny taxi drivers on a bench designed for two underfed bodies. After dinner he returned to the peepul tree.

They weren't there. Gone to a night show, he concluded. Dinner before that, and chai after in Vivekananda Park—he knew the drill. They hadn't thought to ask him. He bristled with indignation. Did they think he wasn't one of them anymore or what? Although he wasn't, he thought, smoothing down his chest. Still, it was a mean dodge, and he would give them hell for it. But wait, would that be seen as weakness? Neediness? Sitting on the curb in the dark, waiting for them... obviously he had nothing better to do.

He drummed his fingers on his knees, his feet keeping time, faster and faster. Around him the walls pulsated with music, voices, laughter. The medley of sounds excited his curiosity, filled him with painful longings. But the doors stayed selfishly shut.

He didn't stand a chance with her. His heart would never find the courage to unload its burden. Because, what could he say that would not panic her, or repel her, or, worst of all, make her laugh? Should he keep his dignity and forget her? If only he knew whether he had a chance...

How long should he wait *now*? What else was there to do, and where else would he go? His new flat? There was only one kind of fun you could have all by yourself and *that* he had renounced. A girl like Dona was expensive! He beat the curb with his palm. It relieved his feelings, but only a little.

He heard the laughter first, and then the voices. Both stopped when he stood up. 'Where were you?' he rapped out.

Nobody answered.

'Movie?'

Dipu nodded. He didn't, as he once would have, proceed to tell him about it. Neither did the others.

Kalol Mondal couldn't demean himself by asking. 'I haven't seen you this whole week,' he said.

Dipu shrugged. He didn't, as he once would have, explain why this was the case. Or express regret, concern, any of that.

Kalol Mondal's jaw tightened. He wouldn't rise to the bait, for bait it was. He wished they would come closer, under the lighted window where he stood, so they could see each other clearly. He would look into their eyes, one by one, look and look and look...

They stayed where they were, moulded into stone by the moonlight. He jerked his head at Raja who was hanging back. '*There* you are, you little bastard!' Say something. *Please say something.*

Raja said nothing.

'I have a new customer for you,' he continued, in a voice that sounded strange even to him. 'Three cars...' He swallowed dry spit. 'I can get rid of his present cleaner.'

Bhola snorted. 'How? By breaking *his* arm?'

For a few seconds he was too stunned to react. Then the familiar, fierce surge of blood galvanized his limbs. 'I'm speaking to Raja, not *you*!'

He checked himself. It was three against one. They could do to him any one of the unpleasant things he himself had taught them.

Bhola turned to leave. Dipu hesitated only for a second before following suit.

Kalol Mondal ground his fists into his thighs. 'You will go when *I* tell you to,' he said hotly. 'Bokachod...' He caught his breath. Raja had stepped into the pool of light under the window, his forearm in plaster.

Kalol Mondal started forward. 'Your arm! What, when did...' His chest began squeezing him. He had realized what and when. When he could speak he said, 'Come stay with me till...till it mends...'

Dipu hooted. 'In your *deluxe* flat, Kalol?'

'Ice-cream every day,' grinned Bhola.

'You keep out of this!' shouted Kalol Mondal.

'Somehow,' drawled Bhola. 'I don't think he'll accept your kind offer.'

'Shut *up*!'

A head appeared at the window above them. 'Chup! We're trying to sleep!'

Kalol Mondal spun around. '*You* shut up! Ki bajey kotha!'

'Don't feel bad, Kalol, rey! My wrist is almost alright!'

'Why're you crawling to him, you fool? After what he did to you?'

Kalol Mondal shook his fist at Dipu. 'Fuck your mother, fuck your sister...'

'Fuck yourself, you mad bugger!'

'Eat shit, pig!'

Another head appeared in the window. 'Quiet, or we'll call the police!'

'Call them!' shrieked Kalol Mondal. He charged at Dipu, swinging his fists.

'Get back,' gasped Dipu. 'Amra...acid. Your girlfriend won't... be...so pretty...if she gets...acid on her...'

Kalol Mondal stumbled. His dinner backed into his throat.

Raja hopped about. 'Jete dao, Dipu,' he quavered. 'Bhola! Stop it! He's our *friend*!'

For this small gesture of loyalty, Kalol Mondal was so grateful his eyes prickled.

The silence in his flat pressed down on him. It made him think of a tomb. He could have never imagined silence and empty space could be claustrophobic.

He had planned to entertain his friends here. For what good is your fortune if it cannot be paraded and envied? He looked at the Primus stove, and the four plates and four glasses he'd bought for the jollities. How hopefully had he enlarged the sense of his life!

They are envious! That explained it. He'd moved up, but they were stuck in their miserable ruts... His eyes lit on the bed marooned on the floor—intended for fun of a different kind—and the gloom returned.

Father John, the repository of his woes, gazed at the cross hanging on the wall as if he was pondering the wickedness of man since the beginning of time. He advised patience and faith—in Jesus Christ.

Kalol Mondal said he would rather put his faith in the Party.

'Isn't that a bit ungrateful, Mondal? When Jesus died for *you*? Believe in Him, my friend.'

'It's not *I* who has to believe. It is *others*—in me. They won't—not in people like me.'

Father John fingered his cross. 'There *is* a place where who you are does not make a difference.'

'Where?'

Father John looked at him for a long moment and then began to speak.

Afterward, lying on his bed, watching a lizard stalk a spider, he went over what Father John said.

Father John poured a pale stream from the teapot and gestured towards the milk jug. Kalol Mondal added too much milk and stared, appalled, at the resultant swill. It looked exactly like the contents of the cleaner's pail in the showroom—after the floor had been mopped. And he would have to drink it because Father John would expect him to. This probably was a test of his suitability or commitment. Something important, anyway.

He thought of Aroma's strong, sugary tea. Life-giving tea. He thought of his mother and sister drinking theirs in Midnapur, insensible to his trials. And of the meal they would be eating later—fried fish, rice mashed with boiled potato and green chillies, drizzled with mustard oil... His eyes as well as his mouth filled. He wondered if he could ever go home after this—whether he could ever *tell* them about this. Suddenly he didn't feel confident. He certainly didn't feel daring.

The clock struck the hour. Seven times. He watched it as if taking his eyes off it would stop it, deflect him from his purpose. He gulped the tea without tasting it.

Father John was peering at him over his teacup. Looking for signs of doubt, Kalol Mondal thought. He trained his yellow eyes on Father John.

He must have overdone it for, 'Are you quite well, Mondal?' said Father John.

Kalol Mondal blinked. 'Yes Father.'

'Good, good,' said Father John. 'You've been a diligent student,' he continued sombrely, 'but I hadn't thought you'd be ready quite so soon.' He pushed his glasses up his forehead. 'Have you thought it through?'

Kalol Mondal nodded.

'And you are quite, quite sure?'

Again Kalol Mondal nodded.

'And you want to do it next Sunday?'

Kalol Mondal nodded for the third time.

Father John opened a notebook, made some notations. 'See me on Saturday evening at 6 o'clock. There are a few formalities to complete. We need to have a little talk first.' He smiled. 'Don't worry, it won't hurt. But first, welcome to our house. It is yours too now.'

Kalol Mondal was overwhelmed by the invitation, and its implications. He'd be an outcast in his family! It never once crossed his mind that his mother might not actively miss him once she'd done with her laments, and that his father might actually be relieved at his departure, and that his sister might have sources of amusement that didn't need him.

Father John's chair scraped the floor like a polite cough.

Taking a deep breath, Kalol Mondal said, 'Is it possible, can I...take the name Anthony Gonsalves?'

Father John's glasses slipped down. 'Of course. May I ask why?'

'He is hero in Hindi fillum *Amar Akbar Anthony*,' said Kalol Mondal eagerly. 'You have seen? It is old but very good.'

Father John said he had not had the pleasure of seeing it but would take Kalol Mondal's word for it.

Kalol Mondal launched into the story. Unmindful of Father John's cooling interest, he told it without missing a single sequence, even singing a snatch of the title song, to explain why he'd picked his new name.

32

Biren Roy was due to arrive at 12.45. By 1.15 p.m. Tuli had finished a bowl of chips. By 1.30 p.m. Dida had peered into the fish curry three times—Dona remarking the third time, 'It will not *evaporate*, Dida.' By 1.40 p.m. Pinaki had gone to the door four times, thinking he heard knocking. (There was load shedding so the bell wouldn't work.) At 1.50 p.m. Rimi muttered *some people*. She was just saying she would take a nap and they could wake her when their guest came, *if* he came, when there was a banging on the front door.

And there at last was Biren Roy, apologizing for his lateness, and presenting Rimi with a bouquet of pink and white lilies, which was the reason for the delay.

Rimi was impressed—she had never received such a grand gift before. (Wrapped in cellophane! With a ribbon!) Dona knew she would rather have got chocolates. But at least she wouldn't have cause to complain.

Pinaki headed the visitor away from the armchair with the broken springs, and hustled him into another, which also sagged but didn't poke. Rimi chose the sofa, Dona the straight chair to Biren Roy's right, out of his line of sight. Tuli squashed himself into the twelve inches between Rimi and Dida.

Pinaki positioned himself by the broken-spring armchair and waited, he couldn't say why, except it seemed the proper thing to do.

He was waiting on Biren Roy's pleasure.

Biren Roy smiled. 'Nice place, Bose. Not quite the alms house you'd given me to understand.'

There was a collective gasp. *Bose*? Not *Mister* Bose?

Pinaki, however, was gratified. He sat down with a thud. The broken spring jabbed him in the thigh, hard. But he was too overcome by the sight of the great man in *his* home, sitting in *his* chair, to register it as more than a pinprick.

Biren Roy rubbed his damaged cheek. Then, as if he'd spotted a friendly face in a mob of stick-wielding strangers, '*Hello*!' he exclaimed. 'You're the boy whose stomach is a sinkhole!'

Tuli squirmed with delight. Dona squirmed too, for him, and for her father chuckling away, and for Dida beaming. What was wrong with all of them? And Biren drawing attention to his cheek—it was aflame now. Her mother was staring openly. Her father was trying not to look—as if that would help!

But Biren was examining the photographs on the table beside him. There was the one of her in that awful fairy costume her father loved. *Put it down, put it down, put it...*

'How's the drawing and painting coming along, Dona?' he asked, looking up so suddenly that she started.

'What?'

Pinaki explained to Rimi and Dida that he had asked Dadababu for advice for Dona's college subjects.

Thankfully Dadababu's (*why* did her father address him so?) attention had moved to the floor. Picking holes in the already pitted mosaic. Next he would mark the bit of plywood in the sideboard that had replaced a broken panel. And the tarnished brass vase of paper flowers on the steel table. Her toes tensed and then relaxed. You're no better than us. Look at *your* studio. Look at your *room*.

But the truth was he *was* better than them. Not that he would give any indication he was. It was just the way he felt about things, and spoke—in that puffy accent he'd got from his school in the hills. The school with a chapel—with a stained-glass window. They weren't to know, as she did, that his clothes were those of a social misfit, not a social outcast.

There *were* giveaways, though. Coming so late, for one, using the lilies as excuse. The lilies, in fact, were a straight giveaway. Their guests, if they brought flowers at all, brought a string of jasmine for Rimi. Or marigolds bundled in newspaper for Dida's thakurghar.

Her ears pricked up. He was speaking to her mother. 'You're fortunate with that corner window, Mrs Bose.'

Don't look so pleased, Ma. It isn't a compliment. Because what he's telling you is, perhaps you should pull back the curtain (they're so shabby!) Besides, is there nothing else in the room to appreciate than a shuttered window?

The truth was there wasn't.

Biren was calculating when he could look—without being observed—at the one thing in the room he could whole-heartedly appreciate. A chance would be a fine thing, though. They were all gazing at him, watching his every move, as if he was a visiting guru about to impart life-changing knowledge. Across him, his host was noddng encouragement (and showing more crotch than was decent).

But the room was infused with her presence. As if she

had been waved around the place like an incense burner to, what, perfume it? Consecrate it? Ward off pests—pestilential intruders?

He pulled out his cigarettes and patted his pockets for a matchbox—and caught Pinaki's anguished expression. The old lady! With a muttered apology he put away the cigarettes.

'Would you like more nimbu pani, Dadababu?' Pinaki asked, miming holding a glass.

'No more, thank you, Bose.' He was hard put to finish the cloudy syrup that had been handed to him seconds after he had sat down—in a glass smelling of mothballs. His seat, covered with a fabric that looked and felt like his eraser, was tipping him forward. The need to smoke grew agonizing.

Rimi heaved herself up. 'I will warm the food.'

'I will help you, Ma,' Dona said, sliding out of her chair. Dida got up too, murmuring about seeing to the curry.

Tuli, marooned in the middle of the sofa, looked at once abandoned and grand. He began flapping his legs, fast, like a butterfly's wings.

Biren began to wonder if he had paid too high a price for a movie in which the billed star was going to make only a guest appearance. Remembering the stated reason for his visit he looked around.

The room was not small as he had first thought—it was just overwhelmed by furniture. Small tables clung to every arm of the sofa set. A three-corner stand displayed a muddle of bric-a-brac. (The wineglass with the red jelly had been given prominent place.) In another corner, the splayed feet of a grimy meat safe clawed at saucers of water. A stained and worn carpet strived (in vain) to make the point that a living room must be carpeted to be respected. It was all as depressing as tea gone cold.

Rimi called out that lunch was ready. Her announcement had

an accusing ring. Lunch, Biren was meant to understand, had long been ready, and was going to taste the worse for the delay, so don't blame *me* if it isn't up to your standards.

She made them wait in the doorway, though, for last-minute arrangements. Dona poured the water. Dida took off a lid from a dish. Rimi fussed with the centrepiece—a menorah the likes of which he had only seen in art books. She was stuffing its holders with flowers. They were his lilies. Decapitated.

A maid walked in with a platter of puris.

'Put it down!' cried Rimi. 'On the table, where else! Oof!'

Pinaki fluttered around. Sit down, please sit! Anywhere! Of course the directive first paralyzed everyone, and then had them making for the same chair.

Rimi took charge. First she directed Biren to a chair—practically pushing him into it. Pointing to the one next to him, '*You* sit there, Ma,' she said to Dida, and to Tuli, 'You here.' Then she flopped on the chair across Biren, and nodded to Dona to sit beside her. (Oh, the unerring instinct of mothers!) But Dida, insensible to these manoeuvres, pushed Tuli away saying, '*This* is my place,' and Dona slipped in beside Biren—earning a muttered reproof from Rimi.

It was rather like the Mad Hatter's party, Biren thought. Minus the hilarity. But *she* had chosen to sit next to him.

He didn't risk more than a glance at her but he could smell her scent. It was citrusy, spicy, hinting at assignations, adventure, amour... You could imagine—at least he did—a cloistered court, shadowy corridors, cunningly hidden staircase. The bedroom, a stately pleasure dome, would have a four-poster bed, and white walls dappled with sunlight. Pomegranate trees glimpsed through latticed windows...

The dream was short-lived. Because there were two kinds of fish. As well as prawn curry. Prawns with their heads on, he noted, in the way one catches the disaster headlines first. Oh, unspeakable. It hadn't occurred to his unfortunate hosts that there could be some Bengalis who didn't like fish just as there might be some Chinese who didn't eat chicken feet.

'Bhetki paturi,' Rimi announced, and in English, 'Fish in mustard masala. Ma's speciality.' Red-tipped claws deposited a banana leaf package on his plate. He could hardly refuse it after that.

'Tuli, Dida wants the pickles.'

'Rimi, pass Dadababu the rice.'

'Thank you, Bose, but I have some on my plate.'

'Dona, your mother is asking for a spoon.'

They were characters in a play, being introduced to the audience in the first scene, and he was the stranger who'd come to town. He felt the responsibility of discharging his role well. He had auditioned for it after all. Lobbied for it, in truth. The fish, which he still hadn't broached, contributed in no small measure to his disquiet. Nobody spoke, except to ask him if he wanted anything. There was no *pass that* or *try this* or *want some more?* They reached across the table, or pointed—or, as Tuli did, just stared at a dish till Rimi noticed. Behind the kitchen door, on which Rimi kept a weather eye, noisy washing-up operations had already begun. She trained it on her guest. 'How do you like the fish?'

Dida stopped eating and looked up.

He packed a piece of it in his cheek, like a doctor staunching a wound. 'It's um, sublime,' he mumbled 'Quite spiritual.' Swallowing, 'So then,' he said thickly, 'let's talk about your new house. How does everyone feel about it?'

Rimi laid down her spoon. 'My question is how can anybody afford to build a house when they can't afford a car? Or even a new sofa?'

'Rimi,' said Pinaki. 'Dadababu is the one to ask the questions.'

She tossed her head.

Poor devil, thought Biren. 'I've come to *answer* your

questions too,' he said. 'After all, it is your house. You must have a say in its design,' he added unblushingly.

Now even Rimi was at a loss for a response. Pinaki's expression struggled between stupefaction and mortification.

'Come on,' said Biren. 'Surely you have discussed it. Unless you don't talk to each other at all?' Now he felt a bully as well as a fraud. 'What do you want in your new home?'

They didn't deserve this. They hadn't invited him—they had accommodated him. On the other hand, they had ambushed him with the fish.

At last, 'Dona wants a dressing room,' Tuli volunteered.

Rimi snorted. 'She thinks she's five-star.'

'Nini has a dressing room,' Tuli said.

Dona gave him a brief glare. 'It's only a converted storeroom. Her clothes smell musty in the monsoon.'

Tuli glanced at his mother. 'One should not be happy at other people's troubles.'

'I *enjoy* other people's troubles,' declared Dona. 'I *thrive* on them.' She leaned across and pinched his chin. He yelped.

'Dona! Ki korcho!'

Quickly Biren pointed to the menorah. 'I've been admiring that. Where's it from?'

'I bought it on this road,' Pinaki said. 'From a man who repairs old fans.'

'Ah. I could be wrong but it's an antique. Early nineteenth-century, Eastern Europe I would say. Quite valuable, if so.'

Rimi sniffed. 'It is useless. Only holds nine flowers. And they keep falling out.'

'Try putting candles in it,' Biren said, smiling at her.

'Ma,' cried Dona. 'I told you it's not a vase!' She reached across and yanked the flowers out. Rimi shrugged but he knew he wouldn't be forgiven.

Tuli took the last puri on the platter, stuffed it into his mouth. 'Are you famous, Uncle?' he mumbled.

'No. But I'm hoping your father's house will change that.'

'It's not big enough,' Pinaki said, with a deprecating smile.

'It's not *anything* enough,' Rimi retorted. 'As far as I can see.'

'Touché,' murmured Biren.

'It would be nice to live in a famous house,' Tuli said.

Rimi snorted.

Biren rubbed his cheek. 'I'm afraid there isn't the remotest possibility of that.'

Upon which everybody turned as one to their food. Dida gnawed on a drumstick with two front teeth. Tuli chewed with his eyes and his mouth open. Dona bent her head so her hair swung to hide her face. Rimi looked hard at Biren, turning him over and over as if she suspected he could be a two day-old catch. It hadn't escaped him that she had been doing that a lot during the meal. There was no fooling her that his interest in them was professional and not something reprehensible. Now she turned her attention to his plate, to the prawn sitting there, awaiting dismemberment. He had to do something, fast, to quell his rising nausea.

'Fame's a social, a cultural, construct anyway,' he said, feverishly. 'With geographic boundaries. A tribe in Borneo won't be interested in who won the Pritzker. In other words,' he said, feeling as though flying into a headwind, 'fame requires some understanding, at least, familiarity with the field in which it is claimed.'

Rimi's eyebrows were semaphoring to Pinaki. *What is going on?*

Stop it, he told himself. Stop *now*. But the prawn! With a head! And a tail! She had put it on his plate without asking him. People were given worse punishment for less. 'Also,' he said, looking at her, 'these days fame is not earned as much as conferred, and for selfish and frivolous, if not downright dishonourable, reasons.' That's put paid to those eyebrows, he thought. He pressed his advantage. 'I'm allergic to shellfish.

I'm afraid I can't eat this prawn.' Struck by a happy idea he turned to Tuli. 'Would *you* like it? I haven't touched it.'

Tuli nodded eagerly. The prawn was transferred. Light-headed with relief, 'So what'd *your* heart's desire, Tuli?' he cried. A miniature Eiffel tower? Sure! The London Bridge? A breeze!

'Nothing,' muttered Tuli, ducking his head.

'Go on, tell Uncle what you told us,' Dona said. 'Don't be shy. Tell Uncle that *all* you want is a window by your study table. What he *needs* though, what he really needs is his own bathroom. Because he is constipa...'

Tuli leapt up. '*No!*'

'My parents' house was in Cossipore,' Dida said. Her eyes filmed over. 'A hundred and ten years old last year. British style, but with a private courtyard for the ladies. In those days there was still purdah...'

'It was a classic design,' Pinaki interjected

'Does hundred years make a building classic, Uncle?' Tuli asked.

'Not if it's a cowshed.'

'What *is* a classic building, Uncle?'

'Good question,' he said, to parry it. (Dona made a gurgling sound. Drat the boy!) He scrabbled in the ragbag of his mind. 'A classic building, a classic *anything*—book, painting—is one that won the popular vote in its time, and continues to sweep the polls.'

'What did they vote for?'

'Incontrovertible beauty. Universal truth and um, cosmic relevance. I thought anybody would have guessed *that*.' He glanced at Dona.

Her eyes were warm and confiding. They were sharing a moment. They were reliving other such moments. The afternoon opened up. Possibilities too.

'Did *you* guess that, Uncle?'

The boy was already the thing Pinaki was. A dentist's drill.

'Actually,' he said, with a straight face. 'It was revealed to me. By angels.' (Dona had a coughing fit.)

'Will our house be a classic one day, Uncle? What will it be?'

He put his spoon down. He must now turn the water into wine. 'Wait and see,' he said.

Dona laughed out aloud.

The sweet, patishaptha, was served. He bit into the pancake—and gasped. The syrup had gone straight to his bad tooth. Through a blur of pain he heard Dida. 'Is it possible to have a small thakurghar?'

And Rimi. '...glass shower cubicle...like our hotel in Digha.'

He gulped water. The tooth hit a higher register of pain. He cradled his cheek and focussed on a poster taped on the wall: *A good Man does not require nor need a character certificate from a characterless subhuman*

'...green tiles. Eijay, you remember the hotel? They changed our towel every single day.'

'We go for a holiday once a year, Dadababu.'

'It was *two* last year. Because Tuli came first in class.'

A fork of lightning split his jaw. A groan escaped his lips.

'He's not interested in our holidays,' Dona said. 'Because I think he has toothache.'

A minor commotion erupted when it was affirmed this was indeed the case. Dida instructed Dona to bring clove oil from her cupboard. Rimi suggested aspirin. Pinaki ran out, shouting for warm water, as if it was needed to put out a fire.

Tuli stood very close to Biren, huffing on his neck while he sipped the water. 'I am very interested in architecture, Uncle.'

Biren pushed him away and stood up. 'Can we see the flat now, Bose?' Another bolt of lightning struck, and he clutched Tuli's shoulder to steady himself. A damp, comfortless warmth emanated from the shoulder, as from a fire made of green twigs.

Pinaki looked anguished. *Why are you plaguing me so?*

'I must warn you it's an old house, sir,' he said, with a helpless gesture towards the noisy kitchen. 'The landlord doesn't maintain it.'

And then Biren was ashamed of his ploy—for what was there to see or understand here that he hadn't the moment he set eyes on Pinaki?

But the tour had begun. His guide was explaining the purpose and situation of each room as if it was a manor of noble lineage. As always, Biren was a little disconcerted at his curiosity (bordering on the prurient), at how people ordered their homes. Or didn't, as was mostly the case in this part of the world, where few concessions were made to the pleasure principle. For example, the predilection for brown, every dreary variant of it. And furniture lathered with black polish, killing every grain of wood. And curtains and carpets that blocked out light, trapped air and stifled life. It must be an atavistic need to recreate cave dwellings.

The flat was not only murky, it was malodorous. Through the pervasive reek of fish he got the poignant whiff of cotton wool marinating in urine. To think of her trapped in this!

On a different note, it was hard to imagine Pinaki making his leap of imagination from here.

He only paid half attention to the flat—he was looking for traces of its resident ghost. A shoe, a bracelet, nimbus caught in the door... Intent on his sleuthing, he volunteered neither comment nor question, pressing a handkerchief to his jaw as an excuse for his abstraction.

He got his break when Pinaki's monologue was interrupted by a trifling catastrophe. A puja lamp had leaked oil on the floor. Taking advantage of the ensuing fuss, he darted into an adjoining room.

And there on the aalna—the ubiquitous coat stand—was his first clue. Under a mountainous pile of clothes he glimpsed a wisp of blue. Her blouse.

From behind him Pinaki had launched into another round of explanations. But Biren was too absorbed, gathering evidence. The toe of a pink sandal nosing the heel of its pair. A green steel desk stacked with college books. A novel (with a lurid cover) face-down on the floor. And two virginally narrow cots.

It *was* her room, this hermitage. She'd told him she shared it with her grandmother.

Pinaki picked up the novel and flipped it over. 'Tch. Children grow up so fast!'

'Not fast enough,' he murmured absently. The calendar (advertising Apollo Tyres) had today's date circled on it—with a tiny indentation on the top of the circle. A *heart*? His own flipped. How susceptible it had become! How beggarly!

But here was his host, beckoning him to the window, twitching with eagerness. He peered at the crush of pedestrians and hawkers, tangle of cycles and handcarts, and the odd car, ploughing through the muddle. The street was as frank and insouciant as a schoolboy's knee.

'Did you see it, sir?' breathed Pinaki. 'There, there, look there!'

'Where? Wha..?' A javelin landed on his jaw. He clutched the window grille. When the throbbing subsided he became conscious of the clanking.

It was a water pump. A knot of women was standing around it, chatting amiably while the water clattered into their buckets.

'The historic shrine, eh? About time you deconsecrated... aaaargh.' Fuck. He shouldn't talk.

Pinaki, probably thinking he hadn't made enough of an impression with the pump, silently (as if *his* talking would worsen his guest's condition), directed Biren's attention to the water stagnating along the curb. One by one he pointed out his grouses—the tattered washing hanging on the railing—which had most of its teeth missing, the three pavement squatters, the garbage heap... *Now* do you understand?

Biren fought the urge to push his face in. He wanted to *savour* the unsavoury scene, and be left alone to do it. *This* was what she woke to every day, had woken to from the day she was born, what she saw when she day-dreamed over her homework, what was imprinted on her eyelids.

Warm saliva flowed into his mouth, embalming the sore tooth. He would have been content to stay there for the rest of the day, nursing it, but Pinaki had already cleared his throat twice. He asked to go to the bathroom. For it had struck him it was a place where he could not only be alone, but on terms of the greatest possible intimacy with her.

Oh, the foulness of his fantasies! The vileness of his desires!

He entered the bathroom, fearful of what he'd find. A comb bristling with her hairs. A mashed toothbrush. Grungy underwear drying on the towel rail...

There was no underwear but there was a nightgown, in a faded green and pink print, bunched beside a threadbare towel—rumpled and still-damp as if its owner had hurried with her bath. Gently he lifted the garment off the rail and shook it out.

How could he tell it was hers? There was only one way to be sure. He drew it to his face. He smelled sweat overlaid with talcum powder, and a less discernible but achingly familiar scent. Her skin. It felt like her skin too. He kissed it convulsively.

He put it back...and snatched it up again. Had he left *his* smell on it? His skunk's spray?

When he returned to the sitting room the faint buzz he'd heard from behind the door stopped. Dida began taking the knots out of her knuckles. Rimi looked as if a careless boot was crushing her toes.

Dona wasn't there.

Pinaki leapt up. 'How are you feeling, Dadababu? Okay, now? Pain gone? Tea?'

Biren shook his head. His whole face was throbbing now, and his head felt hot. It wasn't just the tooth. It was the visit, the meal, the strain of talking, and the frightful woman with the mismatched eyebrows. He had to confess to a bad conscience too.

Touching his jaw, 'I'd better get this seen to, Bose,' he burbled. 'I'm becoming a bore about...aaaargh.'

Pinaki came downstairs with him. To Biren's surprise, Rimi followed them.

He was fitting the key to the car door when he saw a young man hovering around. Thinking he was one of the parking touts employed by the Party to coerce money from timid car owners, but averse to arguing in front of his hosts, he fished out a crumpled two-rupee note and thrust it into his hand.

The fellow looked puzzled. Then his face contorted.

Biren waved him off. 'Not a paisa more. You weren't there when I was parking.'

The fellow flung the two-rupee note into a pool of slime and stormed off.

Pinaki clutched Biren's arm. 'Dadababu! That was *Kalol Mondal*!'

Biren stared after the diminishing figure. 'Really, Bose. You might have warned me. I wasted two whole rupees.' He sucked in saliva. 'Well, at least he didn't drop his pants.'

He had started the car when he heard her.

'Wait, wait!'

She was running up, her bag bumping on her hip. 'Can I hitch a ride to Nini's? Uncle?'

Pinaki said, 'Dona, Nini is in Elgin Road. Uncle is going to Free School Street.'

Dona rolled her eyes. 'Baba, his yoga class is close to Elgin.'

Rimi stared. 'How do you know that?'

'He told us when we went to see him,' Dona said airily.

Pinaki opened his mouth and then shut it.

She banged the car door on the afternoon's humiliations. 'Oof.' Unexpectedly she giggled. 'You didn't come to hear our opinions, did you?'

'Of course I did.'

She giggled again. 'You didn't find out anything!'

'Alas, no. Although *you* found out I don't like fish.'

'I knew that anyway! But I didn't tell them.'

'You know something? You aren't a nice girl.'

'Neither are you! Nice, I mean.' Her eyes danced.

And then he had a powerful desire to take her away from that unspeakable flat to somewhere bright and lively and fun. A Christmas Eve dinner in a restaurant? He imagined the revellers, louts in the main, brutish with liquor, pushing and groping on the dance floor... And he, a fully vested participant in the madness, exchanging the silent companionship of his rum-and-water, the solitude of his eyrie, for this horror. There had to be something else, something classy...

'How would you like to go to Christmas tea at the Grand, Dona?'

He saw the answer in her face.

And so, suddenly, life becomes bearable again.

That night Rimi said to Pinaki, 'She really annoyed me today.'

'She's *old*, Rimi.'

'Oof-o! Everything is not about your mother, okay? I'm talking about Dona! The way she was behaving with...him. Your Biren Roy.'

'But she hardly spoke to him, Rimi.'

'That's what I mean.'

He went into the bathroom. Sometimes it was better not to ask people what they meant just in case they meant what you think they might have meant.

33

A week after the visit, Dona pirouetted round her room, laying out her clothes on her bed—blouse with sleeves making a T, pant legs hanging over the side to the slippers on the floor— so the effect, since the ensemble was all-black, was that of a headless apparition.

Humming, she filled a bucket with hot water in the bathroom, and soused herself with three dippers from it, in quick succession. Wisps of steam rose from her warmed skin. She tipped the fourth dipper in a luxurious dribble that ran from her neck along a breast and fell off the nipple. She shivered with pleasure. Arching her back she held out the cake of soap. *Bathe me, James,* she murmured huskily, imitating Miss Lobo's covert and probably inaccurate—certainly ill-judged—enactment of the movie script of *Dr No* during Class X Chemistry. 'Bathe me James', she murmured again, and then, 'Bathe me, Biren.'

Her eyes flew open. Iridescent rainbows danced over the peeling yellow walls. She blinked to shake the water off her eyelashes—and caught her reflection in the mirror.

Powdery yellow light from the naked bulb had settled on her skin like gold dust. Steam rendered her much-lamented figure voluptuous rather than fat. Her eyes swam up at her. Tilting her chin at the mirror, *Hello beautiful*, she said.

In that moment she knew, with a prescience that took her breath away, that this was the image that would stay with her forever. For *ever*, she thought, awed and not a little scared by the grandeur of the prospect, especially in the context of the shabby little bathroom. When she was middle-aged, when she was dying, this was how she would see herself. What she would look back on at any point in that soaring arc of time.

She ran the cake of soap over her arms, her neck, her breasts. 'Touch me, Biren, hold me...'

The doorknob rattled. 'What's going on in there?'

Fifteen minutes later, when she emerged from her room, Rimi pounced. 'Where are you off to and with whom?'

'Nini's,' Dona said, looking straight into her eyes. 'I *told* you. Movie. What has Daisy had done to your eyebrows? You look like a Samurai!'

'When will you be back? Dona! Come back here!'

'Have fun with Dida!' Giggling, she banged out of the front door.

~

It was only 5 p.m., but the sun had long gone from Park Street. Today the gloom had given way to Christmas cheer. Crowds were already gathering—drawn to the lights like plankton, Biren thought, as he drove under a twinkling canopy. Strings of fairy lights tumbled down Park Hotel, festooned shop windows and restaurant signboards. Star lanterns swung from the trees, and over pavement stalls selling Christmas trinkets—plastic Santa Clauses, tiny plastic fir trees, crackers, whistles...

She had followed the advice of the fashion editor in *The Hoogly Times* (who had recently been pulled off the crime beat) and twisted her hair into a tight coil on top of her head. Her blouse appeared to be made of fused cassette tape reels. It was relieved—unsuccessfully—by a border of polystyrene beads. Her feet were encased in slippers with heels like golf tees. Transparent plastic straps reined in the unruly toes.

But youth wins any debate on beauty. And youthful exuberance as a style is hard to beat.

She didn't seem too confident, though. She kept pulling her blouse over her bosom. She kept running her tongue over her teeth. She kept touching her hair-do to check its stability.

She needed reassurance. (And *The Hoogly Times* needed a new fashion editor.)

But there was Puck, tinkering away in his head as usual. 'Well, well, well,' he said. 'You're going to break more hearts than a patissier breaks eggs!'

Her face fell into confusion.

Damn. A compliment shouldn't be flicked from a catapult.

He hastened to reassure her he meant she looked terrific, and that her dress exemplified deconstruction. Why, it did for fashion what the Parc de la Villette did for architecture!

Double damn. A compliment shouldn't be laid on with a trowel either.

The evening, loaded with anticipation as a boatful of refugees, was in danger of sinking before it even started. They entered the hotel in silence. He was despairing of finding anything in his repertoire of small talk to make amends when he spotted a way out. 'Wait here a minute,' he said, and set off on a run.

By the grand staircase was a log cabin rigged out in all its phoney wonderments—snow, holly, a Santa Claus and reindeer. In addition to the cake and cookies, there were gift-wrapped chocolate boxes. He grabbed one of these, paid, and dashed back to where she was gazing at an arrangement of chrysanthemums and poinsettia.

He would have bought her the entire chalet for a replay of her smile.

'I shall give Tuli *one*,' she said, rattling the box.

'That would be a generous gesture.'

They were seated in the glare of a gaudy Christmas tree, rising from a pile of presents wrapped in shiny coloured paper. The crimson shade of the lamp hanging over their table stained the white tablecloth and napkins, her teeth.

'Those are empty boxes,' he said, following her eyes. 'The

best presents come in small packages, anyway. Unless you like beach balls.'

But she was too enthralled to respond.

'I've never seen anything like this, Biren. And everybody looks so smart! I would love to work here.'

He was wrenched with pity. To *stay* here was beyond the scope of her aspirations.

'*Nobody* here is as pretty as you are,' he said, taking her hand.

She gave him a psychotic red grin and applied herself to the menu.

She put it down with a sigh. '*You* order. It's too fancy for me.'

He ordered prawn toast, corn quiche, mince pie, a slice of stollen. He remembered a childhood favourite that she might enjoy. Chocolate meringue.

'You're so, so, at *home* here, Biren!'

He laughed. That is your spiritual connection. You are both fantasists. And today you have presented her with incontrovertible proof of your other life. You'd been humouring her all along with your ramshackle car and frayed collars, and yes, your junky studio with not one single pretty thing in it. *This* is your habitat. This is the secret you carry around, that other people (those waiters, for example) sense too. It will serve no purpose to point out those waiters would smile and bow at anybody ordering as much as you had. That underneath the glitter lurks the emptiness, the anxiety that haunts all illusions.

She ate with small polite bites, leaving bits on her plate in a show of worldly understanding. Her manner was animated, flirtatious even. She had been so distant in the past month and now she could be eating a meringue from his hand. It was enough to turn a man's head.

'I'll remember this *forever*,' she said, closing her eyes in a parody of rapture that made him think of a baby sated with milk. Was she that simple or merely shallow? An opportunist? It didn't matter, he thought. I'll take anything. Live in the moment. Live for the moment. Happiness will not keep. This wasn't the occasion to point out that when you put lemon in your tea you don't pour milk into it. And if you did, for any reason, nominally absentmindedness, you don't drink the curdled mess, pretending it was fine. You say—like the women he knew, 'Oops! Look what I've gone and done!'

When they left, she cast a last lingering glance at the restaurant, as if memorizing the details.

Chowringhee Road was packed with vehicles and crowds. A curb-to-curb phalanx of cars stretched along its entire length, all honking for no reason other than high spirits. And, of course, just spirits. Revellers were staggering around like antelopes blinded by the lights of beaters. He could think of nothing to say, and she, sweet fool, was too full, too overwhelmed, to talk. Yet, was this all there was to the evening?

At the traffic lights a shrouded figure leapt in front of their car and thrust an arm into her window. She drew back with a cry. On the outstretched palm were two coins and a button.

At a traffic junction he revved up, skittered across the expanse of tarmac, and, pursued by an ear-splitting klaxon, kept going till he reached the dirt strip alongside the maidan. He turned into it and bumped along for some metres, raising a cloud of dust and a storm of protests from her. Then, braking hard, he reversed the car into the great black nothingness of the maidan, and switched off the engine.

'Why have we come *here*, Biren? There's nothing here. And it's so dark!'

He smiled at her. 'I thought we'd wait out the worst of the traffic. But now we're here we can worship at one of my temples.' He pointed at a great white whale rising over the sea of traffic. 'From a distance but still.'

She stared at him. 'That's the Indian *Museum*.'

'I know.'

'What about it?'

'Well, isn't it poetry?'

'It's poetry only if it has to be explained to you. There's nothing to *understand* there.'

He laughed and took her hand, held it to his cheek. 'I would explain if I could do it through osmosis.'

She rolled her eyes. This was exactly the sort of oblique talk that wearied her.

'Come on, let's get out. You can see it better.'

'See what?'

'That its spirit isn't broken, even if its windows are.'

She looked at him curiously. 'How come you admire this kind of building but won't design one?'

He hated the question, which he had been asked many times before. It had no straightforward answer. At least none that didn't involve an exhaustive exposition, failing which he would appear a pretentious snob or an ill-informed fraud.

He became aware she was talking. '...I know it's not grand or anything, but you have a free hand, and that counts for something, doesn't it?'

She was referring to the house. After all, her father's daughter. If it had been her father he would have snapped: Is it outside the scope of your abilities, Bose, to let five minutes pass without mention of your wretched house?

'I'll let you into a secret, Dona,' he said. He pointed to the Museum. 'The original design had *another* floor, and a copper mansard roof. That is, a four-sided curved roof. They ran out of funds. Imagine how it might have been if they hadn't. Try imagining the Taj Mahal with its dome flattened out.'

Her forehead furrowed. 'Why should it matter so much? People come to see the exhibits, not the building.'

'Some of them may be as keen on the container as in the contents.'

'Some of us are keener on the coffee than the cup.'

He laughed. 'You can't want coffee now, surely? After that tea?'

'No, of course not. Do you?'

'I would brave it if it kept you with me for a while longer.'

'You know what, Biren, I think you're *lonely*. I mean, you have nobody to talk to, and share your ideas, nobody who understands you...you're laughing at me.'

'I wouldn't dare.' He brushed her cheek lightly with his knuckles. 'I have you, don't I?'

A curious expression flitted across her face—defiant, shy and determined.

While he was wondering she turned her back on him, reached out, took his hands—and placed them on her breasts.

He had imagined something like this for so long that he thought at first he was hallucinating—and actually wiggled his fingers in lieu of pinching himself.

She pressed them down.

His blood jumped.

When he dared to move he bent his head and rooted around in her neck. Her hair smelled like a basketful of puppies. Her skin was balm for his lips. Was her quiescence a sign of surrender or complicity? Or, or, *pleasure*?

Her breathing was shallow, ragged. Her weight was straining every muscle of his back, his legs. His knees were taking a knocking. But he would continue to stand, stand till, as seemed imminent, the ground gave way. Or the sky descended. Or he died.

None of which happened, of course. Encouraged, he inched his fingers to the edge of her shirt. Then, like a cat burglar, he slipped them inside.

She quivered. But she didn't pull away. Or protest. Stay, though, was that a sigh? What did it mean?

He would wait to find out. To begin with he would leave

his hands there, on her belly. Surely the buttery softness of her skin would repel the callused coarseness of his?

She didn't pull away! Good girl. Lovely, wild, mad girl. Blessed, blessed girl.

What next—up or down?

Up it was. Up was his natural choice and, dare he hope, hers. So, up went his hands. (Hands like scouring pads.) Up and up. Through a fug he heard her whimper. His blood rioted.

Dimly he became aware of his aching back. But he had other, immediate, concerns. His fingers had found the hooks. He paused to savour the anticipation, postponing the climactic pleasure that he'd give an eye for (an eye for an eye!) and that, he was almost sure now, she would share.

He slipped the hooks off their mooring...and was lost. Lost in a cubic foot of her. Adrift and over his head. And she his willing accessory! If she felt his need, his *pressing* need, she gave no sign of it. No confusion, no outrage, no panic. Didn't she know?

She did know. She twisted around to face him. Her eyes were glittering. She was going to scream. She was going to hit him. She was going to make a run for it. His blood backed up.

She smiled.

The bashfulness of her smile was so at odds with what had just passed that he wanted to laugh. To avert the disaster he tightened his jaw.

Her face puckered.

She thought he disapproved! She thought he had found her wanton! Or wanting! Anything but, Dona!

He drew her to him. She put her arms around him.

His blood breached a dam.

You don't know, *really* know, a person unless you've lost someone you both loved. Or been blind drunk together. Or fought together as brothers-in-arms. Or had a heated argument, with both of you leashed to bullmastiffs. You can't know them in other words. For this ignorance he was, for once, grateful.

She had stretched herself on the rear seat of the car, in a show of abandonment. She certainly looked abandoned—tethered and left to her fate. Or to be rescued.

The parodic nature of the scene should have alerted him but irony had deserted him. (A fact that would have been cause for concern at any other time.)

Was he the answer to her prayer? He, the monster, her *knight*? The irony was creeping in. It should have set off an alarm but all he heard was the train thudding through his head.

She shivered. Was she cold? *He* was on fire. His conscience was wilting in the heat of his monster's purpose. Oh, monstrous desire. Wild, savage, straining at the leash. He gulped, gulped again. Great, dry gulps.

He lowered himself on the seat, crunching himself to fit into the tiny space beside her. It was dreadfully uncomfortable, but at least he was on board.

Speak! Is what I want what you want? A word, a nod, a look!

In a fevered dream, he bent his head over hers.

He must have been too rough, too ready, for she cried out.

He clutched the door handle to break his fall.

The blood was pounding like surf in his ears. His runaway train had stopped inches from the cliff.

She was trembling. A butterfly pinned on a mount and still fluttering. The scarf she was tugging at offered as much cover as a yarmulke in a rainstorm.

Touching her shoulder, 'Dona, get up,' he murmured. 'Time to go home.'

She grasped the hand he was holding out and levered herself up, stammering her thanks. The thankfulness of her thanks! He ought to feel humiliated but the overriding feeling was one of weariness.

Smoking a cigarette while she settled her clothes, he found himself hoping that this, that almost happened, would be the worst thing she would have experienced in her life. The thing she most regretted. It was, he stared at the tip his half-smoked cigarette, the thing he was already regretting.

He lobbed the cigarette into the bushes. It cut an orange arc in the darkness. A formless melancholy settled over him. How transitory—and tawdry—was the happiness they had shared!

She was back in the passenger seat, hugging her arms.

'Alright now, Dona?'

She touched her mouth. The lower lip was swollen. There was a bead of caked blood in the corner. It gave him a nasty little thrill.

He braced himself for reproaches, tears...

'Please,' she whispered, 'please don't tell anyone about this.'

'Of course not, Dona. What do you take me for? Um, shall we wait here a bit so you can...'

'No. I...' She broke off with an explosive hiccough. 'I...I...' The hiccoughs cascaded. 'I just want to go...home.'

She sounded as if she never wanted to leave it again.

34

She asked him to drop her at the far end of J. Mullick Road, half a kilometre from her building, no, *one* kilometre, no, right *here*...

He tried to calm her. Nobody could see them. The winter chill had effectively cleared the street, and the lone streetlamp that serviced this stretch was as effective as a firefly in a bush. But her panic blocked out all reason. In the end they compromised on 300 metres from her door. And he would wait in the car till she went inside.

He shook out a cigarette. Before he could light it, he was out of the car and running.

She was arguing with the man rather than fighting him off.

He thrust himself between them, gripped her arm. The man pushed him—hard.

He reclaimed her arm. 'Who the devil...!'

'Chhere dao!' she cried. 'Please, let go. It's alright,' she whispered. 'I can manage. Go, please go.'

'But this fellow is bothering you...'

'You are calling me *fellow*? Who you think you are? Hanh? *You* are fellow!'

'Oh, do shut up. Do you know this guy, Dona? His behaviour is quite presumptuous...'

The man gave him a ferocious shove.

'What the fuck...'

Cathode rays from a shop sign ran down the fellow's face in violet streams. Biren stared. 'Great good heavens. It's *you*.'

Dona gave a low moan. Tearing away from him, she ran.

Kalol Mondal started after her. 'Dhorun!' Looking over his shoulder, '*You* stay,' he said to Biren.

Bugger off, muttered Biren, and then checked his step. A fight would only complicate matters for her. If he kept out of it, she might be able to persuade Kalol Mondal to do the same.

It struck him then—the ludicrousness of his position. He and this lout competing for the attentions of the same girl! He'd touched a new low.

The door flew open the instant she touched the bell.

'Dona! Ki holo? Where had you...*you*! Why, what are *you*...'

'What is *he* doing here?' said Rimi, over Pinaki's shoulder.

Kalol Mondal appeared cool and in control of the situation—whatever the situation was, Pinaki thought, his head whirling. He turned to Dona. 'Dona, bol! What happened?'

Hugging her bag to her chest, Dona sidestepped him, pushed past her mother, and went into her room.

'I can explain,' said Kalol Mondal, giving them a benign smile. For once, Rimi had nothing to say. She turned to Pinaki. Something wasn't right.

'She was walking alone,' Kalol Mondal went on, with the same eerie composure. 'I thought it is not safe.'

'*You* thought,' Pinaki began hotly. He glanced towards the landing. The neighbours! 'Thank you for bringing her,' he muttered.

Without a word Rimi whisked around and marched to Dona's room. Kalol Mondal continued to stand inside the door.

What was he waiting for? A tip? If so, how much?

Dida, who had gone into the living room, called out, 'Bulbul, ekaney esho!'

As Pinaki explained to Rimi later, Kalol Mondal took this request to include *him*. He followed Pinaki to the living room, and sat on the sofa—right in the middle of it, a liberty that was particularly galling, although Pinaki had no intention of sitting there himself, or indeed anywhere within ten feet of his uninvited guest.

In a further show of ease Kalol Mondal threw his arm across the sofa back and began stroking the fabric.

Dida left the room.

Pinaki, oscillating between anger at Kalol Mondal's audacity and anxiety about Dona, tottered into a chair. Kalol Mondal might interpret this as a call for a heart-to-heart but he could do nothing about that. His immediate goal was to put up a show of normalcy so there wouldn't be gossip about Dona.

'She went to a movie with her friends,' he said. '*College* friends. They usually go to the ice-cream parlour afterwards. For coffee. Ice-cream. Coffee ice cream.'

Kalol Mondal inclined his head. He would go along with this story although it seemed a bit too thick on facts.

Pinaki found the gesture insufferably condescending but decided not to react. The fellow would suspect. He would assume. He would expect. Pinaki was hazy about what form the assumption and expectation would take, except that the first would be disagreeable and the second unreasonable.

'Ei, she had informed us she might be late,' he said. It sounded feeble even to him. Rimi's unpunctuated shouting from two rooms away blatantly contradicted this. This was the problem with lying. Something, someone always gave you away even if you managed to pull it off. 'It gets dark so soon in the winter, taito?' he said, nodding at the clock, which showed the time at half-past nine. (Kalol Mondal grunted. The darkness, if anything, should have had her hurrying home early.) 'Her friends brought her back,' he said, with a little more spirit. Perhaps *that* would provoke his tight-lipped guest into revealing the circumstances in which he found her. Kalol Mondal's nostrils widened. He was suppressing a yawn. His expression reminded Pinaki of the crocodile he'd once stumbled upon in Cooch Behar. The same meditative gaze... Unnerved, he began to jabber. 'The movie must have finished later than they planned... It is hard to get taxi at such a late hour... These young people!' He attempted a careless laugh, and made an odd grunting noise.

Kalol Mondal's lips parted like suction pads. 'I saw a car parked down the road.'

No more information was forthcoming. Pinaki was puzzled and irritated, but he didn't dare probe. He stood up to stretch, easing his too-tight sweater from under his arms. 'Tomorrow is a working day,' he said, without much hope.

Kalol Mondal hoisted a leg on to a thigh and began playing with his toes. Pinaki wondered if the fellow *was*, after all, expecting a tip. He was angry with Dona now, for putting him in this new bind. 'It is very late,' he said, and, after a small pause, repeated it with more emphasis.

Kalol Mondal nodded. 'Hein. It was lucky for her I was there. But I won't always be, taito?' He wagged his finger. 'Unnichi, she must not stay out so late, Dada. It is not safe.'

Pinaki stared at the floor. Familiarity and presumption. Could the expectations be far behind? Already the fellow had taken over his sofa. In time would it become his 'usual spot'? Would he become a regular visitor? Cups of tea, advice on cable providers, can I borrow your screwdriver, this and that... Oh, intolerable. How does one discourage such a one? Dislodge him first? He looked as if was there to stay. And there was no lack of entertainment either. The mother-daughter exchange going on inside was entertainment enough, Pinaki thought bitterly. When one of the voices—Rimi's—climbed an octave they both looked up, and caught each other's eye. Pinaki felt as though he'd been caught in an indiscretion. He remembered the scene at the water hydrant and cringed.

Kalol Mondal jiggled his foot up and down, beating a thoughtful tattoo on his knee in time. 'Eta flat khub spacious,' he said approvingly. 'How much rent you pay?'

Pinaki bristled. It has begun, he thought. 'Is Rabin Pal still doing land business?' he asked.

If he hoped that would embarrass his guest, he was mistaken. Kalol Mondal stilled his foot just long enough to rub his chin. 'Must be, I don't know.' He smiled at Pinaki's surprise. 'I have left him. I am now working in Bharat Paints in Wellesley Road. In sales.'

A wail ensued from the interrogation room. Kalol Mondal's expression didn't change but he tensed, like a dog who's heard the key in the front door.

'Thik achhe,' Pinaki mumbled, scrambling up. 'I must leave...I'll see you in the morning.'

I must leave from my own house? See you in the morning?

See *you*? In the morning? He smote his forehead, mentally, again and again.

After he bolted and locked the door on his visitor he darted to the sofa, ripped the antimacassar off and threw it into the dirty clothes bucket.

Rimi turned on him the second he entered the room. 'She came in a taxi. *Alone*. After dropping off the others.'

Dona, huddled on her bed, lifted a tearful face. 'Someone has to be last!'

'Hmm,' said Pinaki, stroking his chin. 'But, shona, see what happens when you do that. You give ideas to all kinds of loafers.'

'Kalol Mondal had ideas long before this.'

Pinaki cleared his throat, although it needed no clearing. He couldn't look at Dona for the guilt whispering to him that he had got her into this scrape in some way.

'You gave him another opportunity,' Rimi said.

Pinaki was impressed. Rimi always found the right words to say and was not afraid to say them. Why couldn't he?

'Jete dao, Rimi,' said Dida. 'She's tired. You can talk in the morning.'

'*I'm* not going to talk about it,' Dona declared. '*Ever*.' She stuffed her face in her pillow.

'Bosebabu! How are you? Well, I hope? And, ah, your family?'

Pinaki stiffened. The wretched Kalol Mondal had already begun talking. For the first time in his life he had harsh feelings about his daughter, even going so far as to refer to her—privately of course—as that stupid girl.

'Good morning, Mr Bose! I heard you had a bit of bother last night. Everything alright?'

'Yesyes,' Pinaki mumbled, and hurried away. They had become news—headline news. He hurried back. 'Sorry, Father. I wasn't, ah, my head is...not working,' he touched his head.

And then because Father John gave him such a sympathetic look the words began tumbling out. 'My daughter came home a little late after a movie. That is all.' *The stupid girl. The stupid, stupid...*

'Well then, all's well that ends well, eh? All the best, Mr Bose. God bless you.' Touched by this unexpected benediction Pinaki ducked his head.

He continued on his way—divining the ground with his eyes. People won't hail you if you don't look at them.

'Nomoshkar, Dada! Kemon achhen? Fine, I suppose?'

He reared back. He wanted to rebuke Kalol Mondal for spreading tales, and then tell him thankfulness was not an ongoing obligation, nor did it imply a lifelong involvement. But, as always, he was unable to articulate any of it. And he had a new fear that saying anything now would aggravate the situation.

'Shall we walk together to the bus stop, Dada?'

'I am busy,' Pinaki said distantly. Busy walking?

Kalol Mondal fell into step with him. 'Same stop, different bus. Yours is Dalhousie, mine is Wellesley Road.'

The fellow knew everything, fumed Pinaki.

When they reached the bus stand in Diamond Harbour Road he was winded and dizzy. He darted behind the guardrail and, keeping his back to his companion, took deep breaths to steady himself. That is, he snorted up the exhaust of departing buses.

When he turned around Kalol Mondal put his hand on his chest and lifted his eyes skywards. 'There is nothing to fear from a sincere heart.'

Anybody but Pinaki would have laughed at this. Even Pinaki, if he had his wits about him, would have recognized the line from *Kya? Hua Kya?*

But Pinaki concluded it was some form of blackmail. 'What do you *want*? Why are you after us?'

Kalol Mondal's muddy forehead creased. 'Kichu na, Dada. I only wanted to help you.' He lowered his head and his voice, 'Shey, your daughter is a good girl. She must be careful.'

Pinaki was speechless with outrage. In that moment a bus hove into sight. He charged to it, pushing past the crowd to squeeze into the doorway. From behind, Kalol Mondal shouted, 'It is not your bus, Dada!'

To crown the aggravations of the day Dona arrived an hour later than usual that evening. She was making a point—simply asserting her position, which she made clear in her response to Rimi's remonstrations.

'It is *my* life,' she said. And with an oblique glance at Pinaki, she said, 'Besides, I am quite safe now. I have *Anthony Gonsalves* for a bodyguard.' She burst into a harsh laugh that made him wince. What did she mean? Even Rimi couldn't get it out of her.

35

Biren walked out of the liquor shop with his modest purchase under his arm. He hadn't gone ten feet when he made a decision—a heroic one, in his opinion. Perhaps meaningless, although perhaps not for someone who pockets his cigarette butts...except that this gesture failed the audit of even that reason. Plus it had the odious reek of sentimentality—like his father turning off the car air-conditioning the first Saturday of every month to be one with the people. And as an act of contrition it amounted to donning a hair shirt over a silk vest. What was the difference between this and kissing the toes of the embalmed St Francis Xavier? He was not about to explain his motive to anybody. All he would allow was that his little sacrifice—a short delay in consuming his purchase—wasn't to propitiate any god. (He was an unbeliever, remember?) And this was the wrong way to appease Bacchus anyway. You could argue that the forfeiture tested your moral mettle. Provided some intangible—and unproven—spiritual benefit. But self-denial never made you feel virtuous or fulfilled. Just regretting a lost opportunity.

But, if put on the rack, this is what he would confess: I make these gestures in the hope the cumulative torment will make me eligible for a reward. The reward being she will call. Or knock on my door. Or, as she had done on one memorable occasion, steal up behind me, and whisper, 'Don't stop. I like to watch you draw.'

Live in hope.

Somehow her breasts were always at eye level. Was that her doing or his imagination? She had a way of easing a strap under her blouse with a soft snapping sound. Had she ever considered the effect *that* had on him? One day she arrived with her hair frizzed, and he'd asked her if she'd touched a live wire, and she said she *was* one, hadn't he noticed?

Memory is an artist's palette left out in the rain.

He had one precious memento of their time together. Her lipstick, which had rolled under the car seat that fateful night. It lived in the bird's nest, among the pins and staples, its red-and-gold gaudiness an impudent intruder in the fold of workplace banality, much as its owner had been in his grey life. He ought to return it to her. How, though? Chuck it into her window in the dead of night? Send it in a jewelled box? For now it rested on its bed of nails.

Loneliness is an abandoned building. Or an abandoned clinic, he thought, as he passed Dr Murray's lightless shack.

~

'*Required* to leave, Biren, not deported. I do wish people would get their facts right. There's no need for hysteria. And it was not overnight. I told you it had been going on for a while, but you don't seem to have registered. The FRO, Foreigner Registration Office to you, found a visa irregularity. It was a trumped-up charge, of course. Try to do good and you become a threat...What? Yes, I did call—several times, but there was no answer. What? This line is so bad. Just a moment. Don't *breathe* down my neck. No, not you, Biren. This is the free phone in the departure lounge. You wouldn't believe the stampede... Well, goodbye then, Biren. I can't thank you enough for being there. And do consider revising your worldview, will you?'

~

Biren took a long drag of his cigarette. He had sadly neglected the good doctor in the last month.

He lifted his head to exhale—and spotted the column. Not his streaming eyes, nor the indigent streetlamp, or the tattered banner *(Happy New Year 1988)* could hide its features. The egg-and-dart motif. The curling horns of the ram. The chiselled flutes... And squatting at the column base was a hunched figure, in an all too familiar stance. Furtive and focussed. Unambiguously exercising a male prerogative.

The fine example of an Ionic column had become a popular urinal.

And he discovered he didn't care.

Nothing had changed in the quad except that winter smog muddled the darkness. The cold had muffled sound too.

Not for long, though. A shriek rent the stillness, unfurled into a wail. A shadow darted across the wall like a harpoon. Atmospheric crackle, portending a fight. Then, like a school of minnows, people began swarming into the archway.

It was a domestic brawl. A woman stood outside an assortment of household paraphernalia, sobbing and complaining in turns. Close by, on a battered tin trunk, a man sat smoking, with the quick, shallow puffs of pretended indifference. Two feet away, a pot had toppled from a still-burning chula. A trickle of dal crept towards a tattered straw mat.

She's been thrown out of her home! Take her back, Dada! You go back in, sister! It's your home!

Biren walked away, marvelling. Every time you think you have it down pat, out it springs. One more surprise. Throwing all your conclusions. A straw mat, a trunk and a chula defining home as inarguably, as inviolably as a lamppost, a bollard and a tree did an eruv. *Do consider revising your worldview.*

Pinaki arrived, breathless and brazen in an apple green sweater, hand-knitted in a lacy design, and caught at the armpits. It reminded Biren of a bed jacket his grandmother used to wear. 'You're looking very festive,' he was moved to comment.

Pinaki's eyes darted to the drafting table, which, for long, too long, had distressed him with its clean-swept look. Seeing the pile of tracing sheets, covered, not with doodles, but clean, bright ink lines, his features lit up—one by one, like mountain peaks at sunrise. His sigh of happiness rustled a loose sheet. He pounced on it.

'Those are structural calculations, Bose. Here, these are the elevations—you want those, I presume.'

Pinaki scanned the drawings with, thought Biren, the eagerness of a new husband waiting to discover virtues in his bride.

After two minutes, Biren realized all was not well. 'What's the matter, Bose? It isn't the notification of cholera outbreak in the neighbourhood that I gave you by mistake, is it? The design not to your liking?'

'No, no sir, it is alright.'

'You must have some reservations, Bose, if it's just *alright*.'

'I don't,' Pinaki mumbled unhappily.

Termites in your rafters, muttered Biren. Then he had a flash recall of his seventh birthday, tearing open Dadu's present and finding a *school satchel.* Dadu! His best friend! To do that to him!

Now he wanted to pat Pinaki's head and give him a biscuit. 'Cheer up, Bose. Take comfort in the thought there is no excellent beauty that hath not some strangeness in the proportion. Whatever else, it will not bore you.'

Pinaki looked as if he might ask why getting bored with the design (or not) should be a consideration. 'Have you designed such a building before, sir?'

'Frequently.'

'And built them?'

Biren regarded him with dislike. 'No. That's a Hume pipe you're looking at.'

When understanding broke, 'A *sewer* pipe,' Pinaki gasped.

'It supports the mid-landing. It took me two hours to get those struts into that grid.'

'*Struts,*' moaned Pinaki, as if they would cudgel him to death at some future date.

'Made from railway sleepers. We can get them cheap at an auction... And I plan to try out a new roof—a sandwich of paddy husk and cement, with clay tiles for insulation. A tympanic membrane. To hear the rain.'

'Won't, won't it leak?'

'Only with the first rains. You can always use a bucket to catch the drip. It should settle down after a couple of years. Besides, the whole countryside is leaky. It's the wetlands after all. Every building has a context, and this one is the wetlands... *wake up*, Bose. You're like a punkahwallah gone to sleep. Can't budge *air* when you breathe.'

'Will it, it will be safe?'

'No building can withstand a determined assault with a battering ram. But yes, it will thwart all but the more determined thrill seekers.'

Pinaki's mouth sketched a poor imitation of a smile.

'You appear underwhelmed. A priori I've slipped in the rankings.'

Pinaki shook his head.

Biren ejected a stream of smoke. You would prefer a spirited dissent to this spineless capitulation. In any case, why do you care? Why do you need, spit it out, *praise,* and from this quarter?

Pinaki made no effort to brush away the smoke. That roused the bully in Biren. 'Well, speak up,' he snapped. 'And don't be tactful either. Tact,' he was spewing smoke, 'is deceitful.'

Pinaki licked his lips. 'It is...like the Jantar Mantar observatory in Jaipur.'

'What the fuck! Are you suggesting I was *influenced*?'

Pinaki's jaw sagged. His sweater felt like a harness.

Biren swept the blueprints off the table. 'I'm not wasting any more time explaining. *Except,*' he jabbed a finger at Pinaki, 'you can tell your daughter there will be no dressing room for her. This is not Xanadu.'

Pinaki surreptitiously wiped away a drop of spittle. 'It's a house,' he quavered. 'A simple house,' he said, more to convince himself.

Biren grunted. 'Yes, that's your party line. Oh, hell.' He rubbed his eyes. Perhaps he was vesting too much in this, his only child, trying it to make a concert pianist of it when, clearly, it was meant to be a nightclub entertainer. 'I'm sorry, Bose. I just feel so, so flayed sometimes. Take the drawings home—show them to your family. Let me get you a folder.' Bending, he rummaged in a drawer. 'Find me a clip will you— there, in the bird's nest...got it? Good man.' He clipped the blueprints together and slipped them into the folder. 'Here you are... What's the matter? You okay? You want some water or something?'

Pinaki swallowed. 'No...o,' he said in a strangled voice.

'I, I... I have to go now.' He got up, groping for the chair's arms like a blind man.

'Aren't you taking these drawings?'

Pinaki gave a small nod. He averted his head as he put the folder in the briefcase. Without a word he stumbled out.

Without a backward glance either, thought Biren. 'And thank *you* too,' he called after him.

Pinaki kept walking.

There's no pleasing them, Biren thought. Any of them. Not the least of them. He aimed a steel scale at the door. It hit the doorframe with a sharp, satisfying crack.

Manu put his head inside the door.

'Why're you holding your hand behind your back like a bloody wine waiter?'

Manu came inside handed him a piece of paper. *Have a nice weekend.*

'Oh, lord. I'm sorry, Sancho. Have a good weekend yourself.'

36

Pinaki stumbled down the stairs, the lipstick knocking in his pocket. Its metal case burned, like a just-fired bullet. But still lethal. His dread of it, his revulsion, increased each time he touched it, which was often. Anger colours judgement, he knew, and distorts the truth. It perverts the course of justice too. But the truth here was all too clear. There had been warnings. He had ignored them because he wanted to believe—how much he wanted to believe! Now they were flying at him, pecking him, battering him with their black wings.

He kept rehearsing what he would say to her. To *him*. To the *police*. There is a monster loose in the city, sir. My daughter has been ensnared by him. She is in his clutches! She has been lured, hypnotized, seduced... *no*! Not that! She's been led astray by him.

When he reached his tram stop, he wanted to run back to the studio, seize Biren Roy by the collar, drag him down the stairs, into the street... And then what?

And then he remembered. *He* had introduced Dona to the monster. He had taken her, his most treasured possession, to his lair. *Given* her to him—as surely as in marriage. Kalol Mondal seemed just a mischievous schoolboy compared to this fiend!

As he climbed into the tram, he recollected reading a story in *The Hoogly Times* about a schoolgirl being raped by a respected lawyer, devoted husband and loving father. Then the case of a girl who ran away with her tutor. Yes, the tutor was evil, he was older, but what about *her*? What sort of girl was *she* to do such a thing?

After that he couldn't keep still. For once he was grateful for the bone-rattling carriage. His head was in such an uproar he didn't notice the conductor collecting the fare, earning him a reproof for not keeping change ready. The lipstick was already bringing him bad luck.

He stood at the door long before his stop, and jumped out before it stopped.

Slow down. You must, you must not... Must not what?

You must not jump to conclusions. A person is presumed innocent until proved guilty, remember? So it is possible the lipstick is not Dona's at all, but belongs to a friend of Biren Roy's. A client. Cherry Brandy is a popular brand.

But Dona had lost hers. She was so upset a fortnight ago, looking for it everywhere. Coincidence?

A new worry stopped him short, right in the middle of the pavement. What kind of house would someone as corrupt as Biren Roy design? Dida always said if you had impure thoughts you could never make good. Should he disengage from Biren Roy then? But the explaining he'd have to do!

More worries followed. He had not seen a single *built* work of Biren Roy's. Perhaps there was no building to see?

Perhaps those drawings on the wall were copied from books and magazines? And *this* man, just because I don't understand his nonsense, treats *me* as if I am nothing.

Dona answered the door. She eased the briefcase from his hand and drew him in. 'You look so tired, Baba. And cold. Shall I make adrak chai for you?'

He shook his head without meeting her eyes, and went into his bedroom. She followed him. Depositing the briefcase on the floor, she took hold of his shoulders and sat him on the bed with a gentle push. 'Lie down, Baba. You don't seem well.' She was so concerned for him. So loving. So...so his child. Who had his nose. His chin. But her own eyes. Bright, naughty eyes. Baby skin. She was a baby still! The innocence of her, the dearness, the preciousness, the heart-breaking trust in his love... She was taking his hand to her cheek to warm it, she was tugging off his shoelaces, she was taking out a blanket to cover him—how could he broach the subject?

He shivered. He *was* cold.

He stood up and groped in his pocket, his fingers so numb it took him some moments to grip the object.

'I...found something...' Once he'd spoken the spell was broken. 'This.' He held out the lipstick. 'Is it yours?' *Say it isn't! Please, please...*

But she was turning it around, excited, delighted. 'Yes! Thank you, Baba! Thank you, thank you, thank you! Where did you find it?'

His vision blurred. He felt as if he was trying to read the dosage on a very small medicine bottle, and if he got it wrong it would have terrible consequences.

'Baba?'

She was frightened. 'Biren Roy's room!' he burst out. '*Your* lipstick was in *his* room! On his table! In that bowl he calls bird's nest! How did it get there? How, I am asking you!'

Rimi called out from the kitchen. 'Is that your Baba, Dona?'

He jumped up, pushed past Dona, and put his head around the door. 'I am home, Rimi! Cha neye esho! Leave it in the veranda!' He shut the door behind him.

She hadn't moved. Her face told him all he needed to know. All he didn't wish to know. Seizing it (how soft her cheeks were!), '*Now*,' he said. 'How did your lipstick get there?'

She tried to pull away but he tightened his grip.

'I must have dropped it when I...returned the book to him. The one I borrowed when we both went to...'

He squeezed her cheeks. Tears started in her eyes. 'Don't lie, Dona. I'm not stupid. That was three months ago. You lost the lipstick two weeks ago.'

'He gave me a lift...'

'Don't *lie*, I said!'

The tears wet his fingers. A string of snot worked down to her mouth. Revolted, he eased his hold. He waited till she wiped her face before grabbing her again, this time by the shoulders.

'You're hurting me, Baba,' she whined. 'I must have dropped it in his car! The day he had lunch here...'

He shook her—hard. 'Then why didn't he return it to *me*? All these days?' He shook her hard and then gave her a violent push. 'What are you hiding? Both of you?'

Her head drooped. 'Nothing,' she muttered.

'What is he to you?' And, hating himself, 'What are you to him?' he cried. 'What do you even have in common that you should...you should...'

Questions that he, *any* father, should not have reason, any occasion to ask. She had dragged him down to this. The anger returned, bruising, scalding.

'What were you *thinking* of? He's old! Old enough to be your... old enough to be *me*! He will never amount to anything! While you... *you* have your whole life before you!'

'Bulbul, ki hoyechhe? Ki *korcho*? Let go of her!' His mother was standing in the doorway.

He threw her a black look. When it came to trouble she had the ears of a piano tuner.

He didn't show anybody the drawings. Before, he wouldn't have had the courage, and now he didn't have the conviction. Thinking of Rimi's reaction sapped what little motivation he had.

'This is a *house*?' he imagined her saying. 'You're going to sink all our money into *this*? The money for Tuli's college, for Dona's wedding, for our old age...into this, this *joke*?'

'No, Rimi. Biren Roy never jokes about his work. It is his religion, the only god he worships! This house represents his philosophy of life.'

'Tell him his life philosophy represents our life savings.'

'You'll see when it's built, Rimi.'

'Will it be built? *Can* it be built? You trust that man too much. He is making a fool out of you.'

'You are right, Rimi. I was a fool to have trusted him. You don't know how much of a fool.' His stomach began folding up again.

'Tell him you will not pay...you haven't paid him yet, have you? Then you can have the last laugh.'

Laugh at him? I have never felt less like laughing! But thankfully I haven't paid him. He hasn't asked yet. Perhaps... because of Dona?

'...I *told* you from the beginning you are making a mistake! But did you listen? At least now admit I was right!'

Yes, Rimi, you are right. More right than you can ever imagine.

All morning he was out of sorts. He could barely manage a civil word to his colleague, who seemed especially frisky. And inquisitive. Then, during lunch break Biren Roy called to ask if he had shown the scheme to his family.

His heart was beating so hard he could hardly breathe when he answered. Fortunately Biren Roy didn't notice anything amiss. 'Really? Not a single suggestion or modification? How about the wife? Your mother? Um, Tuli and...everyone?'

Pinaki bridled. Biren Roy didn't mention Dona. He didn't have to. Because he knows what she wants. He'll give her a dressing room, in spite of what he said. He'll slip it in.

'Well?'

The western sun glared at him through the window. He lifted his arm to block it. 'It is fine, sir.' And then he was angry with the *sir*, angry with the *fine* when it wasn't (nothing was or ever would be), and angry, angry, angry with this man, who, despite everything, could still make him feel so small.

'What? Come on Bose, I don't have all day!'

'I said it is alright! What more do you want to hear?'

'Huh? Are you feeling alright, Bose? I was saying I need a week for the working drawings and then we can begin digging next Monday.'

Pinaki was shaking too much to answer.

He was still hugging the receiver to his chest when Mr Sen came back after his rounds. 'All well at home, Bose? The cat hasn't run away or something?'

Pinaki wilted. Then he dropped the receiver into the cradle. 'Actually, that was my architect. He wanted my final approval for the design of my house.' And he sailed past Mr Sen.

Sneaking a look over his shoulder as he turned at the corner he saw Mr Sen staring after him with a most amazed expression.

He clung to the image for the rest of the afternoon, taking it out to examine every hour, as a lover would a picture of his beloved.

But, when he was locking up to leave, the queasiness

returned—tinged with sadness. This wasn't how he'd imagined it. This wasn't how it should be. This moment he had been longing for—where was the fulfilment? The pride? Where was the *joy*? From a hard-won reward for his perseverance, the house had become a war spoil. Tainted.

His colleague was looking at him over his glasses. 'Life is a bridge, Pinakibabu. Cross over it, but build no house on it. It is a saying, I believe.'

'Thank you for saying it,' Pinaki said, snapping the fasteners on his briefcase.

He was loath to go home. He dreaded meeting Dona. He was afraid of his feelings and what they would make him do to her. He felt as though he was speeding backwards in a tunnel. She was disappearing from his sights. As for the house... That had gone the way of his daughter.

Aroma greeted him frostily, making him wait just long enough for his order to let him know he had lost his favoured status. And, of course, he didn't offer him free sandesh. Pinaki pretended to himself he was relieved, but he felt snubbed.

He couldn't bring himself to leave. Dragging one of the three bar stools in the stall to the far end of the counter, he asked for a plate of samosas he didn't really want.

'*Two* rupees,' said Aroma as he put down the plate. It was his way of informing Pinaki that the days of indiscriminate generosity were over.

That killed whatever appetite he had. Now he had to work up the courage to ask for a square of newspaper to pack them for home. And get two more plates, as this wouldn't be enough. Life was just not simple.

'Nomoshkar, Dadababu! Kemon achhen? You are fine, I think so?'

Pinaki ducked into the tea. His tongue flailed around. *Don't call me Dada! I am not your brother!*

Kalol Mondal pulled up a stool. Before he sat down, he placed an object on the counter, fussing to give it the best exposure. Observing that it had got Pinaki's attention, 'Protects from sun when I go out,' he said. It was a sola topee.

Kalol Mondal angled his head at Pinaki. 'You are habituated to come here, I think so. But not recently?'

Showing off his English, Pinaki thought, shifting his bottom to the edge of his stool. He raised his wrist to his eyes and studied his watch with frowning concentration.

Kalol Mondal pointed to the samosas. 'Bhalo? You advise?'

Pinaki gave a non-committal nod to the counter and then stretched his neck to catch Aroma's eye to ask for the square of newspaper. But Aroma, continuing his policy of disengagement, kept to his wok, ministering to the group there with a genial familiarity that was hard to bear.

A beautiful solution presented itself to Pinaki. Nudging the plate of samosas towards his neighbour, 'Have,' he said. 'I have not touched.' With that, he slid off his stool.

Kalol Mondal leapt up, right in Pinaki's path. 'No, no, Dada! Ami, amar, *I* will also get a plate. We will eat together!'

Pinaki made a frantic effort to abort this plan. No, he was not hungry, he had ordered forgetting he had an urgent errand. He held out his wrist—there was his watch for all to read just how late he was.

Kalol Mondal kept waggling his head, but made no move to get out of the way. 'Okay,' he conceded at last. 'I will eat your samosa. But *only* if you eat *my* sandesh. There is always time to eat a sandesh, taito?' Keeping Pinaki penned with the stool, he called out to Aroma.

Before Pinaki could protest, Aroma, with inopportune— and uncharacteristic—promptitude, was sliding a plate of sandesh down the counter.

Pinaki sat down. His resolve had given way. Certainly his knees had. Under the pretext of finding accommodation for his feet he scraped his stool out a few inches. This new, domesticated Kalol Mondal might, at any moment, throw off his sheep's coat.

The two plates sat side by side, close but not touching, like two strangers, wary of striking a conversation but too polite to move away.

'Nolen gur, Dada,' said Kalol Mondal giving the sandesh an affectionate prod with his repellently long fingernail. 'Special to the season. Please take.'

Pinaki picked the one Kalol Mondal hadn't prodded. Kalol Mondal, who had been waiting for him to do the honours, snatched up a samosa. In a gesture of awful conviviality he raised it high.

Pinaki nibbled at his sandesh with his front teeth, pretending to examine the menu chalked up on the blackboard. In the old days he would have told Aroma 'onnion' had only two ns, not three. He longed for the old days. He longed to get away from Kalol Mondal's elbow, which was nuzzling his ribs, like an inquisitive goat.

'How is *she*, Dada?' asked Kalol Mondal in a confiding murmur. 'Amar bon? My little sister?'

Anger flared in Pinaki. She's *not* your sister! But, 'She is busy,' he muttered. 'Studying for her pre-finals.' He was furious with himself. Was he *still* afraid of this fellow? Was he afraid of *everyone*?

The fellow nodded, his mouth puckering with odious sympathy. 'I also have exams. I'm doing accountancy course. I am no longer active,' he said bafflingly. After a pause, 'In the Party,' he qualified. He made a peculiar scratching noise in his throat. He was laughing.

Pinaki's ears grew warm. 'I have to go,' he mumbled, scrambling up.

Kalol Mondal didn't appear to hear. He had fastened his lips on the rim of his glass and was siphoning off his tea.

Removing the glass with a sucking sound, 'Accountancy has good future,' he said. He bumped Pinaki with his hip. 'When I become manager I can get you discount for paint for your new house. Managers get special discount.'

Get the position first, Pinaki thought, and then glumly, he probably would. Father John had said he was a quick learner. He felt a spurt of irritation at the Father's meddling. Kalol Mondal needed shutting up, not opening out. Anyway, *he* had had enough of Kalol Mondal's enterprising ways. He picked up his briefcase.

He put down his briefcase.

Seize the day, Biren Roy had once said, an expression Pinaki hadn't fully understood, but now he believed he did. It meant *do it now.* Or *it's now or never.* Kalol Mondal was there beside him, friendly, receptive *and* he had brought up the subject himself. Although they had left it behind, Pinaki had the unhappy idea it would not take much to return to it. A simple question... Of course, the answer might confirm what he suspected, and did he really want that?

He didn't and he did. Meanwhile, he wanted another glass of tea.

Aroma himself brought him the tea. He hadn't sent his assistant! He had left his station, left his wok smoking! It was an augury.

'What does it mean, Aroma the People?' Pinaki asked respectfully.

Aroma twinkled at him. '*You* tell me! Call if you want anything else,' he said, bustling off.

Buoyed by this exchange, Pinaki swung around towards his neighbour. 'Ami tomar katha jigesh kortey chai,' he said in a stern voice. 'About that night you came to my house.'

Kalol Mondal opened his mouth in a long grimace to scratch his jaw. Without warning, he snapped it shut. That rattled Pinaki. The tea went down the wrong way and next thing he was bent over the counter.

Kalol Mondal thumped his back with a light, downward sweep. The fellow was patting him! *Stroking* him! Pinaki jerked away, dashing the water from his eyes. 'Why did you come upstairs with my daughter?' he asked.

Kalol Mondal put his head to one side. His expression struck Pinaki as a little too attentive. Even the yellow eyes seemed artificially coloured. Provoked, Pinaki raised his voice. 'The taxi brought her home. What need was there for you to...?'

Kalol Mondal studied a sliver of samosa, turning it this way and that. Weighing different lies, Pinaki thought, his anxiety giving way to irritation. Kalol Mondal tossed the sliver into his mouth and chewed. His Adam's apple bounced like a ball cock in a water tank. Swallowing portentously, 'I didn't see a taxi,' he said. 'She was alone.'

Pinaki gave up. Trying to get the truth from Kalol Mondal was like extracting a tooth with a toothpick.

He seethed all the way home. He was fed up of being the polite one, the one who always gave in, the one who made peace—and kept it. Other people got away with rudeness, bad manners, bullying, breaking the rules. They *thrived* on it. Whereas he was the one who gave up his tram seat—even to men because they looked tired. And they never ever refused. He was the one who gave way to ladies in a queue. And they never ever thanked him. He stopped for the traffic lights on empty, Sunday roads, when everybody else ignored them. Nobody noticed. Nobody cared.

Now he had become the kind of man who distributed information about his daughter as if, as if it was free food at the Kali temple. To, of all people, Kalol Mondal.

She was in the veranda, hunched over her books. Diligence that should have delighted him.

'Sit straight,' he said. 'Otherwise nothing will get into your head.'

She gave no indication she'd heard him.

'Look up, I'm talking to you.'

No response.

He would wait for her to move to make his move. She would have to turn the page. *If* she was studying. Which he doubted—her composure was a little too studied.

She flipped a page.

'Alright.' He wouldn't bother with niceties—she didn't deserve any. 'I want to know about that night—the night you came late.'

She ignored him. But her hands shook.

He snatched the book from her. 'Tell me!' The familiar churning began in his stomach.

'There's nothing to tell!'

'Today that fellow, that Kalol Mondal told me you were walking down the street! He didn't see any taxi!'

There was no mistaking the panic in her eyes. Then, 'You spoke to him,' she said colourlessly. 'To check up on me.'

For an instant he was ashamed. But only an instant. 'See what all I have to do,' he grumbled. 'Because you will not tell me the truth.'

Putting her hands to her face she said, 'I didn't do anything wrong.' The words leaked through her fingers. She was crying! He felt a surge of power. He wanted her to cry.

From the refuge of blindness she muttered something.

He pulled her hands off. 'Did you say I was jealous? Jealous of whom?'

She jerked her head towards the living room where Rimi was watching television.

He longed to be in that blue-sparked gloom. Sit with Rimi and yawn through her serial. Solve a math problem for Tuli. Listen to Dida drone on about the old days. But he'd cast himself out, probably for all time. The sorrow welled up. Pungent, stinging liquid filled his mouth.

'Baba?' she said timorously.

He struck her.

It was a light tap, glancing the side of her head so it wouldn't have hurt, but it was enough. Her eyes blazed.

Incensed, '*You* are giving *me* the red eye?' he cried. 'You think this is the same as breaking a vase? That I should say, "It is okay shona, what is broken is broken, never mind we can get another"?' His brow was clammy. He wiped it with his handkerchief. 'Don't talk back!'

She hadn't said a word.

He put his hand up, and kept it up as if he was taking an oath, although he couldn't swear on what he was about to say. 'I know you had been out with him that Christmas night, Dona. And that he brought you back. There was no Nini, no movie, no taxi.'

Her book slid down her knee. It was a confession. Now there was no going back. Fortunately no one else need know about it...

Kalol Mondal. Kalol Mondal knew who had brought her home.

He had the sense of a picture righting itself. The fellow's knowing smile. His oily concern... Had she plotted with him to keep the whole business quiet? And Biren Roy—was *he* in the plot too? But he, Pinaki, had uncovered the plot!

The elation dissolved. It was a sorry triumph.

He lay on his bed in the darkened room, so disturbed that even this, his haven (when Rimi was away or asleep, that is) couldn't calm him. The scratchy wool rasped against his cheek. Sheta, what all I suffer, he thought. It is not in me to doubt and question, punish—it is not how I am. Anger is *not* my natural state. He snuffled a little, surrendering to the luxury of self-reproach, followed soon enough by self-justification.

At last, and why didn't he think of it sooner, he remembered

Mr Sen's face. How stupefied he had looked when Pinaki told him about the house! How jealous he would be when he saw it!

Soon he was in the middle of a full-blown fantasy, without the limits and brakes of reason. The backdrop was always his tormentor's cubicle, a place that held for Pinaki—even in a dream—all the terror of the headmaster's room. Mr Sen was looking at the invitation card for the housewarming with that wonderfully amazed expression. *You can't miss my house, sir,* Pinaki was saying. *It is the only two-storied building around. Yes, I know a cantilever is expensive but it is integral to the design. It gives the house its crucial balance. Hmm, I suppose it is too elaborate for a bagan badi, but one must think big—otherwise would there have been a Victoria Memorial?*

37

Never again a house, growled Biren, banging down the phone. Housewife or not. In fact, Pinaki had turned out to be more trying than a gaggle of housewives. He was like a bloody coir doormat. Squashy and prickly. Ill-mannered too. Twice he'd broken his appointment, and not bothered to apologize. There was simply no explanation for his behaviour.

But, in the evening, as he waited for Pinaki, he found he was, well, not anxious, but concerned that he just might have lost this one column left standing in the ruins of his projects.

To his relief, Pinaki came.

Inside, Pinaki made straight for Biren's drafting table, and peered at the drawings scattered on it.

'Be my guest,' said Biren sarcastically. 'It *is* your house, after all.'

Pinaki continued to look, hands behind his back and nose pinched with distaste, as if, thought Biren, he'd opened the door of a public lavatory.

'You can touch those, you know. Gauguin's syphilis didn't infect his paintings.'

'The entrance seems to have changed.'

'It has evolved, yes.'

'I hope it won't keep evolving.'

Bugger off, muttered Biren. 'Here, read the contract,' he said shortly. 'I need to pee.'

When he returned, Pinaki was *still* scrutinizing the papers. Biren fought the impulse to tell him if he'd shown a tenth as much diligence when he bought his land, he would have saved everyone a load of trouble. Instead, he commented they were lucky Karim Ali had agreed to do this thankless job—a small project in a remote area.

Pinaki looked up. 'Will he bring his food to the site?'

Biren said he imagined that in the normal course people didn't go without eating for ten hours at a stretch. But what was Bose's concern?

'He may eat beef on the site.'

Biren couldn't find it in him to laugh. 'I hadn't factored that,' he said. 'But it's highly likely, Bose, that this part of the world was once inhabited by cannibals. People may have eaten people on your land. I know for a fact they eat snails. Has a distinctive stink when boiled.' He chuckled at Pinaki's expression. 'I'm sorry for your troubles, Bose, but you must see I cannot share them. While I agree in principle I shouldn't make unilateral decisions, at least not too many of them, you must believe it is in your interests that Karim Ali builds your house. Trust me when I say this beef-eater is the best there is. At least,' he added dryly, 'he won't eat the steel on your site.'

Pinaki pulled a face. 'If there is delay because of Ramzan I will not pay for it.'

After he left, Biren went into the studio. 'What *is* eating the bugger, Manu? He's turned into a werewolf overnight! And you know what? He didn't bring up the matter of our fees. Why is it that clients always get so bloody coy about that?'

He returned to his room and stood by the window, rubbing his cheek. It wasn't just the fees. Pinaki hadn't asked for the estimate either. Either he was afraid to confront it or was still living in his fantasyland. Hard to ascribe indifference to money in an accountant. It was more likely he subscribed to the *if you break it, you buy it* school of thought.

He had misjudged his client. Within the hour Pinaki was back, entering the room without knocking.

Biren bit back a reprimand. 'What now, Bose?'

'How much will this house cost?'

Biren put down his pencil, went to his desk, rummaged in a drawer, and pushed a sheet of paper across. 'These are not the final figures but they'll give you an idea.'

Pinaki studied the paper through his glasses.

Biren studied Pinaki though a cloud of smoke. He looked, Biren thought, as if he'd heard an entire catch of hilsa had been found with mercury poisoning.

Pinaki looked up. 'I cannot afford this.'

'You didn't give me a budget to work with.'

'I had made my financial situation clear.'

'"Clear" implies a figure. You gave me none. Unless it was lost in the annals of our conversations.'

'I told you I wanted a simple house. You didn't take me seriously. You never do.'

Biren controlled his irritation. Infusing reasonableness into his tone, 'Well, it's all done now. A lot of time has gone into the details,' he said. 'So...'

'Two weeks,' Pinaki interrupted.

Biren exploded. 'Twenty *years*, you...!' *Ignorant fool* he had been about to say. He frowned. 'What exactly is the state of your finances, Bose? Let's be frank here.'

Pinaki told him.

'Well, that's frank enough,' Biren said, drumming his fingers on the table.

'So you see you have to modify the design.'

'I have to, do I?'

'Yes.'

'Aren't you rather overplaying your client's role? *You* don't direct *me*, *I* direct *you*.'

Pinaki folded his arms. His stance was like a hunger striker's, Biren thought. Prepared to sit it out for as long as it took to break you down. For as long as it took to kill your design, that is. Line by line.

He took a steadying pull at his cigarette. 'Listen, Bose. You can't add or subtract from a design as if it's a stew. It's an integrated whole, making sense only when executed in its entirety. Without those features the house is as nothing. Nothing.'

'I can't afford them,' Pinaki said. Now his stance was like a parent countering an unreasonable demand.

Biren could have hit him. 'You have no idea,' he said, looking unseeingly at the window, 'no idea at all of what this house stands for, what it means to me...to the city.'

'What has my house got to do with the *city*?'

'I refer to those enlightened few who see the way to its progress. To which faction I thought *you* belonged. You certainly gave the impression you did... But see, you're no different from the rest. Bred in a Petri dish. I wasted my time on you.'

Behind their thick glasses Pinaki's eyes were as stones.

Biren muttered under his breath. *Go easy*. 'Bose,' he said, leaning forward. 'Your *simple* house would have cost, let me see, about seventy-five thousand less, but that's still far more than the figure you gave me. There are always cost overruns. That's one of the reasons I warned you against building a house.'

'I didn't ask for *this* kind of a house.'

'You shouldn't have come to *me*, then.'

There was a minute's bristling silence. Then Pinaki said, 'You should remove that funny window.'

'Oriel. *No*. That gives the eastern façade a focal point.'

'Then cut out the glass pyramid.'

'Frustum. *No*. That's the building's genius loci.'

'You are not a genius.'

Biren let that pass.

'That frame looks crooked.'

'It's a deconstructed portal. The asymmetry is deliberate.'

'You have to cut out *something*. To cut costs.'

'No. We'll manage.'

'How?'

For a long moment neither of them spoke.

Pinaki cleared his throat. 'This is *my* house. Not,' he moved his hand up and down—a crude gesture that deeply offended Biren, 'a laboratory for your experiments.'

'How *dare* you speak to me like this? You little...' Biren checked himself. He walked to the window and peered down.

I am owed.

After a while, soothed by the nightscape, he turned around. 'Right. Let's consider those features you object to. I agree that contrasting styles can get kitschy but this, *this* will be a heavenly union. The copulation of gods.' He put his hands on Pinaki's shoulders and squeezed them gently—as if deflating a football. 'We'll find the money, Bose,' he said. 'I will look for sponsorship from a couple of manufacturers to use their products innovatively.'

The shoulders moved slightly but unambiguously under Biren's fingers. Pinaki was shaking him off.

After he left, Biren yanked open a drawer, pulled out a bottle and snatched up a tea mug—the only clean receptacle he could find. Angry though he was, and more than that, chagrined at the snub to his—gratuitous—self-tribute, he recognized he couldn't entirely blame the little man for it. Because the truth was that the house had become a perverse extension of his ego. It was now a life form, fatted by his hunger, the thwarted longings of a lifetime. The estimate was nowhere near where the needle would come to rest. Although, of course, he couldn't tell Pinaki that.

He would pay for it. He would have to do it with stealth and subtlety (both of which he lacked), because there was no telling how his obstreperous client would view it. He might sprout a conscience, and that would be very inconvenient. One couldn't let a mere *conscience* come in the way of building something the way it should be built. The way he wanted it to be built.

He stared into the mug. To begin with he would have to give Pinaki a revised, that is, a watered down, estimate. Else the fellow might insist on watering down the design. Or dispense with Biren (and Biren had not bothered with an agreement!) and finish it on his own—oh, insupportable! Hard to imagine him doing this, but in his new, strange mood anything was possible. His imprudence was an established fact, but his timidity, Biren now suspected, could inform a low-level cunning.

Pinaki was hurrying down Free School Street. *Believe* Biren Roy? Believe *in* Biren Roy? He had stuck with Biren Roy—enduring slights, sarcasm, bullying—because he believed in him. He had believed in him the way you believe putting sugar in your tea will sweeten it. He had believed in the *goodness* of him. But now Biren Roy's words seemed as fraudulent as the Party's manifesto in election year.

Dona was sitting at her table, chewing the ends of her hair and staring out of the window. Without turning around, 'Are you spying on me again, Baba?' she asked.

His head swam. The old helpless feeling was back. 'Just wondering what you were doing.'

She turned up the corner of her mouth. 'Six of one and half a dozen of the other.'

He jerked her chair. 'I *know* where you learned to speak like that! What *else* does he teach you?'

She jumped up and ran outside. He stood holding her chair, waiting for the trembling to stop.

Dida was standing in the corridor. He gave her a black look. Listening in again! She didn't pretend otherwise. 'You should not disturb the children when they're studying, Bulbul.'

'Please don't interfere in things you don't understand, Ma. And she's not a *child*.'

'I haven't said this before, Bulbul, but I will now. If you go on like this even I will not have any sympathy for you.'

He pushed past her and went to the veranda. She called out to him. 'And if you want to shout and throw things, don't do it in my room.'

This is the last time I'm building a house, he thought, and then remembered it was also the first time. First and last, he amended, but *last* had an extravagant, worldly ring to it so he said it aloud.

Not too far away Kalol Mondal contemplated his day with rather more optimism. He was at last making progress. That morning he'd gone to the Turtle—his private name for the supervisor—to protest against his unsatisfactory status.

'I'm here as a management trainee, not to carry files! If you can't fit me, then tell me! I will find another job!'

This was a wild claim, certainly untenable. *This is the trouble with me,* he thought, as he stood, digging his nails into his palms. *I have a hot head.* Father John said that too. You're a good fellow, Anthony, but hot-headed.

The Turtle didn't say, 'Find another job then,' as Kalol

Mondal feared. He just tucked his chin into his neck and continued with his work.

What did that mean, wondered Kalol Mondal uneasily. He was so relieved not to be thrown out there and then, that he slunk back to his corner without another word. He had best make amends though. He began by offering the Turtle a chew of paan after lunch. The Turtle declined the gift firmly but politely. Kalol Mondal went his way, not too worried. There would be other opportunities.

38

Winter gave way to a long, difficult summer. There were predictions of a heat wave—and the power-grid had collapsed twice already. There was a rumour that the diesel prices were going up. That sparked off a rumour about a transport strike. The impending crises always took a hysterical turn on the road. If *it* happened, *when* it happened (the slightest provocation—your fender brushing a cyclist—was enough to start it) you'd be dragged out and clobbered. The rule was that no matter what, the smaller vehicle was in the right. Those on foot ruled the day.

Biren drove with care, speeding up only on the outskirts of the city. The mud track he turned into, hard and deeply fissured, slowed him again. After ten minutes of bumping along on it, he arrived at the crooked tree that marked Pinaki's site. He'd seen it in many avatars now—heavy with foliage when the footings had been marked, sere and bare when the walls came up, mossy with incipient shoots when the door frames were fixed, and today, with the formwork for the roof slab in place, a pair of orioles gilded its glossy leaves.

Small, naked children sprang out of the bushes and stood picking at their bellies. They did not return his smile. Smiles were easy to come by, sweets were not. He had not thought to bring sweets.

After a couple of nor'westers, an intense green had seeped into the earth. Paddy, ankle-high, pulsated in the pre-lapsarian stillness. Wildflowers speckled the untilled fields. White and yellow butterflies drifted through the sun-warmed air. Surveying this pastoral scene, like a maitre d' in a fine dining restaurant, was a stork.

The half-finished structure looked like the half-picked carcase of a bird. The bird (if anyone cared to know), had a spiritual connection with the Seth's hotel. A genealogical link that evoked it, the way the bump in a nose did an ancestor. The Archimedean parabola in the elder's staircase traced a curve in the progeny's water tank. The colonnaded terrace, of slim round columns marching in geometric progression, was a miniature agora. The original rooftop restaurant was the glass frustum (that Pinaki had objected to, but was destined to be his study), a steel cage just now...

It was unfortunate Pinaki didn't care to know any of this. (And how much that rankled!) His behaviour continued to mystify too. He had shown no interest in his (professedly) life's dream becoming reality. Not even today—and roof casting was a milestone. He had, in fact, visited the site only three times since construction began, and all of them when Biren wasn't there.

Biren flung his cigarette into a bush. Perhaps it was as well the fellow wasn't around, fussing and fretting.

The uncovenanted relief of Pinaki's absence was marred by uneasy speculations for the reason for it. Clients who interfered were a nuisance. But clients who wouldn't meet your eye when they spoke to you? Who were demonstrably unreceptive? Hostile, even? Especially a client who had wooed you—for *months*—with the wearisome ardour of a lovelorn swain? The fellow seemed to be in a permanent sulk. About *what*? At least the Seth had waited till the concrete had set before beginning his grumbles.

Biren could only conclude it was money. Money takes people in funny ways. In this case, it had a bad effect on their character. Perhaps Pinaki thought that if he pursued a policy of conscientious objection to the design he could refuse to pay for the execution of the aspects he disapproved of. Biren wished he could assure him, without rousing his suspicions, that he needn't resort to such a stratagem, because he wouldn't be billed for them. Biren had long decided he would use his legacy to finish the project. *His* project. It had become his through a tacit transfer of responsibility

The sun hit the high notes of noon. Its savagery, unmitigated by the watery landscape, burned his eyes. Before long, he was hot and perspiring, and as scratchy as the untended grass at his feet. Stripping to his vest, he climbed the bamboo ladder to the roof, to inspect the reinforcement. An hour later he jumped down, sat on a half-built wall and shared a packet of chips, very salty, very oily, with a one-eyed village dog.

The rattle and crunch of the cement mixer, the scraping and tamping of the slurry would carry on till the entire roof slab was cast. The water tank too.

By 5 p.m., a slight coolness entered the air. A paw of breeze teased the sweat trickling down his face.

Darkness fell with the suddenness of an executioner's axe. One by one, the Petromax lamps were lit. The unsettling white light deepened the darkness beyond. Work slowed down as everybody's eyes adjusted to the strange largesse.

The lamps spluttered and hissed. Somewhere a child began wailing. Karim Ali put his hand over a lamp as if to silence it, and called a halt for dinner.

The commotion began when the food—rice and fish curry—was being served. Unnoticed by all a group of villagers had come into the penumbra of the lamplight. Biren was alerted to their presence by the altered beat in the aural assault of a busy site. 'Alright,' he said. 'How much now?'

He'd known when he'd first paid the villagers for not disrupting construction that he was buying time. That all negotiations would be prone to distrust and discontent—and regular reviews. Of course, he'd kept Pinaki out of these transactions. He'd been afraid that Pinaki might discover that he did, after all, have principles. Or pride. Some latent, inopportune compunction that might persuade him to stop the work, sell his half-finished house to a canning plant.

So when Pinaki came to the studio the next evening, and looked at Biren as though he'd had beaten him to the last good fish in the stall, Biren expected the worst. He turned down the volume on his transistor radio, prepared to brazen it out. 'Good evening, Bose. What brings you here? Always a pleasure of course.'

'I want an update on the progress of the construction. It seems to be slowing down.'

Biren raised his eyebrows. It hadn't occurred to his impecunious client that, under his circumstances, his attitude was rather haughty.

Pinaki hefted his briefcase on to the table, undid the clasps, took out a package wrapped in newspaper, and hugged it to himself.

'What's that you're hiding there? Hash? I'll take half a kilo, thank you.'

Ignoring him Pinaki tore off the many bits of sticky tape on the package, took out an object and stood it carefully on the table. 'I want to sell it. You said it's valuable. I need the money for the house.'

It was the menorah.

'You can find a buyer for me.'

After the initial ire at this presumption (did Pinaki think

he was a fence? A pawnbroker?), relief flooded Biren. He switched off the transistor radio and stubbed out his cigarette.

A look passed between them, uniting them in their commitment to their venture as nothing before had.

Minutes passed as Biren pretended to give the 'antique' a close scrutiny. Could anyone really believe this piece of metal was the hero saving them from financial ruin?

'Well,' he said at last. 'I can ask a friend who's an expert in the, um, field.' His mouth twisted. 'Let's hope it's worth a really obscene amount.'

'How will we know if your friend is honest?'

Biren almost choked on his cigarette. *What the...?* 'Perhaps you would prefer to sell it yourself?' he asked—and held his breath.

Pinaki shook his head. 'I wouldn't know where to go. I bought it because I liked it. Not for investment.'

Keep it then, Biren wanted to say, *it won't make a difference. How do you suppose we've managed without it all this time?* But something held him back. Prudence? Politeness?

Fear.

'I know I owe Karim Ali another instalment,' Pinaki continued. 'He has not asked yet. But he will—soon. That last cheque,' he said stonily, although his mouth worked, 'finished most of my savings. If I don't get money I may have to...' He turned his palms up.

'I see,' Biren said. He saw only too well. The canning plant option had occurred to Pinaki. And he had intuited that wouldn't suit Biren at all. 'I see,' Biren repeated, slowly.

Pinaki leapt up. 'No, you *don't* see! I don't like owing money! I have never owed money! I am a self-made man, I...'

'Take it easy, Bose.'

'No, it is *not* easy! I have not paid *you* also. Don't think I have forgotten this.'

'All in good time,' said Biren. 'I won't go away. And if this,' he patted the menorah, 'is worth what I believe it is, you won't owe anybody. Leave it with me. If you can trust me with it.'

And Pinaki actually hesitated before nodding!

Biren was debating which he would enjoy more—punching the fellow's nose or throwing his precious brassware out of the window, when Pinaki spoke. 'You can keep it for a week. Then I will see.'

'Good idea,' said Biren, inclining his head. 'You can't be too careful where money is concerned. And careful, don't fiddle with that,' he added, pointing his cigarette at the bird's nest. 'There are pins there.'

Pinaki drew his hand back as if stung.

Biren pushed his chair back. 'You'll get your house. You have my word for it.'

'You mean I will get *your* house. *You* will get *my* house.'

Biren's cigarette fell from his mouth. He snatched it up and brushed the cinders off his shirt. 'Well, well. You *have* come a long way. May I claim some credit for the um, mutation? Or will you debit me for that too?'

Pinaki jumped up. 'I don't want any more of your jokes! I am fed up with them...everything! My mother is *ill*! In hospital! If she dies it will be because of *you*!'

Biren stared after him, astonished.

39

Pinaki hadn't lied about his mother's condition. Early one morning that week, Dona had woken her parents to tell them Dida was having difficulty breathing. She looked 'funny'. Her lips were 'kind of blue.' And she had had a chhotpotey night, tossing and turning.

They knew no doctor who would make house calls. They would have to take her to a hospital. Pinaki chose Halder

Hospital, which had the double advantage of being nearby, and being inexpensive. He had reservations about its reputation till Rimi made his mind up for him. In the careless way of those who believe sick people can't hear, she said, 'I think it is only gastric. She eats all the wrong things.'

Dida made a small protesting squeak like a very small dog whose tail has been stepped on. *That*, declared Rimi, bending over the bed, was the gastric playing up.

All morning they ran tests on her, shunting her from room to room. By afternoon, Pinaki's anxiety about his mother had given way to anxiety about money. When the hospital advised she be left there overnight for observation, he exploded. 'What will you observe when she is sleeping? This place is a money-making machine!'

The matron shrugged. 'You can take her out any time. *Now* if you so wish. We have a queue for admissions. It'll be at your risk, of course.'

After that Pinaki had to grovel. He was trembling with resentment when the matron turned on her heel and left the room.

The next afternoon, the doctor's assistant informed him that his mother's condition was pulmonary arterial hypertension. It could be fatal if not treated and monitored. That is, she had to be on medication for the rest of her life. The list of medicines covered half a foolscap sheet.

He barged into the doctor's room. 'Excuse me, Doctor. I just wanted to tell you that I, my family, doesn't take allopathic medicines. We have faith in homeopathy.'

The doctor pushed up his glasses. Without their friendly cover his eyes were unsympathetic—and shrewd. They divined Pinaki was making a case for cheaper treatment. 'You are asking me or telling me?' he said, his voice crackling like ice in warm water.

'Homeopathy has no side effects,' Pinaki said, jerking his head back.

'Up to you. But don't blame me if anything goes wrong. Homeopathy is okay for headaches and indigestion. And she does not have either. Homeopathy! Why don't you try faith healing?'

Pinaki stroked back the hair from Dida's forehead. 'The doctor said you could take homeopathic medicine, Ma.' Tenderly he adjusted the cushion under her head. 'There is no harm. No side effects.'

'Whatever you think is best, Bulbul.'

'It's not what *I* think,' he said, nettled. '*Millions* of people use homeopathy. Mr Sen in my office...'

'Please, Bulbul. Let me sleep.'

When they were getting into bed, 'I have decided on homeopathy for Ma,' he said. He saw no need to explain why.

There was a rustle beside him. Rimi's hand was fumbling with the sheet. She slipped her fingers through his, rubbed her thumb on his palm. A signal so sparingly given, it should have excited him. Now it roused as much enthusiasm as an alarm clock on a winter morning.

'It is a good decision,' she murmured, pressing her body against his. 'It is gastric, whatever the doctor may say. *I* know.'

'I am tired, Rimi. Very tired.'

But he couldn't sleep. The guilt that had been ringing in his head all day, with the shrill punctuality of a factory siren, wouldn't let him What if the homeopathy didn't work? What if his mother *died*? How trustingly she had given him her fixed deposit! He'd used it up. Used up most of his savings too—and the house only half-done. There was the menorah...and he'd entrusted it to Biren Roy.

Biren Roy! He threw off the sheet and rushed out of the room.

There was a line of light under the dining room door. His

heart warmed. Tuli was working hard. He would go far. An honest and sincere boy.

But it was Dona the Disappointment, not Tuli the Hope, sitting at the dining table. Doing her homework. The lamplight made a golden aureole around her hair. He could see the curve of her cheek, the cushion of fat under her chin.

He should go to her. Speak some words of encouragement, warm, caring words that a father would speak to inspire a daughter engaged in fulfilling her duty to him. Appropriate words, and, crucially, acceptable to her. Such as...such as...

He tiptoed away, crept into bed and pulled the sheet over his head.

~

Biren parked on J. Mullick Road, right outside Pinaki's building. He combed his conscience. He was in the clear. There was nothing owed. Except, if he saw her now, and that was the uncertainty muddying this enterprise, wasn't it, he couldn't guarantee he would not be back in hock.

He was here, ostensibly, to pay a courtesy call to see Dida. And to tell Pinaki his menorah was indeed valuable, that there were several ready buyers for it. Ostensibly. Because he could as well have called Pinaki to enquire after Dida *and* tell him about the menorah. Of course, there was no buyer. The menorah would continue to live in his cupboard as the priceless antique it wasn't, growing in value with every buyer that didn't bid for it.

Nobody answered the bell, but across the landing a door opened. He was informed that the old lady had been readmitted just that morning. The hospital, he understood, was two streets away. And yes, if he hurried, he would make it before visiting hour ended.

He needn't have hurried. The unchecked numbers of people flowing in and out seemed relaxed and confident. Perhaps visiting rules were just an article of intent.

The floor was a mess of mud, courtesy a pre-monsoon downpour. The smell of chicken curry jostled with the reek of clogged drains and medicinal alcohol. At the reception, a phlegmatic girl was dealing with the switchboard, the intercom, an anxious customer and an irate administrator, and clearly making nobody happy. By the simple expedient of leaning over the desk while she was occupied, Biren read Dida's card on the information board. In five minutes he was knocking on a door on the second floor.

Knots of visitors stood in the dank, ill-lit tunnel of a corridor. Three burqa-clad women chatted in the entrance to a dormitory ward. A noisy group of teenagers was horsing around. Everyone seemed to be in party spirits. It would appear that the hospital, nominally a prison—through the doors you got glimpses of inmates shackled to IVs—was a popular club.

Pinaki appeared neither pleased nor otherwise to see him. However, he pressed himself against the open door. Biren took this as permission, if not an invitation, to enter.

Two narrow beds took up three-quarters of the floor space. A fat woman and a little girl hovered around the one by the window. Rimi sat by the one near the door. A shapeless bundle lay on it, covered from neck to toe with a green sheet. The face was obscured by a rubber mask. But for the scribble of yellow-white hair on the none-too-clean pillow, it could as well have been a laundry bag as someone's mother.

He greeted Rimi before turning to Pinaki. 'How is your mother doing, Bose?'

Rimi answered for Pinaki. 'Not dangerous but wheak,' she said, in English. 'The homeopathy did not cure indigestion.'

Pinaki frowned at his wife. 'She is doing well,' he said.

There was nothing about the insubstantial, inert form to persuade Biren that its condition was as stated. Of course there was nothing much to go by, except the obligatory (rusty) IV stand, idling behind the headboard. He traced the origin of the tube snaking out of the mask to an oxygen cylinder—and then wished he hadn't. Because he saw another tube, ending in a transparent plastic sachet clipped to the bed. Straw-coloured liquid dripped slowly into it. It was the only indication of life.

He leaned on the wall, gingerly, conscious that his unfamiliarity with places like this (manifest in his awkwardness), magnified the impropriety of his presence. Patently, Rimi and Pinaki thought so too. Gusts of disapproval were emanating from them.

'I see I'm somewhat of an intrusion here,' he said. He nodded at Pinaki. 'I have some news that might cheer you, Bose. If we could just step outside for a minute...'

He smiled at Pinaki's expression. 'Surprised? I was, too.' Then he realized Pinaki was looking less surprised than sceptical. And about as happy as if he'd wandered into tiger country armed with a peashooter. 'What's the problem, Bose?'

'Is that the best price? Three days are not enough to make proper enquiries.'

Biren took a deep breath. 'You really *are* something, aren't you?' Which was not very original and a poor alternative to a sock on the jaw, but it did relieve one's feelings without courting arrest. Controlling his temper, he dug into his pocket.

'It is not allowed here. This is a *hospital*.' Biren used the sole of his shoe to put out his cigarette. It was a perfectly reasonable rebuke, but it had somehow brought him down to the level of the awful place while lofting Pinaki over it. And it hadn't escaped him that Pinaki had waited till he lit up to tick him off.

'I'll try getting this buyer to up his offer,' he said, commending himself on his restraint.

Now Pinaki looked suspicious. Biren had had enough. He swung around—and ran slap-bang into Dona.

She dropped the bag she was carrying, spilling its contents. Her hands flew to her ears.

Pinaki hurried to pick up the bits and pieces, scolding her for her carelessness and—potentially—breaking the saline water bottle.

Biren handed him a cylinder of plaster. 'It's not her fault, Bose. I should have looked where I was going.'

Pinaki ignored him. Thrusting the bag at Dona, 'You're late,' he said tersely. 'Give Ma the glucose for Dida. Then return the saline to the pharmacy. This time *don't* forget to tell them it's a replacement. And...'

Biren held out his hand. 'I can give it to them if Dona wants to go to the room.'

Pinaki gave him a glare of such intensity that he was stunned. Then he was furious. 'What *is* the matter with you, Bose? I'm getting quite pissed off by your attitude, you know. It's...' He stopped.

Dona was biting her lip, looking so miserable he wanted to put his arms around her. The anger was flatter, less seismic, but he if he didn't get away he might say something he would regret.

Yet he lingered. If asked to explain, he might have said it was for the same reason why you stay on for the second half of a bad play despite all indications it wasn't going to improve. You want to be in at the finish. You might miss something significant. You might hear a line that would change your life.

She might throw him that line.

Her father seized her arm and hustled her off.

Breasting a wave of visitors rising up the staircase Biren reached the lobby. A very crowded, very wet lobby.

It was raining—raining to vindicate every filmmaker and writer who had rendered Calcutta's monsoon as apocalyptic as the eruption of Mt Vesuvius. The noise rivalled an entire army's boots clattering over cobblestones. An easy camaraderie prevailed. This was the sort of catastrophe that had no consequences other than loss of that which everyone had plenty to spare. Time. At least, thought Biren, you could smoke while you waited. He pushed through to the entrance to do just that.

At first he thought he must be hearing things. Then he hoped he was *not* hearing things. The third time, when he realized he wasn't, actually, hearing things, he shut his eyes, held the smoke in his mouth for as long as he could before turning around.

'What took you so long, Dona?'

'Why did you come here, Biren?'

Her mouth was twitching. She was trying not to laugh!

'Shall we make a dash for the car?'

She nodded.

And that's how easy it was.

The traffic on Diamond Harbour Road was moving like ditch water in a drought. He didn't have to think how to spin out the journey to J. Mullick Road, where she wanted to go.

'So Dona, tell me. How have you been since I saw you last?'

As a conversational gambit it was less than tactful. She turned her face to the window.

'Your new home is coming along at a clip,' he said. 'Have you seen it?'

She was doodling on the fogged-up glass. 'Baba hasn't taken us there,' she said in a stifled voice.

'Ah. Perhaps he wants to surprise you with the final product.' When she didn't answer, 'Probably busy,' he said.

'I don't think he's *that* busy,' she said, rubbing off her artwork. 'At least not so that he can't...' The glass squeaked.

He adjusted the rear-view mirror while he considered what to say. For a start, *why do you suppose Baba is the way he is?* Except it didn't seem right to quiz her about her father. 'Well, it *is* the year ending,' he said, careful to keep his tone impersonal so she wouldn't think he was probing. 'That's a stressful time for bean counters, I mean accountants. And building a house is...'

'It's not the house,' she said in a tragic voice. 'It's *me*. And *you*. He suspects that we, he guessed, he *knows* something. About that night.'

The car bucked as he swerved round a non-existent obstacle. 'Kalol Mondal told him?'

'Maybe. But before that Baba found my lipstick in your, in the bird's nest. I must have dropped it in the car,' her voice shook, 'that night.'

He couldn't speak for the turmoil in his head. He'd forgotten about the lipstick. That is, he had marked its disappearance, but hadn't actively missed it.

Her back was unnaturally straight. She was clutching the door handle—in exactly the way, he couldn't help thinking, her father had, that long ago day in the wetlands.

'You know,' he said, keeping his eyes on the road, 'it's uncomplimentary to you perhaps, but all I can remember about that night is the prawn toast. They don't make it as they used to. Shocking, isn't it, how the standards everywhere are slipping? And here we're supposed to be evolving! Is it another casualty of technological progress or...' On and on, till he sensed her distress subside.

He drove right up to her doorway. Pointless to keep up appearances now. In any case it was raining so hard that any neighbour out spying in this weather deserved the reward of his beat-up car making its soggy delivery. Which, he observed, was getting soggier. What was she doing—standing in the rain? *Go inside*, he mouthed, gesturing towards the entrance.

She darted forward to rap on his window. He rolled it down.

'Is it possible, could we...' She was losing words to the rain but was she saying what he thought she was?

Strings of hair stuck to her forehead. Dirty water sloshed round her feet. Was he going to wait for his storm to subside while she drowned? He got out and rushed her into the lobby.

'Now. Did I hear you say you want to see the house?'

She nodded.

'I'm scheduled to go Friday week.' His glasses were misting but he didn't remove them. They were cover. So was his wrist, which he was raising to look at his watch. 'At 1 o'clock.' And he was checking the time *now*? What sort of nut would she think he was?

But her face was serious as she answered, 'That's fine by me.'

It wasn't so fine by him. There were seven days to go. Why couldn't he have suggested an earlier date? Such as tomorrow? Six days earlier wouldn't be counted as unseemly eagerness.

Then he remembered why Friday was on his mind. On Friday morning the formwork for the roof would be taken down. It would be like unwrapping a present for her.

'I can pick you up at Flurys,' he said.

Two distant moons were floating in the blacks of her eyes. Too late he remembered their old meeting place could have painful associations.

'Or anywhere else,' he said, rubbing his cheek.

The moons dissolved. She was smiling at him.

'Flurys corner,' he said, giving her his two-finger salute.

40

Against the hard, particulate light of early afternoon, the structure looked etched in charcoal. A raven, about to take off. The sweeping planes of the roof, a concrete membrane, was its plumage, and the glass pyramid its crest.

'For a change reality trumps imagination,' he murmured. 'It will do. It will do.'

She came up from behind him. 'What will...oh. Oh! I didn't imagine anything like *this*! I couldn't have!'

He laughed and took her hand, tossed it up. 'It pleases, does it? Come, let's go closer. I need to see the contractor first. Walk around. Just be careful of those bamboo poles lying around.'

He was studying the kitchen window, thinking he might have to widen it, when she called out to him.

'What is it, Dona?'

'See those things?'

'What things? Things have names.'

'Well, that glass pyramid.'

'Frustum,' he said mechanically, still intent on the window.

'...and then *that*. The drum.' She tugged at his arm. 'Look *there*, Biren.'

She was pointing to the water tank. 'They look funny together. Is that how it will be?'

He looked, and felt a sharp jab in the region of his chest. He moved a few feet to the left. It made no difference.

Shading his eyes against the light—as if that was the problem—he looked again. No difference.

He stepped back, tripped over a tussock, righted himself, and, his heart thumping, took another step back. Back, back, farther back. Now right, and right again, without once taking his eyes off his target—two targets, as it happened, and that was the problem, wasn't it? All the back-and-forth-and-sidestepping hadn't made a jot of difference to the truth. The truth, the undisguised, *undisguisable* truth being that the two critical features, the frustum and the water tank—the one a light-filled aerie and the other a truncated missile—were fighting each other for dominance. And neither was winning. How hadn't you seen that when you drew the elevations? There had been no ambiguity in your mind *then* which would be the focus. You believed the cylinder would do for the flat planes what a curve did in a Braque.

There was a reason, a rationale! You positioned the water tank for structural economy—to maximize the staircase columns. You had your doubts when the formwork went up. But you believed you could pull it off. Your house wasn't batting platitudes. But there are reasons for rules and rules for reason. Something cold and heavy settled in his stomach.

'Biren! You're *scaring* me!'

You always maintained you cannot have competing focal points in a building. It's like two noses on a face. Two bull's-eyes on a dartboard. And how easily it could have been resolved! You could have placed the tower a few feet clear of the building.

Why hadn't you done it?

The devil always has an ace up his sleeve. Hindsight isn't alternate vision. *You blundered.*

Would you have realized the blunder today, or even in time to come? Or would you—since, of course, only you are competent to judge—have passed off the aberration as an amusing eccentricity? A contrapunctus in a jazz composition? Would you have *lied* to yourself?

'Biren! What is it? Are you in pain?'

It was a panic, not pain, he thought. He recalled, as he had several times before, the first instance of it, that rush of humiliation. Midway during his debut appearance in a kindergarten play he had felt warm liquid trickling down his bare leg. He had run from the stage and hid in the bathroom for the rest of the evening.

An icy shudder went through him. There was no place to hide now.

'Where are you going? Wait!'

He continued walking—on broken knees.

'Did I say something wrong?'

You can't bear to look at her, much less speak to her. How can you? Without any education, sensibility, interest even, she has challenged the conceit underlying your work—all your work.

Why would you care what she, what anyone, thinks? After all, *you* know...

'I'm sorry, Biren. I didn't mean to upset you.'

She was drowning in anxiety. Some acknowledgement was called for, of her keen observation, her timely incursion... Her goddamned perspicacity.

'I'm not upset with you, Dona. In fact, I'm indebted to you.' He took her arm. 'Come. It's getting late. Let's go back.'

'But... but what about seeing the inside?'

'Yes, of course. We must do the grand tour.' He smiled down at her. The kohl was smudged around her eyes. 'You look like a racoon.' He rubbed it gently with his thumb.

Of course he didn't attach any importance to her effusions—how clumsy they were! But he accepted them with grace, with passable gratitude. At the end of the little charade it wasn't clear who was deceiving whom.

~

Late the same evening Pinaki was walking home from his tram stop on Diamond Harbour Road when a scooter drew up beside him. 'Lift, Dada?'

To his surprise Pinaki found himself nodding. Next he knew he was sailing along, gripping the sides of the machine with his knees and holding his briefcase as a buffer against the sticky heat emanating from Kalol Mondal's nylon shirt.

Kalol Mondal's zippy u-turn at the doorway of his building further embarrassed (and almost unseated) him. What need was there for the fellow to fling his legs out, and drag them on the street before coming to a stop? And why was he parking his scooter? Was he—he *was* readying himself for a chat!

'How is the house?' Kalol Mondal asked solicitously. 'Completed?'

Pinaki waggled his head in a non-committal way. He wondered how to indicate to someone their usefulness has expired, and that their continued attendance would be an aggravation.

Kalol Mondal gave the scooter an affectionate thwack. 'Brand new,' he said.

'Ah,' said Pinaki. Thinking this might be a little inadequate after having had a ride on it, ungrateful even, he pointed at the petrol tank. 'Speed?'

Kalol Mondal caressed the tank. '120 kilometres per hour on Red Road.'

They heard a snort.

Dona stepped onto the pavement. She strode past Kalol Mondal, her head held high, but she gave Pinaki a conspiratorial glance in passing. It was gone in an instant, replaced by a grimace.

Flustered, 'He... he gave me a lift,' Pinaki said, waving his hand towards Kalol Mondal. He drew himself up. 'Tell Ma to make my tea.' Turning to send off his pesky escort. 'Ei,' he began.

Kalol Mondal was gazing after Dona. He seemed transcended, as if he had had a divine revelation. Only his tongue flickered over his caked brown lips.

Shock prevented Pinaki from leaping forward and pushing him down.

When he could speak, 'Thik achhe,' he muttered. His ears flamed. *Thik achhe*? I'm saying *it's alright*? Alright to lust after my daughter? What is *wrong* with me? He hurried to Dona, now scrabbling inside their letterbox, and grasped her arm. 'Chol.'

Keeping his back military straight he marched her up the staircase.

Kalol Mondal wheeled his scooter to the road. It had lost its shine. It was also unfortunate that Vinu's scratched, mud-spattered machine was parked just ten feet away, its rear jutting cockily into his path, its bulk and battle scars emasculating his pretty clip-clopping little mount. *Red*! Why had he at least not picked blue?

He ran a practised eye over the motorcycle. Impressive though it was, it was still vulnerable. Tyres, mirrors, leather seat... There were so many possibilities and there was nobody around. It was almost too easy. Except he couldn't do it. Not now. Regretfully he puttered off.

Was it worth it? To give up so much for someone who wouldn't even look at him?

'You can ask for anything and you'll be given it, Father?'

'Within reasonable limits, yes, Anthony.'

'He'll do it for everybody?'

'Well, those who believe in Him.'

It seemed rather a grand premise that millions of people would get what they asked for—with Jesus personally attending to their requests. But Kalol Mondal *wanted* to believe it.

He crouched over the handlebars. If he let go his dreams would go crashing down with him.

He was still dreaming the next day when the Turtle tapped him on the shoulder. 'Come with me, Mondal.'

Kalol Mondal sprang up and followed him into his room. The Turtle sat down, rested his elbows on the table, knitted his fingers and and settled his chin on them. 'We can't fit you into the position you want, Mondal. There is no vacancy.'

'I can wait, sir. I...'

'You can work in the warehouse. One of our workers is injured.'

'But I was told...'

'Management decision,' interrupted the Turtle, clamping his lips over this luscious pellet.

'I won't do that job.'

The Turtle's eyebrows were vestigial, just swellings like incipient horns, but he put them to good effect. 'No? Then you have to leave.'

Kalol Mondal swallowed an ice cube. Now he was being told he would be paid for the whole month, despite being under probation. He was to understand it was a favour. He would have liked to tell the Turtle where to shove the cheque, but he needed the money. And it was futile to argue. They had made their plans, knowing he would refuse their offer. He felt a rattling inside him as of things working loose.

In a stupor he packed his new bag with his few possessions, including a framed picture of Kanchenjunga he'd bought the week before. The sola topee presented a problem. He couldn't possibly wear it and it wouldn't fit into his bag. He carried it under his arm, feeling conspicuous and foolish.

In his bad luck, the owner walked in just as the security guard was checking his bag.

The guard, imagining *he* was under scrutiny too, threw himself into his job, shaking out the sorry bits and pieces. As a crowning humiliation the sola topee fell on the floor with a crack and bounced away.

Now here was the accent you could never copy, not in a hundred years of tutelage by Father John. 'Leaving us— Mondal, isn't it?' said the owner, with that unfocussed smile people give you when they are in a hurry to get away. 'Good luck! Come and see us some time.'

He rode his scooter at a dangerous speed—covering the distance of eight kilometres to J. Mullick Road in fifteen minutes. It should have knocked out all thought but his brain was pumping them out.

He had been employed only to oblige the Chief. It was only a matter of time before the obligation would have been considered discharged. The Chief must have told them this wasn't an important favour. It was the disillusionment that comes with the last spoonful of ice-cream.

By the time he entered the lane he was seething at the

injustice of it. He burst through the red door, his fury raging like wildfire. 'You deceived me!'

The Chief looked at him without expression. 'Who gave you permission to enter?'

'I don't need permission! This is a free country!'

'This is *my* office. And I can have you thrown out.' Without taking his eyes off Kalol Mondal he got up and slammed a chair against the wall.

Kalol Mondal clutched the edge of the table. Sick drool flowed into his mouth. 'I left the job,' he said in a sort of whine. 'I was told to do menial work.'

'So do it! What else are you fit for? First they beg for a bone, then they piss on you!'

'Don't say that, Dada. I respect you.'

The Chief sat down again, leaned back and gazed at the ceiling as if a beautiful picture was unfolding there. His minions wriggled on their chairs.

Maggots, thought Kalol Mondal. *To think I am one of them!* And then he realized he may not be one of them any longer. And what his future would be if he stopped being one of them. He turned to the Chief, who was still contemplating his vision. Bowing his head, 'You have influence, Dada,' he said in a wheedling voice. 'Tell them to...'

The Chief rose to his feet so suddenly Kalol Mondal stumbled. 'Get out!' he thundered. 'Ekhuni!' He unleashed a curse involving Kalol Mondal's mother and a camel. 'Nirobata!' he yelled as Kalol Mondal backed out of the door.

Kalol Mondal took a labyrinthine route, through alleyways and private courtyards, to avoid J. Mullick Road. The sweat dripped unchecked down his forehead. He had the sensation of seeing the credits roll after a movie and having no idea of what the movie had been about.

He longed to see a familiar face, from a different past

though, he thought, someone who didn't give him undrinkable tea and lectures about God. Someone more wretched than he. And *not* the man on the cross.

'Jesus died for us, Anthony...'

He dies every Sunday! That hasn't changed a thing!

He turned a corner, and, 'Raja!' he shouted joyfully. 'Darao!'

Raja glanced over his shoulder. He crossed the road.

'It's *me*, you fool!'

Raja quickened his pace.

When he realized what was happening, Kalol Mondal was furious. 'Eat shit, dog!'

Raja gave no indication he heard.

'I'll kick you all the way to Haldia!'

Raja began running, weaving clumsily across the lane. Sure enough, his feet got entangled with each other and he fell. The blockhead, thought Kalol Mondal. Can't even run.

His laughter died in infancy. The blockhead was shouting for help. There were answering calls, heads bobbed in the windows, pedestrians were stopping to look... He was a perfect target, standing right in the middle of the lane.

Well, he'd go out of the world the way he came in. Bloodied but kicking hard. He was Kalol Mondal. Who would deal with his adversaries like a man, not a boy hiding behind a wall to throw stones. Now he was Anthony Gonsalves too. Let the chinless cowards come. He threw back his shoulders.

To his disappointment—and secret relief—nobody did. Even so, it seemed a long way to the end of the lane.

Once there, his nerve sprang back. He pulled out a soda bottle from a crate outside a booth and heaved it. It landed with a beautiful crash. He sent two more bottles after the first, to different parts of the street. Their splinters polished the dead rays of noon. They would get embedded in the dirt, wedged between the stones. Impossible to clear up. Cyclists, carts, even cars, used the lane as a shortcut to Diamond Harbour Road. Children played barefoot. Pumping his fist in the air, he ran out into J. Mullick Road.

Behind his wok Aroma smiled and shook his head. 'That Kalol. The young are so full of life, taito?'

His elderly customer gave a choleric grunt. 'They have much to cheer about.'

~

'A job,' mused Father John. 'D'Souza Studio wants an assistant—have you used a camera?'

'No,' said Kalol Mondal glumly.

'I'll check with the Oxford Mission. Learn to play an instrument, Anthony. You could join the orchestra and perform at weddings.'

Kalol Mondal said he would give it a thought.

He hurled himself on the bed to think. It was one step forward and two back in this loser's game. This would never have happened if he had been anyone but who he was. And that was never going to change. You can turn yourself inside out to become Anthony Gonsalves but to the world you are Kalol Mondal. Who would always be the first suspect, even if he was miles away from the crime. Whose word would always be suspect, even if he swore on the heads of his unborn children.

He pulled the meagre blanket over his head to block out the unfeeling light. At least he hadn't bought curtains. Or furniture. Now he could pretend he was moving out because he didn't *like* it here. But who to pretend to? Not her, not anymore. Not any of them. Not even Raja.

He plunked on the string of his underwear.

Raja's cowardice. Raja's treachery. The Chief's fury. The Turtle's smile. The owner's accent, which sounded like that old man, *her* friend...

The string bit into his flesh. He writhed in an ecstasy of misery.

Just as he was dropping off to sleep the voice of the salesman in the men's shop—in another age as it seemed now—echoed in his head. *'What are you looking for?'*

He was plunged back into loss and confusion.

41

Pinaki thought it was another of Biren Roy's crazy schemes, except it wasn't obscured in the usual tortuous language. Also he appeared nervous—he was puffing at his cigarette as if he was hyperventilating. What he proposed, however, was only too comprehensible, although, for once, Pinaki wished it wasn't. Biren Roy proposed to demolish the water tank and rebuild it six feet from the main structure.

'They're both too distinctive to share this space, Bose. They need distancing. The tank will go on a tower. It will take your house to new heights. Literally.' His mouth twisted in the offensive way that meant he was enjoying his humour.

At *my* expense, fumed Pinaki. 'It looks alright as it is,' he said.

'That's exactly what it doesn't look. I mean, imagine a Mexican bandit without a moustache.'

'Six feet will make this great difference?'

'It's a critical six feet, Bose. Like a wide ball in a crucial over. It could lose you the match.'

'We aren't playing cricket.'

Biren Roy exhaled forcefully. A long ribbon of smoke curled around Pinaki's head. He can even make his cigarette smoke insulting, he thought, slapping it away. 'You should stop smoking. It is not only bad for you it is bad for others.'

Biren Roy looked startled. Then he tossed the cigarette into the bird's nest.

The minor victory emboldened Pinaki. 'I don't agree to this proposal.'

'You don't have a choice,' retorted Biren Roy.

'*What*?'

Biren Roy rubbed his cheek. His smile was strained. 'Let's try this again, Bose. Suppose the bomb meant for Hiroshima had been six kilometres off course and dumped in the sea...no, that won't do. Cheap Japanese cars didn't change the course of the world, although, arguably, they kick-started the Japanese economy. Okay, I have it. Suppose the fellow who assassinated Archduke Ferdinand had missed him by six feet and hit a lamppost. *That* would have changed the course of history.'

'History of what?'

Biren Roy sighed. 'Jokes apart, Bose, *(as if any of this was funny!)*, this water tank is a bit of a slip-up.'

Biren Roy owning to a mistake! Ha!

The triumph evaporated. The mistake had been made on *his* house. On *his* time and money. And this man was justifying it with his usual tactics. Contemptuous dismissal of those who didn't understand him.

'You see, Bose,' he was saying with that tolerant expression that Pinaki had come to hate. 'There are no absolutes in design. Perfection is a lifelong chase. You can't quit. Or compromise. Apart from anything it's dishonest...I know there is a cost factor...'

Pinaki came to with a start. 'Cost!' he pounced on the only word that made sense. 'It will cost me money, time, peace of mind! My sanity!'

Biren Roy laughed. 'You have a nice touch in rhetoric, Bose. Calm down. Trust me on this.'

'I *don't* trust you.'

'Excuse me?'

Pinaki's legs went cottony. A noose tightened around his throat. He was stricken with a familiar condition. He glared at the bird's nest. 'You can't do it,' he croaked.

Biren Roy muttered something that sounded like *try me*.

Then, '*You* wanted this house, not I,' he said, enraging Pinaki
in just the way Dona did when she argued she hadn't chosen
to be born.

'Yes, I wanted a house! No more changes, no more
evolution, no more... *jokes*!'

Biren Roy squashed his cigarette into the eggshells. The
crunching reminded Pinaki of the time he stepped on a
snail. He winced. 'I'm going ahead, Bose. I thought it would
be polite to inform you first. I'm not sneaking around like a
thief in the night.'

'Shey ki? Of course you have to inform me! It is *my* house!'

'One day, yes,' Biren Roy said coolly.

'What do you mean? I have paid for it!'

Then Biren Roy said something so frightening Pinaki
wondered if he had heard right. He said, 'As a matter of fact
you haven't.' Immediately he added, 'Don't worry about the
money, Bose. This one's on me.' He jumped up and walked
briskly to the grey wash of window.

Pinaki opened his mouth but he couldn't find the words
he needed. His breath escaped in sour gusts. He hadn't paid
for the house? That could only mean there were pending bills
he knew nothing about. And he had almost finished spending
what he'd got for the menorah!

Biren Roy had pressed his face to the glass. He seemed
completely absorbed in the scene below. What did he find in
the street? Signs? Omens? Pinaki wanted to drill a hole into
that insolent back.

Biren Roy swung around. His eyes were alight. 'I see I have
to excite your imagination, Bose.' He sat down and pulled the
accursed bird's nest towards him and stood a pencil an inch
from it. 'So then. This is the house, and this the new water
tank...'

It made no sense at all. There was something about a
fulcrum and a spiral. There was something about the water

tank as a counterpoise. The glass pyramid, the *frustum*, as a centrifugal force. After that he gave up trying to understand.

'...then we'll be in the clear. Literally.'

We, thought Pinaki blackly, it's become *we* now. A mistake has collective ownership, Biren Roy had said once. Success stands alone. He was tripping on his own words. The elation died. De facto, certainly by *default*—in this case hiring and then not firing Biren Roy—Pinaki was co-owner of this mistake.

Biren Roy was sweeping his hand over the table, pushing away papers, pens, pencils, clips. 'It's like beginning with a clean slate.'

Pinaki grew cold. *A clean slate*? The house was almost finished and this man was talking of starting over?

'We're building something for future generations, Bose.'

'I want to see it built in *my* lifetime.'

Biren Roy didn't appear to have heard. He was up and pacing the floor. To the door and back, again and again, reminding him of that first time—a lifetime ago!—when he was standing in the studio, hearing the very same footsteps, imagining the caged beast inside, and how true *that* had turned out!

The beast stopped mid-stride to grin at him.

It was too much. 'Why are you so *joyful*?'

Biren Roy laughed. 'Because this is going to be better than before! But yes, it must be finished in your lifetime.' He waved his arms. 'So avaunt into the darkling streets!'

Pinaki stopped at a snack stall in Free School Street (which was indeed dark from a power outage), and ate two punitive puri-and-potatoes, cold, oily and over-spiced. He crumpled and wiped his fingers on his leaf plate, and, after only a moment's hesitation, threw it down on the road instead of the bucket provided for it. How mad Biren Roy would be!

A bubble of sour liquid exploded in his mouth. The

small act of rebellion, the futility of it, only drove home his powerlessness. He could not fight Biren Roy.

'Ei, babu! Don't think so hard! Who are you murdering? Walk faster or give us side!'

His hands flew to rescue his face from his thoughts. Could people read what he was thinking? Could they see he was walking behind Biren Roy's hearse?

Death wasn't a nice thing to wish on someone—it would bring bad luck on oneself—but how about disease? Hospital, oxygen mask, ventilator, coma...

~

'How much will this new folly cost you, Pinakibabu?'

'Well, it is *his* fault and *his* idea so he has to bear the...'

'Arre Pinakibabu. Whether the knife falls on the cucumber or the cucumber falls on the knife, it is the cucumber that gets hurt, no? You will pay, my friend.'

~

Waiting for his tram home he felt the stirrings of a solution. He pushed it down. Whereupon it took root like—he was struck by the simile—the pristine lotus in mud. Mud is where good things have their beginnings. Flowers, paddy, Durga statues, and bricks of course...

You can't do it. You take *that* road, you walk alone. Or with people you don't want to rub shoulders with.

But isn't guilt a form of self-indulgence? Like atheism is a religion? Guilt is a luxury for you now, at any rate. You can't afford it.

Biren Roy once said great buildings owe their existence to corruption, pillage, slavery... So behind lesser buildings— houses—there could be cheaper compromises. Such as lies? Lies have such shifting boundaries, though. One's man's lie is another man's delusion. That could be said for truth too. Truth is rooted in belief. (But this goes against every grain of your belief!) Truth is fundamental to...everything. The world revolves around truths. It flounders on lies.

Perhaps you had misread the situation. You were too hasty, too judgmental...certainly too harsh. Now you must backtrack... You have to be *flexible*.

But without conviction? That *is* lying.

You're taking a new position. Revising your premises, rejecting your prejudices, using your imagination as Biren Roy once advised. *Be a bit more adventurous, Bose.*

Biren Roy *again*.

The tram arrived.

Dona, I have something to say to you...

His throat dried up.

It is regarding this lipstick business...

He ran his tongue over parched lips.

I was too hasty...you did *drop it in his car when, when...*

He belched. Those puris!

You're not dishonest. Thoughtless, yes, headstrong, disobedient...

He clutched his pitiful hair.

True, I got angry, but if your own child disobeys, deceives, lies...

He was back to accusing her.

I worry for you, child! You see, there are things you don't know about men—men like Biren Roy. They are from a different world. They have no morals, no principles, no conscience... Look how he used you.

No, he couldn't say that.

It's like this, Dona. There's a side to this man that...

Side? Biren Roy was only a side? Biren Roy was the top, bottom, middle of, of everything! He opened and shut his palms to pluck the appropriate words out of the air.

I was thinking only of you—your safety, your happiness, your future... Even this house is for you!

By the end of the tram journey he was sniffing and wiping his eyes.

After dinner, which he barely touched, he waited for Rimi's television programme to begin before making his way to Dona's room.

She was lying on her bed with a book but sat up when he entered. Good, he thought. At least she shows me respect. He turned to his mother, to ask if she had taken her medicine, did she need more water, was that pillow comfortable or should he...

Dida flapped her hand. 'What do you *want*, Bulbul? You're making me tired.'

'*I* don't want anything, Ma. But now I'm here it occurs to me I haven't spent time with Dona of late. Isn't that right, shona?' he asked in an awkward falsetto.

Dona flicked back her hair as if to say, since when do we spend time with each other in this house?

He abandoned the effort at pleasantry. 'I want to talk to you, Dona. In the veranda so Dida won't be disturbed.'

'Dida *likes* being disturbed. She's always complaining nobody gives her attention.'

'Actually I would like to sleep now,' Dida said.

Dona gave her grandmother a reproachful look. But she got up.

The fluorescent tube light leached the chlorophyll from Rimi's plants, rendering the walls a sickly mauve. Everything else looked both over and underexposed. It was flickering too. Rimi had asked him to change it two weeks ago.

Dona declined to sit in the chair he indicated, choosing instead to lean on the balustrade. Not quite turning her back but cutting off as much of him as she dared.

He cleared his throat. 'So, Dona. What have you been doing?'

'Studying. I have exams.'

'Shey ki? I thought they were over.'

She turned around. 'They haven't begun.' Her mouth twisted in a sardonic smile. If he didn't know *this* vital fact about her life he had no business to be saying he missed chatting to her.

'So when are they?'

'End of June.'

'I hope you are studying hard.'

'I *was*.' She crossed her arms on her chest.

'Don't speak to me like...' He checked himself. Pretending to search in his pocket for a handkerchief, he wiped his hands on his pants. 'Darao, don't go. I want to talk to you.'

The tube light stilled for ten seconds, allowing him to see her as if for the first time. The lower lip sticking out, the cheeks slopping over. The wobbly chin, the indistinct jaw line... There *was* no line. She was so unformed still...Beads of sweat popped up on his brow.

A light came on in the building across the street. If it went out he wouldn't go on. He wished it would go out. He hoped it wouldn't.

A wave of self-loathing swept through him. *Stick to the plan*! Think of the house, finished, beautiful. Think of showing it to Mr Sen... You're almost there!

'It's about...your lipstick,' he croaked.

It was not easy to drum up the conviction he needed to make his story—the vindication—credible. He hoped the fidgety light would hide his jumpiness.

The tension in her face eased as he spoke, but her eyes moved uneasily. The effect was like a clumsily dubbed movie shot. 'Why are you telling me this now?' she said when he paused. 'Has something happened?'

He felt a pang of irritation. Did she have to be so astute? Or was he that transparent?

'I want you to know I don't blame you. I admit I was too harsh. Even though it was for your own good.'

'Thank you. If that's all may I go?'

'No, wait. There's more.' His ribs were squeezing his chest. 'Something *has* happened.'

'I thought so,' she said dryly.

That ripped the plaster from the wound. It came spewing out—Biren Roy's latest iniquity, his own frustration, anguish. Struggling for breath, 'He's going to demolish it,' he wheezed. 'Soon. He will bankrupt me. And he just laughs! He's a madman! I should never have engaged him. *Never.*'

She was chewing a strand of her hair. 'Tell him to pay for it,' she said.

'He said he would but I don't believe him! I don't believe anything he says after...' he caught her eye. 'He will add the cost to something else,' he said. 'And what about the delay? Today it's the water tank, tomorrow it will be the staircase, day after something else! All for his ego. Six feet!' He slapped at the sweat trickling down his face. 'Of course, I'm not a hotshot architect.'

Something flickered over her face. Something warm, like pity.

Pity? He bristled. Then he crumpled. It was the old— humiliating—helplessness.

She was watching him. 'In any case, what can *I* do about it?'

And the best he could come up with (a poor best, as he knew too well,) was, 'This is *your* house too.'

'Is it really?' she asked, with the sort of smile you wanted to smack off. He couldn't speak for rage. And the longer he didn't speak the more difficult it became to do so. Muscles and mind conspired to cleave his tongue to his palate.

She was looking at her watch. 'I have an essay to write, Baba.'

The armrests cut into his palm. 'Wait,' he said thickly.

The light in the window was still there. A cathartic breeze fanned him. *There's no rightness or wrongness per se, Bose. Whatever results in the general good can't be bad.*

'Baba, I must *go*.'

'Every man has a weakness,' he said.

Her brow wrinkled. 'Shey ki?'

'Maane, he is not an exception.'

'So,' she sounded amused, 'what is his?'

Was she really that obtuse? Or was it an act? It was not unreasonable to suppose she hadn't guessed where this could be going.

The light was shining. Shining like a beacon.

He crunched his stomach. In a voice he didn't recognize and yet knew to be his, the way you know the honking you hear on the Hoogly belongs to a foghorn and not a wild goose, he said, '*You.*'

The colour left her face. Perhaps it was the tube light.

He spoke, pushing the words through a nozzle. '...will listen to you...would never ask you if I thought for even *one* second that you were in any...danger.'

She was looking at him with a disbelieving expression, which turned speculative and then mutinous.

He had the dizzying sense he might have miscalculated. Out of the blue he recalled a long-ago yearning for a kitten, which he had vocalized to a plea charged with emotional overtones as his sixth birthday approached. Almost immediately upon getting it he had thought: *I don't want this.* There was the opportunity cost as well. He'd refused the option of a football. The opportunity cost of *this* was incalculable. From now, he thought, with a flash of terrible insight, I will be a stranger to myself. I will be lost. My past will be as if it happened to someone else.

But he had to see this through if he didn't want to make a

complete fool of himself. The attributive *complete* stung him. Why had he thought of it?

'I was wrong about the lipstick. I overreacted.' Even to himself he sounded petulant.

'Yes, you said so.'

In an attempt at dignity he made a cage with his fingers and held it to his nose. 'Parents make mistakes too—we are only human. But we always act in your interest.'

'Do you?'

Pinaki thought, I am making no progress. 'He is not bad,' he said bleakly. 'Only—only...'

'Imperious,' she supplied, and had a minor fit of coughing—or laughing, he couldn't tell which.

'Ki?'

'Nothing.' She composed herself. 'So you think he'll listen to me?'

'Well, he likes your company.' Enough to want to be with you and, and I don't know what else. I prefer not to know... why do you look at me like that? The way *he* does, in fact? As if I'm the class duffer whom the teacher said you must not tease? 'He has a special regard for you,' he said, stonily. 'Like a professor for a good student.' He heard a sound suspiciously like a chuckle. He ignored it although it riled him. Then he remembered Rimi's long-ago taunt. 'He's your friend, philosopher and guide, taito?'

Now there was an unmistakable giggle. Bowing her head, 'Yes,' she said. 'I suppose you could say that.'

She was mocking him. First the mother, then the daughter, he thought, with dull resentment. In the semi-darkness he could not see whether the mocking had become full-scale scorn, or whether she was just buying time for her answer, which would be...what? He had the peculiar sensation of things going very fast when they hadn't moved at all, and he felt the injustice of this keenly.

The silence was pinning him to his chair. 'My feeling is he may really not want to do this thing, once he realizes how much trouble it is. But he has too much of, ke korey bolbo, *ego*, to go back on his decision. All he needs is a little...' He mimed a push, which was so absurd applied to Biren Roy that she burst out laughing.

He wanted to shake her. 'Chhere dao,' he said, through stiff lips. 'What has to happen will happen. I was wrong to ask you. I've been wrong all along. About everything.'

After a pause, 'I'll talk to him,' she said quietly.

There was an indiscernible shift in the mood in the veranda.

The light in the window had gone out.

42

Pinaki said he would go with Dona to Biren Roy's. Not all the way, you understand... At which she exploded into giggles. He didn't ask why—he guessed he wouldn't get a straight answer. She said, (with a straight face) she hadn't expected him to. That caused him a twinge of anxiety. What did she mean? With Dona one could never be sure. He said firmly he would walk her to Marquis Street.

Meeting at Flurys corner was her idea, although, for some reason (and this was the reason one could not be sure of her), she had laughed again when she suggested it, and wouldn't explain what was so funny.

Flurys' window displayed an arrangement of pink-and-green papier-mâché cupcakes to lure passers-by. He turned his back on this synthetic cheer. Having succumbed once to window dressing—the *wall* dressing in Biren Roy's studio—he wasn't going to fall for it again.

There was a newspaper stall set up against the roadside

railing. He picked up a magazine at random and flipped through it, glancing at the crowded pavement every ten seconds. She said she would come after evening class—if there was class. With Dona you could not be sure of that too. Always a little undependable, she had now proved to be deceitful. Perhaps, he thought with a touch of bitterness, she always had been and she had slipped it past him.

He had fixed for late evening because Manu would have left. He caught his breath. *Alone with Biren Roy?*

Don't think, don't doubt, don't, don't change your mind.

There she was. He put down the magazine and hurried forward. His relief gave way to irritation. 'Couldn't you have cleaned up before coming? Look at you!'

She blew out a pink bubble, and kept going till it burst. She picked the rubbery strings off her face and stuffed them into her mouth.

Infuriated by her disrespect, 'At least you could have combed your hair,' he snapped.

'At least you could have bought that magazine,' she said. 'Not diddled that poor man of two rupees.'

He felt a rare pang of sympathy for Rimi.

'You've done this on purpose,' he scolded as they set off down Free School Street. He stopped in his tracks. 'Wait here a minute. Mind my briefcase.'

He plunged into the busy road, holding up his arm to warn the traffic. Within minutes he was back with a pack of wet wipes (imported!), panting and relieved to see she was still there.

The wet wipes turned out to be dry. She pinched out a lifeless square, held it between finger and thumb, and dropped it on the pavement. He snatched the pack from her, tore out a clump and rubbed her face—nose, cheeks, chin and her neck for good measure—obstructing (and entertaining) passers-by. A strong scent of patchouli hung in the air.

'Do you have a comb?' he asked, fussing with the fluff sticking to her skin.

For answer she gathered her hair and pulled it back—revealing a shining bump on her forehead.

He clicked his tongue. 'You need powder.'

'I need to hurry. It's almost six o'clock.' Then, with that half smile that had begun to madden him, 'I'm actually looking forward to this,' she said. 'It should be fun.'

'It is not supposed to be,' he began, frowning. Catching her eye, he fell silent.

She ploughed through the crowds, swinging her satchel, uncaring of who it might hit. As they neared Marquis Street he seized her arm. 'Okhane dekho—Rizvi Tea Corner. I'll wait for you there, okay?'

She thrust her head forward as if to battle an unseen storm, and sped away.

'At least see where it is!' he cried. Shrugging angrily, he went into the teashop.

~

Biren hadn't heard her footsteps, and she hadn't knocked either, so when she walked into his room he was taken by surprise, and then by delight. He jumped up and came round the table. Holding both her hands in both his he said, 'I can't believe you're here! But how cold your hands are! And how scruffy *you*!' He pulled her arms apart. 'You little ragamuffin!'

She gave him an affectless smile. Then, divesting herself of her satchel, she hooked a foot round a chair leg and sat down.

He pulled up the second visitor's chair for himself and took her hands again.

She appeared tense. And, really, she was appallingly grubby. Her tee looked like a white page gone over, over and over, with a decayed eraser. There was a blackish smudge on her neck, and what was that peculiar scent? He toyed with the idea of teasing her—that only her mother could love her in this state, and then remembered the mother in this case was not exactly sympathetic.

He went to make tea, giving himself time to think. Why was she visiting him in such a condition, and in such a mood? Their last meeting hadn't exactly been propitious but the parting had been cordial. Arguably the drive back from the wetlands wasn't much fun but it was peaceful enough. Perhaps she sensed his distress and blamed herself for it?

Perhaps she had come to make amends?

Handing her a mug, 'Are you alright, Dona?' he asked.

'Long day at college,' she said thickly. 'Two tests.'

'Poor you,' he murmured, rubbing her cheek with his knuckles. That scent! Holding his breath he tucked in a strand of her greasy hair.

She shied away and hid her face behind the mug.

'What *is* the matter, Dona?'

She took a swallow of the tea—and grimaced. He relaxed. You'd have to be extremely stressed not to register how bad the tea was. Ergo, she wasn't in such a state.

The tea roused her from her lassitude. 'I came because of the house,' she said in a sepulchral mutter. 'I didn't...'

'It would facilitate communication if you got rid of the mouth guard. It's not exactly an amplification device, you know.' He mimed lowering the mug.

She obeyed. 'I didn't mean to criticize your design. I spoke without thinking.' Her throat contracted. In the hushed quiet the gulp squelched like a bubble in a swamp. 'I mean, the drum, the water tank. And the triangle thing. It was just a...a...'

'A casual observation?' The apology was excessive. It certainly sounded rehearsed.

She knotted her fingers around the mug. 'Yes! That's it. So you shouldn't take it seriously.'

'I didn't. No harm meant. No offence taken.'

'It's the same as an abstract painting,' she said in the same stilted manner. 'You once told me an abstract painting means different things to different people.'

'Or nothing at all,' he murmured, but she was too agitated to catch that.

'And you can't say one is right and another wrong.'

Oh what nonsense, he thought.

'In any case I don't understand design. So I had no business to comment.'

'Don't worry, people are always doing that. Everybody has an opinion, which is the only correct one, as it happens.'

'But mine was *not* is the point I'm making!' she wailed. Embarrassed, she began nibbling at her mug.

This was getting tiresome. 'You were a clever girl to spot what I'd missed. You helped avert a disaster.' Which was not only blatantly insincere but substantially untrue. He hadn't been at all grateful for her input.

Something of what he was thinking must have shown on his face. She shook her head so vehemently her teeth clattered against the mug. 'Right,' he said, wearying of the subject. 'You were a meddlesome pain. Now what?'

The eyes watching him over the mug pleaded with him to understand.

The blackness was gathering, thick and fast. He had no patience with mysteries. He got up and poured himself a rum-and-water, taking his time over it.

She had slid down in her chair, legs splayed, and was cleaning her fingernails with the point of a compass she'd picked up.

He put his glass down with a force that spilled some of its contents. It interrupted her unsavoury occupation at any rate. 'About the water tank, Biren...'

'Yes?'

Her forehead was dotted with perspiration. She brushed it with her wrist, leaving a smear. He started out of his chair to wipe it off and then sank back. Old habits. He finished the rest of his drink in a single swallow.

'It actually makes a fantastic contrast with the triangle...the pyramid. *Frustum*,' she said, with a smile of relief that might have stirred him to tenderness any other time. But now he was precariously close to a tantrum. Some undignified and childish outburst anyway. 'It's pure geometry.'

He laughed without mirth. 'Sweet words don't stick to me, Dona. I'm too fly. And surely you haven't come here to praise me.'

She sat up and grinned at him. 'As a matter of fact I haven't,' she said in her normal voice.

He smiled back. It had been a near thing. He had been about to tell her he had to go out. 'So what's this charade?'

'Don't demolish the tank, Biren. It'll only delay everything. And add to the costs. And really, nobody will even notice it.'

'*You* did. First thing.'

'But *you* hadn't.'

'I would have. Eventually.' His goodwill was quite gone. 'So you see why I can't oblige you.' He frowned. 'How do you know I was planning to demolish it?'

'Well...' She tugged at her t-shirt.

'I see,' he said slowly. '*Daddy* told you. And Daddy sent you to dissuade me. Plead on his behalf. He forced you to,' he said narrowing his eyes at her. 'Threatened you is my guess. Not beating you, is he? Somehow I can't imagine that.'

'Worse,' she said dismally. 'He lied to me.'

'That definitely qualifies as blackmail. First degree.'

'He said,' she began worrying her t-shirt again, 'he'd been wrong about... us. I could tell he only said that so he could send me here. You don't have to,' she raised her head, 'do anything you don't want to because I asked.'

She has more principles than her father, Biren thought, impressed, and a little sickened. Squinting at the tip of his cigarette he asked, 'How, pray, did he think you would bend my will? Tears? Or indulge my deep dark desires?' He blew a smoke ring. 'And if your eyes don't water or my knees turn to water, you are to do—what?'

'What?' she said, bewildered.

'Of course it hasn't occurred to Daddy, that any promise made under duress—in this case the fatal hold you have over me—is as creditworthy as a politician's pledge.' He blew another smoke ring, tossed the cigarette through it, potting it in the bird's nest. 'It's too late anyway. The tank was demolished today.' Suddenly he laughed. 'What Daddy doesn't realize is that this is an assignment for a woman, potentially a siren. Not a girl who, technically, has inky fingers. And who, by the way, is smelling like a mosque on Eid.'

She sniffed at her fingers. 'It's the wet wipes. He bought them for me. They turned out dry.'

'Typical. But why are you such a mess? Is it an act of defiance or something else?'

She ducked her head and wriggled down in her chair.

'You thought I might get ideas if you prettied yourself up. Aha, you're looking sneaky! I was right. I'm disappointed, Dona. That you should think I'm so shallow.'

'No, that's not it! Well, not exactly.'

He wanted to put his arms around her and tell her, without prejudice or perjury, that she wasn't going to affect him in quite that way again. 'Anyway, it was considerate of you. But you know what? We have to do something about Daddy. Else he'll continue this foolish line of persuasion. Perhaps,' he gave her a speculative look, 'we should keep you here till the house is finished.'

'Where would I take a bath?'

'How practical you are, Dona!'

'How silly you are, Biren!'

'I'm losing my edge.' But he was depressed. Shading his eyes from the light, 'Get away, Dona,' he said.

'Whaa...t?'

'I mean, from him, your mother, the lot of us. Especially this city. Don't get rooted here as I did. At least not out of some misplaced sense of loyalty or idealism or nostalgia. Go to Bombay, Bangalore—any city where people aren't so obsessed with the past. Find yourself a *life*.' He smiled at her. 'Or find yourself love—if that's what you prefer. Chances are you'll find it in a sales engineer whose idea of happiness is samosas on the beach. Take that chance and run with it. I say this quite sincerely. Don't go looking for some chimerical paradise. That kind of chimera is only for the silver screen. And the paradise is behind an unscalable wall. *I* should know.'

To his surprise, she began crying.

He ought to give her a hug, he thought uneasily. Pat her head, give her his handkerchief—wasn't that what you do? He put out a feeler, his hand, and withdrew it. There seemed no appropriate place for it. And he could think of no appropriate words to say either.

He returned to his chair and picked up his glass.

She mopped her face on the hem of her t-shirt. In her woe she was insensible to the fact she was exposing her belly. (The soft roll of fat, that cheeky little knob!)

He felt nothing. She could be a footballer wiping down after a game.

'What came over you?' he asked. 'Are you afraid of telling your father your mission was unsuccessful?'

She pushed her hair back and stood up. 'No,' she sighed. 'It's not that.' Before he got over his surprise, she was out of the door.

'Dona, wait! You left your books!'
But the studio was empty.

~

Pinaki's stomach was giving him nasty little jabs. Intimidated by the tea boy, who had come four times to fill his water glass, three times to flick a duster over the table, and once to quip that customers staying more than half a day would be charged rent, he had eaten a potato chop, four onion bhajas, and drunk three glasses of syrupy tea. It was this cowardly submission that was the cause of his discomfort. And his conscience had combined forces with his stomach to torment him.

Time moved like a lame tortoise. He made a couple of unsuccessful attempts to ingratiate himself with the teashop owner. He read and reread a newspaper someone had left behind—two days old and the personal column pages, so no wonder. He scribbled illegible notes on the margins, to prove to an idle observer or undercover agent that he was engaged in a business that required the anonymity of this sorry little place. The metrical regularity with which he peeped at the single flyblown window gave the lie to this ploy.

He leapt up. 'Dona!'

His legs buckled under him like a faulty undercarriage. Undigested food backed up in his throat. 'Ki hoyechhe? Your face, your eyes, you're...what did he, was he...'

Without a word she walked out.

The tea boy chased him with the bill. He rummaged in his pocket and shoved a crumpled note at him and, without waiting for the change, charged after her. 'Wait, Dona! Amiyo aschi!'

She was walking on the edge of the pavement to avoid the pedestrians and the stalls. 'Darao, darao!' he cried, stepping on to the road and endangering the cyclists coming at him full tilt.

She didn't stop but several others did—to stare. He didn't call out to her after that. As a matter of habit he never said her name out aloud on the road, in case the territorial louts picked it up to put to some lewd use. It struck him now that had he shouted her name from every rooftop in Calcutta he couldn't have done worse by her.

He got his opportunity when a balloon seller lurched into her path. She hesitated just a few seconds for a cyclist to pass before jumping off the curb but it was enough. With a final spurt of speed he caught up with her and seized her arm.

'Stop,' he gasped. 'Amra taxi nobo.'

He feared she would run again, but she stood still while he hailed a taxi.

During the (interminable) journey he did not try to speak to her—did not move even—for fear it might set her off. Anything could. At every speed bump he clutched the door handle. She might fly at him. At every traffic light he tensed. She might jump out.

By the time they entered Diamond Harbour Road he was a sorry wreck.

Plucking at her sleeve, 'Did you ask him?' he asked. His pulse was racing, and against time too—they were almost home. 'Could you persuade him...what did he say...did he agree?'

She turned her head a fraction, then the other way, and back again, in a barely perceptible but unambiguous negation.

He sank back on the broken seat, the stuffing knocked out of him.

His ears flamed. *I lowered myself. They made a fool out of me. Again.*

After a while he raised the leaden lump of his head. 'You didn't ask him,' he said. 'I should have known better than to depend on my own daughter...'

She yanked open the door.

'Dona, what...wait till we stop!'

43

She was running. She had landed on her feet. Pinaki's relief was short-lived. As he was paying the driver Kalol Mondal bobbed up at his elbow.

'Nomoshkar, Dadababu.' He nodded after Dona, who had disappeared into the lobby. 'Is something wrong with Didi?'

'No,' Pinaki said, counting his change.

'But her face was swollen! Her eyes were red!'

'Allergy,' Pinaki said, and then was irritated. Why couldn't he just ignore the fellow? He pocketed his wallet and turned around.

Kalol Mondal was giving him a strange, almost accusing, look. He thinks *I* hurt her, Pinaki thought, now angry with Dona for putting him in yet another ridiculous situation. On top of everything else, he must explain himself to this fellow. He stared at the disappearing lights of the taxi. How would all this end? Would it ever end?

Kalol Mondal touched his arm. 'Ki hoyechhe, Dadababu? You look tensioned.' His voice was furred with concern—bogus concern, Pinaki thought, drawing his arm away from any further demonstration of it.

'If anyone has hurt her I will...' Kalol Mondal feinted with his right and then with his left. Right, left, right, left.

Pinaki glanced up at the windows, hoping nobody had seen this byplay. He hurried into the lobby, hoping Kalol Mondal would take the hint.

Kalol Mondal had other ideas. He followed Pinaki in, right up to the staircase, stopping, mercifully, at the foot. 'If you need help just ask me, Dadababu! *Any* time. I am always here.'

Pinaki, who'd reached the first landing, stopped and peered down. His breath came in short, angry bursts. 'Ask *you* for help? What can you do? Beat up Biren Roy?'

'*Who*?' Kalol Mondal started forward. 'Why, did he, was he, what did he do?'

Horror-struck, Pinaki scrambled to retrieve the situation. 'No, no. I was speaking about myself. It is *I* who has the problem with him.' He smote his forehead. 'It was an unlucky day I met him! I should have never got into this house business! It's been nothing but trouble from day one!'

In the hush after the outburst, Pinaki, worrying that it might have been a little too theatrical, resumed climbing up.

Kalol Mondal thwacked the newel post. 'Then we should do something about him!'

Pinaki stumbled over a step. *We?*

'I know where he works.'

Of course you would, thought Pinaki. 'So?' he said, with a touch of hauteur. 'How does that...?' He swallowed a hairball.

Catastrophe focuses the mind. A conspiracy of fate had led him to Biren Roy, a concatenation of fateful events to the building of the house. The time had come to take fate in hand. *Kalol Mondal* as the means to it was not what one would have wished, but in the spot Pinaki was in he had few choices. He sleepwalked down the stairs. Kalol Mondal was still there, cracking his knuckles with ferocious concentration.

Pinaki braced himself. 'I trusted that man,' he said heavily. 'I trusted him with my life's dream, my life's savings, my family...' His shoulders slumped. His lot was indeed heavy. 'He doesn't deserve my trust.' He doesn't deserve *me*. He stared unseeingly into the distance thinking how to put into words just what Biren Roy deserved. Becoming aware of his audience's keen eye, he clenched his fist.

Kalol Mondal patted his shoulder, and how far gone was Pinaki that he should allow this!

'Ei, but Didi, Dadababu? My sister? You mentioned her?'

Pinaki tried not to let his irritation disrupt the furious computations going on in his head. 'She was getting advice from him about college,' he said primly. He allowed some seconds to pass, containing his impatience by counting them. 'I don't know what happened. She will not tell me' The resentment was not an act.

Kalol Mondal gave Pinaki a final, business-like, pat, as if to dust off past misunderstandings. His lips parted with a sucking sound. 'Maybe she can't tell you, Dadababu.' Training his eyes on Pinaki, 'He is not a good man,' he prompted.

'Not good?' said Pinaki. The outrage was not an act either. 'He is evil! Immoral! He...he *drinks*.' It was the only suitable damning trait that came to mind. His pulse jumped. Perhaps this was the key he was looking for. 'In his office,' he added.

Kalol Mondal's eyes were burning like fog lights. Pinaki put his hand up to shield himself from the blaze. 'Every evening,' he said. And, since Kalol Mondal may not know—although he had made it his business to know, especially about Dona (here the anger resurged, threatening to derail purpose), 'Alone,' he added, looking up because there ought to be no ambiguity about *that*.

The understanding in the yellow eyes was like a handshake.

Pinaki was obscurely peeved. Somehow, even when he was cooperating, Kalol Mondal managed to be awful. Ahead of even Biren Roy, who was not awful as much as diabolical. To be obliged to this lout for the rest of one's life! The very idea was oppressive. Perhaps one could reduce the debt?

He made himself look at the fellow. 'Ei, you mentioned buying paint from your company for my house,' he said, trying to sound as if he was bestowing, not taking a favour. Kalol Mondal stiffened. 'I will buy from you,' continued Pinaki. 'Not because of the discount but because you can make a commission...'

Kalol Mondal made an odd sound, halfway between a groan and a howl. He turned on his heels and clattered off. Pinaki stared after him. Had he said something wrong?

~

Biren stood by the window. A low and livid cloud, the cumulative emission of city lights, hung in the sky. A marriage was in full swing on the street. The noise would last all night. The stench of stale food would linger all day. The litter would stay on the street all week. (It's a year-round carnival here, Doc. For some, anyway.)

You had upset her with your take on her future. That *was* a little brutal. But you meant no malice!

Perhaps it was the cavalier—alright, insulting—manner in which you dismissed her father. Face it, you are responsible for his moral corruption. She should hate you for it. You don't much like yourself either.

Yes, she had cried. But she had stopped at the door and looked back at you.

That's why you will not walk out of that door. You will not walk away from the project. That option is out of the ambit of conjecture even. You aren't the walking away kind.

So you drag a stool to the drafting table, pin a fresh tracing sheet on it, draw a vertical and a second, a third, a fourth, a fifth, and keep going till there's a grove of lines, a virtual clutch of them, a cacophonic debate ... You balance a drum on this jungle, erase it, substitute a sphere, then draw in rapid succession a dodecahedron, a cube, a trapezoid, an egg...

He studied the sooty smokestack moodily. What's the point? The exercise was another search for a truth that has so many versions you can spend an entire life looking and not find it. More and more you doubt if there is a single one, and whether you will recognize it when and if you stumble upon it. The need to *get it right* no longer seems the imperative it was. (What difference does it make to the milkman doing his rounds? War and vaccines change the world.) Perfection, as you know only too well, is a vanishing point. The more you chase it the faster it recedes.

Perhaps the tears were for a father who had let her down. The first of all the men in her life who would. Prescient tears. Truth be told, *you* were the first. You did not take her to the Tolly, remember? He felt as guilty as if he had not fulfilled the last wish of a child in a cancer ward.

When the drawing was done, he folded it into an envelope to courier to Karim Ali. As he was addressing it he had an idea. There *was* something he could do for her. He pulled out his cheque book and wrote out a cheque and a short covering letter, put them in another envelope, and took both to Firstlight Couriers down the corridor. He could brook his guilt with a lighter heart now.

He had just poured out his second drink when the studio door whinged. Muffled sounds followed. Footsteps.

He froze, the glass halfway to his mouth. Had she returned for her books? It was almost eight o'clock. What a tenacious salesman hope is! Hand on the knocker, foot in the door! And he had imagined he had put all that behind him! The betrayal of one's flesh was cruel.

He quickly drained his glass. He sniffed at his armpits. He arranged and rearranged his features. Every muscle was pressed into service. Every nerve had been alerted.

What *was* she doing? Looking at the wall of drawings? Dousing the furniture with petrol? He picked up his cigarette and counted five before he called out. 'I'm in here, Dona!'

The footsteps stopped outside his door. His heart back-pedalled. 'Dona?'

When the door opened he almost bit through his cigarette. Recovering, he drew on it—only to find it had gone out. He tossed it into the bird's nest and leaned back in his chair, smiling, although he was wild with disappointment. 'Well, well, well. If it isn't the lovesick parvenu.'

His visitor hesitated at the door.

'What brings you here, Mister, Mondal, isn't it?'

'My name is Anthony Gonsalves,' said the intruder, with a pugilistic swagger.

'It could be Mohammad Ali for all I care. What the fuck are you doing *here*? And what's eating you?'

For Kalol Mondal radiated hostility. It was coming off him in waves. Garlic was, at any rate. Biren wondered if he was another emissary sent by Pinaki—this time to threaten him into submission. He knew himself to be less intimidated than irritated that his temple, his monastery, was being desecrated by this oaf.

He reached for the matchbox and relit his cigarette. 'So. Are you here to canvas for your Party goons? Or have you come with a message from Bose—as a friend of the family now?'

Kalol Mondal continued to glower. It was obvious he had understood very little, and that was riling him. And it was true that the fellow's eyes were markedly yellow. They also looked a little deranged. And they did not leave Biren's untended for even a second. Without moving his head Biren scanned the table. The bird's nest appeared to be the only object approximating a weapon. He pulled it towards him, fished out the half-smoked cigarette. 'Well, state your purpose.'

Kalol Mondal yanked out a chair, sat down, hoisted up a foot and placed it over a knee. That done, he picked up a pen, uncapped it and scribbled experimentally on a pamphlet.

'That's right,' Biren said. 'Don't mind me. Me casa es tu casa.'

Kalol Mondal looked up. 'Ami tumake cheeni,' he said. 'I know what you are up to. I know very well.'

'Really,' murmured Biren. 'You're one up on me then. I have no idea what *you* are up to. Except that you're using up my supply of oxygen.' He returned his visitor's stare, but when he tapped ash he took care to keep his movements unhurried. Somewhere in the depths of the building a motor began running. His head vibrated in sympathy with the hum.

Kalol Mondal reared up and snorted. (Like a prize racehorse reined at full gallop, Biren thought.) 'What did you say to her, eh? What did you do to her? Dushkormo! I saw her just now!'

Biren saw no point in pretending not to know what he was talking about. With an insouciance he knew wasn't very smart, he blew out a coil of smoke.

Kalol Mondal slapped the smoke this way and that. 'You will be punished,' he hissed.

'Oh, I don't think so,' Biren said cheerfully. 'So don't bank on it.'

The blast of a foghorn startled both of them. 'Kidderpore dock,' said Kalol Mondal. He clicked his tongue in exasperation. That was not what he had meant to say.

Biren felt almost sorry for him. The poor idiot would always be staring into windows. And knocking on doors. He would be a trespasser in his own home—the one he imagined he would share with Dona. The inevitability of his dispossession was what fuelled his rage. Biren just happened to be its focus. Don't fret, pal. Neither of us is going to get the lady. Within the year her father will marry her off to a struggling PhD student in the US.

He was wondering where this would go, where it *could* go, when Kalol Mondal thrust his head forward as if he had just remembered a new outrage. 'You *old* man. You *ugly* old man!'

Biren winced. 'Don't rub it in, there's a good fellow.'

'I'm not fellow!' shouted Kalol Mondal. Half-standing, he held up the fingers of both his hands and stabbed the air. 'Pachis barsh! There is *twenty-five* years between you and her!'

Twenty-four in point of fact, Biren thought, massaging his temple. His head had begun to ache. 'There's 100 years between *you* and her,' he said. 'Hundred years of evolution, that is.'

Kalol Mondal's face darkened. 'What?'

'Nothing.'

Kalol Mondal nodded grimly. 'Okay.' He thwacked the table. 'Better it is nothing.' Sitting down again, 'Shameless,' he growled.

Biren rubbed his cheek. Actually this, that was happening, was more shameful than shameless. A random image flashed across his mind, of himself at some not too far away future, slouching around Free School Street, ducking into dives, a figure of such seediness his old friends would not recognize him, or wish to acknowledge him if they did. An overpowering yearning took him, to dive into the Hoogly, for the spiritual dunking religious fanatics went for, in their hordes, on full moon nights.

Kalol Mondal, now at a loss, followed the cigarette to and from Biren's lips, as if it was a snake charmer's pipe.

The muezzin unleashed a shattering wail, breaking the spell. Kalol Mondal cocked his head at the window, patently relieved at the interruption.

Biren raised an eyebrow. He finished half his glass in one gulp. A mistake. His head began throbbing. 'Now that you have had your say perhaps we can continue with our evening. Preferably not together.'

Kalol Mondal shot him a vindictive look. He was being mocked again. 'So what will you do?' he said belligerently.

'Finish my drink in peace,' Biren said, indicating his glass.

Kalol Mondal leapt up. 'You, you drunkard!' His hand shot out and swept the glass off the table. It landed in smithereens, five feet away on the floor. 'Leave her alone!' Engorged veins fanned his forehead. The eyeballs, enmeshed in a web of pink capillaries, bulged. And, because his shirt was unbuttoned halfway down his chest Biren also had a gratuitous view of his pectorals—girlishly smooth, and globular, as in an advertisement for one of those chest expander gadgets he and his kind no doubt used to boost their miserable little egos. This fellow seemed to have overdone it though. He had incipient breasts. To think this strutting peahen, this gelded donkey, had set himself up as his rival *suitor*! It would be farcical if it wasn't so sordid.

He scraped back his chair, 'I'll give you thirty seconds to get out. After that I'm calling the police.'

Kalol Mondal's lips parted in a snarl. '*Police*!' He snatched up a pencil stand and overturned it. '*I* will call the police!' Then, as if unsure how to proceed, 'If I *need* to,' he added, scowling.

Biren inferred he wouldn't need to. He didn't reply. He had begun to hear the drone of low-flying fear. All of a sudden the room seemed too quiet. It had become dark too. At some point the neon sign had gone out. The darkness, the isolation, removed him absolutely and irrevocably from the cheerful chaos on the street four floors below. He would gladly open his gates to the pavement people. They were fellow-men. He gathered the pencils and mechanically began popping them back into the stand, one by one.

Kalol Mondal's features convulsed in a fresh paroxysm of rage. 'If you go one *inch* near her I will break your bones! I will...tomakey shesh kore debo! *Finish*!'

The fellow was insane. A second frisson of fear rippled through Biren. He felt as vulnerable as a naked shin in a football scrimmage. Ducking his head to pick up his cigarettes, he gauged how quickly he could get at the phone. He may be able to reach it but chances were he wouldn't get very far with it.

Fortunately Kalol Mondal was strutting off to the door. There, striking a triumphalist pose, 'Not *one* inch near,' he grated. 'Bhujo? Understand me?' He jabbed his finger into his head to drive home the point.

'Bloody impertinence,' muttered Biren. Something snapped in him. 'It won't progress *your* case, though,' he said. 'Because,' he glanced at Kalol Mondal's sparsely whiskered chin, 'she likes men who need to shave at least every third day. Also,' he looked pointedly at Kalol Mondal's chest, 'she doesn't go for men with...' It came to him—to his surprise—the Bengali vulgarism for breasts. 'Buk,' he said—and regretted it the instant it was out. He was plumbing new depths.

Kalol Mondal's face contorted. Grinding his fists into his ears, he opened his mouth in a soundless scream.

Biren lunged for the phone. Before he could reach it his collar was seized, and his chair kicked from under him.

From the floor he glimpsed his assailant picking up the bird's nest. He experienced real terror for the first time in his life. It was paralyzing. Through a mist, he saw a brawny black arm suspended over him like a building crane. He lifted his own arm, to shield his head, but his muscles had seized up. *Don't*! It was a stillborn cry. The crane came swinging towards him. He heard rather than felt his head explode. A searing light blotted out all sensation except the sound of, of all things, applause.

Voices were piercing the din.

'You can't talk to them like that, Biren...'

'You say such funny things, Biren!'

Darkness chased the light down a tunnel.

'Biren!'

'*Biren*!'

The ovation became deafening. The light became a pinpoint. *So this is how...*

~

At 10 p.m. Kalol Mondal banged on Pinaki's front door, incoherently accusing Pinaki of inciting him to 'do this thing'. Now what were they to do? Pinaki had a hard time shushing him before he woke the household. After making sure there was no one on the landing, he pushed his caller there. '*Now* tell me,' he hissed. 'And keep your voice down.'

'Are you sure? How do you know that he is, that he is...But you are mad! I never meant that you should... Hey Ma! Ekhon ki kora jaye?'

'Did anyone see you go in? Only the watchman? He is old...
Even so, you have to get away from here. *Tonight*!'

'No, you fool! Not to your village! Go to Bombay, Delhi,
Kerala—far away!'

At last Pinaki shut the door, shooting the bolts, every one of
them, including an iron crossbar unused since the time of the
Naxalites. Then he rested his forehead on it to catch his breath.

It had been a terrible ten minutes. Kalol Mondal, his face
the colour of stale coffee, had sweated and jerked the whole
time, as if reliving a bad dream. Pinaki felt *he* was in the
dream too.

After a while, he calmed down. The dreadful business had its
upside. It had rid him of *both* his worries. Biren Roy and Kalol
Mondal. And he hadn't planned it, not quite in this way, so his
conscience was clear. With a sigh of relief he turned around.

The shock came like a kick in the chest.

Dona was slumped against the wall.

44

A month after her visit to Biren's studio, Dona received a
package by post—a sealed manila envelope festooned with
stamps. It was tucked into the door handle because it was too
large to fit into the post-box in the lobby. She had to read the
sender's name over and over—the words kept blurring.

Thanking her stars that it was she who had found it, and
not her father or brother, or worse, her mother, she clutched
it to her chest and hurried to her room.

It was a magazine. *Japan Architect*. The cover was a house
balanced on a cliff, all angles and glass.

Why? But first, *how*?

Perhaps there was a letter to explain. She ripped off the
cellophane wrapping, and rifled through the lushly illustrated

pages. A small card fell out. She pounced on it. It was a coupon, urging her to gift twelve issues of the magazine to avail a 20% discount for next year's subscription. Now she was disappointed. That was all? Still, why? Was there a coded message in it?

Too practical to be scared away by thoughts of the supernatural, she hid the magazine under her pillow to look at when Dida was asleep.

Four sentences into the lead article she realized that reading it with understanding and an intelligent engagement, as was expected, since it had come to her in this mysterious fashion (which was the other bothersome aspect of it), was beyond her capacity.

She drank some water and tried again. She felt she owed it to the sender.

Architectural creation is a form of comprehending reality…it works to transform reality through the construction of a substantial object of use. Form has the two-fold quality of both mirroring and enriching reality. The understanding of this reality, which takes place through architectural creation, requires that the anatomy of reality, its substantial and spiritual structure…

Her eyes closed.

A second magazine arrived in the following month, and another the next… How many more before she would be allowed to forget? Would she *ever* be allowed to forget?

She got the message. The magazines were opening up other worlds for her, pointing her to them. *Follow me.* Or was it *don't* follow me? Since he'd told her to leave the city?

Her throat ached from swallowing the tears. All the symptoms again. The guilt. The regret. And a weird kind of longing.

She needed no encouragement to get away. Her parents all but pushed her out. Pinaki had become querulous and needy, tin cup at the ready for the coins Rimi deigned to drop into it. Grateful to be allowed to live in his own house, frightened he may be sent back to the hell he'd escaped. Rimi harangued him night and day about the 'country house' he'd sunk all their money into, that they never stayed in a single day.

Only Dona knew the reason for the abandonment, and it haunted her for years.

Immediately after she finished her BA exams, she landed a job in Bombay, in a shipping company. She moved into a small flat with two others, girls with whom she giggled and sang, and squabbled and cried, and clubbed resources to buy a hairdryer, a Primus stove and a backless gold-embroidered blouse—the prime reasons for the squabbles. After that she had an unsatisfactory affair with an older man, moved in briefly with an even older man, moved on to another...

Predictably, Tuli won a scholarship to do his graduate studies in a prestigious college in the US. Less predictably, he married an American girl—a bookish, straggled-haired blonde, who Dona privately thought was a drip. Fortunately her first visit to Calcutta was her last. Now Tuli timed his visits to Calcutta with his sister. With the years their childish animosity had gone, replaced by a common dread of spending time alone with their parents. 'Ma,' Dona said, 'had become hysterical. Every minor infraction set her off. As for Baba... He's like a prisoner on parole. An apology of a man—he'd say sorry to the executioner before his head was chopped off.'

'Well, he did behave very irresponsibly over the house.'

She flopped back in her chair. 'Don't let's think of it now. Let's enjoy your cognac.'

It was late at night and they were sitting in the veranda. Pinaki and Rimi had long gone to bed. Glimpsed through the balusters, J. Mullick Road looked much as it had sixteen years ago. The road was still pitted and the streetlamps like dying match flares. But there was a brash new building in the place of Daisy's Beauty Parlour, and a mini supermarket had replaced the modi's shop. Of course, a significant section of the dramatis personae was no longer there. Vinu turned out to be a surprisingly successful painter and had moved to Delhi. Aroma had retired to his village, leaving the teashop to his son, who covered the walls with mirrors and doubled the price of everything. Das Engineering had sold his shop. Nobody's Dog was run over by a truck.

Kalol Mondal had not been seen since that fatal night.

~

'By the way, Rabin Pal's a minister now, would you believe? Tourism Development.'

'Whoever Rabin Pal was.'

'The swindler who sold Baba the plot.'

'Ah.' Tuli shifted in his chair. 'You know, I have one rather frightening recall of that time. A couple of men came from Biren Roy's bank, to investigate some transactions. Cheques made out to one Karim Ali. Baba looked shaken—I was terrified they'd take him away. Put him in jail or something. But the entries turned out quite legit. Biren Roy's father had sent them around to intimidate Baba into a confession or something.'

'What a little snoop you are,' she said pleasantly. 'But you've cleared up a mystery for me. How the house was paid for. Biren, um, Roy paid for it—most of it. It must have been a significant amount. It was quite an edifice—as I remember.' She turned her face away.

He leaned over to take her glass. 'I wouldn't know that, would I? I never saw it finished. Is it still there?'

'Well, it seemed quite indestructible.'

He splashed some brandy into her glass and handed it to her with elaborate care. 'You know, I never did understand what affected *you* so. I thought—years later, of course—that perhaps you had a...thing for him. Biren Roy.'

'*Baba* had a thing about him. He never quite got over his...' She tapped the rim of the glass against her teeth. 'Recklessness.' She'd almost said *treachery*. 'His behaviour was inexcusable.'

Something in her face told Tuli not to ask whose behaviour was inexcusable.

'He did rather lose his head,' he mused. 'Baba, I mean. Showed poor judgement too, but that's not a sin.' He put down his glass. 'Listen. Why don't we go see the place?'

'Well...'

'Come on Didi, it's been *years*! Long enough to forget all that happened.' And, as though the matter had been settled, 'Tomorrow, then,' he said. 'I'll hire us a car.'

With his new sensibilities, exacerbated by a wife who had washed the vegetables with soap solution on her one visit here, he started complaining five minutes into their journey. 'This is a rag picker's landscape! You have to scavenge for a decent sight. And the city's *sneaked* into the countryside. Behind my back!'

'You grew up,' she said, pulling his nose in the old way.

'It hasn't just greyed, it's *browned*. And the pollution! You can scoop the air with a spoon!'

'Don't worry,' she said kindly. 'It acts like nerve gas.'

But his attention was on the road divider. 'Look at those concrete camels! Who are they fooling? *We'd* rather do a long dirty railway journey to Rajasthan to boast we've seen the real thing, wouldn't we?'

She laughed. 'You sound like...' She bit her lip.

'Who? *Watch it*!' An overloaded state bus bumped hips with their taxi. 'God,' he breathed, peeping through his fingers. 'That driver shouldn't be on the loose.'

Her patience had run its course. 'We can always...hmm.' *Turn back*, she had almost said. She wanted to see the house.

'I wonder,' she continued, a little unsteadily, 'what became of Manu. He found the...body. The police gave him a rough time.'

'Now who was he? You forget I wasn't as involved as you and Baba in...that business.' He shot her a sidelong glance. 'How involved were *you* anyway?'

'Less than you imagine.' *More than you'll know.* She inched away to the window.

'I remember there was quite a row one night. Ma shouting and Dida hushing her, Baba wilting as usual, poor guy. And that lout, Kalol Mondal, sitting in the living room. You'd been a bad girl, I gathered.'

'Very astute of you.'

He reached across and picked up the skin of her hand with thumb and forefinger, as if it were a bit of fluff. She pulled her hand away, and didn't speak to him for the next two kilometres.

'What did the police do to Manu, Didi?' he asked humbly.

She didn't answer immediately. Her stomach was misbehaving again. 'What do you imagine the police do to people in custody? In *this* country?' Then she relented. 'Biren Roy's father got him out. He tried to kill himself in his cell— that was in the papers. He worshipped Biren Roy.' She felt a little silly about the appendage *Roy*. 'Biren,' she said, clutching her purse, 'was the world to him. I'm sure he, Biren, that is...' Now that she had started she couldn't stop saying his name. '... would have made some provision for him although he couldn't have foreseen...' She looked at her hands as though she wasn't sure what they were for.

'He must be okay, Didi,' he said, with synthetic cheer. 'You'd have heard otherwise. The newspapers love bad news.'

She didn't retort that no news was not necessarily good news in this part of the world.

They were in the wetlands. Palm fronds fluttered like pennants beside the iridescent ponds. The fields were lush with mustard.

Two freewheeling egrets cut white lazy white circles in the tall winter sky. Tuli heaved a sigh of pleasure. 'I feel I understand Baba better now. He got *something* right.'

Somehow they found the house. As Tuli said, it found them. A grey smudge appeared on the corner of the windshield, expanding, as they neared, to fill it.

They sat without speaking. It was the anti-climax of arrival. She was too overcome, too conflicted, to speak. And he seemed out of his depth. *Which was in itself an achievement for Biren*, she thought, wryly.

The cry of an egret, plangent, insistent, broke the spell. Tuli stirred. 'It looks like a paper boat left in the gutter,' he said.

She had to laugh. It was a pretty accurate description. The structure was listing at a precarious angle on the groundswell. The hull was a tilting concrete wall, and the pyramid, now just a skeleton, its ghostly sail. Biren would have laughed too. He'd once told her he preferred outright derision to cautious praise.

'Rather tactless, isn't it? A cultural, geographical anomaly.'

'Biren said there's no point building if you don't explore ideas. If you can't experiment.'

'And to *this* experiment Baba commended his life's savings!'

'It's quite functional actually.'

He gave her a sceptical smile. 'What's with that grinning slit?'

'It ventilates the utility,' she began to explain and then thought, *why bother? Those who can, do. Those who can't, sneer.* But she cringed for Biren. That window, located under the roof, would have been impossible to use. The glass pyramid— the beacon for futurists—would have been a furnace in the summer. (And how would you clean the glass?) All those innovations—the sawn-off sewer pipes, the gantry girder, were too like the affectations he so despised... Just how would he have defended this? Postmodernism or cynicism? Nihilism? Sophism, absolutism...?

But he had had belief. Her eyes watered. She fumbled in her bag for her sunglasses, and jammed them on.

'I wonder if the guy had a touch of megalomania. What think you?'

What think you. Who spoke like that? She exhaled forcefully. '*I* think this is not a house for everyman.'

'Or any man—as it's happened.'

'Well, in some quarters it might be considered...' *A masterpiece.* She caught his eye. '...as making a point.'

'Is there a philosophy to the design? There *is* a philosophy, I suppose?'

She whirled around so fast her skirt snapped at his legs. 'How about this? That there is an understanding beyond ours, even yours.'

He raised his eyebrows. 'Do you suppose he was any good?'

'He was before his time.' Make what you will of *that*. 'In fact, I don't think his time will come, not *here* at least, for another twenty years.'

'If at all.'

It would have, she thought. If there's anything I can be certain of it is that.

Jete dao, Biren. There's nothing left for you here.

They were outside the gate—barbed wire looped over two concrete posts. Absently he put his hand on it. 'There's a Turkish proverb... ouch.' He rubbed his palm on his leg. 'When you finish building a house death walks in.'

She didn't respond. She had spotted the bush. Winter jasmine. In full bloom. *He* had planted it.

'Something to remember me by, Dona,' he had said on her their fatal visit. 'Although an Agave Americana would be more apt. It could even work as my epitaph—flowers once in its lifetime and then dies.' He had smiled but sounded a little sad.

Now her eyes were filling again... Jete dao. You *have* to let go...

'Are you okay? Where are you going? Didi!'

She had begun walking towards the unruly thicket bordering the lake, tripping over tussocks in her hurry to get away from him because he *will* ferret and analyze, and I don't want to talk to him. I just want to sink into this grass that is climbing up my skirt and teasing my thighs... I want it to tear into me, relieve the itch that has tormented me for years, and staunch the weeping gash, heal my heart...

Her lungs were sawing her in half. The thin soles of her sandals offered no resistance to the stubble of the recently harvested winter rice. She smelled the scent of crushed vegetation—young plants, new grass, wild flowers and the tears began again—what, was she weeping for those now?

When she judged she had put enough of a distance between herself and her brother (who was now hallooing fit to scare the fish out of the ponds) she dropped down. Her skirt, white, wide, settled around her. She must look, she thought distractedly, like a felled egret.

Her haunches moved, cautiously at first and then with uncontainable urgency.

The healing was under way.

The minutes dribbled through the sunlight. Her face grew sticky with sweat. Faint sounds drifted down from another world—bird cries, the susurrus of leaves, the whir of insects, children from the village...

Tuli gave her a curious look when she staggered back, but didn't comment on her state. Instead he drew her attention to the windows. '*Plastic* sheets!'

Why does he sound so awestruck, she thought, irritated. What did he expect? Lace curtains?

'No panes—and the frames have been removed. Vandalized ...look, there's someone.' A woman emerged through the burlap hanging on the front door.

'I didn't know it's been let.'

'It hasn't.'

'Sold then?'

'No. The villagers just occupied it, Baba said. In effect, we've lost it.'

'Well, then, we'll have to get them evicted. Get a court order...'

'Forget it,' she said shortly. Her thighs were sore and scratchy.

'But we'd be within our rights.'

She clicked her tongue. Was he that distanced from the realities here? 'And what would you do with it?'

'We could start a wetlands research centre in it.'

'Do that. Come and run it too.' She punched his arm. 'Let it go, idiot.'

Biren would have—and he paid for most of it.

Jete dao, jete dao.

'Perhaps you're right, Didi. Best to let go.'

'What? Oh, the house.'

'Well, we *were* talking of the house. Oh well. Write it off as a bad debt, I suppose. I wonder what your architect would have said to such cavalier treatment of his magnum opus.'

He wouldn't have cared. He just wanted to build it. She pulled at her lip. 'He once said that his life was work-in-progress. Or was it his *work* was his life-in-progress?'

'Which is apropos?'

'The house wasn't the culmination of his life's work. It's his mortal remains. As it turned out.'

'What a morbid pun.'

She tossed back her hair. 'He'd have appreciated it.'

Tuli jiggled the change in his pocket. 'Well, at least one of them realized his dream.'

'Ye...s. But which one?'

'Does it matter?'

She looked at him with sudden respect. 'No. No, it doesn't.'

Acknowledgements

Thank you to Renuka Chatterjee, Vice President Publishing at Speaking Tiger, and to Shalini Krishan for her editorial inputs. Special thanks to Shomit Mitter whose invaluable advice helped shape this book and made me see what I never could have otherwise. Thank you too, my first readers Shantha, Kalpana, Anand and Basak, who caused me many an 'ouch' and 'oops' moment, but they were right! Well, mostly.